PRAISE FOR

THE RULE OF LAW

"*The Rule of Law* cements Lescroart's status as the undisputed master of the courtroom thriller, as always spiced with richly drawn characters and genuine emotion. Neither he nor Dismas Hardy have ever been better."

—*Providence Journal*

"Lescroart's novels are known as much for their abundantly human characters as they are for their rigorously plotted stories, and this one is a showcase for both of those attributes. Also impressive is the way Lescroart has kept his long-running series fresh by allowing Dismas to grow over the years. . . . Lescroart is a certifiable A-lister. His series entries and stand-alones always draw a crowd."

—*Booklist*

"Lescroart plots so cleverly that he has you believing his split-level thriller is really a single foreshortened novel. The perfect read for those who agree that "it's only trouble if somebody's shooting at you."

—*Kirkus Reviews*

"Enthralling. . . . Sharp dialogue and a timely plot help make this entry a winner."

—*Publishers Weekly*

"*The Rule of Law* is vintage Lescroart, drawing on parallels between real-life and hot-button issues while also providing top-notch entertainment."

—The Real Book Spy

Also by John Lescroart

Poison

Fatal

The Fall

The Keeper

The Ophelia Cut

The Hunter

Damage

Treasure Hunt

A Plague of Secrets

Betrayal

The Suspect

The Hunt Club

The Motive

The Second Chair

The First Law

The Oath

The Hearing

Nothing But the Truth

The Mercy Rule

Guilt

A Certain Justice

The 13th Juror

Hard Evidence

The Vig

Dead Irish

Rasputin's Revenge

Son of Holmes

Sunburn

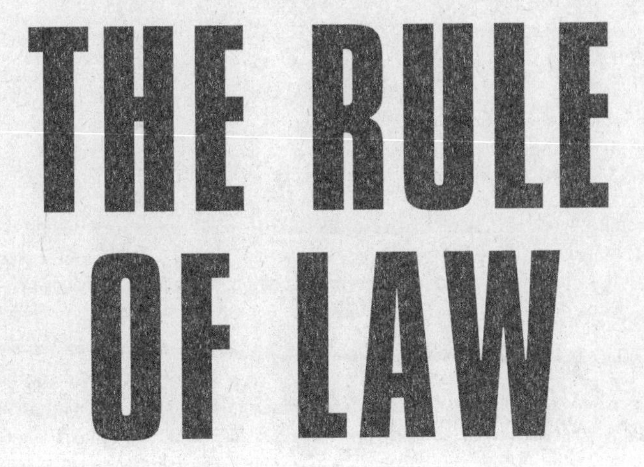

THE RULE OF LAW

A Novel

John Lescroart

ATRIA PAPERBACK
New York London Toronto Sydney New Delhi

An Imprint of Simon & Schuster, Inc.
1230 Avenue of the Americas
New York, NY 10020

First Atria Paperback edition September 2019

ATRIA PAPERBACK and colophon are trademarks of Simon & Schuster, Inc.

For information about special discounts for bulk purchases, please contact Simon & Schuster Special Sales at 1-866-506-1949 or business@simonandschuster.com.

The Simon & Schuster Speakers Bureau can bring authors to your live event. For more information or to book an event, contact the Simon & Schuster Speakers Bureau at 1-866-248-3049 or visit our website at www.simonspeakers.com.

Manufactured in the United States of America

10 9 8 7 6 5 4 3 2 1

Library of Congress Cataloging-in-Publication Data

Names: Lescroart, John T., author.
Title: The rule of law : a novel / John Lescroart.
Description: First Atria Books hardcover edition. | New York : Atria Books, 2019. |
Identifiers: LCCN 2018029488 (print) | LCCN 2018032713 (ebook) |
ISBN 9781501115752 (E-Book) | ISBN 9781501115738 (hardback)
Subjects: | BISAC: FICTION / Suspense. | FICTION / Legal. | GSAFD: Legal stories. | Suspense fiction.
Classification: LCC PS3562.E78 (ebook) | LCC PS3562.E78 R85 2019 (print) |
DDC 813/.54—dc23
LC record available at https://lccn.loc.gov/2018029488

ISBN 978-1-5011-1573-8
ISBN 978-1-5011-1574-5 (pbk)
ISBN 978-1-5011-1575-2 (ebook)

This book is dedicated to
Barney Karpfinger, Al Giannini, and Lisa Sawyer

It is easier to resist at the beginning
than at the end.
—Leonardo da Vinci

A man cannot be too careful
in the choice of his enemies.
—Oscar Wilde

THE RULE OF LAW

PROLOGUE

AFTER YOU MURDER someone, life is never the same.

Ron Jameson found himself thinking about this all the time; he couldn't get over the before and after differences.

Before, he'd been a hardworking mid-level attorney, billing his mega-hours, fair to both clients and opponents, responsive to his partners, honest to a fault.

Before, he had been a compassionate yet somewhat stern father to his two children, a righteous man who both taught and modeled the importance of respect—for property, for their mother, for other political, social, and religious viewpoints.

Before, he'd lived a circumspect, modestly successful, controlled existence, neither particularly happy nor sad, vaguely content most of the time, occasionally a bit bored, going through the motions.

Before, he'd been half-alive.

That had left the other half.

After he'd murdered the man who'd slept with his wife, it had taken him a while to get his bearings. Most of that time was spent worrying about what would happen if he were caught, about what he would tell his children and his wife. How he could justify himself and what he'd done to those he loved.

Every day he had lived with the constant fear that the police would catch onto him, that in spite of his best efforts he'd left a clue somewhere, key evidence that would convict him. He worried about going to jail, about spending the rest of his life in prison.

He was the sole support of his family; how would they all survive?

After, above all, he worried about how he could have turned into the man who could have actually done what he'd done.

When the police had found the incriminating evidence—a shell casing from the same make and caliber of the gun he'd used—on the boat of Geoff Cooke, his former best friend and partner in the law firm, it had taken him a while to understand. Mystifyingly, Geoff had apparently then used the same weapon to kill himself, which meant that the case was closed.

The police no longer believed that he'd done it. He was no longer a suspect.

It appeared that his law partner had in fact killed the philandering bastard.

When in reality—he came to understand—it had been his wife expertly shifting the blame from him to Geoff, protecting him and their marriage and their family, shooting his law partner and convincingly making it appear to have been a suicide, then planting the incriminating shell on Geoff's boat.

Which meant that both of them, husband and wife, were killers.

And after you murder someone, life is never the same.

1

"PLUS ÇA CHANGE, *plus c'est la même chose.*"

"I hate it when he does that," Wes Farrell said.

Gina Roake nodded. "He knows that, and that's about half the reason he does it."

"Seven-eighths of the reason, to be precise," Dismas Hardy said, "and precision is my middle name."

"Dismas Precision Hardy," Roake said. "It doesn't exactly sing."

"He just wants to rub it in that I don't speak French."

"That hardly qualifies as French," Hardy replied, "since anyone with even half an education should have run into that phrase somewhere and figured out what it meant."

"Well, I didn't."

"Tant pis pour toi."

Farrell threw his hands up. "I rest my case." Then, to Roake: "Maybe this isn't going to work out after all."

"It means 'The more things change, the more they stay the same.' "

"Thank you so much," Farrell said, "whatever the hell that means."

On this late Tuesday morning in early January—a clear and crisp day outside—the three of them sat around the large mahogany table in the circular conference room of the stately Freeman Building on Sutter Street in downtown San Francisco. Because of its domed glass ceiling that rose to a height of fourteen feet above their heads, the space had earned the nickname of the Solarium. The room also featured a forest of assorted indoor plants at its periphery.

Dismas Hardy, the nominal host and managing partner of the law firm

Hardy & Associates, leaned over and filled Farrell's wineglass with Jordan Cabernet Sauvignon. "That should ease some of your pain. Meanwhile, I'll try not to lapse into French again, since you're so sensitive about it. Although, to be honest, I don't seem to remember sensitivity as your most shining virtue."

"That was before I was the district attorney. Now I'm sensitive about everything. Do you know how many sensitivity training classes I've taken in the last eight years?"

"Twelve?" Gina guessed.

Farrell shook his head. "Seventeen. I counted."

Hardy snorted. "I don't think I even realized there were seventeen things to be sensitive about. I mean, after gender and poverty and the homeless, the list shortens up real quick, doesn't it? Oh, except, of course, women . . ."

"Watch it, buster," Roake said, but leavened things with a smile.

Farrell swallowed some wine. "Add at least four subsets under each of those, you're still not really close. You didn't even mention animal rights, and those subsets, too. Grandparents' rights. Left-handers' rights. Fish."

"Fish?" Hardy asked.

Farrell shrugged. "Probably. I tell you, the sensitivity epidemic is out of control."

"Hey," Roake said. "Our firm could have a motto. 'Sensitive about everything.' "

"That would bring in a lot of work, that's for sure." Hardy sipped at his own wine. "But way to bring us back to the point, Gina."

"Which was . . . ? Oh yeah, the new firm."

"Are we really going to do it?" Farrell asked.

"Up to you," Hardy said.

Ten years before, these three attorneys, plus one, made up the core of the firm Freeman, Farrell, Hardy & Roake. But then, in rapid succession, David Freeman had died; Gina Roake, who had inherited the building after Freeman's demise, had decided to take a sabbatical to pursue novel writing full-time; and Wes Farrell had stunningly and unexpectedly won election to district attorney, which necessitated the removal of his name from the firm's roster.

But two months ago Farrell had been defeated going for his third term as DA, and at his wake of a victory party, which Gina and Hardy had both attended, someone had floated the idea of reconstituting the old firm—or what was left of it.

Hardy, who was looking to reduce his hours in any event, had followed up in a low-key yet persistent way, and now here they were.

An hour later, the three of them were in a booth at Sam's Grill, celebrating their decision to go ahead with the firm's resurrection. Assertions about his sensitivity notwithstanding, Farrell rather famously wore a themed T-shirt every day that always pushed the limit on that score. There were those among his political supporters who believed that this was what had eventually caught up with him and cost him the election. Warmed up by the wine in the Solarium and a preprandial martini here, Farrell was midway through buttoning up his collar, having shown off today's T-shirt, which read: "Alcohol—because no great story ever starts with a salad."

Someone knocked on the panel and threw open the curtain.

"Ahoy, commoners," Abe Glitsky said by way of greeting. "I thought I heard familiar voices behind this shroud."

"He's a trained detective," Hardy said. "Nothing escapes."

"Former detective," Glitsky corrected him, not that anybody needed to be reminded. All of the voices he'd heard behind the curtain were indeed familiar to him. Hardy had been his best friend since they were beat cops together nearly forty years ago. He knew Gina from her days with the earlier iteration of Hardy's law firm. And he'd worked for Farrell in the district attorney's investigative unit until only a few weeks before, when he'd retired as the new DA's administration had gotten itself settled in.

Tall and broad, with a scar through both lips, milk chocolate skin, and blue eyes—his mother had been black and his father Jewish—Glitsky projected a threatening and, to some, even terrifying demeanor. Before he'd gone to work for Wes's DA's office, he had risen through the police department—patrolman, Robbery, Vice, head of Homicide—until he eventually became the deputy chief of inspectors. "A former detective, I might add," he said, "now well and truly retired."

"And how's that going?" Farrell asked.

"He hates it." Glitsky's wife, Treya, appeared from behind her husband. "He'll tell you he's loving it, but that's a lie. And I don't like it so much, either." Treya had been Farrell's secretary during the eight years of his administration, and like her husband had resigned when her boss had left office.

"Well," Gina said, "maybe our new firm can dig up some work for both of you. Would you like to join us for lunch and talk about it?"

Glitsky jumped at the invitation. "If it's no trouble," he said. Coming forward, he pulled one of the chairs back, stepping aside to hold it for Treya. "So," Glitsky said as he took his own seat, "is it just me? Or does this little gathering smack of conspiracy?"

"Nothing so dramatic," Gina said. "We're just reconstituting the old firm. Or talking about it, anyway."

"We're thinking we could have more fun than just each of us working alone," Hardy said.

"Lawyers looking for fun," Glitsky said. "There's something you don't hear about every day."

"We're breaking the mold," Farrell said. "It'll be a brave new world."

DIZZY FROM THE wine and more than a little breathless from the climb up the hill from Sam's, Hardy ascended the eight stone steps that led to the doorway of the Freeman Building. Opening the brass-trimmed door to the circular lobby with its marble floor and upholstered wallpaper, he caught his breath for the next twelve steps up the ornately filigreed cast-iron spiral staircase that led to the first floor and its wide-open oval reception area.

Halfway across that space, on his way to his office, Hardy stopped again, made a face, and changed course. Seated behind the low wooden wall that delineated the workstation of his long-suffering secretary, Phyllis, sat another woman whose name, he was pretty sure, was Karen, the secretary to one of the junior associates.

He checked his watch. It was 2:30, long after Phyllis in the normal course of events would have returned from lunch—if she had taken one in the first place, which was a rare enough occurrence. Most days, loath to abandon her post, deeply committed to her sacred mission of controlling access to visitors to Hardy's office, Phyllis ate from her little plastic salad container and drank her bottled water at her desk.

But she wasn't there now.

Karen—Karen?—had a phone bud in her ear and was speaking with someone, and Hardy waited in front of her until she bid good-bye to whoever it was and looked up at him, stood with a smile, and extended a hand. "Hello, I'm Kathleen. Mr. Peek's secretary?"

Hardy shook her hand. "Yes, of course, Kathleen." His famous though sometimes AWOL memory suddenly kicked in. "Kathleen Mavone Wheeler, if I'm not mistaken."

"Wow," she said. "You got my whole name. I'm impressed."

Hardy shrugged. "Old party trick. But what are you doing up here? Is Phyllis all right?"

"I really don't know. Mr. Peek just asked me if I could handle the phones for a while and here I am. She had to leave unexpectedly."

"There's a first," Hardy said. "But thanks for filling in. I appreciate your flexibility. Would you ask Don"—Mr. Peek—"to come down when he gets a second? Oh, and when I get calls, would you please buzz me on the intercom to let me know who it is before you patch them through? I've got my cell for my friends, but business calls I like a little warning. Good?"

"Of course."

"Excellent."

Less than a minute later, Hardy had just hung his suit coat over the chair behind his desk when he looked up, frowning at the knock on his door. Hadn't he just told Kathleen-not-Karen that he liked a little advance warning before . . . ?

But no. He'd only mentioned phone calls. And he'd asked her to call Don Peek and have him come down, so that was almost undoubtedly who was now at the door. But if Kathleen stayed on, even for a short while, he'd need to bring her up to speed on how he liked things handled. The revelation struck him that Phyllis was more valuable to him than he might have realized. It brought him up short. But for now: "Come in."

Don Peek, large and genial, with a horsey smile, opened the door and took half a second to acclimatize to the grandeur of the managing partner's office, with its Persian rugs covering the hardwood floors under the two separate seating areas—one formal, one less so—the wet bar, the espresso machine, the wine cooler. Nodding approval, he came around to Hardy. "You wanted to see me?"

"I did. Do you know what's up with Phyllis? She just left in the middle of the day?"

He nodded. "About an hour ago. Norma"—the office manager—"was still at lunch and I was the first office down the hall, so Phyllis came to me and said she had to leave right away: some crisis in her family."

"In her family?"

"That's what she said."

What family? Hardy thought. He'd never heard her talk about any siblings, and both of her parents were deceased. "How did she seem?"

Don Peek shrugged. "Pretty much regular Phyllis-like," he said. "No offense."

"No. I know what you mean. No mention of when she might be coming back?"

"No. And I didn't ask. Sorry."

Hardy waved away the apology. "No worries. I'm sure she'll let us know the second she's able to. It's just a little odd. No. A lot odd, actually."

"Well, as you say, she'll probably call. Meanwhile . . ." Peek made some vague motion back in the direction of his office and showed off his grin. "Billables await."

"Go get 'em," Hardy said. "Don't let me keep you. Thanks for coming down."

EITHER KATHLEEN HAD held all of his calls as Hardy had requested or he hadn't gotten any. When, at a quarter to five, he woke up from the hour-long nap he'd taken on his office couch, he sat up and walked over to his espresso machine, got a cup going, then crossed to his desk and pushed the intercom button. "Yo, Kathleen," he said. "I'm back in the land of the living. Did I get any calls during that little hiatus?"

"Nothing, sir."

"Slow day on the prairie, I guess. And still no word from Phyllis?"

"No, sir."

"Hmm. Is Norma in her office?"

A pause while Kathleen turned around to look. "Yes, sir."

"If she tries to make a getaway before I come out, please ask her to wait for me."

"Yes, sir."

Straightening, he checked the mirror on his closet door, buttoning up his shirt and tightening the knot of his tie. The machine finished spitting out his two-ounce cup of coffee and he drank it down black. Going around his desk, he grabbed his suit coat and put it on, then once again noted his reflection in the mirror. Good to go.

For an old guy, he didn't think he was doing too badly.

Hell, he thought, he was about to launch a new firm, or relaunch an old one. Either way, the idea excited him. He still had his energy and his wits about him, to say nothing of a wife whom he loved, two healthy grown-up children, and a small but select coterie of close friends.

In fact, he suddenly realized that, except for the somewhat disconcerting disappearance of Phyllis, his life was all but perfect.

And even the Phyllis situation, he thought, would probably . . .

2

"It'll probably, I hope, turn out to be nothing," Hardy said. It was just after six o'clock in the evening the next day, Wednesday.

"Do you really believe that?" Glitsky asked. "And if so, tell me again why there's a hurry here when it's just as likely you'll be able to ask her tomorrow when she comes to work."

"Okay, you win," Hardy said. "In fact, I'm officially worried. This is her second full day of missing work. I've been waiting for her to call but we haven't heard a word. She's never done anything remotely like this before and it's just plain not who she is. She's not answering her cell phone and there's no pickup on her home phone. I think she might be in trouble."

"Then this isn't probably nothing, which is how you and I got started here. You've got to make up your mind: probably nothing or probably something."

"I've made it up. I'm going down to her place as soon as I can."

"And do what?"

"Knock at her door. If she's not there, take a look around the neighborhood."

"Why don't you ask Wyatt"—this was Wyatt Hunt, Hardy's go-to investigator—"to run down and have a look?"

"He's stuck at home with a sick kid. Out of commission."

Glitsky let a silence build on the line.

Finally, Hardy said, "Look, Abe, your lovely wife mentioned yesterday that you were perhaps a little bored with your retirement, and I thought it wasn't impossible that you'd like to go for a ride-along just for the thrill of it all."

After a pause Glitsky said, "When were you thinking of heading out?"

"How fast can you get here?"

"Fifteen minutes."

"Great. I'm still at the office. I'll meet you out front."

HER APARTMENT WAS a flat on Silver Avenue, near the south edge of the city. From the street, it looked to be a twin of Glitsky's own two-unit building, with an exposed stairway on the left beside the garage leading to a second-floor entrance to the apartment proper. When they got there at 7:25, Glitsky pulled up to an open space at the curb directly across the street. "This can't be the right address," he said. "The parking place is way too close."

"Divine intervention," Hardy replied. "It's a sign we're supposed to be here." He pointed out across Glitsky's chest. "That would be her apartment above the garage, I think."

"Pretty dark."

"It is." Hardy let out a breath, then another one. "Well," he said, suddenly opening his passenger door, "you coming?"

The street was light on both car and foot traffic and featured about half residential flats like Phyllis's and half commercial storefronts: a body shop, an electrical supply store, a laundromat, a nail salon, a mom-and-pop grocery store at the corner, a few empty windows. Streetlights cast their feeble glows intermittently.

Hardy, his breath vaporing in the chill, stopped and shined his cell phone flashlight at the mailbox built into the stucco at the bottom of the stairs. As Glitsky came up alongside him, he said, "This is her, all right. McGowan."

Glitsky leaned in to verify. "McGowan. Check. Okay, now what?"

"Now we knock on the door."

A minute later they'd done that to no avail and Hardy had also called her landline number. They stood on the cold outside landing and listened to the phone ring inside the apartment until it stopped and her voicemail picked up.

"Well," Glitsky said, "this has been a treat. I'm glad I got to know a new place." He started back down the stairs.

"Abe."

Continuing down for a step or two, he finally stopped and turned. "Now what?"

"I still don't like it."

Glitsky said nothing. Sighing, with a pitying expression he shook his head, then looked up at his friend.

Hardy went on. "This woman has worked for me for over twenty years. Before yesterday, she has perhaps three times called in sick. She doesn't have a family member or any next of kin in her HR file. In fact, she doesn't have an alternate contact at all. This flat is the only address we have for her. So where can she be? Where did she go?"

"Someplace. It's just possible she's developed a life, isn't it?"

"Maybe, but unlikely. No sign of it until yesterday in any event."

"So what are you thinking?"

"You might not like it."

"Well, there's a promising start."

A FEW MONTHS before, Wyatt Hunt had had occasion to break into the apartment of a murder suspect, and what he found there had led to that man's arrest and a dismissal for Hardy's client. After the dust had settled on that case, Hardy had begged and pleaded and finally persuaded Hunt to give him a few lessons in lock picking. Just for fun. It wasn't as though he was ever going to use the information, but what a cool thing—Hardy had argued—to know about.

Now he and Glitsky stood inside the front door, which Hardy had carefully closed behind them. Turning on the main room lights, he folded his burglar's tool kit back up and dropped it in his pocket. Grinning like a fool, he said, "That was way easier than I thought it would be."

Glitsky didn't share his enthusiasm. "This is just wrong on so many levels."

"You're right, of course. But since we're here . . ."

"We make sure she's not dead, Diz. That's why we're here, even though it's no excuse for us being inside her apartment. If she's not here, then we get out fast." His face clouded with a new thought. "But even so, if she is here and dead and we call it in, how do we explain . . . ?"

"She gave me a set of her keys long ago for just such an eventuality. She'd basically invited me to come in and check if I got worried about her."

"Did you just come up with that?"

"Situations like this, it's better if you have a plausible story."

"Sometimes you're a little scary, you know that?"

"I like to think more than sometimes, but thank you."

The front door opened directly into the living room and now Hardy crossed the room and turned into another doorway, flicking on more lights in the kitchen. "I'll take this side," he said.

Leaving Glitsky to his own devices, turning on lights as he went, Hardy went into the kitchen, where several dishes and mugs were neatly arranged on a counter drying rack. Turning left out of the kitchen, Hardy entered a short hallway, checked out a tidy bathroom with a glance, then got to what obviously was Phyllis's bedroom.

The queen-sized bed was neatly made up, with some flounce pillows at the head and a quilt of bright yellow sunflowers. Two matching mahogany nightstands with reading lamps flanked the bed—the left one held a stack of six paperback books, *A Man Called Ove* on the top. Pulling the sleeve of his dress shirt over his hand so he wouldn't inadvertently leave any fingerprint or other trace of his presence, Hardy reached down and opened the drawer and was surprised to see a semiautomatic handgun that he had to force himself not to pick up or even touch. He closed the drawer just as he'd found it.

Across the bed, the other nightstand was bare except for a doily under the reading lamp. He went around the bed and, still careful with his fingers, opened the other drawer, but this one contained only a Costco-sized bottle of ibuprofen.

The small clothes closet held no surprises, nor did the six-drawer dresser or its surface. Everything was as he would have predicted from what he knew of Phyllis and her personality and habits. For a last couple of seconds, he stood at the doorway looking back into the bedroom for something he might have missed, and then, marginally satisfied, switching off the lights as he passed them, he headed down the hallway back to the kitchen, then into the living room again, where there was no sign of Glitsky.

Hardy took a few steps down the other hallway, which led off toward the back half of the apartment. "Paging Dr. Glitsky?"

"Down here."

Hardy got to the second left door and, looking in, saw Abe leaning over a desk, scowling. "I'm trying not to touch anything," he said. "But it's a challenge."

"I had the same experience in her bedroom. She's got a gun in a drawer next to her bed. What do you got?"

"Envelopes addressed here, this address, to Adam McGowan."

"Her brother?"

"Or maybe cousin? You want more?"

"Always."

Glitsky reached behind him and opened the closet in the opposite wall, which contained some men's pants, a pair of men's shoes, a few hanging shirts, and a pile of dirty clothes on the floor. "This is a guy's room. Adam's. Who, I might add, might come home at any moment, and that would be awkward, to say the least. I've heard a rumor that an unlawful-entry beef might cost you your bar card."

"Thanks for the reminder." Hardy, his adrenaline suddenly pumping, took a quick last glance around the small second bedroom: a thrift store dresser, a single unmade bed. "You're right," he said. "We need to leave."

But when they got to the front door again, Glitsky told Hardy to wait a minute as he walked across to the nearer of the two couches. Removing the cushions, he nodded with satisfaction, then leaned over and lifted out the fold-a-bed, this one casually made up with a sheet and a plain green blanket.

For a second or two he seemed to be studying the room in this new light. Reaching over, he pulled all of the magazines out of the leather rack next to the fold-a-bed and flipped through them, then put them back as he'd found them. Folding up the bed, he replaced the cushions as they'd been, then went to the couch across the room.

At the open front door, Hardy stood waiting. "Anytime today, huh?"

Ignoring him, Glitsky held up his index finger, then turned back around and directed his attention to the second couch. Once again removing the cushions, he found himself looking at another fold-a-bed, which he didn't bother to open out. Instead, in an obvious hurry now, moving quickly, he put the cushions back, gave the room a last look, and strode over to where Hardy had already stepped outside.

"Lights," Hardy whispered.

Nodding, Glitsky hit the switch, checked to make sure that the place was completely dark and that the doorknob, locked from the inside, wouldn't turn. "Relock the dead bolt?" he asked.

"I think not. Let them believe they forgot to lock it going out."

"Fine by me."

At the bottom of the steps, the quiet street remained deserted. Hardy stepped onto the sidewalk, swung around to his left, and checked the shoulder-high window in the garage door. "Nobody home," he said, "but we already knew that, didn't we? Are you having a heart attack?"

"Pretty close," Glitsky said.

"Me too." Hardy had his car keys out and started jogging across the street. "Let's get the hell out of here."

3

When Hardy arrived at the office at 9:00 the following Monday morning, Phyllis was fielding phone calls, typing at her computer, and otherwise being her usual multitasking self behind the low oval wall that delineated her space in the firm's main lobby. On Sunday she had called and with no further explanation left a message on Hardy's office line that she would be back at work at the start of the week—just to let him know. So he wasn't so much shocked to see her at her workstation as surprised that she appeared none the worse for wear.

When she saw him, she was talking into her headpiece, but held up her index finger in greeting—she'd be with him in a minute—and then spun away from him to continue her conversation. Hardy paused as he came up to her, took a beat, then shrugged his shoulders and continued around to his office.

He'd barely gotten into his chair, getting some papers out of his briefcase, when his intercom buzzed. Thinking that he might as well follow Phyllis's lead and get back to normal, he said, "Yo," which drove her crazy, because this was not the mature response she expected of a professional attorney like himself. Then he doubled down. "What up?"

He noted her gratifying sigh of frustration before she said, "Mr. Farrell would like a moment."

"Well, then, by all means let's give him one. Is he out there now?"

"He is."

"Send him on in. Oh, and, Phyllis . . . ?"

"Yes, sir."

"Is everything all right?"

"Fine. Thank you."

"Good. But I did want to mention that if you get a few minutes later on this morning, maybe you could stop in for a minute or two. Say hello."

After a split-second hesitation that he might not have even recognized except that he was so attuned to her rhythms, she said, "Of course."

"Maybe after I finish up with Wes. How's that sound?"

"As you wish, sir."

"I think I do. Let's call it a plan. Meanwhile, you can send Wes on in."

"Yes, sir. He's on his way."

Five seconds later Wes knocked and then pulled open the door. "I want to have Phyllis guard my office like she guards yours."

Hardy shook his head. "Can't do it, and even if I could, beware what you wish for."

"People always say that. I don't really get it. I don't wish for something if I don't really want it. So what's to beware of?"

"Unintended consequences. Phyllis stands guard outside your office, she scares away clients, and next thing you know, you go broke. Or you get your million dollars and lose your friends because you don't share it enough and they think you're selfish. Or you get elected DA and you prosecute some guy whose mother hates you and unexpectedly shoots you in the head."

"Oh yeah, stuff like that happens all the time."

Hardy grinned. "Just sayin'. Unintended consequences. So what can I do for you?"

Wes cocked his head, sparrow-like. "Give me a minute. All that philosophy derailed my train of thought. It'll come back to me. Meanwhile . . ." Plopping himself down onto one of the chairs in front of Hardy's desk, he put an ankle on his knee and brought a hand up to his chin.

"Something to do with the office?" Hardy prompted him.

"Probably." Suddenly his eyes lit up. "Ah. Got it. Treya, not Phyllis.

I'm thinking about bringing her on board here as my assistant. She's been with me eight years and I don't really think she's ready to retire. She doesn't think so, either, I believe. She just felt like she couldn't work for Ron Jameson."

"She's joining a big club," Hardy said.

"Not big enough. And I'm not saying that because I was the greatest DA in history—I made a lot of mistakes—but at least I tried to be fair and do the right thing most of the time. I don't think Jameson gives one little tiny shit about any of that. I still can't believe the whole office didn't walk out when he won by a whopping nine hundred and seventy-two votes."

"They've got jobs they need, Wes. They're waiting for their pensions. They're choosing to believe it won't be so bad."

"They are wrong, you know. It's going to be that bad. The guy's a true menace."

"Well . . ."

"You're just thinking this is me being a sore loser."

"Not at all. And by the way, even if you were, you'd have every right. He probably scared away twenty thousand people, and certainly nine hundred and seventy-two, who would have voted for you if he hadn't convinced them that having their name and address on the ballot rolls might attract attention to their families and have their grandparents or parents or siblings, or even their friends, turned over to ICE" —Immigration and Customs Enforcement, also known as *la migra*—"and sent back to Mexico or El Salvador or wherever."

"And all the while pretending he was on their side, just trying to protect them. Don't vote and stay safe. It makes me sick."

Hardy shook his head, then straightened up behind his desk. "But, hey, we've been through this ad nauseam, haven't we?"

"And then some. I know. Sorry. It's just so damn hard to accept."

"Yeah, but on the bright side, you can run again in four years and then go back and get him arrested for everything he's done wrong—which, believe me, by then will be a lot."

"Ha! If he doesn't have me killed first."

"I doubt that. Let's not go there."

"No? Really?"

"I know the rumors, but I don't think he's quite down to that level, Wes." The rumors were that Ron Jameson had killed his wife's purported lover, another attorney named Peter Ash, a couple of years before, and then framed his law partner, Geoff Cooke, for that murder . . . before killing him, too, and making it look like a suicide. In spite of the rumors, no charges had ever been filed, and the whole affair got written off to dirty politics. "The guy's an asshole," Hardy said, "but I don't believe he's an actual killer, and—no offense, Wes—when you bring that up, you sound just a smidge paranoid yourself."

"Just 'cause *you're* paranoid—"

Hardy held up a hand. "Don't go there. Especially when you've got a bunch of real, verifiable, awful things the guy's done. The election being one. But thinking he's actually capable of murder, that just undercuts your legitimate concerns, is all I'm saying."

"I hope you're right."

Hardy scratched at his desk for a long moment.

"What?" Wes asked. "You're pissed off at me."

Hardy shook his head. "Not really. Just trying to pull the reins on you wasting your time. You got beat, he probably cheated or at least played unethically, and that really sucks, I agree, but it's done and he's not going to come back at you."

"He might if I come after him."

"And why would you do that?"

"So I can beat him in four years."

"Okay, but this campaign's over. Beating Ron Jameson is just not your job anymore."

Wes considered, then let out a heavy sigh. "All right. You win. But it really is just a bitch."

"I hear you, and I'm not trying to win anything. But it's ugly enough out there, Wes. No reason for you to add to it, not when you've got good work you can do here, make a little money, lick your wounds. Life's good, or can be. Our job is to spread the word."

"All right, all right." Wes was up on his feet. "So, back to the point: How do you feel about Treya?"

"I love her," Hardy said. "And always have."

"I mean working here."

"You're a full partner here, Wes. If you need her, you need her. Bring her on. It's entirely your call."

"I like that answer."

Hardy broke a small grin. "What's not to like?"

"YOU WANTED TO see me, sir?"

"I did, Phyllis. Come on in. Have a chair."

"Thank you."

Hardy's secretary/receptionist was sixty-three years old. She cut her hair short and did not dye it, nor did she use much makeup. Tall and slender, she wore wire-rim glasses and no-nonsense footwear. She favored pale dresses and skirts that reached below her knees and the tops of those dresses or blouses or sweaters around her neck. He'd never seen her in pants.

At one of Hardy's earliest office Christmas parties, just after he'd come on as an associate in the firm, Phyllis—in tasteful makeup, eye shadow, and mascara—had arrived in low heels, a fashionable dark green and red dress revealing some cleavage, and a stylish shoulder-length haircut that showed off the blond highlights in her lovely tawny hair. At first glance Hardy had thought she was one of the new young secretaries he hadn't met yet, and a cute one at that.

Now, as she sat down across from him, he could not find much of a trace of the young woman she'd been back then. In many ways, he had to admit, her graceful surrender to age was enviable. She was who she was: efficient, competent, tireless—a jewel, perhaps in the rough, but valuable and valued nonetheless. Even a few days working with Don Peek's secretary Kathleen as her replacement had reassured him on that score.

Hardy decided to get up from behind his desk and take the matching chair across from her, and as he sat down, he broke what he hoped was a welcoming smile. "So," he began, "can I get you anything? Cup of coffee? Tea?"

"Thank you," she said. "I'm fine. You wanted to see me? I've left Kathleen at the desk. She's holding your calls."

"Great. Let's see if she does."

"Sir?"

"Never mind. A bit of a lame joke, I'm afraid."

She sat waiting, finally clearing her throat. "I'm assuming that this is about last week."

"You'd be assuming right," Hardy said. "Only in the sense, though, that we all were worried about you."

"I'm sorry for that, sir. I didn't mean to upset anyone. I had a personal issue come up that I had to take care of. If I would have known beforehand, I would have given you some more warning, but there just wasn't time. I had the vacation accrued . . . Norma said it would be all right—that I could also have charged it to sick time—so I didn't think it would be a problem."

Hardy held up a hand. "There's no problem with the time off, Phyllis. I'm sure we owe you a month or maybe two or, between vacations and sick days, probably close to a year. I don't remember the last time you took a sick day. That's the least of my concerns."

"Well, then . . ."

"But then you didn't pick up any of your emergency numbers, and that was disconcerting."

"I'm sorry about that."

But still, Hardy noticed, no explanation why. "Well," he said, "I guess I'm just checking to see that you're all right. If there's anything we can help you with."

Phyllis straightened her back, coming forward in the chair. She looked down, then over at Hardy with a small smile that all but failed. "I appreciate that. Thank you. But as I said, it was a personal matter. I'm sure that things are now under control."

"That's good to hear. But even if the immediate emergency has passed, or you could just use a little more time, I'm sure we could work something out. And you know the firm has resources that might be helpful if you or somebody you know is in some kind of . . . situation."

"No." She shook her head with some emphasis. "It's just something I had to take care of," she said. "And now it's all good. Really. All worked out."

Hardy, wishing now more than ever that he'd never entered her apartment and found the gun in her bedroom drawer and learned of her brother or cousin or whatever he was, spread his hands, then brought them back down to rest on his knees. "Okay, then. If anything changes, you know where to find me."

"I do. Thank you, sir. I'm sure nothing like this will happen again, and I'm truly sorry for any inconvenience."

"If you apologize to me one more time, Phyllis, I'm going to have to fire you."

"Yes, sir. I'm sorry."

"I won't count that one."

"What? Oh, I'm . . ." She brought her hand up to her mouth.

"Good catch," Hardy said.

WHEN HIS LANDLINE phone jangled on his desk, Hardy jumped about a foot from the surprise and slammed his thighs into the underside of his desk. Swearing aloud, he wondered if Phyllis had left her station again and, if so, who might be out manning the phones. He reasoned that it couldn't be Phyllis because she would have, as always, used his intercom after first vetting the caller and getting Hardy's approval to put the call through.

But meanwhile the phone rang again and he grabbed at it. "Dismas Hardy," he growled.

The voice on the phone replied, "Adam McGowan."

"Well, Mr. McGowan, you sound exactly like my friend Abe Glitsky."

"Yeah, but you'll want to hear about Adam McGowan."

"What about him?"

"Six weeks ago, guess where he got out from? Here's a hint. Avenal State Prison."

"That's kind of a big hint. What was he doing there?"

"Twenty-five to life for armed robbery, for which he served the minimum twenty-five. He got arrested when he was twenty-one, which, if my math holds up, makes him forty-six now."

"And living with Phyllis upon his release."

"Looks like."

"Where did you get this?"

"The inter-webs, with a little help from some friends in law enforcement."

Hardy digested that for a minute. "Well, whatever it was," he said, "it appears to be all cleared up, and Phyllis doesn't want to talk about it."

"You've talked to her?"

"I have. Not that it was the most scintillating conversation of my life. But she's back at work as of this morning and everything's fine. She had a family crisis that's all been taken care of. And whatever it was, it wasn't any of my business, so that's the end of that."

"I bet it's not. The end of it, I mean."

"Well, you may be right, but it is for the moment, and until something else happens, she made it pretty clear that she doesn't want anybody else involved. Like, for example, me."

"She's protecting Adam from something, you realize. He's back in trouble."

"Not unlikely, I grant you. But I'm not inclined to try to find out whatever it is on my own. And I think you and I have already gone about as far down that road as I'm comfortable with. In fact, quite a bit farther."

"You don't have to remind me. But"—Glitsky's voice went down a notch in volume—"since nobody interrupted us, it breaks my heart now we didn't stay around a little longer."

"Oh yeah. And then we could have watched me get a real heart attack."

"You would have been fine. That was just a little adrenaline rush."

"It didn't feel so little. It felt like a sledgehammer beating my heart to a pulp."

"It never would have hurt you."

"Maybe, but I didn't want to find out. Besides, what would we have been staying around longer to check out that we hadn't already seen?"

"How about what was going on in her living room?"

"Was something going on in her living room?"

"Undoubtedly."

"You never mentioned that at the time."

"I didn't? I guess I was busy with our getaway. But something was happening there besides Adam and whatever he was doing in his back room. The couches both folded out and had been slept on."

"And this means?"

"Well, from what we know about Phyllis, she isn't exactly the have-friends-over-for-a-sleepover type, is she?"

"Probably not."

"To say nothing about the magazines."

"What about them?"

"Half of them were in Spanish."

"Really?"

"Really. So what do you suppose that means?"

Hardy rubbed the phone against the side of his jaw. "I don't know. But it's a little odd, to say the least. If she speaks Spanish, I've never heard her, and there's been plenty of opportunity here in the office for that over the years."

"See what I mean? Mysteries abound. We should have stayed awhile longer."

"Except for that whole unlawful entry thing. Oh, and let's not forget her absolute right to privacy, which we've already pretty severely compromised."

"Picky, picky."

"Maybe, but we're just going to have to live with the mystery. And while we're talking, I think Treya's right about you maybe getting a little bit bored with retirement."

"No, I love sudoku. It's really great."

"I'm glad to hear it. But would you like me to keep my eyes open for the random investigator moment—maybe talk to Wyatt—just on the off chance?"

Glitsky hesitated. Hardy heard him draw in a breath. "I don't see how it could hurt."

4

HARDY COULD BE as glib and even self-righteous as he wanted with Glitsky, but the news about Adam McGowan's criminal record—to say nothing of the gun in Phyllis's bedroom drawer and the fold-a-beds and the Spanish magazines in her living room—was playing havoc with his conscience. These were facts that in the normal course of his life he really shouldn't know anything about. If he'd simply minded his own business and, by the way, not broken the law, then none of this stuff would be plaguing him the way it was.

On the other hand, though he was sorely tempted, he couldn't very well bring up any questions he might have with Phyllis without admitting what he'd done. And what he'd done had been unequivocally, perhaps unforgivably, wrong. For the first time in a decade or more, Hardy found himself wrestling with his childhood Catholic demons. Breaking into Phyllis's home—and the justification for it that he'd conned himself into believing—felt in his heart like what at one time he would have called a mortal sin.

And adding to the gravity of the situation, he was sure that Abe was right: whatever had caused Phyllis to take those days off, in spite of her protestations to the contrary, was very probably not over. She'd either volunteered or been pressured into taking into her home a relative with a serious criminal record, and regardless of which one it was—brother or cousin—the basic situation was unlikely to be a recipe for a tranquil and uneventful future. Hardy knew that it might be irrational, but he suddenly felt in his gut that some terrible thing was going to happen to Phyllis, and because of his indefensible behavior he couldn't discuss with her that possibility and/or some strategies that might prevent it.

He stood up, came around his desk, walked over to his door, and opened it. Phyllis was once again not at her station. While this explained Glitsky's phone call coming directly to him at his desk rather than the normal route via his intercom, it was also a sign that all was not back to normal in Phyllis's world. This was a woman who never even so much as went to the bathroom without making sure that someone else was covering the phones, especially Hardy's, and access to his office.

Off to Hardy's left, Norma's door yawned open, and seeing the office manager working at her desk, he crossed over and knocked on the lintel. "Sorry to bother you," he said, "but have you seen Phyllis recently?"

Norma leaned over to get a view of the receptionist's area and, confirming that it was unoccupied, said, "I think she must have just gone down the hall for a minute."

"Would you mind checking?" Hardy asked. "After last week, I'm just a little worried about her."

"I am, too, to tell you the truth, sir. She's been a little distracted all morning. I mean, for Phyllis. Plus, it's not like her to leave without coverage."

"That's what I was thinking."

"Okay, then." Norma, up and moving, came around her desk. "I'll be right back."

"I'll be at Gina's," Hardy said, and headed out behind her.

Roake had given up her active law practice to pursue a second career writing novels. She'd since published three books to modest critical acclaim and much more modest financial reward. Her connection to the firm had remained strong during this time, since the original firm's founder, David Freeman, had been her fiancé and he'd named her in his will as the inheritor of the building. After his murder, she had never even vacated her large corner office.

Hardy knocked at her door.

"It's open. Come on in."

Hardy complied, saw Gina standing over by her bookshelves, and said hello.

"Rats," she said. "I thought you might have been my first real new client."

"On day one?"

"The word's out that I'm back in the fight, Diz. I was marketing like a crazy person all over town last week. I thought they'd be knocking down my door by now."

"You know that many active criminals with money in need of counsel?"

"More than you'd believe, I'm afraid. Where do you think I got the grist for all of my books? You think I could have made up all that stuff?"

"Given your imagination, absolutely."

"Well, actually, you're right. I did make 'em up. My plots, I mean." She ran a hand through her thick black hair and broke a wide smile—all white teeth and sparkling green eyes. "But I always liked to keep up connections with my clients for deep background. I'm thinking they ought to start showing up here anytime now. And between you and me, I just can't wait to rejoin the billable world, those lovely six-minute increments where if you put in the work, there's a pretty good chance you're going to be compensated."

"As opposed to . . . ?"

"As opposed to another industry I could mention if I were a bitter failed writer type of person, which of course I am not."

"Of course not. And hardly a failure. Three novels. All outstanding."

"And strike three you're out, too, though you're nice to say so."

"Well, in any event"—Hardy closed the door behind him—"can you spare a minute?"

"Sure." She boosted herself up onto some low file drawers under one of the corner windows. Unlike Phyllis, who was about the same age, Gina had no compunctions about showing off her legs or any other part of the rest of her zaftig figure. Now, getting herself comfortably arranged sitting on the table, she crossed her shapely ankles and swung them back and forth like a schoolgirl. "What's up?"

For all of the lighthearted bonhomie between them, Hardy and Roake had spent significant time in the legal and ethical trenches together. Each knew secrets about the other that, if revealed, would have ruined reputations and careers.

"Our Town"

by Sheila Marrenas

Perhaps the most sensational unsolved crime in the recent history of San Francisco is the so-called Dockside Massacre, which took place eleven years ago this month on Pier 70, in the industrial wasteland just north of Hunters Point. On that cold afternoon, police responded to reports of multiple gunshots only to arrive and discover five bodies, including that of Chief of Homicide Lieutenant Barry Gerson, where they had fallen after what the evidence indicated was a horrific gunfight—over two hundred spent casings from at least nine different weapons littered the pier.

The other four dead men included John Holiday, a former pharmacist and current owner of The Ark, a seedy downtown bar, and three off-duty Patrol Specials—Nick Sephia, Julio Rez, and Roy Panos. (For those unfamiliar with the term, Patrol Specials are supplemental private security forces licensed and supervised by the city's Police Department. They wear uniforms that, except for a small logo on the shoulder, are exactly like those of regular city policemen. They are allowed to carry weapons and to make arrests.)

The question is: What was Barry Gerson doing on that pier, far from his normal place of business in the Hall of Justice, and what was the relationship between him and the other four men? Why were they all there? And who else had been there and apparently escaped untouched?

For reasons that no one has ever adequately explained, it seems that Gerson had made arrangements to meet with John Holiday on the pier to arrest him for the murder, which had occurred the week before, of a pawnshop owner named Sam Silverman. After the event, speculation had it that Gerson had second thoughts about meeting Holiday by himself in such a remote location, and for some reason enlisted the aid of these Patrol Specials rather than regular city police officers as he drove down to the meeting spot. Whatever the actual reason, it is indisputable that some sort of ambush transpired.

In the wake of the massacre, police inspectors went into overtime. Then mayor Kathy West issued an Event Number that essentially guaranteed unlimited city funds and man-hours to investigate the slaughter. Three teams of homicide inspectors worked on the case for six weeks and came away empty handed—no suspects and no arrests.

They did, however, uncover several provocative connections between Gerson, other members of the city's legal community, and the Patrol Special licenses controlled by Wade Panos, brother of the victim Roy Panos. Specifically:

- Matt Creed, the Patrol Special who had discovered the theft and murder at Silverman's pawnshop, was shot to death making his rounds within that same week.
- Also in that same week, David Freeman, a veteran attorney involved in a lawsuit against Wade Panos, was mugged walking home from work and subsequently died from his injuries.
- On the morning of the day of the massacre, Paul Thieu, a homicide inspector assigned to the Holiday case, apparently committed suicide by jumping off the roof of the Hall of Justice.

- John Holiday's lawyer, Dismas Hardy, was David Freeman's partner.

In spite of all of this smoke, police discovered no fire in this neighborhood. Because the Panos Patrol Special organization provided security for the Georgia AAA Diamond Center, and because massacre victims Sephia and Rez had also been part-time couriers for Georgia AAA, inspectors eventually came to concentrate on that business's owner, Dmitri Solon, a young Russian immigrant with a luxurious lifestyle. Solon apparently was smuggling diamonds into this country from the former Soviet Union, using the proceeds to procure drugs and launder money. The dominant theory among police inspectors was that the intimate and perhaps conflicting connections between the Panos group and recruits from organized crime syndicates in Russia may have played a significant role in the shoot-out at Pier 70. Certainly, the amount of firepower expended seemed consistent with a paramilitary organization. After the gunfight—or assassinations—the perpetrators may have used diplomatic immunity, and Georgia AAA's Russian-built helicopter, to effect their escape.

But to this day, the crime remains officially unsolved—yet another blight on the record of what has to rank as among the most inefficient, unprofessional, and scandal-ridden police departments in the nation.

(Today's *Our Town* column is Part IV of a seven-part series on unsolved major crimes over the past twenty years in San Francisco.)

IN POINT OF fact, after death threats to Hardy, Glitsky, and their children, and the murder of David Freeman, Hardy and Roake had both been participants in the gunfight that the media had dubbed the Dockside Massacre. This had left five dead people—one of them Barry Gerson, then the SFPD head of Homicide—shot up on Pier 70.

More recently, Gina had provided an alibi, under oath, that may not have been true for Moses McGuire (Hardy's wife Frannie's big brother and the last participant in the Dockside Massacre) during his trial for the murder of the young man who'd allegedly raped his daughter. Gina testified that on the day that the murder had taken place, she and Moses had been in bed together. And based on that alibi—which Hardy had made up and supplied to her the night before her testimony—McGuire's jury had acquitted him.

And now Hardy, sitting on the corner of Roake's desk, without ever consciously deciding to do so, found himself making a confession to her of his break-in at Phyllis's apartment the previous week and the dilemma he faced regarding the facts he was now aware of but could not reveal. "I'm almost certain," he concluded, "that she's still, at least potentially, in some kind of trouble; but unless she confides in me, which doesn't seem to be happening, I can't really do a thing to help her."

"That sounds about right," Gina said after a slight pause. "I don't think you have a choice. Unless you want to tell her . . ."

"No. That's pretty much out of the picture. I don't know if she'd forgive me. Hell, I don't know if I forgive myself."

Gina nodded. "It is a little bit outside of the playbook, I'll give you that."

"More than a little bit." In a defensive tone he added, "For the record, I wasn't spying. I really was worried about her."

Gina held up a palm. "Hey, no judgment here. I believe you. And I'm sure you did what you felt you had to do at the time. But now what you have to do is forget about it. If she gets in trouble again, maybe you can push a little harder, get her to open up. But, for the moment, you're just going to have to live with it."

"That's what I was afraid you were going to say."

"Sorry."

"Yeah." Hardy pushed himself off the corner of the desk. "Well," he said, "back to the grindstone. Good luck on those new clients."

"I'll get 'em, you wait."

"I'm sure you will. Anyway, thanks for listening."

"Of course."

But he hadn't yet taken a step toward the door when they both heard some commotion out in the hallway, followed by an urgent knocking and the door opening to the usually unflappable Norma wearing a look of panic. "Excuse me," she blurted, "but there are a couple of investigators from the DA's office in the lobby who say they've got a warrant to arrest Phyllis. You need to come down and . . ."

5

Including the brand-new presence of Farrell and Roake, the firm comprised five partners, six associate attorneys, six paralegals, eight secretaries, two mail room guys, three bookkeeper/admins, and Norma, the office manager. Of those thirty-one employees, thirteen were already gathered around Phyllis's workstation in the lobby, all of them probably obstructing justice if one wanted to get technical, when Hardy got there.

Also present, in an unusual turn of events, were two DA investigators, whom Hardy recognized as Glitsky's former office mates, Chet Greene and Terry Simms. Literally surrounded and obviously hostile, they'd already been drawn into some kind of engagement and interaction with the restive crowd. Hardy arrived in time to hear Greene raise his voice and show himself as every bit the asshole Glitsky had often described.

"All right," he boomed, "I need all of you people to back off and let us do our job. So we need you to—"

Hardy raised his own voice, cutting Greene off. "What's the problem here? You know me. I'm the managing partner of this firm and I need to know what you think you are doing here, disrupting our workday."

"We're here serving a warrant on this woman here. Phyllis McGowan."

"That's absurd," Hardy said. "Phyllis is my personal secretary and the firm's receptionist. She is not involved in any criminal activity. Who issued this warrant, and what for?"

Greene's tone hardened. "Yeah, Hardy, I do know you. And I brought extra handcuffs in case you decided to act up, as Mr. Jameson warned me you might. The grand jury has indicted this woman as an accessory to murder. We have a warrant, and she's coming with us whether you like it or not. Now, one last time: you and your people get out of the way and let us do our job, or, I swear to God, I'll call a wagon and we'll bring in the bunch of you."

Hardy backed away a step and took a beat. Then, in as calm a voice as he could muster, he said, "Could I take a look at the warrant?"

Greene's face was granite. "I don't need to show you anything. This is an arrest warrant, not a search warrant. I don't need to have a copy, and if I did, I wouldn't have to show it to you."

"I didn't say or imply that you needed to show it to me. I'm asking as a matter of courtesy."

Greene took his own beat, obviously trying to decide how far he wanted to take this thing. Finally he nodded. "We can do courtesy, too. Terry, show him the warrant."

The other inspector pulled some papers from his breast pocket and reached across where Phyllis sat. Greene took them and handed them to Hardy, who scanned them quickly and then said, "Accessory after the fact? On a murder indictment?"

Greene shrugged. "If that's what it says, that's what it is."

"It's ridiculous is what it is. Phyllis, what do you know about this?"

"Nothing, sir. It's the first I've heard of it."

"The police didn't interview you? You didn't get subpoenaed to appear before the grand jury?"

"No, sir."

"So this woman's been charged without so much as being asked to tell her side of the story, and with no evidence? Please." Hardy held on to the warrant and snapped out: "One last courtesy, Inspector. I'd like to put in a call to your boss, get to the bottom of what's going on here."

Greene, now a study in frustration, looked over to his partner, then scanned the hostile faces still pressed in all around them. He decided on the better part of valor. Grabbing the warrant back from Hardy, he barked, "One call."

"One ought to do it," Hardy said. "Phyllis, you know the number. And hand me the headset, please."

• • •

"Hello, this is Dismas Hardy. May I please speak to Mr. Jameson?"

"Just a minute. I'll see if he's in."

Hardy waited for ten seconds until the voice returned. "I'm sorry. Who did you say this was again?"

"Dismas Hardy. Wes Farrell's law partner. Regarding the Phyllis McGowan matter. It's rather urgent."

"One moment. Please hold."

Another extended silence. Finally, "I'm sorry, but Mr. Jameson has stepped out for a minute and is not available."

"Well, excuse me, ma'am, but I got the very distinct impression that he was available until you told him who it was calling him. As a courtesy, I'm trying to save him from a very embarrassing situation. It won't take more than two minutes of his time."

"I'm sorry, sir. I'm afraid I can't help you. Mr. Jameson is unavailable."

His knuckles white, Hardy held on to the receiver until he heard the dial tone start up again; then, letting out a lungful of air, he passed the apparatus back down to Phyllis. Turning to Greene, he said, "Mr. Jameson isn't able to get to the phone, but I assure you that I've found compromises in these kinds of situations dozens of times. And my earlier offer to you stands. There's no reason to subject Ms. McGowan to this whole arrest procedure. Why don't I just drive her down to the Hall and you guys follow me and we'll get all this worked out?"

With a flat gaze, Greene shook his head. "You got your phone call, Hardy. I don't want to be forced to call in a backup team, but that's my next step if there's any more resistance here with you or your people." He looked around the assembled employees and raised his voice. "All right. The show's really and completely over here," he said. "Let's everybody break it up, get back to your offices." He came back to Hardy. "Get your people out of here before this turns ugly. And I mean now."

Hardy didn't like it, but there weren't a lot of other options. After nodding to Don Peek across from him, and Graham Russo and Amy Wu, all of whom nodded back in tacit agreement, he said, "You heard the man, team. They've got a warrant. They're just doing their job. I'll be following them downtown and making sure Phyllis has representation. That is"—he looked down at his secretary—"if you want us as your attorneys?"

"Of course." She closed her eyes and sighed as a wave of relief seemed to wash over her, almost as though she hadn't been sure that Hardy would be her lawyer. "Thank you, sir."

"All right, then," Hardy said.

But it wasn't all right, because an intimidated Greene had suddenly had enough. Stepping over and reaching out, he grabbed Phyllis by the arm and twisted it behind her back, spinning her around and bringing her other arm up to fit the cuffs.

She let out a yelp of pain.

The onlookers reacted almost as a single body, surging, as Hardy pushed himself forward, trying to intervene with Greene's unexpected and violent manhandling. Terry Simms, who'd been on full alert, jumped forward, stopping Hardy, pushing him backward.

Hardy pushed back. "You bastards! Let her go."

But Simms ignored him, turning to grab Phyllis's other arm.

"Let's go," he screamed at Greene. "Let's go! Let's go! Now!"

Greene threw a last malevolent look at Hardy and then the two inspectors pushed their way through the gathered mass, knocking people back when they blocked the way.

They marched Phyllis across the lobby and down the stairs.

6

Over the past eight years—and even though he was technically on the wrong (that is, defense) side—Hardy had gotten used to fairly free access to the district attorney, who had after all been his friend and former partner Wes Farrell. Whenever he felt the need, even when—particularly when—he and Wes had been at significant legal odds with one another, he always felt that he could drop in on the third floor, appointment or no appointment, where he would often pass some pleasant time of day with Treya Glitsky before she would admit him to the sanctum sanctorum if Wes was around. And if he wasn't, she would tell Hardy where he was and when he was expected to return.

Under the new Jameson administration, clearly things were going to be different.

It started outside the main doors that separated the public area from the working offices of the DA and his assistant DAs. Formerly, Hardy would get to the admission window, nod at the clerk, Linda Coelho, who knew him, and wait for her to hit the buzzer that unlocked the door. Today, at the window, a line of more than a dozen people stood waiting to show their IDs and get individually admitted.

Hardy, already starving from lack of lunch, and in a foul dark humor over the humiliating arrest of Phyllis, then his inability to intervene in any way while they got her processed into the system, did not feel like his most patient self. By the time he got to the window, it was nearly 2:30 and he'd been in the Hall of Justice, knocking on doors and accomplishing nothing, for three hours.

Nevertheless, Linda Coelho knew him. So when the lawyer in front of him finished her business at the window and turned toward the admission door, Hardy dredged up a smile and pointed after her, indicating that he'd just fall in behind her when she got buzzed in and save them all some time on this bureaucratic nonsense.

But then Linda Coelho was knocking on the window, shaking a finger at him. She did not buzz through the woman in front of him. Hardy, his smile by now a little bit shaky, pointed again at the door. The clerk shook her head. After a theatrical sigh, which probably didn't help his case, he came back to Coelho's window, much to the displeasure of the guy who had finally gotten to it as well. "I'm sorry," Hardy said.

"Hey," the guy said, showing every sign of not being willing to cede his place, "same rules for everybody, pal."

"But I know Linda, the clerk here. I thought . . ." Hardy calmed himself down, decided that this was not the hill he wanted to die on. The line at the window was now at least as long or longer than when he'd first arrived twenty minutes before. With an apologetic shrug for the guy at the window, he said, "Excuse me, please. I'll just be a second."

After a moment's hesitation, and with an ill-disguised disappointed shake of his head, the guy finally backed up a half step and let Hardy lean in to the window. "Linda. What's up? You know me."

"Yes, sir, I do. But I need to see your ID. New rules for the new DA."

Hardy, taking care not to sigh again, fished out his wallet and flashed his credentials.

Meanwhile, Linda buzzed in the woman who had remained waiting at the door, then glanced at Hardy's driver's license, nodded, and asked him who he was going to see.

"Mr. Jameson."

"Do you have an appointment?"

"No." Another hopeful smile. "Not specifically, but I thought he'd give me a few minutes."

Linda obviously didn't think that this was a feasible plan, but she simply nodded wearily and told him to hold on. She picked up her phone, punched in some numbers, had a short conversation, then came back to him. "I'm afraid you'll need to make an appointment. Mr. Jameson's schedule is completely full this afternoon."

"But I'll only be—"

"Mr. Hardy, please."

From behind him: "C'mon, pal. We don't have all day."

Hardy half turned, noted the line starting to look like it might get proactive against him. Blowing out heavily, he gave up and said, "Okay," then excused his way past the muttering line and back out into the wide-open hallway.

DEVIN JUHLE WAS a close friend of Hardy's main investigator, Wyatt Hunt. He was also the head of Homicide and, Hardy was beginning to think, besides a couple of judges, perhaps the only person left in the entire Hall of Justice with whom Hardy did not have an adversarial relationship.

Or so he hoped. His faith had been pretty badly shaken so far today.

Still, he thought it was a good sign that he could walk up to the fourth floor and knock right on Juhle's open door without being molested or hassled for his identification. The lieutenant was sitting at his desk, immersed in some paperwork, and when he looked up at the knock, Hardy asked, "Got a minute?"

"Hey." He pushed away the papers. "How you doin', Diz? Come on in."

"You're sure I'm allowed?"

"Sure I'm sure. Why?"

"I thought you must not have gotten the 'Don't talk to Dismas Hardy' memo."

Juhle sat back, smiling. "Maybe the interoffice mail's late. But before it gets here, what can I do for you?"

Hardy had gotten to the closer of one of the small chairs that faced Juhle's large desk and sat down on it. "I don't know exactly, to tell you the truth. I've been sorting my socks while they get one of my clients—my secretary, as a matter of fact—processed into the jail."

"Your secretary? You mean Phyllis?"

"That's her."

"Processed into the jail?" Juhle did a double-take. "The jail? You mean *the jail*?"

"Yeah. The real jail."

"For what?"

"You'll love this." Hardy spent a minute with the short version of his day so far.

When he finished, Juhle wasn't smiling anymore. "I don't get it," he said. "Why would they want to put her in custody at the jail? She'll get arraigned tomorrow or Wednesday at the latest anyway, right? Then she makes bail and she's released."

"Correct."

"So why wouldn't they just have called you as a courtesy and let you arrange bail in advance? Then asked you to bring her in to get booked and processed, and then bailed out without a night or two in the slammer?"

"I don't know. Maybe it's another one of Jameson's new policies. He's not into the traditional courtesies. Or maybe it's something to do with Wes. Jameson's heard the word that he's coming back to our firm and so, by extension, I'm the enemy, too. And so is Phyllis. Or maybe hassling her is just a way of getting at us."

"So what'd she do that they thought they had to put her in jail?"

"They've got her charged with accessory after the fact."

"The fact of what?"

"Well, that's why I thought I'd come talk to you, as head of Homicide and all. This is all around a murder."

This news all but blew Juhle back in his chair. "Phyllis is involved in a murder? Whose?"

"I thought *you* might be able to tell *me*. They had a grand jury about it, since that's where the indictment came from."

"That narrows it down. Seriously. It would have been Tuesday of last week. That's the only murder grand jury we've had in a while."

Hardy immediately realized that this was the day that Phyllis had disappeared, but for the moment he kept this to himself.

"And if it was then," Juhle went on, "the victim was a major piece of work named Hector Valdez. Shot, apparently, by one of his girls, Celia Montoya, which is who they brought the indictment down against. And who, as far as I've heard, has since disappeared. So here's one for you: Does Phyllis know Celia?"

"I don't have any idea. I've never heard either of these names. But when you say this Valdez is a major piece of work, what are you talking about?"

"Pretty much you name it. His cover is that he runs a bar, El Sol, down in the Mish. Out of which he was into extortion, petty theft, drugs. At least, early on in his career. Mostly, lately, he was doing pretty good as a coyote bringing girls up from Mexico or El Salvador or both. Told them he had salon or waitress work for them, but guess what?"

"Maybe not so much?"

"Maybe never, more like it. And Celia was evidently one of these girls. Somehow, Hector let his guard down and left a gun where she could get her hands on it and she grabbed it and took him out. So if Celia knew your Phyllis somehow . . . and she must have had some connection if the grand jury . . ." He hesitated. "But why wouldn't they have picked her up until this morning? I mean, if the indictment came down last Thursday . . ."

Hardy said, "She left work in the middle of the day last Tuesday and only just came back this morning."

"Where'd she go?"

"No clue, Devin. Truly. I asked her about it this morning and she wasn't saying. I have a hard time believing that she is connected in any meaningful way to this guy Valdez or his murder."

"Well, somebody must have testified against her to the contrary. Or they must have some pretty good circumstantial evidence, and the grand jury bought it."

"I'll find out. If they ever let me talk to her again." Hardy checked his watch—just after 3:00. "Speaking of which . . ." He got to his feet. "Oh, do you mind letting me know which inspectors drew this Valdez case? Maybe I could finagle a word or two out of them, if they'd talk to me."

"You can try. Tully and McCaffrey. I could mention that you've already talked to me. That might help."

"You're a prince."

"Yeah, well, keep that to yourself."

More times than he'd care to remember, Hardy had been shocked almost to the point of nausea when he met clients in the jail's attorney visiting room, seeing them for the first time dressed not as regular citizens but as de facto criminals in their bright orange jumpsuits. No belts, some variation of flip-flops instead of shoes. And, of course, for the women, no sign of any makeup. They might, technically, be innocent until proven guilty, but with this garb they certainly didn't look it. This seemingly innocuous step effectively began the transformation of suspects from innocent citizens to dehumanized animals who needed to be caged.

When Phyllis finally appeared with an accompanying guard where Hardy had been waiting for her for another interminable hour, the sight of her nearly broke his heart. Her right arm was in a sling, her hands almost ludicrously still cuffed together in front, and she was in obvious pain.

Behind her desk at the firm, and in spite of Hardy's teasing at her expense, she was a formidable presence, not only as Hardy's gatekeeper but in her own right as a personality. Indeed, Hardy would never have considered needling her at all if he wasn't absolutely sure that she could take it and maybe even enjoyed it on some level. And, more than that, he knew that she could in her own subtle way dish it out as well, and had done so many times.

Now, after Hardy had insisted that the female guard undo her handcuffs, Phyllis waited patiently until she'd done just that and then left the two of them—now lawyer and client—alone in the large, ovoid-shaped room.

Rubbing her chafed wrists, she turned to face Hardy and surprised him again as a trace of a smile played at her mouth. Meeting his eyes, she said, "Yo," echoing Hardy's default wiseass response whenever she reached him on their intercom. The smile grew more pronounced. "And ain't this a fine kettle of fish?"

Relief washed over Hardy in a wave. They hadn't broken her spirit yet, not by a long shot. "Yo yourself," he said. "How are you holding up?"

"I've been better, to tell you the truth. These people in here are a lot crueler than they have to be. You know that?"

"I've heard rumors. But no actual abuse?"

Her smile went prim. "Well, the handcuffs seem a bit much. But when I mentioned it nicely after they took the first pair off, when they came to bring me down here, the second pair seemed tighter. I didn't take that as a fluke. Of course, they did give me a sling and an Advil, which doesn't seem to me to be overmedicating what feels like a dislocated shoulder."

"Shit. Really."

She shrugged. "I'll get over it."

"I know you will." Hardy sighed. "Why don't we sit down?"

"All right." She pulled around one of the steel and plastic chairs—chained down to the floor—and waited for Hardy to get settled in his own chair across the table. Before he could say anything, she preempted him. "First of all, let me say how sorry I am to have gotten you involved in this, to say nothing of the disruption to the firm today. I had no idea anything like this was going to happen."

"Well," Hardy said, "just so you understand why you're being fired."

"Of course. I'd expect nothing less. It's the only thing to do."

Just for a second, Hardy wondered if she realized that he was kidding.

"Great," he said. "Now that that's settled . . ." But the joking had quickly run its course. Hardy gave her a straight, no-nonsense look. "But seriously. Do you want to tell me what's going on? I'm assuming this has to do with your family crisis last week."

"Of course."

"I'm afraid I didn't realize that you had a family. I know that's unforgivable with all the time we've been together, but—"

"It's not a whole family, sir. It's a younger brother. Adam. And most of the time I'd rather forget that we are related."

Hardy sat back in the hard seat and crossed a leg. He nodded encouragingly.

She went on. "He's eighteen years younger than me, so we were never close growing up. I left my mother's home when I was eighteen and he'd just been born, and I never moved back in with them. And by that time my father was long gone, too." She steeled herself, taking a breath. "Anyway, I got some student loans and did two years at Heald here in the city and learned how to type, and then David hired me, so I've been lucky. I've always had a job."

"Maybe because you are really good at it."

"Maybe. Thank you. But meanwhile Mom and Adam moved to Bakersfield, where she'd gotten some work in a hospital down there. Mom died from throat cancer about ten years after that, when my brother was eighteen. I went down for the cremation and hung out for those couple of days with Adam, who was already pretty much of a mess."

"In what way?"

She chuckled mirthlessly. "You name it. He'd fallen in with a different culture: dropped out of school, worked on motorcycles all day, long hair, dirty jeans, dirtier T-shirts, tattoos, drugs and alcohol. He tried to keep himself relatively straight when I first got down there, but he was strung out enough that he couldn't even keep it together to make the appointment we'd made to go scatter her ashes. I went by their house with the urn and he made it all the way to the front door, where he told me he was just too hungover. Why didn't I just go and do it myself? And, PS, the place also smelled like marijuana, and lots of it. Anyway"—she shrugged her shoulders and winced at the pain—"he got his first prison sentence within a year or so after that—carjacking—and of course got in touch with me. Could I help him out with his attorney fees? Which, stupidly, that first time, I did."

"You're saying there were more times?"

"Three." She leveled her gaze at him. "The last one was for armed robbery. It was his third strike and he was just lucky that he didn't kill somebody. He could have, and maybe should have, been doing life without. But anyway, he got out of Avenal six weeks ago."

"And somehow got in touch with you."

A bitter smile. "One of the drawbacks to living at the same address for forty-three years—thank you, rent control—is that people can generally find you in a pinch."

Hardy breathed a sigh of relief, albeit one laced with guilt. This was information he never should have acquired in the first place through his snooping with Glitsky, but now she was giving it to him firsthand, and so anything he collected from here on out would be fair game. He hoped. "So he contacted you?"

Nodding, tight-lipped with frustration, she said, "He needed, he said, a few weeks to get himself together. Someplace to stay short term while he looked for a job. He'd promised me that he was a different person. He'd changed. Which I doubted, because, you know, people don't really ever change, and especially in prison, except maybe to get worse. But he was my brother, my only living relative. And I convinced myself that he sounded different. Older, more mature, which of course he was, although not necessarily better. I told myself I owed it to my mom's memory, at least. All the usual stupid excuses why this time it was going to be different."

"So he moved in with you?"

"Temporarily. Until he found his own place and a job to make his rent. Ha!"

A tentative silence descended into the room. Through the building's walls, they heard car horns blaring on the freeway, punctuated by the clang of metal on metal—a cell door slamming?

Phyllis let her shoulders settle; her free hand dropped into her lap.

Hardy in a brown study scratched at his jawline. "So how is your brother connected to Celia Montoya?"

For an instant Phyllis's eyes widened in surprise. "How did we get to Celia?"

"You got arrested as an accessory after the fact of the murder that Celia's charged with. A guy named Hector Valdez. Which means the grand jury believed that you knew something about that murder, specifically that Celia committed it or had been charged with it, and then you harbored, concealed, or aided her to avoid arrest, trial, conviction, or punishment. Not to sound too much like a lawyer. Does that pretty much sound like what you might be involved in?"

For a few seconds Hardy wondered if perhaps Phyllis had gone into a trance of some kind. He felt he could almost see her mind accepting and rejecting responses to what he'd asked her. Finally, in a quiet and controlled voice, she said, "I don't mean to sound like a vigilante, sir, but if she did, I believe that she would have had every right to kill him—out of pure self-defense. Adam told me he'd evidently bragged that he'd killed a few girls himself when they'd tried to get out of the life once they got here. And the poor other ones that he sent back to where they'd come from? Guess what? They got killed by their handlers as an example to the others. It's a humanitarian nightmare, sir. The sex trade. And this time it caught up to Celia."

"And you could somehow help her? How was that?"

Phyllis brought her hands up to her mouth in a prayerful attitude. Closing her eyes briefly, she sighed into her hands. "I don't know what else I should tell you, sir. There's more to this than just Celia's story. And Adam's."

"You can tell me anything, Phyllis. I'm your lawyer. Anything we say to each other is covered by the attorney-client privilege."

"I understand that. But I've also seen how privileged communications sometimes get out in the real world."

"Not in my world," Hardy said, although he knew part of that answer, at least, was a lie.

"Maybe not on purpose," Phyllis shot back, "but you can't deny it happens. I've been in the law business long enough, too, sir. You can't let a drop through that dam or the whole thing comes down. And this is a big dam. It's not just Celia. And if they've connected this to me—my goddamn brother selling me out for a plea deal or a cup of coffee, if you want my bet—well, it's bigger than you think."

7

Among the amenities that had improved his life, Hardy ranked the garage he had finally rented as right near the top. In an enclosed street-level spot four buildings north of Geary, it was on the west side of Thirty-Fourth Avenue, on the block where he lived.

In the old days, before he'd started shelling out the $850 a month for the parking place, it was not uncommon for him to wind up finding some legal spot three, four, even six or seven blocks from his home. He would regularly trudge home carrying his twenty pounds of lawyer's briefcase, often buffeted by the wind, soaked and chilled through and through by the shroud of misty fog. Out in "the avenues," San Francisco often rivaled winter in London or Moscow for the inclemency of its weather, and the search for curb space nearly always left Hardy dispirited and, at least in the short term, exhausted.

Tonight, though it was dark, windy, and low-50s, the walk from the garage to his home took him less than five minutes. When he got to the picket fence bordering his property, he stopped for a moment and took in the place: with the porch light on, the two-story bungalow was by far the most inviting building on the block, huddled as it was between two four-story apartment buildings. He caught a whiff of smoke and looked up at the chimney. No doubt breaking some law against the burning of wood, Frannie—God bless her—had apparently started a fire going in the fireplace.

Opening the door, in sudden high spirits, he put his briefcase down on the floor and sang out in his best Ricky Ricardo voice: "Honey, I'm home."

Dressed in blue workout clothes, Frannie appeared, walking through from the dining room carrying a wineglass in one hand and a leaded crystal cocktail glass half filled with amber liquid in the other. "I took the liberty," she said, handing him the glass and leaning up for a quick kiss. "Macallan 12 and one ice cube. Dinner in a half hour. Meanwhile, you take off your coat, sit in your chair, enjoy the fire and your drink."

"Well, all right, if you insist. But to what do I owe all this fanfare?"

"The Beck"—their daughter, Rebecca—"called and told me about the showdown you had in your office over Phyllis."

"The bastards."

"They really walked her out in handcuffs?"

"Well, you know, because she's such a danger to the community."

"Right. So, anyway, then I get your text that you won't be home until at least seven thirty. You're at the jail. So I put two and two together and realized it probably hasn't been your favorite day of all time. Maybe you could use a drink and a fire and a little relaxation when you finally get here."

"Even if you didn't do stuff like this, I'd still love you. You know that?"

"Of course. And why wouldn't you?" She kissed him again. "Now give me your coat," she said. "And sit down."

THE DINNER WAS simple—filet mignon, green beans, orzo, a bottle of Hafner Cabernet Sauvignon. Frannie had set out the good china and several candles. They sat across from one another rather than at the opposite ends of the table as they did more often. Frannie was a marriage and family counselor, and one of the couples she'd been working with for several months had just decided to reconcile and were moving back in with one another, which she was taking as an unqualified success.

On the home front, Frannie had talked to both of the kids, the Beck and Vincent. They were both going to try making it over for Sunday dinner, and how about if they also included the Glitskys?

"Oh," she added, "and Vincent sounded like he might be thinking about bringing a young woman with him as well."

"He's going to *try to* make it Sunday and he's *thinking about* bringing a girlfriend with him if he comes? God forbid he just says 'Yeah, we'll both be here. See you then.'"

"He'll probably commit by Saturday."

"Probably, though, you notice. Not definitely."

"He's just having some issues with commitment."

"Who isn't?"

"Well, you and me, for example."

"We don't count. We're an anomaly."

Dessert—a rare event—was a brownie and a scoop of vanilla ice cream. Hardy took a first spoonful, rolled his eyes, and feigned a swoon. "Can I get three more of these?"

"Sorry. The limit is one each."

"I could take yours."

"I don't think you could."

"I'm bigger and stronger than you are."

"You don't want to try, Dismas. It won't turn out well for you."

He sighed, theatrically. "Ah, well. So do you want to hear about Phyllis?"

"If you're up for talking about it."

"I figured for a bite of your ice cream and brownie . . ."

Frannie shook her head. "Nice try, but it's not that important to me."

"How can you say that when you don't know what it is? It's really pretty darned amazing."

"I'm sure it is." She spooned another bite into her mouth and gave him a tolerant smile. "I can't wait to hear. It can't really be that she's involved in a murder, can it?"

"It kind of depends on what you mean by 'involved.' I don't believe she had anything to do with killing anyone herself, but as it turns out, I could be wrong about that, too."

"What do you mean, 'too'?"

"Well"—he popped the last bite of dessert—"you think you know somebody, especially if you've worked with them for twenty years or so, but it turns out I really didn't have much of a clue about who she really is."

"And today you found out?"

"Got some idea, at any rate."

"And who, really, is she, then?"

Hardy, hesitating as if he had to process his answer internally one last time so that he could believe it, finally said, "She's part of . . . of this underground railroad system that helps undocumented immigrants get out of the country and up to Canada before they can get themselves deported."

"But that's not happening here. Not in San Francisco. We're a sanctuary city."

"Right. That's the theory. But that doesn't mean it's not happening. There's evidently still a huge community of people right here in town who get the word somehow while they're at work or hiding out, lying low, that ICE knows where they are and is on their case. According to Phyllis, we're talking hundreds of people, maybe thousands, who've just slipped through the cracks up to now. They can't get their green cards; there's no way they can get to citizenship or even on the road to citizenship. They get picked up on a sweep and there's nothing they can do."

"And Phyllis got herself involved in this? How did that happen?"

"It's still not completely clear to me. It seems one day five or six years ago—"

"Five or six years ago? You mean pre-Trump?"

"Several years pre-Trump. Obama had a pretty vigorous deportation policy in place, too. Don't kid yourself."

"I didn't realize that."

"Lots of people don't, but it's true enough. In any event, this one day, Phyllis got off from work early and went home and found her housekeeper, Luisa, sitting crying at her kitchen table. So she asked what was the matter and they started talking and one thing led to another and it turned out a couple of her brother's co-workers at the restaurant they worked at had gotten picked up by ICE the day before.

"Her brother had just been coming in for his shift and saw what was happening and managed to get away, but that was the end of that job and, even worse, he knew it was only a matter of time before they found out where he lived and busted him there, with his wife and two kids under five, all of them undocumented. If he didn't want to have them all deported and wanted to have some kind of life, he had to get out of the country, probably to Canada. But how could he do that without any papers or even ID?

"Luisa said they could all stay with her for a while, but that only increased the risk for her, too. Because, of course, she was undocumented as well. She didn't know what any of them were going to do. So Phyllis said, 'Why don't you tell them they can stay at my apartment until we can find out where they can go?' "

"Just like that?"

"Apparently."

"That's an enormously big step out of nowhere."

"Tell me about it."

"We're talking about the same Phyllis McGowan who works for you?"

Hardy nodded. "I know. It's hard to imagine. But evidently she did some homework and got in touch with a whole bunch of other people up and down the state who were smuggling these immigrants up to and across the border. Before too long, her place became one of the regular stops for either the locals or people passing through on the way up from LA or San Diego. Three, four, five times a month she'd have people come by for a couple of days, crash at her place, then head up to the next station in Santa Rosa or Ukiah or someplace."

"Except this last time she got caught?"

"She thinks more ratted out than caught."

"By who?"

Hardy spelled out Phyllis's theory about her brother being the source of the betrayal, although many of the details about that remained vague.

"So where is he now?" Frannie asked. "Adam."

"Not clear. Evidently he's still in and out of her place. Lately out. But his clothes are still there, so he'll probably be back."

"And how does he fit in with this murder?"

"That, too, I'm afraid, is unclear."

"So what happens next?"

"In a perfect world, tomorrow morning Phyllis gets arraigned and I get her out of jail with little or no bail. Then we start trying to get our hands on some facts that might explain some of what really happened.

I'm tempted to believe that the worst is over, all that crap they pulled on us today, but of course with our new DA there are no guarantees. Jameson seems to be playing by a different rule book, and it ain't the rule-of-law book, but maybe it feels like that just because of my former access to his office and Wes being my pal."

"And partner, don't forget."

"I never would. But the new guy, Jameson, couldn't pick me out of a lineup, I'm sure. I can't believe it's anything personal to do with me."

"You hope."

Hardy shrugged. "Well, even if, how bad could it be?"

AT 9:00 P.M., Ron Jameson sat behind the oversized cherry desk that he'd had brought in on the day after he took office. He wanted to send a strong message right away, distancing his administration from that of his predecessor. Wes Farrell may have enjoyed not even having a desk, the informality of his two library tables, the foosball and Nerf basketball games, the dartboard and chess table, the framed poster of Che Guevara amid the diplomas and celebrity shots of himself with Tom Hanks, Beyoncé, Madison Bumgarner, and other stars, but these accoutrements didn't even begin to deliver the impression Jameson wanted to convey—not approachability. Not friendliness. Not competence or efficiency or justice or even simple fairness.

No. His office and its formality would reflect what he was about, and that was power.

Now, behind his desk, he sat upon his red leather throne—$12,000 from Gump's—and surveyed the space in front of him. The two Queen Anne chairs on the Persian rug; the floor-to-ceiling bookshelf filled now with leather-bound law books rather than the hodgepodge collection of mostly paperback fiction that Farrell had collected; the three-foot-diameter $4,500 globe. In all, the space was nearly flawless and sufficiently intimidating. Leaning back in his chair, he crossed his arms and nodded with satisfaction.

A knock on his door, which then opened to reveal the shapely form of his secretary Andrea O'Riordan, in Jameson's opinion the most beautiful woman in the building. His own wife, Kate, was another world-class beauty, in some ways Andrea's superior in that realm, but that did not necessarily mean that he could not appreciate both of them equally as objects. Men defined themselves, he believed, by the objects with which they surrounded themselves. These things made a difference.

He came forward in his chair, hands on his desk, and nodded pleasantly. "Ah, the lovely Andrea," he said. "Time to go?"

"If you have nothing else. The decks are cleared for the morning. You did get another call from Dismas Hardy, who was hoping to either talk with you or make an appointment for tomorrow before the McGowan arraignment."

"But I still wasn't in, was I?"

"No, sir, as you instructed. And I informed him that your morning calendar was already filled."

"Nice. Thank you. That guy's got some balls, doesn't he? How many times did he try to get me today?"

"Three times by phone. Once dropping by outside with no appointment."

"You'd think he'd be starting to get the message by now. Wes Farrell's friends aren't any friends of mine. You think we haven't made that clear enough?"

"I think we must be getting there."

"I mean, the guy lobbied everybody he knew against me. He thinks I wouldn't have heard about that? And I'm going to forget? Is he dreaming?" He paused for a moment, quickly gave Andrea what he thought was a subtle once-over, thinking anew that she was one magnificent hunk of womanhood, and the plain fact was that he wanted to keep talking to her for another minute or two, bask in her glow. "And speaking of McGowan," he said, "we've got her locked up for tonight in the jail, right?"

"Yes, sir. Mr. Hardy talked to her until nearly seven o'clock, but she's back in her cell now."

"Where she belongs."

"Yes, sir." Andrea briskly looked around the corners of the room, came back to her boss. "Is there anything else?"

Jameson hesitated and finally shook his head. "No. I think that'll do it." He pushed himself back and up out of his chair. "And I've got a big day tomorrow myself. The DA shows up in court. That ought to make a headline or two, don't you think?"

"Yes, sir."

"All right," he said. "Let's get going while the getting's good."

8

On reflection, in spite of telling Dismas Hardy that he'd put in a good word with the homicide inspectors who were working the Valdez case, to increase the odds that they'd talk to him, Devin Juhle decided to speak with them himself, give them a heads-up about what might be in store.

This was why, at a few minutes past 8:30 on Tuesday morning, Beth Tully and Ike McCaffrey sat across from Juhle in one of the booths at Lou the Greek's, a bar-restaurant directly across Bryant Street from the doors of the Hall of Justice. They could have all been either in Juhle's office or at the inspectors' desk area in the Homicide Detail's bullpen, but since Ron Jameson's election to DA, rumors had swept through the Hall that many of the private offices—and even seating areas—were either bugged or in the process of getting there. Although not exactly believing the truth of this, Juhle didn't want to take the chance, and so had invited his inspectors across the street for their little chat.

Three untouched mugs of coffee sat on the table, one in front of each of them. Ike hunched all the way back, expressionless, his eyes heavy-lidded, almost reptilian, as if he were only a spectator to these proceedings.

His partner, by contrast, was all attention, ramrod straight, focused on her lieutenant across the table. "I just don't see what we want to talk about with McGowan's attorney," she was saying. "These defense guys . . . well, you know."

"I do, of course," Juhle said. "You don't have to talk to him at all. He asked me to ask you as a courtesy. And, for the record, I gathered he was only interested in your suspect insofar as his client got implicated with her, what came down with the grand jury that put the McGowan woman into the picture."

"In other words, he wants to hear about what happened in the grand jury trial—which, even if we'd been invited, we're not allowed to disclose?"

"Wait a minute," Juhle said. "You're saying you didn't testify? Neither of you?"

"Not for this one, no."

"And they still had enough to indict this Montoya person?"

"Apparently. Ike writes a good report," Tully said. "Plus, there are three eyewitnesses: Mel Bernardo, the bartender where the shooting went down; his girlfriend, Rita Allegro; and McGowan's little brother, Adam. Who, you'll probably not be surprised to hear, is a recent graduate of Avenal U."

"Who is? The brother?"

"Yes."

McCaffrey finally bestirred himself. "We didn't have squat to do with or say about McGowan, Devin. You want our opinion—and here I'm sure I speak for Beth as well—as soon as it became clear that this was going to have elements of a sanctuary case, this was all driven from above. Give it a higher profile."

Juhle's voice took on a lower tone. "I didn't know it was a sanctuary case."

"Yep," Beth said.

Juhle waited for explanation or comment. He continued to wait. Between the sanctuary issue and the nonappearance of his inspectors before the grand jury, this was getting interesting, but no questions leapt to his tongue. The inspectors were playing eye tag.

Finally, Ike picked up his mug, drank, made a face, and cleared his throat. "Celia Montoya is undocumented, Dev. In theory, as you know, we're not supposed to turn any information we have on her over to ICE. But then she went ahead and allegedly killed her handler, or pimp, or whatever else you want to call Mr. Valdez. And then she had to get away from us fast and that put her in the undocumented pipeline, which apparently connects her to Mr. Hardy's client. And not only puts ICE in the picture, but . . ." Suddenly out of steam, Ike looked sideways at Beth.

"What?" Juhle asked. "Not only puts ICE in the picture, but what?"

"But effectively takes us out," she said.

"How's that? She's a murder suspect. You guys are homicide inspectors. Whatever happens, you're in it hip-deep."

"Except if we're not," Beth said.

"And how could that be?"

"Well, if, for example, Mr. Jameson runs the case entirely through the DA's Bureau of Investigations and freezes us out. Then, win, lose or draw, he turns Montoya over to ICE for deportation."

"He's not going to do that. His whole campaign was based on no deportations ever. And she's still up for murder. Jameson's not going to try to get her deported before she goes to trial."

"No. She'll be going to trial all right, if they catch her," Beth said. "But in spite of the grand jury and the indictment, the case against Celia isn't all that strong and his backup play is to have her deported, even if he can't make the criminal charges stick."

"Wait. You just told me the case wasn't that strong, but you said there were three eyewitnesses."

"Right," Ike said. "We questioned these three individuals and all of them told the same story."

"Which doesn't mean that it's a true story," Beth put in. "It might be, of course, but we—Ike and I—hadn't decided yet to press for her arrest, or even to settle on Ms. Montoya as our prime suspect, but Jameson decided he had enough for the grand jury, and I guess he was right."

"Enough for the grand jury." Juhle chuckled. "There's a high bar."

He knew, as did his inspectors, that the grand jury was a blunt instrument. When a DA brought a case to the grand jury, the result was nearly always an indictment. This was because no defense attorney was allowed to cross-examine witnesses, nor was a judge present at the proceedings to rule on techniques or testimony that might not be admissible at trial. The grand jury essentially heard only one side, one version of the story, and, not too surprisingly, they more often than not swallowed it hook, line, and sinker.

Not for nothing was it said that if the DA wanted, he could get the grand jury to indict a ham sandwich.

Juhle sat back on his bench. "I don't get it," he said. "Who wins in this scenario?"

"Well," Ike said, "clearly it's a work in progress, but whatever shakes out, it looks like Jameson is going to be in the middle of it, since he's gone out of his way to put himself there."

"Okay, but what for?"

"Media," Beth replied. "Attention. Publicity. This is a seriously hot-button subject, and he gets to play all sides against the middle. And then he starts to set himself up to run for governor. After which the sky's the limit."

"She's not a fan," Ike said.

Juhle flashed a tight smile. "I'm picking that up." He picked up his mug, looked at it suspiciously, put it back down. "So . . . Jameson's cut you out. That's what I'm hearing."

"Pretty close," Ike said.

"If you want to get back in, Hardy's client might be a way to go. Just sayin'."

"Except that the McGowan woman is not really a part of the homicide case," Ike said.

"Well, you never know. From what I'm hearing here, she might be, after all."

LIKE MOST OF the paired-up partners in Homicide, Ike and Beth had front-to-front adjoining desks. Still, when they wanted to talk about something sensitive or at a little lower volume, Ike tended to come around and sit on the corner of Beth's desk, which he was doing just now. "You should have told him what you really think about our new DA," he said as he made himself comfortable. "You came across as reasonably rational about him."

"I *am* reasonably rational."

"You think that he actually worked around us so we wouldn't get to give any of our testimony on Valdez?"

"Absolutely. And not 'we.' Me. He wants to keep me at arm's length, and that's generally okay with me. Except, truly, if it could do our case any good, I am beginning to be tempted to talk to this Hardy guy. Do you know him?"

"Only by reputation. Hard-charging, straight shooter. Sometimes gets outside the box entirely. He and Abe Glitsky and Wes Farrell are all apparently close, which speaks well of him. And then, of course, Devin and he get along. So, for a defense guy, he's got reasonable cred on our side. He started out a hundred years ago as an assistant DA, so he's got some kind of clue about how things really work. Let's not ever forget that he's a defense guy, but if he wants to talk to us and you, Beth, set the ground rules, I don't see how it could hurt. Although I think I'd prefer myself not to be there, so we have the lowest possible profile. In any event, maybe he'll let out something that will help with Celia, if they ever bring her in."

"Maybe."

"You say 'maybe,' but I'm hearing 'no.'"

Beth pushed her chair back to look up at her partner. Then she pulled in closer so that she could talk in a near whisper. "You want to know the truth, Ike, Jameson scares me a hell of a lot more than I bet I scare him."

Ike's face showed his frustration. "I know that's what you think, and it's why I'm not thrilled with the idea of you talking to this guy Hardy. It might stir it all back up. I think what you've got to do is let that go. There's no sign that your job's in jeopardy."

"Except he doesn't call us to the grand jury."

"That's just politics. Beyond that, the man might be a prick, but he's not a literal killer."

Beth let out a dry little laugh. "Yeah," she said. "Except that I believe he is. I almost had him two years ago, if you remember."

"And if you remember, that turned out to be someone else."

"No. Ron and his wife just framed their pal and set him up as the perfect suicide."

"His wife, too?"

"Kate, yeah. My friend since college. Maybe my best friend. Which speaks rather strongly against my judgment, wouldn't you say?" After a moment's hesitation she said, "Maybe I should just transfer to another detail—fraud: nine-to-five, paperwork, humans for witnesses, long lunches. What's not to like?"

"That's a bad idea."

"Not if I'm so hamstrung that I can't do my job."

"You're not that."

"Maybe not all the time." She paused again. "Do you really think we shouldn't talk to this Hardy guy?"

Ike shrugged. "Not we. Maybe you, if you're comfortable with it. But no pressure. Devin says he's got some questions for us, but he might inadvertently give us some answers, too, slipping out through the cracks. And we can be pretty sure of one thing around that."

"What's that?"

"He's not going to be sharing what we all have with Ron Jameson."

DISMAS HARDY WAITED in stony silence in the gallery of Department 22 (in San Francisco, the courtrooms are called departments) on the second floor of the Hall of Justice. He checked his watch for the twentieth time, noting that a full two minutes had passed since the last time he'd looked.

It was now 10:18. He'd been in the building for an hour and a half, in the courtroom for an hour and fourteen minutes. The judge today was Marian Braun, with whom Hardy was on poor terms. Her presence at the bench was not a propitious sign.

After all this time, Phyllis's case had still not been called, although Hardy had arrived early and talked to the clerk and should have, in theory, been third on the list. Instead, the judge seemed to be calling cases in no particular order but studiously avoiding his line number.

He didn't know for sure, and certainly had no proof, that this was another random bit of bureaucratic abuse that someone was trying to heap on him through Phyllis.

But he thought it anyway, and something in his gut told him that he was right.

From her ignominious arrest at the office yesterday, to the refusal of the DA inspectors to grant her a night in her own bed before Hardy would bring her down for a prearranged arraignment, to the delays in her processing, the handcuffs, the dislocated shoulder, the jumpsuit—all of these spoke to a gratuitous animosity in the handling of her prosecution. Hardy didn't quite understand what this was all about, but there was no denying what it was.

He rubbed at his burning eyes, forced himself to pay attention. They were currently on line 13, a domestic disturbance case that was about to fall apart and be dismissed due to the wife's withdrawal as a witness. Hardy could have left the courtroom and taken a break and a breather, perhaps grabbed a soda or a cup of coffee, but he was certain that if he left the room even for a minute, somehow the fates would conspire to call his client next, whereupon—given his absence—the matter would be dropped to the end of the calendar. This was an immutable law of nature, and he would ignore it at his peril.

So he sat, fighting sleep, and waited.

At 10:55 the door behind him opened. He turned on his bench at the intrusion and, at the sight of Ron Jameson, the arresting officers Greene and Simms, and three other members of what Hardy took to be Jameson's staff, suddenly found himself completely awake and energized. There could be only one explanation for this show of prosecutorial firepower, to say nothing of the DA's personal appearance in the courtroom.

Could it be that Jameson himself was going to represent the People against him and his client?

Apparently so.

When Judge Braun called his case, clearly in response to Jameson's entry, Hardy grabbed his briefcase and stood up. Passing through the swinging gate that separated the courtroom from the gallery, he took his place at the right side table where the defense always sat, farthest from the jury. This morning, there was no jury, but over on the prosecution side the admitting DA—who'd handled every earlier case of the morning—had left the table and gone back into the gallery, and now Jameson and his two inspectors were getting themselves arranged, the DA in the middle.

No glances at Hardy. No handshake. No acknowledgment of any kind.

Well, he thought, if it was hardball they wanted . . .

The clerk called line 19, Phyllis Anne McGowan. The side door, which Hardy knew led to a holding cell in the hallway behind the courtroom, opened, and Phyllis, again in her orange jail jumpsuit and—sling and all—those damned handcuffs, and accompanied by a female bailiff, came forward to where Hardy stood at his desk.

But she had barely gotten there before Hardy spoke: "Your Honor, before we go any further here, I'd like to request that Ms. McGowan have the handcuffs removed immediately. They are painful and unnecessary in a woman who has been my personal secretary for nearly twenty years, as she has, and who has no criminal history of any kind. For heaven's sake, Your Honor, her arm is in a sling—a sling, I might add, that is there because of the brutal and unnecessary force employed by the two DA investigators that Mr. Jameson apparently has brought with him to gloat over the results of their handiwork."

In the blink of an eye, Jameson was on his feet. "Your Honor, Ron Jameson for the People—"

Hardy interrupted. "Well, well. I see that Mr. Jameson himself has come down for this arraignment, and I think he should be ashamed of himself for this grandstanding."

"Your Honor!"

Hardy knew that he was completely out of line, and didn't care. "We all know," he went on, "that Mr. Jameson isn't doing this case himself, since he's never done a criminal case from either side. In fact, it appears he requires two assistants to help him find the prosecution table. So his only purpose for being here must be to pose for the reporters and photographers outside the courtroom."

"Your Honor, Ms. McGowan all but resisted arrest yesterday when—"

But Hardy was ready for this, and slapped his hand on the table in front of him, stunning the court and shocking even himself. "Your Honor! Please. Eighteen people have appeared before you so far today, and only two before Ms. McGowan have been handcuffed. Both of those individuals were charged with violent crimes and were facing enhanced charges for use of weapons. In Ms. McGowan's case, this is unconscionable bullying of a kind and gentle woman and has no place in this courtroom."

On the bench, Braun clamped down her expression and banged her gavel. She cast a withering glance at Jameson, held up a finger to him, then—in an obvious high fury but in tight control—spoke in a near whisper. "I will be the only one slamming tables or gaveling for attention in this courtroom, Mr. Hardy. Is that clear?"

"Yes, Your Honor. But I didn't want to allow the district attorney to waste time in a futile argument while my client stands here in handcuffs. They need to be removed before we can proceed."

"Again, Mr. Hardy, I will not be dictated to in my courtroom. I make the rules here."

"Of course, Your Honor. I apologize for my sense of urgency, but this degree of restraint is completely unnecessary."

Somewhat to Hardy's surprise—because this was about as hard as he'd ever pushed in a courtroom in his career, certainly right to the edge of contempt—with a shake of her head conveying her disappointment in the DA, Braun brought her gavel down and said, "Bailiff, please remove the handcuffs."

A minute later Phyllis and Hardy stood at the defense table and Braun had the clerk read the charge again: accessory after the fact.

Hardy waived instruction and arraignment.

The judge herself then asked the question: "Ms. McGowan, how do you plead?"

She and Hardy had gone over all the details in the jail the night before, and now Phyllis raised her head and said in a clear voice, "Not guilty, Your Honor."

Since the charge had come about because of an indictment by the grand jury, there was no need to schedule a preliminary hearing. Instead, the judge asked Hardy if his client wanted to "waive time" before scheduling a trial. In the normal course of events, defendants had the right to trial within sixty workdays of their arraignment, but if they chose to waive time, the trial could be postponed almost indefinitely, certainly for several months if not a year or more. Hardy did not choose to waive time. So this trial would be on the fast track.

None of this took much more than another minute.

So far, except for his outburst against Hardy's objection to the handcuffs, Jameson had no further comments.

That was about to change.

"Now," Judge Braun said, "moving on to the matter of bail: Mr. Jameson, I'm wondering if what I have here in front of me is a typo. The People are requesting ten million dollars for bail?"

Jameson got to his feet. "We are, Your Honor. And I might add, that is in lieu of denying bail altogether."

Braun made a guttural noise, cleared her throat, and looked out over the bench to the defense table. "Well, I'm just guessing, but I'm thinking Mr. Hardy might have an objection to this request."

"I do, Your Honor, of course. The bail amount is absurd on the face of it. Ms. McGowan has deep and strong ties to the community and a full-time job working at my own law firm for nearly forty years. She is an exemplary human being and a valued employee. She has never run afoul of the law. She is no flight risk. She poses no threat to society in any way, shape, or form, and to imply that she does is nothing short of a deluded fantasy or a publicity-seeking abuse of power."

Without waiting for the judge to call for his response, Jameson started right in. "It is no fantasy that the defendant has been indicted and charged with accessory after the fact to the crime of murder, and in this case murder connected to human trafficking. This is a form of organized crime where she has been smuggling people, perhaps hundreds of them, out of the country for several years. She could just as easily make herself disappear."

Hardy snapped back without benefit of the judge's invitation. "Except that she has no reason to want to make herself disappear, Your Honor. She has a steady job and has lived in the same apartment for over forty years. Forty years, Your Honor! She is not going to be running away rather than show up to face her accusers at her trial."

"Thank you, Mr. Hardy, I believe you've made your point." Braun looked over at the DA. "Mr. Jameson, I will set bail at the statutory amount of fifty thousand dollars. Is there anything else?"

Hardy briefly considered letting things stand as they were. He had already succeeded in getting the handcuffs removed and the ludicrous bail lowered to a more reasonable amount. He might as well call it a day and get his client released and back to life outside of the jail. But his blood still ran high, and he wasn't really inclined to stop himself or even slow himself down. Instead he said, "Yes, Your Honor. There is something else."

"And what is that, Mr. Hardy?"

"I want a gag order."

Over at Jameson's table: "Oh, for the love of Christ."

Hardy said, "I believe this prosecution to be unfounded and political. The way Mr. Jameson got this indictment, the way he sent his henchmen to make this arrest, the brutal and unnecessary force employed against my client, even Mr. Jameson's personal appearance here smacks of prosecutorial misconduct. The district attorney should not be permitted to taint any potential jury pool by making inflammatory and frankly false statements about my client to further his own vindictive, personal, *political* agenda."

"Your Honor, objection! These are just lies meant to discredit me and my office. There was nothing irregular about Ms. McGowan's treatment by any of my staff. Getting arrested is not a pleasant event, granted, but my inspectors followed protocol in spite of the hostile and even dangerous atmosphere at Mr. Hardy's office. There is nothing unfair about arresting someone involved in human trafficking who has helped a murderer escape."

In his anger, Jameson betrayed his lack of courtroom experience by asking his opponent a rhetorical question. "Besides which," he said, "why would I treat this one defendant unfairly?"

Hardy had given this question a lot of thought and come up with what he believed to be the answer. "Because this one defendant, Your Honor, as I've mentioned, happens to work at my law firm, which is also where Wes Farrell, Mr. Jameson's predecessor in the DA's office, is about to come on as a partner. And the DA's behavior in this matter is just pure harassment of his former political opponent—"

"I don't have to harass Mr. Farrell. I already beat him. And now he's got you out fighting his fights with these baseless accusations. Which, frankly, doesn't surprise me in the least."

"Look at the sling on Ms. McGowan's arm. Tell me why two large cops have to dislocate the shoulder of a nonresisting woman of her age and stature to take her into custody."

Braun picked up her gavel, ready to slam it down. "All right, all right. That's enough. Mr. Hardy, this is neither the time nor the place to air out this issue. If you think you've got grounds, you can file the appropriate motions and the two of you can fight it out in another courtroom. In the meantime, Mr. Jameson, if you're not interested in a gag order in this case, you might want to temper your public pronouncements. But having said that, I think we're at the end of the arraignment process for this defendant. If Ms. McGowan can meet her bail today, she'll probably want to get out of these buildings as soon as she can."

9

Rigoberto Alvarez came to the United States with his Mexican parents in 1995 when he was two years old and lived with them first in Modesto in California's Central Valley, then in Napa. Finally as an adult he moved by himself to Ukiah, a small Northern California town with a burgeoning wine industry.

During the Obama administration, he had qualified to become a DREAMer under the Development, Relief, and Education for Alien Minors Act. He fit the bill to a T. Under thirty-one years of age, he had entered the US before he was sixteen and had lived continuously here for more than five years, had never been convicted of a felony or "serious" misdemeanor (or three misdemeanors), and had earned a GED or general education high school diploma. Beyond his native Spanish, he spoke fluent vernacular unaccented English.

Although of course his immigration status remained problematic and a force in his daily life—he was, after all, technically an undocumented alien—it was something he'd long ago come to grips with, thinking that it was only a matter of time before he could find some kind of path on the way to citizenship. In the meanwhile, he'd keep a low profile, do his vineyard job very well, obey the law, and enjoy his life.

Which he did until the day after last Thanksgiving, when he was just walking away from an ATM with eighty dollars. Three white guys with guns had been waiting by their pickup truck in the parking lot. Hemmed in, he gave up all the money, and was just starting to consider himself lucky to get away with his life when one of the guys clocked him from behind, hard, with his gun, knocking him to the ground, whereupon at least one of the other muggers, and maybe both of them, joined in, kicking him wherever he/they could land a foot—head, body, legs, groin.

When he came to, bloody and battered, they were gone and a couple of local town cops that he vaguely knew were there and had already called an ambulance. Rigoberto cooperated with them in every way, including supplying them with a description of the pickup and its license number, which he'd noticed and memorized before the fracas had developed.

Two days later, the guys who'd mugged and robbed him were in jail and the local cops from the other night stopped by out at the vineyard, where Rigoberto lived in a two-room apartment behind the barrel storage barn. They told him that he needed to come down to the jail and identify his attackers, but he told them that he wasn't inclined to do that. He just wanted to get his money back.

But the cops explained the situation: he wasn't going to get his money back—and these hoodlums probably weren't even going to jail—if he didn't show up to be a witness against them. Because he, Rigoberto, was the whole case.

And besides, they asked him, did he want these guys to go unpunished so they could keep on beating and robbing innocent people like himself? If Rigoberto was afraid that they'd come after him and hurt him again in exchange for his testimony, the cops understood that, and the prosecution could accommodate him by helping him relocate.

Whichever way it went, it was perfectly safe.

Rigoberto had nothing to worry about.

But he had to point the finger at these bastards if he wanted to get them off the streets, if he ever wanted to have a chance to see his eighty dollars again.

Eventually, he'd given in.

Officers Dyson and Simonds—who by now were Brad and Chester—picked him up Monday morning and took him down to the courthouse, where it all went as they'd predicted it would. Rigoberto identified his attackers in a lineup and by noon he was back outside, waiting for the patrol car to pull up and take him back out to the vineyard.

But just in front of that patrol car as it was pulling up, a black sedan slid itself to the curb and four men wearing black parkas with the acronym "ICE" on the back were suddenly all around him. One of them had his ID out, demanding to see Rigoberto's. Brad and Chester jumped out of their car and tried to intervene, but these ICE people clearly had rank over the locals. Unable to provide anything like sufficient identification, Rigoberto got taken into custody and put into another cell in a different building to wait while the feds clarified his documentation and immigration status.

To the new administration, he was no longer a DREAMer but an illegal alien, an undocumented immigrant. He was in the country illegally. That was the bottom line. And the crime of entering the US without documentation—never mind that Rigoberto had "committed" that "crime" when he was two years old!—was now in many jurisdictions prima facie evidence of guilt. So, upon apprehension and identification, he could legally be immediately deported back to Mexico, where he knew no one and had never even visited, without further administrative interference.

Just as though he were a burglar, a rapist, or a murderer.

THEY HAD KEPT him alone in his cell—no food and no water—for seven hours, until the man who'd originally flashed his ICE badge when they'd taken him into custody outside came to the cell door with one of the guards.

"Rigoberto Alvarez?"

He had been sitting on the edge of his cot, and now he stood up and turned to face them. "That's me. And I'd like to see a lawyer. You've got pro bono lawyers here, right? And public defenders. I want to see one of them."

The man nodded and then said something, dismissing the guard. Coming back to the prisoner, the cell door still closed between them, he said, "Your English is excellent."

"Yeah, well, it's my native tongue, so that makes sense, doesn't it? Did I mention I want to see a lawyer?"

The man simply shook his head, his expression flat and unyielding.

"My name is Philip Newton, Rigoberto. And as a pending deportee, you don't have a right to a lawyer. Once we've verified your immigration status as illegal, it's pretty simple. We put you on an airplane and fly your ass back home."

"This is home. This is where I live."

"Alas. I'm afraid the government doesn't see it that way. By all accounts, from what we've seen since we've picked you up, you cannot prove that you are an American citizen, and therefore that you have the right to live in this country. You don't have any kind of green card or other documentation that will allow you to stay here."

"I've been here my whole life. I was born here."

"Really? Where, precisely?"

"LA?"

"What hospital?"

"I wasn't born in a hospital. I was born in my aunt's house."

"Very good. What is her name and the exact address? We'll check her out."

"She doesn't live there anymore."

"That shouldn't be a problem. Do you have her current address?"

"She moved, and then she died."

Philip Newton clucked. "I'm sorry to hear that. Did she have your birth certificate?"

"No. My mother kept that."

"And where is she? Your mother."

"We've lost contact over the years. I don't see her anymore."

"That's sad. You don't know where she lives?"

"No."

"Any other relatives, especially citizens of this country?"

"No."

"Well, that's unfortunate, Rigoberto, because in this matter the burden of proof is on you. We need to see documentation that proves either that you are a citizen or that you have permission to be here, to work here, anything like that. And so far we have none. Can you think of anyplace else where we might look and find something of that nature?"

"Being born here, I never worried about that stuff. I'm as American as you are."

"I don't think so. I think you're as Mexican as I'm American."

"Well, you're wrong. And how about, if I can't have a lawyer, can I at least make a phone call?"

"I'm afraid not. The presumption is that you're in this country illegally and therefore that you don't have the same rights as a citizen would."

"This is just so wrong. You guys are so wrong. I've got a good job here. You can check. Parinelli's Winery. I'm the vineyard manager there."

"We did check. What do you think we've been doing all day while you've been in here? But Mr. Parinelli had no papers on you, either. Neither did Mr. Bosche down in Napa, who was your reference for Parinelli. Oh, and your social security number is for a guy named James G. Cooley, who died in Boise, Idaho, in 1991. I'm afraid we've got you nine ways from Sunday, Rigoberto. I could have you on a plane to Mexico by the end of the week and nobody would blink or think twice about it. And I'd be that much closer to my bonus. You understand me?"

"You ought to be ashamed of yourself."

"To the contrary, I'm damn proud of what I do. I'm helping to keep this country safe from people who lie about their background and their activities. Who come to this country either criminally or to commit crimes, as so many of your people have done."

"My people are Americans, just like you are. You're not listening. And the bad Mexicans or illegals you're talking about? You're saying white people don't commit crimes? Tell that to the punks I identified today in the courthouse. So, yeah, are there bad Mexicans? Sure. So put them in jail or deport them or whatever the hell you want to do with them. But don't confuse me with them. I've never even spit on the sidewalk and all of my friends are the same way."

"All of your friends? Where are they? And would any of them be able to vouch for your citizenship?" He waited and got no response. "That's what I thought. This is a losing fight for you, son. Nevertheless, I'm here to offer you a deal."

Rigoberto cocked his head, interested in spite of himself. "What kind of deal?"

"Well, first, the kind that will keep you in this country and could, if you play your cards right, get you in line for a legitimate green card."

The young man scratched at his shirt over his chest. He only just now realized it, but he was exhausted—not only from the stress of his identification of his attackers that morning, and then from his arrest and the long empty afternoon in this cell, but from the effects of the beating he'd taken that previous Friday night. His head throbbed, his back ached, his ribs—two of them broken—stabbed at him. "I'm listening, but first could I get a little water?"

"I could do that. Give me a minute."

It was more like five, but when Philip Newton returned, it was with a couple of plastic bottles of water, ice-cold, as though they'd just come out of a refrigerator.

Rigoberto drank his down in one long gulp. "Thank you," he said when he'd finished. "What's your offer?"

PHILIP NEWTON ASSURED Rigoberto that, in spite of his own case, ICE was not really interested in deporting simple undocumented aliens. The agency's focus—especially in California, where there were over a hundred thousand DREAMers and at the same time so many sanctuary cities—was apprehending felons: drug dealers, sex traffickers, gang members, killers.

The problem was that these people might be identified by local police in whatever sanctuary city in which they'd committed their crime. But the city police were not mandated and mostly did not attempt to turn these suspects and criminals over to ICE, whose mission was to take them into custody and then deport them to their country of citizenship. Instead, these people, often posing as DREAMers, would get released from custody, making bail or getting released from jail or prison after serving their time, and then, instead of hanging around where ICE might find them, would hook up with a loose network of activists—an underground railroad—who helped them disappear into another community or out of the country entirely.

Rigoberto knew about this underground railroad and was of the opinion that a vast majority of the people it facilitated were, like him, innocent of any real crimes. Most of the runaways felt that they needed to relocate because they had come to believe for whatever reason—often a sibling or a cousin plucked from their waitress or picking or warehouse job—that they'd hit the government's radar and were in imminent danger of being picked up and sent south. They had to leave everything on little to no notice with no independent means of transportation, no valid IDs, no credit cards. If they could just make it to Canada, they could start their lives over again without the constant fear that they would be deported.

Apparently, according to Philip Newton, ICE did not care about these people, who were essentially deporting themselves to the north instead of south. Canada was much more tolerant of them and Canada was welcome to them. But there was a host, a veritable plague, of other people, who used the well-meaning but sometimes clueless station masters of the invisible railroad to escape from the law and evade prosecution in the cities where they'd committed their crimes, resettling and causing havoc wherever they chose, setting up their drug and sex traffic networks, connecting with their fellow gang members, intimidating any population with which they came in contact. These people were criminals, wanted by ICE not for their documentation irregularities but because they were lawbreakers, often violent and dangerous, who gave a bad name to all of Rigoberto's countrymen.

Philip Newton thought that, as a victim of a violent crime, Rigoberto might be willing to connect himself with the local underground railroad stops and help ICE identify these people as they passed through town. In return for this information, he could avoid his own deportation and put himself—finally—on the rocky road to US citizenship.

It seemed like a reasonable trade.

10

At a little before 4:30 on the day they'd had the arraignment, Hardy walked down the lengthy corridor that led to Gina Roake's office. The door was open, but Hardy knocked anyway, and Gina looked up from the green leather chair in which she sat over by the corner window. "Hey," she said, closing the copy of the *New Yorker* she'd been reading.

"Hey yourself. You busy?"

She made a gesture at her reading material. "Overwhelmed, as you can see. Reading this damn magazine every week is a commitment and a half. But if I don't, I feel guilty. Of course, if I do read the whole thing, there's an hour of billing gone, so I feel guilty about that, too. It's such a joy being me. What's up?"

Hardy took the identical chair across from her. "Celia Montoya."

"Do I know her?"

"I doubt it. But I think, with any luck, she'll be in your future."

"Who is she?"

"Allegedly, she killed Hector Valdez. That's the murder Phyllis is charged with being an accessory to."

"Okay." Gina laid her magazine on the low table next to her. "What about her?"

"They just got her into custody up in Ukiah. Evidently ICE picked her up on some kind of anonymous tip and is bringing her down to the city tonight. And she's going to be needing a lawyer."

"I like the way you say that. Does she have any money to pay such a lawyer?"

"I doubt it. Phyllis said she was essentially broke."

"Don't we still have a public defender's office here in town for, you know, like, poor people?"

"We do. And a fine office it is, too."

"And yet you're bringing her to my attention. I should take her on as my client, right? And pro bono, I assume."

Hardy nodded. "That's not really an issue. The case will be worth its weight in gold as advertising for the firm, but that's not really it, either."

"I'm listening," Roake said.

Sitting back and crossing his legs, Hardy took a beat and let out a breath. "The real answer isn't much of a legal argument as far as that goes. The plain fact is that somebody's going to have to take on that son of a bitch—"

"You're talking Jameson, I presume."

"No flies on you, Gina. If the way he's handled Phyllis is any indication—and I believe it's just the tip of the iceberg—he's going to be a procedural nightmare every step of the way. He just doesn't care about how things are supposed to be done. He doesn't care about the law, period, which he made pretty clear this morning. Plus, it was abundantly obvious this morning that he's still got his personal grudge with Wes. If we let this case get away from us and go to the PD, it'll disappear into the bureaucracy instead of showcasing what an incompetent and immoral asshole this guy is. Which, if we take her case, especially alongside Phyllis's, we're in a perfect position to do."

"And we want to do this because . . . ?"

"Because this guy's a menace and somebody's got to sign on to take him down."

"So it's personal?"

"For me it is, and I know it would be for Wes, too. And I'm inviting you along just for the sheer thrill of it."

"You're sure this is not just politics?"

"Maybe a little of that, okay. That's why I'm coming to you rather than Wes. If he took on the case, it would be just politics and nothing else, and there'll be some of that no matter what. But if it's just you and me, we can expose the many ways Jameson plays it wrong, and maybe even make a difference. I thought that might appeal to the idealist in you."

Gina broke a wide smile. "Has anybody ever mentioned that you are a shameless flatterer?"

Hardy grinned back at her. "Only rarely. When I really want something."

"Which is not to say that it isn't effective."

Hardy waited.

Gina glanced at her watch, then sighed extravagantly. "Okay, okay. You've got Phyllis, so if I take Celia, I'd have a conflict. But, assuming she waives it, I'll take her. When is she going to arrive at the jail?"

HARDY COULDN'T BELIEVE it when he came out of Gina's office and there in front of him sat Phyllis, at her reception desk, doing what appeared to be some filing. He had posted her bail himself, in cash, but had never expected to see her so soon. He came around and stood in front of her until she looked up. Before she could say anything, he said, "Do I vaguely remember telling you to take the rest of the day off, or was that someone who looks exactly like you?"

"Yes, sir. But I wanted to get a jump on tomorrow's work and catch up on what I missed last week."

"Of course you did. Or how about take tomorrow off as well and not worry about whatever it is you're catching up on?"

"I'd rather get caught up so I don't have to worry about it, if that's all right with you."

Hardy all but rolled his eyes. "It's all right with me, but I thought that after a night of no sleep and then all the emotion of your arraignment this morning and then posting bail . . ."

"And by the way, thank you for that. I promise I'll pay you back."

"In your dreams, Phyllis. There's nothing to pay back. I put up the bail myself so that when this trial is over I get it back, unless you're planning to skip town. But as I told the judge, I really don't believe you're a flight risk, so I'll get back every cent of it when you show up for your trial. How's the shoulder, by the way?"

Phyllis looked down quickly, then back up at Hardy. "I took another Advil," she said. "It's fine."

"Did you see a doctor and tell him to send the medical records as I requested?"

"Yes, but . . ."

"No buts. Did you tell him to send them?"

"I did."

"Good. I want a record of what they did to you. Clear?"

"Yes, sir."

"And so I guess your presence back here at your desk today means that you're planning to be coming in tomorrow?"

"Yes, sir. Of course."

"Of course." Frustration bleeding out, Hardy said it half to himself. This woman, he was thinking, would try the patience of a saint. "Why would I even ask?"

When Devin Juhle received notification that ICE had picked up Celia Montoya in Ukiah, the first thing he did was call Beth Tully and Ike McCaffrey and tell them about it. After all, they were the inspectors of record in the Valdez murder, and even if they did not get to testify before the grand jury that had indicted Celia Montoya and Phyllis McGowan, they still had a vested interest in that case.

The second call he made was to Dismas Hardy, relaying the same information. This was the call that had driven Hardy to walk down to Gina Roake's office to try to persuade her to get on board with Celia Montoya's defense.

Now Hardy was on with Juhle again, letting him know that, with the suspect's approval, Gina was going to be representing Celia pro bono, a fabulously unusual occurrence in a murder case of an indigent suspect. This was another in the series of events that had begun with Tully and McCaffrey not being called to testify before the grand jury, then the theatrical arrest of Phyllis McGowan and her mistreatment at the jail and in the courtroom for her arraignment.

Juhle, frankly, just didn't get what was going on, and he posed the question to Hardy.

"What do you mean?" Hardy asked. "Other than that Mr. Jameson wants to do things his way, even if it's illegal? Even if he ignores everybody's civil rights? And he doesn't like people trying to stop him?"

"But why these two cases—McGowan and Montoya—which in the normal chain of events wouldn't be close to the highest-profile cases he'd be prosecuting as time goes by?"

"Well, one reason is the connection to Wes. Here's a chance to take his political rival down a couple of notches so he won't be as much of a threat to Jameson's power next time—if there is a next time."

"But this whole sanctuary question, Diz? Of all the political stands to take, how does this help Jameson when the city's, like, ninety percent behind it? Being a sanctuary city, I mean. We don't hand our immigrants over to ICE, even if they're going down for something as large as murder. Period."

"Yeah, but how about if ICE hands its suspected killers back over to us and we put 'em on trial? For the crime but not for their immigration status. That way, he's tough on crime and at the same time appears relatively sympathetic to the whole deportation issue. Or at least not hostile to it. That, in spite of the fact that he's on the record as saying that he's not opposed to rounding up everybody who's undocumented; that in itself is the crime. But since that doesn't fly here politically, he has his murder suspect brought in and that changes the message a bit. In spite of the rhetoric, he's not turning people over to ICE. Only the bad ones, after they're actually convicted, with the tacit understanding that he's leaving the good ones—the hardworking, tax-paying immigrants—alone. It's bogus, of course, but bogus is his game and he's playing this one pretty well."

"Okay. So if you don't mind my asking, why are you so involved?"

"Well, the easy answer is that I really don't feel like I've got much of a choice. Phyllis is my secretary, and if she's in legal trouble, I've pretty much got to help her out if I can."

"Sure. That's understood. But it's not exactly what I was asking. This isn't just you taking Phyllis's case, or even Roake getting on board with the Valdez killing."

"Yeah."

Nearly half a minute passed in silence, until Juhle said, "Diz? You still there?"

"I am. I'm thinking about why I'm so pumped up around this, and I'm afraid the answer I give you may not redound to my credit."

"'Redound'?"

"Redound."

"I'm afraid I don't know 'redound.' Is it a lawyer word?"

"It might be, at that. But it's also open to use by the general public, I believe."

"What's it mean?"

"It means to lead to something. Like, if I tell you why I want to go up against Jameson, my motive might not lead you to think I'm the paragon of virtue and goodness that I try to project. It might not redound to my credit."

"Okay. So what is it? Your motive?"

"I want him stopped. I want to end his political career before it goes any further because I firmly believe that he is one dangerous motherfucker. I don't want me and the rest of the legal community in this city to have to live the next four years playing by his rules, which—trust me—are not the rule of law. And now that I've fallen into them, I think these two cases—Phyllis and Celia—might give me a platform to get the man's character out there in front of God and everybody, where it will not thrive. And neither will he."

"And that's it?"

"That's it."

"But still, why you? How'd you get that job?"

"I didn't," Hardy said. "It came out of nowhere and got me."

11

When Phyllis had gotten home on Sunday, she had been exhausted and, after calling the office to apologize for her absence and to tell Mr. Hardy that she'd be in the next day, she'd gone to bed and slept right through until Monday morning. She noted that they had made a mess of the place in the wake of the service of the search warrant, which had apparently taken place the previous week while she was holed up in Ukiah with Celia, but she hadn't had the energy to do anything about it.

Then, on Monday, they'd arrested her and she'd spent that night in jail.

Finally home again today, it took her over four hours to get the apartment back to the way it had been before the search.

The most disturbing element from her perspective was the absence of the gun that she had left in the drawer next to her bed but which was gone when she'd gotten back. According to Adam, it was the murder weapon used by Celia, and no doubt—if Adam hadn't in fact stolen it—the inspectors had taken it for testing and then kept it locked up as evidence.

The big problem was that the gun would, she knew, have her fingerprints on it, not that anyone was accusing her of actually being the murderer. But that, she believed, might change, although how remained a mystery.

She was also worried about Celia. Over the years, she'd taken perhaps three hundred immigrants in transit into her apartment—some in more desperate straits than others, but all of them trying to get to the next station, whether it was the one in Santa Rosa or Vallejo or Ukiah—on their way to Canada.

Because of the murder, Celia had been among the most desperate, so she hadn't even stayed a night in Phyllis's apartment. Instead, on that Tuesday afternoon when Hector Valdez had been killed, Phyllis had driven them both up Highway 1; but when they'd arrived and she had called her connection Muriel Windsor on the throwaway cell phone she used, Muriel had told her to lie low at the local Motel 6 and hold off dropping Celia for a while—that there was some question about whether their security and secrecy had been breached.

Apparently, three other *migrantes*, all wanted on criminal charges in various jurisdictions down south, had been picked up by ICE in Ukiah in the previous six weeks. Somebody, Muriel believed, was turning these people in. Maybe one of their neighbors. She just didn't know, but didn't want to risk it with someone as high-profile as Celia.

Muriel was in contact with another family—unbelievably, a superior court judge named Jared Rosen and his lawyer wife, Stephanie—who'd confided to her that they could take people in and get them on the road to Red Bluff or Redding or even Ashland, Oregon. So Phyllis and Celia had stayed in Ukiah's Motel 6 for four days, until early Sunday morning, when finally the Rosens thought it would be safe and Phyllis had dropped Celia at their front door.

Usually, passing off the runaway was the last time that Phyllis would hear about the person she'd helped. And she knew that this was probably the case with Celia. The judge and his wife weren't going to call her back and report on the success of the next leg, on how it had gone. No news was good news.

Now it was closing on ten o'clock and she took the burrito she'd bought down at the corner from the refrigerator and put it in the microwave. She'd just sat down to wait for it when her cell phone rang. Seeing that it was her brother, she sighed and picked it up. "Where are you?" she asked.

"Up at Mel's, but you know fish and guests stink after three days, and now it's been a week. I think he and Rita are getting tired of me."

"You haven't been back here?"

"Not since," he said.

"What are you wearing, then?"

"Dirty clothes. Mel's about my size anyway. And they got a washer."

"So you didn't take the gun?"

"No. What? It's gone?"

"They must have gotten it in the search."

"They searched the place, huh? I thought they might."

"You thought they might? Adam, you sent them here."

"Not on purpose. And I knew that you'd be gone by the time . . . I had to give them something or they might have taken me in again. Hey, and you were gone, weren't . . ." He trailed off. "Anyway, I tried you last night, too. No answer. Where have you been? I thought it was just gonna be a night or two you were gone."

"Well, it wasn't, as it turned out. I had to hide out in Ukiah for four days before I could drop Celia. Then I got back and got arrested and last night I was in jail."

"Get out of here. Jail where?"

"Downtown. Here. You really have screwed things up for me, Adam. Do you realize that? They've charged me with helping Celia escape. That's a felony. I'm out on bail right now. I could go to jail myself."

"Hey, I never meant for that."

"No. I'm sure you didn't. But sometimes you do something and that makes something else happen. That's called having consequences."

"Yeah, well . . . but the thing is . . . I'm sorry and all about that. But it's not like if it was me. I mean, if it had been me they arrested, then we're talking real time."

"It felt real enough to me. One night."

"Okay, yeah, but . . . anyway, the thing is, if you don't mind, they're kind of kicking me out . . ."

"And you want to come back here?"

"And get some clothes at least. Maybe a shower. I'm starting to put something together with Mel, but nothing steady yet, no guarantees. You know how people are if you been in jail."

"No. But maybe I'm about to start finding out."

Adam let the silence build. Finally he said, "So . . . what do you think? It wouldn't have to be too long."

Phyllis sighed heavily. Her brother, she thought, was unbelievable. He seemed to have no feelings at all for what he'd put her through, and clearly expected her to simply step up and offer her home to him again until he could get himself settled somewhere else.

She sighed again, astounded anew by his near-bottomless selfishness.

On the other hand, he was after all her only blood relative in the world. He'd grown up without a father and with an overburdened mother. And in spite of all his weaknesses, in spite of what he'd done to her, she thought he was really trying to turn his life around. How could she abandon him at this point? Where was the goodness in that? She sighed a last time. "And where are you now, Adam? Where's Mel's place?"

"Just off Dolores," he said. "At Twenty-Second Street." Then, hopefully: "I could be down there in, like, an hour. I still got my key."

"You won't need it," she said. "I'm sure I'll be awake."

BETH TULLY KNEW Abe Glitsky by sight and by reputation, but she had never before met the former deputy chief of inspectors personally. When he stood up to greet her from his booth at Gaspare's Pizzeria, she was unprepared for the sheer presence of the man close up, which from her perspective was intimidation incarnate. And yet he shook her hand with a gentle touch, then gestured her into the seat across from him.

"Thanks for coming down to meet me so late," she began. "When I called to ask you if we could get together, I didn't necessarily mean in the next fifteen minutes, but I really do appreciate it."

Glitsky shrugged. "You say you're in Homicide, you can generally get my attention pretty quick. From my days in the detail, I don't remember paying much attention to the clock. By the way, I ordered iced tea and a pepperoni and mushroom pizza, if you'd like a slice or two, or even half. My cardiologist would kill me if he found out, so we need to keep it between us."

"Sounds great. I'll never tell."

"Deal," Glitsky said, then leaned back as the waitress came by and poured, leaving the pitcher. After a sip, he put down his glass. "So, how can I help you? You said this was the Valdez case? I can't say I've really been following it."

"There's not much to follow. Valdez got shot a week ago today by one of the girls he was running. We have three witnesses . . ." She ran down the particulars of the case and her role in the investigation, concluding with the information that she and her partner had been effectively cut out of the investigation by the DA's decision to go forward with the grand jury proceeding but not have them testify.

When she finished, Glitsky said, "I'm not sure I see the problem. Sometimes inspectors don't have to testify in front of grand juries, especially if it's a particularly strong case."

"Well, maybe that's the point," Beth said. "It was one of those cases that looks strong until you stare at it a little more closely. If my partner and I would have testified, we might in fact have introduced some doubt, but the DA didn't want any doubt, so we got called off, or never got called on."

They took a small hiatus as the pizza got delivered and they took their slices, their bites.

Glitsky swallowed, then drank some tea. "I'm afraid I still don't see the problem," he said. "If it's a loser, they'll lose at trial, your suspect walks, and that's the end of it. I don't see how it would wind up being a reflection on you or your partner. Especially if you didn't testify for the grand jury. It's the DA's problem. Am I missing something?"

Beth took an extra moment chewing, swallowed carefully. "Here's the thing, sir. A couple of years ago, you might remember a lawyer named Peter Ash got himself killed."

Glitsky, to whom all things bearing on homicides in the city seemingly became part of his DNA, nodded. "Geoff Cooke," he said. "Another lawyer. That's who shot him, right? One of Ash's friends. Then when you guys were closing in, he killed himself, if I'm not mistaken."

Impressed by this instant retrieval, Beth sat back. "You've got a good memory," she said. "That's pretty much the story."

"Okay. What about it?"

"Well, it leaves out something of some importance that never made the record. It was my case, so I know."

"What was that?"

"Peter Ash had had an affair with Ron Jameson's wife, Kate."

It was Glitsky's turn to sit back. He picked up his iced tea and took a long drink. "How did that not make the record? Didn't anybody interview her on tape or video or get some kind of statement?"

"She was my best friend. I found out about the affair on my own—or more like put it together at the time—by stuff she'd told me before he was killed, before there was any investigation. And then, afterwards—I mean after Ash washed up dead on the beach and I drew the case—when I called her on it, she acted like she didn't know what I was talking about. She told me she'd never had any kind of thing with Mr. Ash. I had misinterpreted what she'd said. She'd barely known him. She couldn't even remember what it might have been or what could have made me think it. I was just flat-out wrong."

Glitsky chewed some ice. "You're saying that Ron Jameson had a motive to kill Ash."

"Yes."

"But so what, if Cooke actually did kill him? Which I thought was pretty well established."

"Not that well established. Which is my point. I don't believe Cooke killed him at all. I don't believe Cooke killed himself, either."

"Although his death was ruled a suicide?"

She shrugged. "Suicide/homicide equivocal. You know how that goes."

Glitsky did. He nodded. "So you think what? That Jameson killed Cooke?"

"No. Ron had an airtight alibi for Cooke's death. He was at some business meeting with a dozen colleagues from early till late." She sucked in a deep breath, let it out heavily. "But Kate, Ron's wife, didn't have any alibi."

Glitsky cocked his head to one side, his brows drawn together. "Okay.

No alibi. Not the strangest thing in the world. Certainly not unheard of. How about motive?"

"If we close the case, which we did, nobody's looking at her husband for Peter Ash anymore."

"So then," Glitsky asked, "you're saying your friend Kate killed both Ash and Cooke?"

"Not exactly. I'd bet a million dollars she killed Cooke, yes." She paused, took a beat, then went on. "I believe that Ron himself killed Ash."

Glitsky's eyes went wide for an instant, then squinted down. "Ron Jameson. Our DA, you mean? That's quite an accusation."

She nodded. "Well, you wonder why he wants to keep me marginalized, like for example away from a grand jury."

"Do you have proof of any of this? Both the Ash case and the Cooke case are closed, aren't they? If there had still been questions, shouldn't they . . . ?"

"That's the point. There weren't any unresolved questions. They got a ballistics match on some shell casings. Nobody seemed to have any doubt about the cover story: Cooke killed Ash and then in remorse or guilt killed himself."

"And why again did Cooke kill Ash in the first place?"

"I didn't mention that? Ash had hit on Cooke's wife, too. So we've got the same motive, jealousy. It all worked for everybody."

"Except, apparently, you."

"Apparently. Yeah." She dipped a finger into her glass and gave it a little stir, then brought her finger to her lips. "I'm sorry that this is all so nebulous," she said.

Glitsky waved that off. "I don't care about that. But I'm afraid I'm still up in the air about why we're here. You and me, now, I mean. Not that it's not great pizza and good company, but I thought you wanted to talk about something a little more specific, where I could help you somehow. You know that I'm completely retired, right?"

"Yes. My lieutenant—you know Devin Juhle—told me that."

"So, then . . . ?"

After a last moment's hesitation, she said, "So I understand that you're on pretty good terms with a defense attorney named Dismas Hardy."

Glitsky broke what might have passed for a smile that faded as quickly as it appeared. "You could say that. Is he involved in this?"

"Not specifically. Not the cases we've been talking about, anyway. But Hardy passed the word along through Devin that he wanted to talk to me about why me and my partner got passed over with the grand jury on the Valdez case we started with here."

"Back to that? How does he . . . ?" Glitsky shook his head. "I'm sorry, but I'm not sure I get the connection, if there is one."

"I'm not sure there is, sir. At this point, I admit it's obscure. Mr. Hardy's got a client who's been arraigned as an accessory after the fact in the Valdez case. Evidently, Jameson at the very least condoned if not ordered her being mistreated at her arrest. Of course, this could also be just the typical defense attorney moaning and groaning about how his clients are disrespected and abused by law enforcement, but Devin knows Hardy a little bit and says that he seems to have a legitimate complaint, to the extent that he's filed some legal papers on Jameson."

"Okay . . ."

"Okay. So Hardy apparently wanted to talk to us to see if something happened in our investigation of the Valdez case that might connect to his client: why we got bypassed for the grand jury, and if there might be something he can point at with Jameson to show some kind of pattern of abuse or misconduct that might help his case. And, not incidentally, land a good hit on Jameson's reputation. And if it also helps to take Jameson down, he's all over it."

Glitsky nodded. "Sounds about right. It also sounds to me like you might want to talk to Hardy."

"Well, that's why I'm talking to you first."

Glitsky made a face. "You just lost me."

"Well, the sad truth is that my experience with defense attorneys in general hasn't been a big bowl of cherries. I wasn't about to go talk to Mr. Hardy cold and essentially ally myself with him against the district attorney. Don't get me wrong, I'd like nothing more than to see

Jameson shut down, if not in a perfect world arrested for murder. But these are some pretty serious stakes: Jameson knows what I think he did and that isn't going away, so he wants to keep me at arm's length or more. So I'd be a fool if I took step one without a pretty darn strong recommendation from a reliable source on our side assuring me I could trust this guy."

"That sounds about right. And I'm that source?"

"Yes, sir."

"Well, I'm flattered, I think. And no doubt you're smart to check. As to Diz—Mr. Hardy—I don't know if you know, but he actually used to be a cop himself: he and I walked a beat together when we were both just starting out, and we've been friends ever since. Which is not to say he can't be a pure pain in the rear, but you can trust him and he doesn't lie, which are not the same thing."

"I don't mean to sound paranoid, sir. It's just if Jameson gets any idea . . ."

"I hear you. Especially if you're right about him and Peter Ash."

"I am." She nodded with finality. "I'd bet my life on that."

Glitsky reached over and patted her hand where it rested on the table. "Let's hope it doesn't come to that."

In his raggedy old terry-cloth bathrobe, Hardy sat alone on the couch in his family room just off the kitchen. He'd just done a tour of the whole house, front to back, and the entire place was bathed in a darkness that would have been pitch except for the dim bluish light in the tank that held his tropical fish.

Just before getting into bed with his wife, he'd turned his phone back on to see if he had gotten any messages—he'd turned it off for dinner as he usually did—and saw that he'd gotten a text from Glitsky in the last couple of minutes saying that they needed to talk.

So, in spite of the late hour, Hardy knew that Abe was still awake and he'd called him and learned about his talk with Inspector Tully. It woke him all the way up.

He couldn't have said how long he'd been sitting there, more or less mesmerized by the gentle bubbling of the tank. The eleven fish swam about in their random fashion and he watched them without conscious thought.

Eventually, though, the staggering reality of Beth Tully's information—her belief that San Francisco's newly elected district attorney, Ron Jameson, was a literal murderer—forced him to give it some, then a lot, and finally all of his attention.

Of course, he couldn't be sure that it was true. Abe had told him that Tully hadn't been able to build a righteous case against Jameson; that she had little or no evidence to back up her claim; that, in fact, the case had been closed and considered solved, with another suspect, Geoff Cooke, widely considered the true culprit.

This was all not exactly persuasive. And, beyond that, both he and Abe knew nothing about Tully's character, habits, state of mind, or record as a police inspector. It wasn't impossible, for example, that she'd had her own affair with Ron Jameson and that he'd broken up with her, or perhaps she wanted to have one and he'd rejected her. By keeping her from testifying in front of the grand jury, Jameson might have been trying somehow to marginalize her career, and this was her chance at payback. She might be a congenital liar. Or just a bad cop. The possibilities were endless.

And yet . . .

Her talking to Glitsky was a bold and dangerous move, and reaching out to a defense attorney such as himself even more so. Why would she put herself at that kind of risk? If Jameson got wind of it, he could lobby—and probably successfully—that she did not belong in the Homicide Detail, and maybe should not even remain on the force. And if her suppositions about Jameson were in fact true, she might actually be putting her life on the line.

Hardy knew that he himself had brought up with Devin Juhle the long-shot idea of speaking to the homicide inspectors who'd been working the Celia Montoya case to see if they might be able to help him in his defense of Phyllis. But he had not in his wildest dreams thought that one of them might contact him through his friend Abe, and with such explosive information.

Getting to his feet, he crossed the room and stood for a last moment staring at his tropicals. Then, not completely understanding why he had opened this can of worms, and vaguely wishing that he had not, he walked back up through the house to triple-check the dead bolt at the front door, then the dead bolt to the back. From long experience, he knew that he would not shake this sense of unease until he got some sleep, but that sleep would probably not come easily. Giving one last careful listen to the silence around him, he finally turned to mount the stairway that led up to his bedroom.

12

AT THE BREAKFAST table in his home the next morning—Wednesday, February 8—Ron Jameson put down his morning *Chronicle* and stared across the room.

Kate looked up from her coffee. "Are you all right?"

After a moment he shook his head. "A little frustrated with this coverage is all."

"Isn't that what you wanted?"

"Yes, but I thought it might be a little more positive."

"Says the man who believes that all press is good press."

He frowned and looked over at her. "I mean, who is on the side of someone who helps a murderer escape? Especially when you can tie that person, as I did, to show the kind of people who are in the Farrell camp. The McGowan woman works for the firm he's joining up with, for Christ's sake. It's pretty obvious that these people don't give a thought to obstructing justice. They really think they can do anything they want, and get away with it because they're so special. That's the real story here, and I'm just a little disappointed, though not particularly surprised, that the *Chronicle* apparently doesn't see it that way."

"The *Courier* liked it." This was the city's second newspaper.

"Nobody reads the *Courier*."

"Yes they do. And a lot of them are your fans. You might not want to forget that." She pointed down at the paper in front of him. "It was the dislocated shoulder," she said.

"This just in," he said, "the function of handcuffs is to bind and constrain. They're not supposed to be loose. And I wanted to make the point that this woman was very much, in fact, dangerous. They found the gun in her apartment. This is an armed woman helping a murderer escape. She'd damn well better be restrained. Wouldn't you say?"

"It seems completely defensible to me. But do you really think this lawyer, Hardy, is going to sue you personally?"

Jameson considered for a minute. "At least he's told the papers he's doing the whole trifecta. First, he's filing a complaint with the state bar. He's also suing me and my two inspectors for the injuries to his client. Those two are no-brainers for us. Then, my personal favorite, he's filing a recusal motion, which is the only one we actually have to deal with in the criminal proceeding. He wants the whole DA's office to be kicked off the case and the attorney general to take over the prosecution because we are bad, mean, evil, and generally prejudiced people. All the typical crap. But in fact we followed protocol every step of the way. No judge on the planet would rule we didn't, and Hardy knows that. He's just showboating. Welcome to the world of the sleazy defense attorney."

"It's a little worrisome."

"No. It's just what it is."

Their eyes met and held.

Finally, Kate dabbed at her lips with her napkin. "And it's not only just what it is, Ron. Let's not kid ourselves. If this man Hardy picks a judge with a grudge . . ."

"Judge with a grudge," he said. "Good one."

"It's no joke," she said. "I'm just trying to make sure you're aware of all the elements that are out there."

"I think I am, thank you."

"Don't get mad at me, Ron. You can't blame me for being protective. It's for both of our sakes. And though maybe you don't think so anymore, I don't think it would be smart to let down our guards and invite too much trouble. It may all be in the past, but that doesn't mean it isn't something we need to be aware of. Constantly."

This, between them, was the great unspoken truth.

Ron let out a heavy sigh that could have been boredom at the topic, or frustration. Or both. Wearily he said, "I have never been anything but grateful to you, Kate, and you know it."

"Except now, after you've won this election, I'm a little worried that maybe you've got a tendency to feel a bit invincible, more or less bulletproof. And I'm just saying you might want to think about being a little cautious."

"And it's your job, somehow, to shut me down."

This straightened Kate right up in her chair. "Don't you *dare* even start to imply that. I'm not trying to shut you down, Ron. No one has ever been more supportive of you, and proven it time and again, than I have. Do I have to even mention this?"

"No. I know what you've done, for both of us. Do you think I could forget that even for a second? Beyond the fact," he added, "that you would never let me forget it."

Infuriatingly, Kate's eyes suddenly filled with incipient tears. "Goddamn it," she said. "That is just not true, Ron. How can you even say that? You are always free to do whatever you want to do. Always. But you and I have been partners long enough to know that we both have the right to call each other if one or the other of us thinks we're skating a little too close to the edge. And this is one of those times for me. So I'd appreciate it if you'd at least take seriously what I'm talking about. Where I'm concerned, I've got every right to be concerned, and you'd be foolish if you didn't at least acknowledge what I'm talking about."

"And you don't think I'm doing that?

Kate paused to let her anger and hurt subside a bit. "I don't blame you for being confident, especially after what we've been through and where we are now. Where *you* are now. But I am your muse, or at least I used to be . . ."

"And still are."

She shrugged. "Maybe not in the same way, but I still feel that I am, too. I don't want to have us fight over how you want to live your life."

He reached over and put his hand over hers. "I don't want us to fight, either. And I want to live my life with you. Period. That's not changed in any way."

She let a breath of relief escape. She put another hand over his. "I just worry."

"I know you do. I can't blame you. But all that's happened, that's behind us now. Nobody's interested in what may or may not have happened two or three years ago."

"That's my point, Ron. I think now, especially, we don't want to push that. You have political enemies that you never had before. If they find any way to take you down, they will try and try again. And you may not think I've got a role anymore, but I've got your back. I'm always going to have your back, even if you think it's not necessary."

"And I appreciate that," he said. "I really do. And you know, I've got yours, too. Really. All the time."

"Okay," she said. "Okay."

Then Ron's cell phone chirped at his belt. He picked it up, glanced at it, and made a face. "I'd better get this." Connecting, he said, "Andrea, what's so important it rates a call at home?"

Listening, his face clouded further. "No, I see," he said. "Yes, I get it. Any other details? Okay, well let me know. I know. No, I didn't expect anything like that, either. It's a major shock, I admit. Yes, I'll be in soon."

Ending the connection, he held on to the cell phone, looking at it as though it might bite him.

"What?" Kate asked.

"Celia Montoya," he said. "She killed herself."

HARDY SAT AT the big table in the Solarium. Next to him, Phyllis was going through a lot of Kleenex as she wiped a steady flow of tears spilling from her eyes over onto her cheeks.

A couple of seats farther along, Gina Roake leaned back in her own chair, arms crossed over her chest, her face closed down tight. "Somebody should have been able to predict this," she said. "Put her on a suicide watch, if nothing else. If that's what it was, after all. A suicide, I mean. What do you think, Phyllis? Was Celia someone who you think might have killed herself?"

Phyllis sniffed and wiped her nose. "I don't really think so," she said.

"We were only together those four days, hanging out at the motel, watching TV, and eating junk food. So she wasn't in a very good place emotionally. Naturally. I mean, imagine the stress. But she never mentioned even thinking about killing herself. If anything, she was upbeat that she'd made it as far as she had. It seemed to me she just wanted to get out of Dodge as soon as she could and start over again. She talked about looking forward to that. So I'd have to say no, she wasn't really acting like she was thinking of suicide."

"Okay," Hardy said. "But then she got betrayed somehow and she knew she was coming back to stand trial for murder. That could have pushed her over the brink."

"Agreed," Gina said. "Something seems to have, anyway. It's so senseless."

"I'd like to know how the betrayal happened," Hardy said. "Who turned her into Immigration." He turned to Phyllis. "Any ideas there?"

She shook her head. "I'm afraid that wasn't my part of it. I heard they were having some trouble like that in Ukiah, but there were always those rumors. To me, she was just another in a very long line of very scared people."

"Well," Gina said, "although I hate to say it, except for the murder part."

"If you believe that," Phyllis said, her voice taking on a bit of an edge.

Hardy put his hand over hers. "Wait a minute. What are you saying?"

"What do you mean?"

"I mean it sounded for a second there like you don't think she killed anybody."

"That really wasn't my concern, but if I had to say, I'd say I never thought that."

Gina asked, "You didn't think she killed anybody? This Mr. Valdez, for example?"

"No."

"Then why did you . . . ?" Gina asked. "How did you get involved at all?"

"Well, the main thing to me is that she was undocumented. Those were the people I'd been helping for the past several years, so I had some idea of what I had to do and the urgency of it, before ICE got any wind of it. It was nothing to do with anybody murdering anyone. My brother Adam knew Celia from a bar named El Sol, and when he called me, he told me he had to get her out of town right away, that she was the main suspect in this murder."

"Why was that?" Hardy asked.

Phyllis shrugged. "Because she . . . well, no . . . not she. Valdez had brought her up from Mexico a few months before and apparently they had an ongoing relationship, though Adam said she was more like his sex slave, with every reason in the world to have shot him. Anyway, it was all rushed and crazy and we had to get on the road immediately."

"Didn't you ask her?" Gina asked.

"If she killed him? I mostly just assumed she did. I think she brought the murder weapon to my house with her."

"You *think*?" Gina asked.

Phyllis nodded. "Well, it was there for the police to find later when they searched, which is probably a big part of the reason why they charged me with being an accessory." She turned to Hardy. "Wouldn't you say, sir?"

"It wouldn't have hurt," Hardy said.

Phyllis went on. "But whether or not she'd actually killed him wasn't my issue. If she did, he sounds like he deserved it. Celia didn't have anything good to say about Valdez, but she never said she killed him, either."

"That was just being smart," Gina said.

"Maybe that." Phyllis dabbed at her eyes again. "This is such a tragedy. That poor girl."

HARDY SPENT THE next couple of hours in his office, writing up his motions against Ron Jameson.

The complaint to the state bar was the easiest. Because Jameson had abused his office and charged someone without probable cause for political reasons, he should be disbarred.

The civil suit he farmed off to one of his associates with instructions to name the two investigators and Jameson personally, and to include a demand for punitive damages.

He kept the recusal motion for himself.

Fun stuff.

But for all the fun, about two minutes after he'd sent his document to print, he found himself again having slumped into what was becoming an all-too-familiar anger, or was it melancholy? Unconsciously he must have gone over and opened the doors to his dartboard, because now he was standing at the throw line, three darts in hand. He took up his throwing position, set himself, and then stopped.

If he thought he'd been enraged over Ron Jameson's treatment of Phyllis—and he was—he was suddenly and acutely aware that the DA's indictment of Celia Montoya for the murder of Hector Valdez—whether or not she had in fact been guilty of that murder—had been far more consequential, and more tragic. It had forced her to go underground, where she had somehow been betrayed, and this had apparently driven her to a despair that led her to suicide.

He walked back to his dart cabinet and put the darts in their slots.

His hands were shaking, blood ringing in his ears.

13

For well over twenty years, Jeff Elliott had been writing the "CityTalk" column for the *San Francisco Chronicle*. Hardy had made his acquaintance early on and the two had formed and maintained a friendship that had served them well over the years, both personally and professionally. Back when he'd just been starting out, Jeff had been a slender, clean-shaven guy who soon enough would be struck by multiple sclerosis. Now he got around mostly by wheelchair, and his most striking physical features were his full gray beard and a substantial potbelly.

Hardy had brought with him a couple of *bánh mì* from a place down Mission Street, and now Jeff was just swallowing the last of his. "Well, that hit the spot, thank you."

"You are most welcome."

"History argues, though, that bringing this lovely lunch down here has a price."

"Absolutely not. I was just in the neighborhood and thought I'd drop by, and then I noticed the *bánh mì* spot and thought you were probably starving yourself and could use a bite."

Elliott nodded. "But what, really? Since you already came out smelling like a rose in today's column from your court appearance yesterday. And Jameson? How do you not look like a horse's ass if you ask for ten million dollars, not to say dislocating the shoulder of a sweet, elderly woman. How is Phyllis, by the way?"

"She's fine. And her shoulder has a ping-pong fracture, clearly visible on the X-rays. They offered her Oxycontin, but she's taking Advil instead. Sometimes as often as twice a day. I had to speak to her about addiction."

Hardy was scrolling through his cell phone, looking for the copy of the X-rays. "Here you go. Check that out."

Elliott squinted at the screen. "You want my honest opinion, Diz? This doesn't look so bad."

"It doesn't look bad. It just hurts a lot. Off the record, I was thinking about asking her to scratch herself up a little, make it look a little worse. But that would be unethical, wouldn't it?"

"Some would say so." He brushed his hands on his pants. "So what can I do for you?"

"Really"—Hardy sat back in his chair—"I'm not sure, to tell you the truth. Have you heard about Celia Montoya?"

"Killing herself? Yeah. Awful stuff."

"And another connection to Jameson."

Elliott frowned. "I must have missed that. I heard she hung herself in her cell."

"Yeah, but why was she in a cell to begin with?"

With another shake of his head, Elliott said, "I still don't get it, Diz. She was in a cell because Immigration picked her up, right? To say nothing about being charged with murder. Either one of those will get you in a cell. What's it got to do with Jameson?"

"How about if she didn't kill anybody? If the indictment was rushed and flawed?"

"Do you have any proof that it was?"

"Not yet. Maybe I will before too long. But in another sense it doesn't even matter. Even if she did kill this Valdez guy. The way Jameson handled it all, forcing her to run, no real investigation. You see what I'm saying?"

"Sure, and I'm not denying it's sad as hell and bad luck for her. But getting all the way back till you blame it on Jameson—that's a reach. Not that I don't think the guy's a cretin."

"He's more than a cretin, Jeff. That's my point. I think he's ultimately responsible for this girl's suicide, and I think you've got a real opportunity here to put it out there. It's a hell of a story, don't you think?"

"If he were closer to it, maybe. But not the way you spun it right now. There's no context. You're just pissed at him."

"No. It's more than that."

"All right. Then give me some more to tie it together. But right now it's just your assertions and not much connection between them. If this poor girl hadn't gotten herself caught in—where was it? Ukiah?—she'd probably be in Canada by now. It's not Jameson's fault she got picked up, is it? Could he have even seen that as a possibility and done something to avoid it? I don't see how. And without that, she's still alive."

Hardy sat all the way back in his chair, slumping, his hands crossed over his chest. "How about if I could prove that he fast-tracked the indictment?"

"Doesn't matter, Diz. Fast-tracked or not, he got a righteous indictment. Which means he had enough evidence for the grand jury. End of story."

"There's more to it, I'm sure."

"Well, get it to me and I'll see where it leads. You know my door's always open for you and whatever lunch you happen to bring around. Or it would be if I had a door."

BETH TULLY WAS waiting in the lobby when Hardy got back from Mission Street. After they'd gotten settled in his office with the door closed behind them, Beth finally let out a pent-up breath and extended her hand, which Hardy took, and they shook. "Nice to meet you at last," she said.

"How'd you know I'd be here?"

"I just took a shot. Lied to my partner and cleared an hour or so."

"I appreciate that. But your partner's welcome, too."

She clucked. "He's a little . . . skeptical . . . about working with defense attorneys."

"But you're not?"

"Sometimes. Anyway, Ike basically doesn't want to hear about it." She shrugged. "Your friend Glitsky had some nice things to say about you."

"That's always good to hear."

"I could never have an affair," Beth said. "I told Ike I was meeting my daughter for lunch, and now I'm a wreck he's going to be driving by when I leave here and find me out."

"You don't want him to know you're talking to me?"

"Probably not."

"Well, in case it's ever needed, we've got a secret underground tunnel that runs from here down to the Hall of Justice, so you can just show up there and say you were in the bathroom or something."

"Really? Are you kidding me?"

"Yep." Hardy broke a grin. "No secret passage, I'm afraid."

With a look of chagrin, she said, "Glitsky didn't mention you being funny."

"Well, you know his nickname?"

"No."

"People Not Laughing. That's because, wherever he is, he's surrounded by people who aren't laughing. That's his true nickname, by the way. Not a joke."

"I'll keep that in mind if I ever see him again. Meanwhile, you wanted to talk to me?"

"Yes. I did." His grin faded. "The woman outside the office here is my secretary, Phyllis McGowan."

Beth nodded. "Adam's sister," she said. It wasn't a question.

"Yes. He ratted her out, didn't he?"

"Well, he put her in the picture as Celia Montoya's accomplice, if that's what you mean."

"Accessory after the fact, if you want to get technical. And, based on what Adam told you, you then got a warrant to search her house and found the purported murder weapon. Is that about right?"

"Not exactly. We didn't do the search. That was DA investigators."

"Why was that?"

"I think Lieutenant Juhle might have told you, the case went upstairs pretty fast. We hadn't come anywhere near finishing our investigation, when suddenly it had become the DA's case. His people searched her apartment and found the gun, then he took the case to the grand jury and got his indictment, and me and Ike, we were out of it."

"How'd you like that?"

A bitter little smile. "About like you'd expect."

"So when you got called off—"

"Excuse me, but it wasn't exactly like that. We weren't called off as in dismissed. When the indictment came down, that was just the end of it bureaucratically. Nobody actually told us to stop or back off. We had other cases."

"But you didn't think the investigation was complete?"

"Not even close, really. Can I ask you something?"

"Sure."

"I know why this matters to me, but why does it matter to you?"

"Well, a couple of reasons. The first one being Phyllis out there. If you, the inspectors assigned to the case, weren't sure that Celia killed Valdez, why in the world would Phyllis have jumped to that conclusion? And if Phyllis didn't think that, and if she didn't have a reason to believe that Celia was going to be charged with murder . . . you see what I'm saying?"

"Not quite."

"Okay, if Celia to her was just another immigrant who needed to get to Canada to keep from being deported and didn't know anything about any murder or even the likelihood of Celia getting charged, then Phyllis is technically not an accessory after the fact. And if I can make a jury see that you and your partner—homicide inspectors, for God's sake—had serious doubts about Celia's guilt, or whether at the time of her flight she would even be charged, then certainly Phyllis wouldn't have much of a reason to believe it, either."

"So at her trial you'd want us to testify that our investigation wasn't complete?"

"In a perfect world. That's the general idea. When defense attorneys call cops to testify, it tends to be a bad day for the prosecution."

"After which I'd bet it's often a bad day for those cops, isn't it?"

Hardy showed her another tight grin. "It might be at that. But that would tend not to be my problem. In any event"—he spread his hands—"all that is by way of explaining why I hoped to be able to talk to you—why this all matters to me."

"What's the other reason?"

Hardy cocked his head, a question.

"You said you had a couple of reasons why it mattered to you. What's the other one?"

"Ahh." Hardy met her gaze. "The other one's more personal. You may be aware that I campaigned pretty hard for Wes Farrell in the DA race. So when Jameson realized that Phyllis, with a little finessing, could be dragged into this case and that she worked for me, there was an opportunity for some payback and he was going to make it as humiliating as possible for her—and, by the way, she is a true saint—and at the same time rub my face in the shit. He wants to play that game, I'm going to take him down if I can."

Hardy stood up and walked over to the windows, where he held back the curtains and glanced down briefly to the street outside. Turning back, he said, "I understand that beyond getting dumped off Celia's case, you've got some personal issues yourself with Mr. Jameson."

Beth hesitated, taking in the corners of the ceiling. Finally, coming back down to Hardy, she nodded. "I hate him," she said. "I believe he's lying in wait for a way to plausibly get me fired, if not worse. It's only a matter of time."

"Because he knows that you think he killed Peter Ash?"

"I *know* he killed Peter Ash. And I know his wife killed Geoff Cooke. In fact, Kate—his wife—she might be the only thing keeping me alive, because as you pointed out, he's a vindictive bastard without an ethical bone in his body. If it were up to him, I believe I'd be gone. And I don't just mean off the force."

Hardy, back in front of her, boosted himself onto his desk. "Given all that, I can't really thank you enough for sneaking down here to talk to me."

She shrugged. "This has got to end. Someone's got to figure out how to bring this guy down."

Hardy nodded. "I'm assuming that you've heard about Celia."

"Of course."

"All right. Let's pretend for a minute that she didn't kill Valdez, and let's say you're not sure of that. Are you?"

"Not entirely."

"So if that's true"—Hardy pushing it now—"she's another innocent victim in Jameson's wake. He rushes the case, kicks off the regular inspectors, chases Celia out of town as the suspect, gets her in custody, and then she kills herself in jail. Doesn't anybody else see this except me?"

"I do. I completely agree with you. But again, what are we going to do?"

Hardy gave it a couple of seconds. "This is me just thinking out loud," he said, "but what do you think about the idea of reopening the investigation into this case?"

Beth sat back, surprised. She, too, took a moment to pause. "You're talking Valdez?"

"Right."

"Well." Another pause, the outrageous idea perhaps starting to resonate. "First, sir . . ."

"Please. Dismas. Or even Diz."

"All right. What kind of name is that, anyway? Dismas?"

"Dismas was the good thief, crucified up on Calvary next to Jesus. He's the patron saint of thieves and murderers, which is handy if you happen to be a defense attorney. It's always good to have a saint on the home team."

"I'd imagine so. It couldn't hurt, anyway." She ran her hand through her hair. "But back to reopening the case . . ."

"Okay."

"Well, maybe not so okay. I don't really see how we could make that happen. There are procedures, as I'm sure you know. Celia was the indicted suspect and now she's dead, so the case is technically closed, or on the verge of it. But beyond that, what would it accomplish in terms of Jameson?"

"Those are good questions and reasonable objections, and I can't say I've got any quick answer for either. But Jameson clearly interfered with you and your partner and the pace of your investigation, and the way it played out ended in tragedy. If you come up with another suspect—I mean the bona fide, convictable killer of Mr. Valdez—that you missed the first time because Jameson was in such a hurry, pulled you off the case, and screwed it all up, then his decisions and actions led to the unnecessary death of an innocent young woman, and the whole thing can be laid at his feet. At the very least, he's seriously embarrassed. Definitely it'll hurt him politically. He won by only a thousand votes, and this ought to eat those right up. And then some."

"Wouldn't that be sweet?"

Hardy shrugged. "It might be worth a look. That's all I'm saying."

Beth nodded. "It might at that."

14

In Devin Juhle's office, the door closed behind them, Beth had barely started in on her pitch, when her partner cut her off. "Are you out of your mind? You want to *what*?"

"I want to solve a homicide to my satisfaction. Which is, if I'm not mistaken, the job we both do."

"Except that we've already done that case." Ike turned around and motioned to the whiteboard that covered the wall behind him. "Check it out, Beth. Devin's even got it crossed out on the magic whiteboard. Valdez is done."

"And who killed him?"

"Celia Montoya, indicted and now deceased."

"You're not sure of that, and neither am I."

"It doesn't matter what we believe . . ."

Juhle, seated behind his desk, straightened up a bit and raised a finger. "Wait a minute there, Ike. It does in fact matter what you believe, to some extent. At least, to me it does. Do you have some real serious doubt about that case?"

Ike huffed out a breath, looked across at his partner, came back to Juhle. "No case is perfect, Dev. We all know that. This one may be a little less perfect than others. But do I have real serious doubt? I don't know. I do know that the grand jury indicted her. After that, traditionally it's up to a trial jury to decide if she's guilty. Not us. Am I wrong here? And if I am, tell me where."

"No," Juhle said. "You're right as far as that goes. But after today we're not ever going to get to a jury trial on Celia Montoya, are we? So if there are some unanswered questions, I'm reluctant to formally close the case, even if it's lost its place on the whiteboard."

"It's not impossible she would have been cleared and we would have closed in on somebody else if we'd just had a little more time," Beth said.

"Who?" Juhle asked.

"I'm going to say one of our eyewitnesses."

Ike all but exploded. "That's the other thing. We got testimony from not one, not two, but three eyewitnesses, Dev."

Beth was shaking her head. "But none of them even close to rock-solid. Maybe mutually collaborative, but that's one fifteen-minute conversation among the three of them. None of them said they actually saw her take the shot. So they agree on what they're going to tell us, and lo and behold, amazingly, they all have the same story. Not too many details, but the same basic idea. And before we get the time to go back and ask a few of the hard questions, suddenly we're off the case, so the grand jury only sees the first pass."

"So what do you want to do, Beth?" Juhle asked.

"I think we ought to talk to these eyewitnesses again. See if the stories hang together like they did the first time, or maybe they start to fall apart. See if any of them decide they want to lawyer up before talking to us again when they see which way the wind might start to be blowing." She turned to Juhle. "These are not people without their own agendas, Dev. One of them is fresh out of Avenal. The other couple—the bartender and waitress—it's possible they had a little more to do with Valdez's business than just with the bar, although we never really got around to asking about any of that. But when you're talking rock-solid eyewitnesses, these people don't spring immediately to mind."

"So why—" Juhle began.

Beth was a step ahead of him. "Because Jameson took the case away. That's my point. It never should have happened, but it did and left us strung out."

"And why are you only now getting around to this?"

"Because before today, Dev, Celia Montoya was going to trial. There'd be more investigation and lots of it. And call me optimistic, but maybe the truth would have come out, and conceivably she could have even been cleared. And at least if she got convicted, we would know that she was guilty. Now, if the three of us don't do something to follow up here, there's a chance the real killer—if it's not Celia—is going to walk. And that's just something I'd prefer not to live with. It's our case, and if we don't do something now, we'll never get another chance to close it."

Juhle scratched at a peeling piece of lacquer at the corner of his desk. "She makes a good case, Ike. What do you say?"

"After all that," he asked, "do I really have a choice?"

THE OWNER OF the building that housed El Sol was Miguel Maria Larson and he didn't much care about who managed day-to-day operations at the bar, just so long as they made the monthly nut. Hector Valdez had held the job for a couple of years, and the way these things went, the position was probably overdue for a turnaround, although Miguel wouldn't have necessarily hoped for Hector's murder as the vehicle for the personnel change.

But hey, what were you gonna do?

Hector Valdez knew that the game he played came with its risks as well as its rewards. When he'd first come on, he was as low-profile as anyone could be, actually working the bar, dealing most of the common drugs right out of the back room. From that inauspicious start, he'd graduated to some protection work in the neighborhood, brought on his strong-arm partner Mel Bernardo, and Mel's girlfriend, Rita. And soon enough realized that the money and possibly a little more of the fun was in girls. The building was perfectly suited to this endeavor, since its three upper stories were all divided into SRO (single room occupancy) units, which meant a place for up to thirty girls to stay while Hector shopped them around and Mel and Rita made sure they felt both secure while they were waiting and too afraid to try to escape.

But again, none of that was Miguel's business.

And now, with Hector's passing, apparently at the hands of one of his girls—Miguel didn't care—he was having to negotiate terms with Mel and Rita, who were more than ready to step into Hector's shoes. And he gathered he was supposed to somehow include this new guy, Adam, just out of the joint. And who, frankly, scared the shit out of Miguel.

Well, he was thinking, change happens. He'd just have to see how this new team worked things out, how they were going to play it.

The bar opened for business at 3:00, and when Miguel knocked at the door at the exact time of their appointment, 2:30, it was dark inside. He put his face up against the glass and saw movement, and in another few seconds Mel turned the dead bolt and opened the door, a big smile on his face, and reached out to put his huge arm around Miguel's shoulders. A greeting more for family and friends than for business partners. "*Buenas tardes, buenas, buenas.*"

And then they were inside, the door locked again behind them, moving to a round table in the back where another guy was sitting, his back to them.

That man turned out to be Adam, a shot glass of tequila in front of him. Miguel hadn't expected him to be here for this meeting, and his presence was a little unnerving. But now, getting to his feet and turning, he stuck out his hand, a welcoming smile on his face as well. "How are you doing, Miguel?" Old pals shaking hands. "Good to see you again."

Switching to English for Adam's benefit, Mel asked, "Can I get you something to drink? *Cerveza*? Tequila?"

"Sure." Miguel nodded. "Tequila would be nice."

"So"—Mel coming around with a bottle and shot glasses—"you hear the good news?"

"What's that?"

"Celia," Mel said. "The girl who shot Hector. She killed herself this morning in her jail cell." He poured two shots and topped off Adam's. "God rest her soul."

The men picked up and shot their drinks. Mel filled them all again, and everybody sat.

"Why is that good?" Miguel asked. "Her dying."

"Because it ends the investigation," Adam said. "And we can get back to business."

"She can't talk anymore," Mel said, "and so her story never changes."

"Trying to save herself," Adam added, "she could have made trouble for us. Now there is no danger of that."

"What kind of trouble?"

The two younger men shared a glance. "Rita and the two of us," Adam said, "we are the only ones who know what happened, what she did. And that's what we told the police."

"But she might have pointed back at us," Mel added. "And now that can't happen."

"I don't pay any attention to much of that," Miguel said. "Hector and his girlfriends, huh? He picked the wrong one this time. That's what I heard."

"That is the truth. And fortunately"—Adam raised his glass again and drank—"all that is over now."

"And they, the police, they know she did it?"

"Hey," Mel said, "she shoots him and that same day she runs. There is no doubt."

Adam nodded. "You don't run if you didn't do it."

Yes you do, Miguel thought. You do if you're an undocumented alien. You do if someone like Mel or Adam makes you believe that the police will think you did it anyway. Or if they told the police you did. You'd run if you didn't think the system is fair.

Miguel could think of a dozen reasons—beyond that she was guilty—why the girl had run, but that was not what he was there to talk about today. Taking another sip of tequila for courage—the more he sat facing Adam, the more nervous he became—he put the glass down and said, "But the water—what do they say—is no longer muddy?"

"Right," Adam said. "We are ready to pick up where Hector left off. Mel manages and I help out at the bar."

"And Rita, too, of course," Mel said, "with the girls."

"That is just a rent issue," Miguel said. "Hector kept the upstairs rooms filled is the important thing. He had, I believe, connections. We don't want to get behind on the rents there."

Mel nodded. "I know his people. I've been on that side of it for a year now. He was just making promises and taking money. And also, the other business at the bar."

Miguel shook his head. "That is also the rent. I don't care where it comes from. But I need to clear twenty thousand from you on the first, in cash, every month. That is all that matters. Then we can do business. As Hector and I did. There is enough for everybody here to be comfortable."

"We can do that," Mel said.

"I know you can."

"But eighteen would be better." Adam gave him a frigid smile. "At least until we set up a little better and get our feet on the ground."

"Eighteen will not work."

Another look from Adam that was nothing like a smile. "For Hector, I understand, because he told me, it was fifteen."

"That's a lie." The two men stared at each other until Miguel's shoulders sagged. "For Hector it was eighteen."

Adam's smile returned, his hands held wide and welcoming. "Which is all that we ask for. In all fairness." He lifted his shot glass and drained it. "Eighteen," he repeated.

Miguel let out a breath. He glanced at Mel, who gave him an ambiguous nod. He then came back to Adam. Through clenched teeth he said, "Eighteen," then pushed his chair back and got to his feet. "On the first. In cash."

He gave each of his two partners one more nod each. By the time he'd cleared the table on his way out, he realized that he was no longer going to be dealing with Mel but with Adam, who had arrived only a few weeks before and then, obviously, seen a situation here that he could take advantage of. He could simply convince Mel and Rita that they didn't have to take leftovers from Hector. They could run the whole show themselves.

Of course—and Miguel saw this clearly—Adam knew that he would go on to be in control of the business. All he had to do was get rid of Hector and then somehow make it appear that his girlfriend had killed him, when in fact . . .

Miguel didn't want to burden himself with these speculations. The only thing that really mattered to him was that his rent got paid.

But he could not ignore the plausible truth.

. . . when in fact Adam may very well have killed Hector, then convinced the poor girl that she needed to run. The police wouldn't even listen to her denials if she tried to make them: as an undocumented person, and the girlfriend of the murder victim, she would have been seen as Hector's killer. Adam could have told her that, even if she didn't kill Hector, the cops would jump to that conclusion and arrest her. She had to run. She had no choice.

Once she did that, the police wouldn't be looking at anybody else.

And Adam—protected by his new partners' conspiracy, then by the young woman's flight, and today by her death—would move into Hector's position.

A cold, clean, and efficient takeover by a very dangerous man.

15

Because it was a Wednesday, which had been his and Frannie's traditional date night for most of the past thirty years, Hardy left work early and drove out to the Little Shamrock, the bar he co-owned with his sister-in-law, at Lincoln and Ninth Avenue. Frannie would be coming over by Uber at around six, and the two of them would head out to some worthy destination in this endlessly fascinating city.

Meanwhile, before she got there, he liked to put in a couple of hours bartending every week or so, feeling that it kept him in touch with the real world of regular people: working stiffs, teachers, musicians, construction guys, young professionals, service people, a few retirees—real human beings not involved as he was in the universe of criminal law.

The Shamrock was in some ways a touchstone, as important as his home. He had essentially spent all his waking moments there, behind the bar, in a haze of Guinness stout and Bass ale, for the decade after he lost his first son, Michael. That tragedy had also destroyed his first marriage and detonated his first career as a young, red-hot DA ready to conquer the world and bring all criminals to justice.

Now it wasn't so much that he wanted to relive any of that painful time as to remind himself how fantastically well his life had turned out when it had seemed for the longest time that it would never have that chance.

Two hours behind that bar with these regular good people showered him with an almost primeval sense of hope, of possibility, of the future, even as he cruised past sixty.

Who would have thought he'd have gotten to here?

Certainly not him.

And now here he was, pouring drinks, his suit coat hung on the peg behind the bar, his tie off. The place was starting to fill up, and it was that magic time before it got crazy but still was busy enough to set up a nice mindless rhythm. He and his cohort Lynne worked together seamlessly, their waitress Noni appearing promptly at 5:00 and starting to place orders for the folks who didn't have a spot at the rail.

Hardy, in the zone, was loving it. When Frannie sidled up to the bar and ordered her Chardonnay, he checked his watch and saw that it was already 6:15.

"Where are we going?" he asked her.

"Locanda," she said. "Seven thirty."

One of his favorite restaurants.

"Perfect," he said.

Hardy wound up parking on Sixteenth Street, around the corner from the restaurant. Now sated and happy after their dinner of rigatoni alla carbonara and grilled whole trout, he and Frannie had just about gotten to his car when Hardy touched her arm, stopping her.

"What?" she asked.

His eyes were still focused across the street and it seemed that only reluctantly he came back to her. "That's the El Sol."

" 'El' means 'the,' Dismas," she said. "So it's just El Sol, not *the* El Sol."

Hardy slapped at his cheek in mock dismay. "You probably can't see it in this dim light, Fran, but my face is red with shame and embarrassment. *The* El Sol indeed. What was I thinking?"

"It must be that, just for the moment, you weren't. Strange though that would be. What about it, though? El Sol? Why is it on your radar?"

"It's where Hector Valdez got himself killed last week. The case Phyllis got involved in. Or I should say *is* involved in."

"But this place is back open already? What about that whole crime scene thing? Closing the place down? Getting all the evidence?"

"They got what they needed. One bullet in the guy. It's a bar, so prints and DNA are useless. No security camera. So, as I understand it, the investigation wouldn't have taken very long."

They stood looking for another few seconds. At last Frannie sighed. "Okay."

"Okay what?" Hardy said.

"Okay, we can go in so you can check it out."

"I wasn't—"

"Shut up, Dismas. Of course you do. Since we're already here."

Hardy gave it a few seconds of hesitation. "Just a couple of minutes," he said.

He took her hand and they walked across the street.

THE CROWD INSIDE El Sol extended to the doorway, salsa blaring and an overflow crowd spilling out into the street. Hardy and Frannie, still holding hands, made it to the edge of that crush and Hardy said, "This might be more productive earlier in the day."

"You're sure?"

He nodded. "And maybe not even then."

He had started to turn, to recross the street back to his car, when suddenly a familiar female figure materialized out of the throng and he stepped over in front of her. "Phyllis!"

She straightened up, shocked. "Mr. Hardy. What in the world . . . ?"

"I could ask you the same thing. How are you? And what are you doing here?"

"Well, I was just moping around the apartment. I mean, after today and Celia and everything that has happened." Shrugging, she forced a pathetic smile of sorts. "Anyway, Adam thought it might be good for me to get out and try to cheer up a little, although I didn't think that was likely to happen. And certainly not here, where all these young women just remind me more of her.

"But Adam just got what he said was a real job here, and I think he wanted to show it off to me and have me see that he was back on his feet and everything was going to work out now. But really . . . as you can probably see, this is not my kind of place. Although maybe, for Adam, especially after being in prison . . . well, you can see." She leaned to one side. "Is that Mrs. Hardy?"

Frannie stepped forward. "It is. How are you, Phyllis?"

"Well, as I was just telling your husband . . ." She sighed. "It's just been a terrible few days. I'm so sorry."

"Nothing for you to be sorry about," Frannie said. "We're sorry you have to go through all of this. And, by the way, Dismas has told me about all you've done helping those poor people without documentation all these years. I am so impressed."

Phyllis shrugged again. "Well, we all do what we can. The system is so unfair. Somebody's got to step up and help."

"Yes, but not many actually do," Frannie said.

"Well, thank you."

"So," Hardy broke in, "are you on your way back home?"

"Yes. I was just going to get an Uber."

"How about if we just take you there in my car and drop you off?"

"Oh, that's too much trouble. I couldn't . . ."

"Yes you can," Hardy said. He pointed. "We're parked right there, across the street. We'll have you home in ten minutes."

FRANNIE INSISTED THAT Phyllis sit in the front seat, and by the time they arrived and parked at the curb in front of her apartment, she and Hardy were deep in the kind of conversation that had eluded them while she'd been in custody.

"No," Phyllis was saying, "Celia wasn't Adam's girlfriend. She was this man Hector's, his woman, but it was more like his slave. He owned her. Evidently that was what his business was: bringing girls into the country with the promise of work—good work, clean work—and then keeping them until he could sell them to other men or put them to work in massage parlors or even just brothels. But Hector kept Celia for himself."

"So what happened? The day Hector got shot, what did Adam tell you?"

"Well, it's a little hard to understand if you haven't seen the layout at the Sol, but after I saw it just today I got more of an idea." Her hands were in her lap and she looked down at them and sighed. When she spoke again, it was so quietly as to be nearly inaudible. "There's an office in the back behind the bar," she said, "and behind that is another room, mostly for storage, but it's also got a bed and a dresser—more like for naps, though, than a real bedroom."

"So somebody stayed there part-time?" Hardy asked.

"Well, I think that's kind of the general situation in that building. One person per tiny little room, one shared bathroom per floor, that kind of thing."

"And Celia lived there, in this one, downstairs?"

Phyllis shook her head. "No. She evidently stayed with Hector at his apartment. He didn't want to let her out of his sight. Anyway, the morning of the shooting, they came in together—Hector and Celia—and it was clear that they were having some kind of serious disagreement, so Adam and his partners gave them kind of a wide berth."

"I don't think I've heard about Adam's partners yet," Hardy said.

Phyllis nodded. "Mel and Rita. They were the couple Adam had gotten friendly with, who had kind of brought him on and given him work."

"Okay." Hardy decided to prod gently. He had her talking and he wanted to keep her at it. "So Hector and Celia are having a problem and Adam and this other couple are trying to stay out of their way?"

"Right. Then finally they disappear through the back door to the office."

"The one with the other room behind it?"

"Yes." Phyllis hesitated again. "All the rest of this, I'm afraid, is pretty much conjecture on Adam's part. He didn't know exactly what happened back there, but evidently Hector was threatening her—that's what it sounded like from the bar where Adam was—and he had a gun that in the struggle somehow Celia must have gotten ahold of. In any event, Adam heard the shot, so he went back there and she was in the office, the gun was right on the desk, and Hector was dead or at least dying on the floor. And so he asked her what she'd done, and she told him it hadn't been her. She'd locked herself in the back room to get away from him. It must have been one of the people from upstairs: the office also opened to a hallway and the stairs leading up. Anyway, Adam didn't believe somebody coming from upstairs had shot Hector. It was obvious to him that Celia had killed him, and he told her that there was no way that the police wouldn't see how it had happened. She had to run. He'd already told her about me—that if she could get to me, I could help her get away. Then he called me and said he had an emergency: I needed to be home to meet this woman."

After dropping Phyllis off and waiting for her to get safely inside her apartment before he started up, Hardy drove about three blocks before he asked Frannie: "On a scale of one to ten, how credible do you think that story was?"

"Does it have to start at one?" she asked. "If it started at zero, I could get closer."

"Are there any parts of it you believe?"

Frannie gave it a moment's thought. "None of the important ones. How about you?"

"I'm having some difficulty thinking about Adam as the good guy. I mean, Celia kills her boyfriend, and all he can think about is getting her to his sister so she can make a getaway to Canada? When, coincidentally, her disappearance just happens to be good for him in every way possible? Mostly that he's not a murder suspect."

"That does seem coincidental." She paused. "Do you think Adam killed Hector?"

Hardy nodded. "I'm starting to think that. Let's work this backwards. The murder weapon is at Phyllis's home. That's the big reason she got indicted. I don't think there's any doubt Adam brought it there. Now, Adam says he got it from Celia, who he says is the murderer. But if she's not, she didn't have the gun to give him. So where did he get it? Answer: He had it all the time. He's the one who killed Hector. It's the only way this fits if we assume Celia didn't do it."

"And what about Celia? Why go to Phyllis's if she knew Adam was the killer?"

"Well, good question, but a couple of good answers spring to mind. First, what if she was afraid that if she didn't leave town, Adam would kill her next?"

"Why would she think that?"

"Because he shoots Hector right in front of her, then tells her she has two choices: he can shoot her right now and make it look like a murder-suicide, or she can do exactly what she did and get out of town. She can't go to the police, so which one do you think you'd choose?"

"He might have shot Celia, too? Do you really think that?"

"It wouldn't have been a gigantic reach. The idea of shooting Celia wouldn't have slowed him down much if he felt he needed to. Instead, way better, he put all the blame on her, plus he had two other witnesses willing to swear that Celia had done it. Everybody wins. And that was exactly how it played out, with the bonus round going his way when Celia killed herself."

"So Celia, she just let herself be framed?"

"Not much choice. Dead or framed. I'd take framed any day."

"Okay, but once she'd gotten away with Phyllis, and no chance that Adam's going to kill her now, why didn't she tell her?"

"You mean rat out Adam to his sister? What good would that do? Celia's got to believe that Phyllis is going to be on Adam's side no matter what, isn't she? And Adam saw that, too. Once he got her to start running, she wasn't ever going to tell. Which, I wouldn't be surprised, might have played a role in her killing herself."

"What a cretin," Frannie said.

"But not a stupid cretin."

"No. He had it all figured out, didn't he?"

"That's how I read it."

"So what about Phyllis?"

"What about her?"

"Is she in danger?"

Hardy cast her a glance. "What do you think?"

16

Beth and Ike agreed that the most emotionally vulnerable of the three eyewitnesses was Mel's girlfriend, Rita Allegro. That Thursday morning, after Beth had gotten an update call from Dismas Hardy, they'd both reread the transcript of Rita's earlier statement when they'd interviewed her on the day of the murder, and it seemed that she had the most tenuous grasp on what may have actually happened, so she was the one they wanted to talk to.

Ike, now on board, albeit unenthusiastically, with the clandestine reopening of the case, had called Rita and set up an early (10:30) appointment at El Sol. No, Ike told her, it wasn't necessary that Mel come along with her, not for today's meeting, anyway. They just wanted to clear up a couple of questions that remained now that Celia had died. And, no, she wasn't in trouble. It was just routine business, some last-minute paperwork, so they could close the case.

They parked right in front of the bar, and by the time they were out of the car, Rita was standing in the bar's doorway, smiling uncertainly. In her early thirties, with shoulder-length black hair and deep, smoldering brown eyes, she projected a heavy sensual aura. Flattering blue jeans with a men's white dress shirt tucked into them added to the effect.

She nodded hello and led them inside. After pouring them coffee from a pot behind the bar, she came back around and led them to a table where they all pulled up chairs and got settled.

Beth had a sip of coffee and then took out her cell phone. "We're going to be taping our conversation if you don't mind, Rita. Just so we don't miss anything."

"It's not really a question," Ike told her, a little on the gruff side.

"Of course," she said. "Last time we did that, too."

"That's right." Beth smiled at her and pushed her cell phone to the center of the table, then recited her standard introduction: the date and time, her badge number, the case number, memorializing the presence of both Ike and Rita, and ending with "Okay, now, we're on the record."

Ike had brought inside a leather binder, and while Beth had been doing her spiel, he pulled out a few typed pages—the transcript of Rita's earlier statement—and laid them out in front of him.

"Inspector McCaffrey and I have gone over what you told us last time, and we've just got a few questions. The first one is this: Before the morning that he was killed, did you ever see Hector Valdez in possession of a gun?"

Rita's face clouded over in confusion. "Did I ever see him with a gun?"

"Right," Ike said.

"Did I ever say I did?" When she got no answer, she said, "Well, no. I don't think so."

"Did you ever see a gun in the office?" Ike asked. "Maybe in the safe? Did you ever look in the safe?"

"Yes, I've seen in the safe, and, no, we don't normally have a gun back there."

"All right. Did you see him bring in a gun that morning?"

She shook her head. "No." Turning to Beth, she said, "I don't know where the gun came from. But he was wearing a Giants jacket. You know, the black and orange one. He could have tucked it underneath somewhere. But I never saw no gun."

"Not with Hector? Not with Adam?"

"Neither one. Not that I was looking. I was working, like I said."

Beth was all understanding. "That's all right. Let's forget about the gun and move along to the moment when the shooting happened. Where were you?"

"In the front here, stocking behind the bar. It was before we were open."

"About this time in the morning, then?"

"Close. Yes."

"And while you were here, stocking," Beth asked, "who else was with you in the bar?"

"I already tol' you that last time we talked." She pointed at the papers on the table in front of Ike. "Don't you got that down?" she asked, then came back to Beth. "Mel and me and Adam. And then Hector and Celia in the back, in the office."

"So five of you." Beth let her eyes sweep the room. "And Adam. Where was he?"

Rita pointed. "Back there, by the register."

"The one at the end of the bar?"

"Right."

"Would you mind, Rita, showing us exactly? If you'd just go down and stand where he was the last time you remember seeing him."

Showing some impatience, Rita hesitated, then got up and walked on the customer side of the bar to the back, and then around behind it.

"About there?" Beth asked. "Just before you heard the shot?"

"Yeah."

"And what was he doing there?"

"I'm not sure exactly. Counting the cash, I think."

"All right. Stay there just a second, please." Beth walked over to the front end of the bar, swung underneath and behind it, then walked a few steps down toward the waitress's station. From there, she looked down toward Rita. "So you were here, prepping the limes, right?"

"Exactly."

"And where's Mel?"

"He's back behind where we were sitting, but at the corner table, wiping it down."

"So he's in the corner, you're here where I am, and Adam's down by the register? With Hector and Celia in the back office?"

"Yes."

"Okay, so now you've got a sharp knife in your hands, you're concentrating on cutting limes, and you hear the shot. Boom! What did you do?"

"First thing, I ducked."

"Then what?"

"Then I call out, see if everybody's okay."

"And they are?"

"Yeah, but Mel's yelling, 'Stay down, stay down.' So I stay where I am and cover my head and do that."

"You covered your head and you're protecting yourself, looking down?"

"Yes."

"And what about Adam?"

"What about him?"

"What did he do?"

She paused. "He was behind the bar, like I said."

"Down in a crouch like you were?" When she didn't answer right away, Beth pushed. "Was he down in a crouch, Rita?"

"Yes."

"You're sure. You saw him, down in a crouch at the end of the bar?"

"Yes, I just said."

"I know you did say that. But I wonder how you could have seen him when you were crouched, looking down with your head covered."

"I must have looked over. I was afraid he was shot. I saw that he wasn't. I was sure of that. That's all I remember."

"Did Adam call out to you or Mel, or did either of you call out to him?"

"Did Adam call out?"

"That's what I'm asking."

And again, dredging up her answer took Rita a second or two. "I don't remember exactly. I know I yelled to see if everybody was okay and Mel said to keep down, so I did. It all went so fast. One minute we were scrunched down, and then Celia was coming out of the office, still holding the gun, and she ran through the room and out of here."

"You stood up to see her running?"

"Yes."

"Did Adam go with her?"

"No. Why would he do that?"

"What did he do then? Adam."

"He went back into the office, where the shot had come from and where he found Hector, so he called nine-one-one and then he waited for somebody to arrive, just like we did. All of us the same, waiting, just sitting here, with Hector dead in the office."

WHILE IKE WAS finally finishing up with Mel's interview about a half hour later, Beth walked out to the sidewalk and put in a call to Dismas Hardy, who had after all been the prime mover in convincing her to take another look at the details of Hector's murder. She told him that she felt they'd made some marginal progress in their talks with Mel and Rita, and that it had certainly been worthwhile to reopen the case, at least informally.

"So you got something real?" Hardy asked her.

"I don't know about that, but we did ask a few questions we didn't get around to last time, when we got there and everybody seemed to agree that Celia had been the shooter."

"Such as what questions?"

"For starters, just their physical location when the shot went down. Rita had herself and Adam behind the bar and Mel across the room wiping down a table. Mel said he was wiping down a table all right, but it was by the front door, and Rita was behind the bar, but at the end nearest him, not halfway down at the condiment tray cutting limes."

"And what about Adam?"

"Behind the bar, back by the office, same as Rita said. But actually Rita couldn't have seen him because she said she was squatting, covering her head to hide behind the bar."

"Oops."

"Right. So, with Rita's statement, Adam could easily have been in the office shooting Hector. But Mel, of course, said he never lost sight of him standing behind the register, looking around apparently to see if the shot had caused any damage inside the bar itself. Oh, and Rita said she called out to see if everybody was all right, and Mel told her to get down, but Adam didn't answer at all, or if he did, Rita didn't remember. Of course, if he was in the office shooting Hector, the whole calling-out moment was bogus. It never happened. Rita just made it up. And Mel never mentioned it at all."

Hardy was silent for a beat or two. "They got the basic story right but never worked out all the little details."

"That's how I read it. The important thing they had to remember, and to tell us, was that Adam was behind the bar the whole time and never wandered into the office so he could shoot Hector. So they both tried to put him there where he needed to be, but he was either squatting or standing, certainly not both, and he never answered when Rita asked if everybody was all right, which probably never happened. Rita made that up because it seemed the logical thing that somebody would have done."

"Right. And also," Hardy said, "in the excitement of the moment when there's shooting going on, people's memories can get squirrelly real quick."

"Thanks for reminding me," Beth said, "but at the same time, it's good to see some inconsistencies."

"True. Don't let me rain on your enthusiasm. When are you going to talk to Adam?"

"Uh, he's been a little hard to get ahold of. His contact information when we interviewed him last time turned out to be unreliable."

"Not a big surprise. He's staying at his sister's apartment; if you'd want to drop by, I can get you the address. Phyllis, my client, his sister, says he tends to sleep in. He might still be just waking up, and it would be better to talk to him before he's had a chance to check his story against his partners'."

"Yes, sir. I think I got that part down in theory."

Hardy paused. "Sorry, Inspector. That was just me being a jerk. Of course you know what to do next. I apologize."

"No worries. I'll get over it. And I'll take that address if you have it."

"Well, also, in the small world department, I happened to run into Phyllis last night. She told me a little about Adam's version of events, which may not have been exactly what he's told you. If you've got another minute . . ."

PHYLLIS WAS RIGHT. Her brother tended to sleep in.

Beth rang the doorbell to Phyllis's apartment and Adam answered the door barefoot in jeans and a *Willie Nelson & Family* T-shirt. His hair hung in dirty-blond strands. With barely a glance at the IDs that both inspectors proffered, he nodded affably and invited them inside.

Beth and Ike didn't seem inclined to make friends. This was, after all, a career criminal fresh out of prison and—at least to them—quickly becoming a prime suspect in a murder case.

They walked through the apartment, following him into the kitchen, where they each took a seat at the round linoleum dining table. Beth took out her cell phone again, explained that she'd be taping this discussion as they had before, and then recited her standard introduction.

When she was done, she said, "All right, Adam, we're ready to go. We've got several questions about events on the morning that Hector Valdez was killed."

Still acting as though he didn't have a care in the world, Adam gave both of the inspectors an upbeat, sincere look and said, "Why?"

Ike didn't like that answer. "What do you mean, 'Why?' We've got questions because we've got questions. You got a problem with that?"

Adam raised his hands, palms out. "No problem, not at all. But I was thinking that with Celia out of the picture now . . . Well, I mean, she shot Hector and then lit out. Right? What more is there to know? She ain't likely changing her story now, is she?"

"She never gave anybody her story, Adam," Beth said. "We got that story from you and your partners down at El Sol, if you remember. We just want to make sure we got it right. Do you remember where you were when you heard the shot?"

"Yeah. Sure. I was down by the register at the back, behind the bar."

"Standing up?"

"What else would I have been doing?"

"Maybe ducking after you heard the shot."

"I don't think so."

"And how about Rita?"

"How about her what?"

"Where was she when the shot was fired?"

For a second the question seemed to stump him. Then: "I wasn't really looking around for her when I heard the shot, which was obviously in the office. I was looking that way."

"From behind the cashier's station?"

"That's right."

"Where was she the last time you remember seeing her?"

"Behind the bar, I'd say. Down the other end someplace."

"And Mel? Where was he?"

"Well, same thing. I wasn't looking at him. I was getting the cash station ready, counting the money in the till. Paying attention to that. You don't want to get the money wrong."

"If you had to guess? At the moment you heard the shot?"

"Somewhere up by the front door, if I had to say."

Beth threw a frustrated look at Ike, who took over. "Okay, then, let's talk a minute about right after the shot. What did you do?"

"Not much. I'm mostly just waiting, see what's going to happen."

"You're behind the bar the whole time?"

"Yeah."

"Did anybody call out?"

"Like who?"

"I don't know. Anybody."

"Why would they do that?"

"To see if you were okay?"

After his longest pause so far, Adam finally shook his head. "I don't remember nobody yelling anything."

"All right. Let's move on. You don't go toward the office?"

"No way. I don't want to get shot, man. Somebody in there's got a gun that just got fired. No way am I going in there."

This response, in direct contradiction to what Phyllis had told Dismas Hardy the previous night, seemed to energize Beth, and she leaned forward in her seat. "I want to be real clear on this, Adam. You never went into the office until Celia had already come out?"

He made a little show of pondering the question. "That's right."

"And when you did go in there, you never saw a gun?"

"No. Celia's already gone with it. I'm around a gun and I go running nowadays. Police see me with a gun, I go back to the joint, so I got no truck with no gun. Besides, Celia, when she comes out, as I said, she's got that gun with her, so I'm just trying to stay cool, not rile her up, let her walk away, gun and all."

"Walk away? Not run?"

"Pretty fast. Maybe not running, but in a hurry."

"And the other two—Mel and Rita?"

Adam bobbed his head up and down. "Same thing. Celia just shot Hector, and we are the only witnesses. Who's to say she don't panic and start shooting at us? So we just let her go, get her out of there, and then I go in to see about Hector and call you all. There really ain't no doubt about what happened, you know. Couldn't have happened any other way."

"There wasn't another way in or out of the office?" Beth asked.

"Yeah, there's another door leading upstairs, but so what? Somebody happens to come into the office with a gun when just at the same time Celia's ducked out someplace? How does that happen? You got any evidence like that? And then what? That shooter comes in and does Hector and leaves the gun so that Celia can have it? I don't think so. That don't happen. That's 'cause she did it, then kept the gun and ran."

"Right to your sister's house. Here," Beth said. "Isn't that right?"

Adam nodded. "That's what she did."

"And how again did Celia know about Phyllis to begin with?"

"I told her. Before, I mean."

Ike butted in, asking. "Just like that? Why'd you do that?"

"Because she was in trouble. Hector, he was keeping her like a slave."

Ike's voice dripped with sarcasm. "And you were going to be her hero and save her from all of that?"

"Not so much that." Adam shrugged. "Look, you don't believe me because I'm an ex-con. That's cool. I get it. But me and Celia, it was just what it was. She told me a couple of times that she was looking to get away, and I knew what my sister did, the immigrant stuff, so I gave her the address if she ever could break away without him hunting her down. So I think she had it planned if she ever saw her chance. Hector having a gun with him that day was just his bad luck. And hers, too, as it turns out."

"And she left the bar with the gun?" Beth asked.

"Yep. Ask Mel and Rita. They'll tell you."

"Well, thank you," Beth said, reaching over, picking up her phone and turning it off. "You've been a help."

"Hey, check it out. I ain't lying."

Ike gave him a curt nod. "Nobody said you were."

17

Chet Greene, the man who had arrested Phyllis, was the least senior inspector in the DA's Bureau of Investigations, but his star was rising fast. He intended to keep things moving in that direction.

Before the arrival of Ron Jameson on the scene, he'd spent his entire adult life as an SFPD cop, and he'd become both bored and cynical: the city was either going or had already gone to hell with its anti-police bias and its mollycoddling of criminals, illegal aliens, immigrants, gay people, and the homeless (or, as Greene thought of them, bums). He'd come to wonder what the point was of identifying, locating, and arresting people who broke the law—murderers, rapists, gangbangers, whatever; it didn't matter—only to see them released by juries at trial. The citizenry of San Francisco believed that they shouldn't be punished. No, what they needed was sensitivity training and counseling, understanding and forgiveness.

It made Greene crazy, and for the past couple of years, even though he'd been a homicide inspector, he was basically marking time until he could maximize his pension and get out.

Then, during the last election cycle, and at first strictly for the money, he'd volunteered to moonlight doing security for the Jameson campaign. Eventually, over fifty or sixty events, the candidate and the cop formed a connection based on all the things that the city—and Wes Farrell, the sitting DA—did wrong over and over and over again. Eventually, Greene became Jameson's driver and confidant.

And a true believer.

Behind the sometimes ambiguous rhetoric—so essential to electoral success in San Francisco—it was absolutely clear to Chet Greene that

Jameson was going to do his damnedest to make things in the city right again. Right, that is, for the good guys. Beleaguered cops would be able to fight back when they got attacked making righteous arrests of criminals; illegal aliens taking so many jobs from his kids and their friends—they would be deported; they'd sweep the Tenderloin and Hunters Point and take the vicious animals off the streets.

And all this talk of "sanctuary": Greene admiringly thought that it was nothing short of amazing the way Jameson managed to talk out of both sides of his mouth on the issue. One of his campaign promises had been that he wouldn't turn one innocent or unconvicted soul over to Immigration, but there were any number of ways to get around the letter of the city's proclamation, this Celia Montoya case being a perfect example. You're Ron Jameson and you have a clandestine meeting or two with supervisors at ICE, who somehow find informants like whoever it had been in Ukiah to turn in people who'd committed crimes and were simply running from the law. They go to trial, then they serve their terms, then they get sent back where they came from.

Why, Greene wondered, would anybody be in favor of letting these people simply escape justice, where they could terrorize and victimize good citizens again and again? He just didn't get it.

And now Greene, who'd quit the PD and gotten hired by the new DA to his new position replacing the one that Abe Glitsky had abandoned on the day the election results became final, was taking the slow route through downtown, driving his boss to a Knights of Columbus meeting at Washington Square. When Jameson had first gotten into the back seat, he'd spent the first few blocks polishing up his remarks. Say what you will, the man worked like a dog.

Until finally he closed his binder and sighed audibly.

"You all right?" Greene asked.

Another sigh. "Maybe a little frustrated still about the McGowan arraignment. It shouldn't have gone down like that."

"Yes, sir. It sucked, I agree."

"I'm hearing this guy Hardy might actually file suit against us—not that he's got a chance of making that stick."

"What an asshole," Greene said.

"I hear you. I ought to try to get Her Honor Marian Braun challenged out of the building, show her who's holding the cards. And that would be me."

"Good idea. Get the word out to the others."

"Fucking judges."

"Really."

Greene caught a red light on Sansome and came to a stop.

"None of that was anything you did wrong," Jameson said. "The arrest, all that. Booking her in. I know I've said it before, but you went exactly by the book. I just wanted to let you know I've got your back. Still."

"Yes, sir. I appreciate that, though I never really had any doubt. Dealing with these defense guys, that kind of thing comes with the turf."

The light changed and they began to roll again. Their eyes met in the rearview mirror.

Jameson said, "You ever have dealings with that guy before? Hardy?"

"Not one-on-one. But for a defense guy, he got to be pretty well known around the detail—Homicide, I mean. He and Glitsky palled around a lot. I always thought that was weird."

"Hmm. You know he also used to be Farrell's law partner?"

"No, but I'm not surprised." A connection fell into place, and Greene said, "So if Hardy's with Farrell, he's with Gina Roake, too. And her I do know."

"The four of them, yeah. Thick as thieves. In fact"—Jameson paused while they bumped through another intersection—"I had Andrea do a little document searching this morning. She didn't have to dig too deep to get wind of some bad shit they were all around."

"Yeah," Greene said, "the Dockside thing. I remember those rumors, but in the end I think they came down with it being some Russian mob hit, didn't they? Blood diamonds or something."

"Maybe. But according to Andrea, evidently not everybody bought that. Hardy's client at the time was one of the victims, and another victim was Barry Gerson."

"Gerson was running Homicide when I came up," Greene said. "Great guy, good cop."

"Yeah. A good cop who got promoted when Glitsky got himself shot. And after Gerson died, guess who got his old job back in Homicide?"

"You're saying Glitsky . . . ?"

"Just sayin'. Some people believe it. Andrea got a whiff of it. But guess who was Glitsky's alibi for when the shooting was going down? Ten points if you say Roake."

"Roake."

In the rearview mirror, Greene saw Jameson nod. "There you go. Maybe worth looking into. What's your workload like down in the unit? You think you could find any free time? Maybe if I put in the word?"

"I'm sure I could squeeze in a few hours."

Another nod in the mirror. "It might be worth your while. Get Hardy off my ass. Hell, get him off your own for that matter. Give him something else a little closer to home that he has to worry about. That's what I'm saying."

INSPECTORS BETH TULLY and Ike McCaffrey sat in the two folding chairs in front of Devin Juhle's desk. On the drive in from their interview with Adam McGowan, they had kicked around the results of their interrogations, and finally Beth had overridden Ike's reluctance about reopening the investigation into the murder of Hector Valdez. Ike was now about as enthusiastic as his partner that they'd gotten to some new truth.

Their lieutenant, upon whose shoulders the burden squarely rested, wasn't so sure. "All you've got," he was explaining, "is two small discrepancies among three witnesses about what this one guy did in the aftermath of what must have been a pretty uptight moment."

"Adam said he never went into the office either before or after the shot until Celia had run out of the bar, but according to Hardy he told his sister he did. That's not a small discrepancy, sir," Beth said. "And neither is whether anybody called out afterwards. Between them, that's a whole new ball game."

"That's the part I'm not getting too clearly," Juhle replied. "Maybe you could explain to me one more time why it's important. He went into the office after the shooting, right? He admits that. Found Hector dead on the ground and called nine-one-one like a good citizen."

"Yeah," Beth said, "except if in fact he went into the office with his own gun and shot Hector, then explained the situation to Celia and told her he'd help her get out of town."

"Why wouldn't she then just have called the cops?"

"Because," Ike said, "the simplest answer is that she's undocumented. All she wants to do is get out of there alive, and Adam's telling her how she can make that happen. 'Go to my sister's and she'll get you out of here. Otherwise you're a hooker and everyone will think you did it.' "

"But she just witnessed him do it, according to your theory. She knew he had done it."

"Yes, she did," Beth said. "But she knows his threat to her is righteous—that there's three people right there who are going to swear that Adam was behind the bar the whole time; he never went into the office until Celia was gone and he called nine-one-one. Which meant that as far as we—the cops—were concerned, she had killed Hector. She knew he was framing her, but there wasn't anything else she could do except run. Have I mentioned this? She was undocumented. She *had* to run, and that's of course exactly what she did."

"Got it," Juhle said. "I might have run, too. But why does this make Adam the killer?"

"Because the story he told his sister is different," Beth said.

"And also because what he told Phyllis makes no sense," Ike added. He settled back into his chair. "First of all, neither of the other two witnesses saw Hector with a gun. Ever." He held up a hand. "Small point, I know, but if he doesn't have a gun, the idea of Celia taking it from him makes no sense. But beyond that, even if he does have a gun, how do the witnesses not see it, and how does Celia get it from him in a fight? Unlikely at best, right?"

"I'm still listening, at least," Juhle said.

Beth picked it up. "Adam told Phyllis that after the shot he went into the office and Celia was standing there with the gun on the desk in front of her, Hector dead on the floor, and Celia saying she hadn't done it.

Some mysterious other person from upstairs happened to come in while Celia was locked in the back room and not only shot Hector but left the gun there. Are you kidding me? That's the stupidest thing I've ever heard. Adam is just making up something that his sister might believe. What he's not making up, though, is that he went into the office, which is why his two partners get it differently about where he is right after the shot. Rita says he's crouching behind the bar, and Mel says he's standing up, looking toward the office. Fundamental difference. He never hears Mel calling out, asking if he's all right. That's 'cause Rita made that part up.

"Then we've got Adam himself telling his sister that he went into the office right after the shot and discovered Celia in the back room, where she'd locked herself. If you'll pardon the phraseology, sir, the whole thing's a clusterfuck. None of it happened the way they originally said it did, and now our three witnesses are going to be tripping all over themselves trying to get their stories straight—which, because they're all lies, is going to be difficult."

Juhle had listened to this with his elbows on his desk and his hands steepled at his lips. Now he put his arms out in front of him, resting on the desk. "I'd feel a little better," he said, "if we had something in the line of physical evidence to support any of these theories. You guys come across anything like that? Anything on the gun?"

Ike's face reflected his disappointment. "Unfortunately, no, sir."

"Because it's going to ruffle some feathers with the DA if we go ahead on this without any new evidence."

"It'll serve him right," Beth said. "He rushed the indictment and got it wrong."

"But how are you going to prove that?"

"We push harder on Mel and Rita next time and get one of them to change their story and put Adam in the office before the shot. Which will pretty much have to mean that he did it."

"You think you can do that? Put him there?"

The two inspectors shared a glance. "We got a definite window with witnesses who've got to be getting nervous, keeping their lies straight, and knowing that Adam would probably just as soon kill them, too, as look at them," Ike said. "If we turn up the heat, everybody involved is going to feel the pressure."

Beth nodded in agreement. "We'd like to give it a try. Dev, these witnesses stink. We've talked to them and, cop to cop, they just stink. We can just tell; you know what that's like."

"Yes," he said, "I do."

18

Hardy hit the button on his office intercom and heard the buzz in his ear. Hoping to inject some relative normalcy into his interactions with Phyllis when she picked up, by way of greeting he said, "Yo." Hearing the rewarding sigh of her frustration came close to warming his heart. "Do you have a couple of minutes?" he asked.

"Certainly. In your office?"

"Please."

"I'll be right in."

Seeing her drawn look as soon as she appeared, Hardy immediately realized that no amount of superficial levity was going to make this any easier. Things in Phyllis's world were obviously still in turmoil.

He stood up and came around his desk, indicating that she should take one of the Queen Anne chairs in the major sitting area while he took the other one. "You don't look very happy," he said gently.

She drew in a deep breath and released an almost audible sigh. "The police came by today and had another interview with my brother. It doesn't seem like he's out of the woods yet. Once you've been in prison, he says it's always like this. You're near any crime that gets committed, he says, and you become a suspect. Now he thinks they're going to go after him for the Valdez murder."

With a straight face, Hardy asked, "How are they going to do that with Celia Montoya already indicted? They'd have to reopen the whole case, and I don't see Mr. Jameson moving in that direction. They're just probably trying to answer any remaining questions."

"Do you really think so?"

Hardy temporized as he nodded. Phyllis was going to need a little more preamble before he got her to the nitty-gritty. "If Adam was really in trouble, they would have brought him in for the interrogation. He's on parole. He can't refuse to talk to them. It wouldn't be uncommon for them to go back and tie up loose ends. Was Adam any more specific? Did they say they were going to charge him?"

"No. At least, I don't think so. He didn't say that. But he was pretty sure that that was where they were headed. As you know, he's been through this kind of thing before. He says he knows it when he sees it."

"Did he tell you if he'd changed anything about what he said to the grand jury?"

"No," she said. "What would there have been to be changed?"

"I don't know specifically. There's usually something. The cops come in chipping at the details, that's all. As long as his story stays the same, he's probably got nothing to worry about."

"Why wouldn't it stay the same? He just told them what happened. The pure facts aren't going to change. I mean, how could they?"

Hardy allowed himself to sneak a quick glance at his secretary's guileless face. Was it possible, he thought, that she could remain so naïve after a forty-year career in a law office? Could it be the power of genetics—that she was just going to believe her only brother no matter what he told her? Or could it possibly be that the woman just had as trusting a nature as he had ever seen—so trusting as to be dangerous?

"Do you think," he asked her, finally broaching the real topic, "there might have been something else going on? With Adam."

She met Hardy's look. "Well, of course, given his history, I'd be silly if I believed every word he said. But this was a murder . . ." Her expression betrayed a glimmer of hope. "He may not be a particularly honorable or good person, but it's hard for me to believe that he could really be a killer."

"Really?"

She leveled her gaze at him. "He's my brother, sir. We've got the same blood. I don't want to think about what he's capable of, but maybe I'm being unrealistic, aren't I? It's just so hard to imagine, but if I'm being honest with myself . . ."

"You're afraid of him?"

She nodded. "Maybe I shouldn't be, I know, but . . ."

"He's nothing like you, Phyllis. You're a good person, maybe to a fault."

"It's just so hard to accept. How could he and I start at the same place and turn out so different? It's so hard to wrap my head around it. That he could have just . . ." She trailed off again.

"Okay," Hardy said, "I've got a confession I've got to make to you, if you want to hear it."

"About this?"

He nodded. "You're going to be mad at me, but I knew that the inspectors were going to go by and talk to him again. In fact, I probably played a role."

Her face clouded. "Why would you do that?"

"Because of the story you told me last night about what happened before and after the shot was fired at El Sol. What Adam told you isn't what he told the police, either originally or again today. Which means he either lied to you or lied to them, and neither of those scenarios is particularly pretty."

"So you're saying you think he did it? Killed Mr. Valdez?"

"I'm saying there is some question about what happened, and that is one very real possibility. And then setting it up so that Celia comes to you and you help her run away—it turns all eyes on her and away from him as the killer."

Sitting all the way back in her chair, Phyllis closed her eyes for a moment and took a few breaths. A tear escaped and trickled down her cheek.

Hardy went on. "I told Inspector Tully your version, what you told me last night. So it's not that she thinks Adam's a liar because he's an ex-convict. He's a liar because that's what he seems to do whenever he gets the chance. It's who he is. Now he's got himself set up at El Sol with a great new job and a couple of partners who don't really seem that sad about losing Hector Valdez, even though they'd been working with him for years."

She opened her eyes and wiped at them with an index finger.

"So what he told me wasn't true? What part was different?"

"He didn't go into the office after he heard the shot. In all probability, he went in and was the actual shooter. Celia wasn't ever locked in any back room. She didn't struggle with Hector, and it wasn't Hector's gun but Adam's. Take your pick."

Again she closed her eyes and shook her head. "God," she said, "how stupid can I be? What am I going to do now?"

"Well, the first thing is what you're *not* going to do, which is get into any kind of a discussion with Adam about what he told you versus what he told the police."

"Why not? Maybe I could—"

"No." Hardy cut her off abruptly. "I need you to hear me very clearly on this. You won't mention any of this to Adam because then he'll see you as a potential threat, the only person with an alternative version of events that can get him in trouble. That's why you're not going to talk to the police, either. As things stand right now, you've told me your version, but I'm your lawyer and so our conversations are privileged. Even if I've told the inspectors what you told me, it wouldn't be admissible in court—not unless you tell it directly to them. So as long as Adam doesn't believe that your version of Hector's death is the source of the police's interest in him, you're okay."

"So you're saying I should be afraid of my brother?"

"Maybe we could just go with 'wary' or 'cautious.' "

"You're saying you believe he'd hurt me?"

"I'm saying it's not impossible," Hardy said. "Maybe he wouldn't, and maybe being your brother matters. But still, you'd be wise not to give him a reason."

Phyllis sat there looking drawn and devastated. "I'm sorry, sir," she whispered at last, "but I'm afraid I don't really know what to do about all of this. I'm so much at a loss, even just to understand exactly what's going on. Adam's my brother and of course I care about what happens to him, but I don't really want to defend him or hide him or anything if he killed Mr. Valdez and then placed the blame on poor Celia. And that sad, sad girl . . ." Her shoulders sagged as the memory deflated her. "Do you think I'm safe going home?"

"I'd hate to guess and be wrong, Phyllis. But as long as nothing changes—as long as you don't become some kind of threat, as I talked about earlier—I'd say you ought to be all right."

Hardy must have made a face, because Phyllis leaned over toward him and said, "What?"

"I didn't say anything."

"But you thought something. Your eyes just lit up."

"No," he said. "It was nothing. Nothing reasonable, anyway."

"At this point, sir," she said, "I'm willing to listen to unreasonable. As far as I can tell, my other alternative is living in fear in my own home, worrying about if my own brother is going to murder me. So let's hear unreasonable and then decide."

Hardy pushed himself back an inch or two in his chair. "Well, the other thing you can do is talk to the homicide inspectors and give them your version of events, told to you by Adam, which might go a long way—maybe all the way—toward getting him back into custody for the murder of Mr. Valdez. Or—and this is really getting out there, at least in terms of what you could live with . . ."

"What?"

Hardy hesitated, then went on. "Well, the inspectors might also want you to wear a wire—a recording device—to get Adam to contradict himself in his own words. And if they did get to arresting him again, there might be some other ramifications—this is just occurring to me now—such as the charge you're facing."

"What about that?"

"What about that is that if Adam gets charged with the murder, it's going to be that much more difficult for Mr. Jameson to make the charge against you stick. If Celia didn't kill Mr. Valdez, and now it sure as hell looks to me like she didn't, then you can't very well be an accessory after that fact, now, can you? And let me just add while we're being hypothetical here: rubbing it in Jameson's face if we could get Adam charged as a legitimate suspect wouldn't exactly break my heart, either. Maybe it would teach him a lesson about how to proceed on these matters. Which is not how he treated you."

Phyllis crossed her arms and after a moment let out a long sigh. "This may be horrible, but given what has already gone on, all of that doesn't seem that unreasonable to me."

"When I say it out loud, it doesn't to me, either. But I don't want to kid you: this stuff is no joke. And even if it all goes exactly right, that probably means your brother winds up in prison again, maybe for the rest of his life. Do you think you'll be able to live with that?"

She hung her head.

Hardy let her live with the idea for a long minute. Finally: "Phyllis."

She raised her eyes to meet his. "You really think he killed Mr. Valdez, don't you?"

"I'm afraid I do."

"And he might kill other people if they get in his way?"

Hardy nodded. "I don't think we can rule that out."

"Oh, Adam," she said. "How could you have come to be like this?"

Another long moment.

"If he's really done all this bad stuff"—Phyllis paused and swallowed—"you're saying he probably needs to be in jail again, doesn't he?"

"I'm afraid so. I'm so sorry, but I think that's what needs to happen."

"So what do we do now?"

"Now," Hardy said, "I think we might want to do the polar opposite of what I had in mind when we started this conversation."

"And what's that?"

"We call the police."

Phyllis visibly wilted, head down, shaking it from side to side.

"This is horrible," she said.

LATE AFTERNOON NOW, and Adam, Mel, and Rita had postponed opening the bar for the time being while they sat at the round table near the front and talked out their story, making sure the inconsistencies got ironed out. "The main thing, Rita," Adam was saying, as patiently as he could muster, "isn't whether I was down behind the bar, but that you were looking directly at me when the shot got fired. You saw me clearly, no question, outside here. The whole point is that none of us were in the office. The only people in the office were Hector and Celia. We, the three of us, we were all out here, you cutting limes, me setting up the cash register, and Mel wiping down tables; it doesn't matter which table, but let's say this one we're at now to make it easy if there's a next time."

"So where?" Rita asked.

"Right here," Adam said. "This table."

"But how do we—"

Suddenly Adam's anger flared and he slammed his palm down. "God-*damn*, Rita! We've been over this. Why'd you have to go and say that Mel called out to see if we were all right? Why'd you make that shit up?"

"Because I thought it's what he would have done if there was a shot he didn't know was coming."

"But how am I supposed to know that's what he does?"

"Hey, sorry, Adam. I'm sorry. But it's no big deal. You just say you were excited on hearing the shot; maybe a little deaf, too. It makes sense."

"Sense. Fuck." Shaking his head, Adam looked over at Mel. "Talk to her," he said.

"She gets it," Mel said. "The question is: Did I yell? Rita says I did, so we say the same thing, and you didn't hear because you were closest to the shot and it must have fucked up your ears for a minute or two. This is not a crisis. We stick with what we said and we're fine."

"You better be right, both of you," Adam said.

19

Chet Greene had a lifetime of investigative experience. He didn't believe you always had to struggle to get your hands on information. Sometimes it was right in front of you; more often than not, in fact, if you knew where to look.

While Ron Jameson was giving his well-received speech with the Knights of Columbus—a speech that ended with a standing ovation and then all kinds of compliments from the crowd—Greene was checking out "San Francisco Dockside Massacre" on his cell phone. It took him about ten minutes to identify Sheila "Heinous" Marrenas, the columnist who wrote "Our Town" for the city's second newspaper, the *Courier*, as his most likely source of background material on the misdeeds of Hardy, Farrell, Glitsky, and the rest.

As soon as he dropped off the DA back at the Hall of Justice, he beelined it for the outer Mission and the *Courier*'s main offices on Dolores Street. Parking in front of a fire hydrant and leaving his business card visibly displayed on the dashboard, he locked up and walked the half block in a freshening wind to the front door. Inside the lobby, although two young women handled the reception duties behind an enormous counter, the place had a deserted feel, and Greene suddenly remembered that the newspaper had recently announced its new publication schedule, cutting back to four days a week. Tough times everywhere, it seemed.

Still, from Jameson's Knights of Columbus venue, he'd called Marrenas and made an appointment and in theory she was waiting for him. The receptionists pointed him in the right direction and he walked down a long, deserted hallway until he came to the last door on his left, slightly ajar, and knocked.

"It's open. Come on in."

Pushing at the door, he entered and crossed to where Marrenas sat behind an all-purpose table. Half rising, she reached over, shaking his hand with a firm grip. "It is such a pleasure to meet you," she said. "I must say that it does my heart good to see an official person deciding to take a look at some of the things you said you wanted to talk about. After all this time, I keep hoping something someday is going to make a difference." She pointed to a chrome and leather chair. "You want to grab that seat? You can take off your jacket. We're pretty casual around here."

As a divorced man, Greene liked her right away. Short and compact, she had a bright and ready smile and intelligent green eyes. Her face was attractive without being distractingly pretty. With a riot of frizzy black hair lightly streaked with gray, she'd probably been called cute a lot when she was younger, and maybe more recently than that. No wedding ring, he noticed.

His jacket hung over the back of the chair, he got himself situated, his legs crossed. "Well," he began, "thanks again for seeing me on such short notice. I really do appreciate it."

"Are you kidding me? Anybody wants to talk to me about this stuff, I'm all over it. I can tell you honestly, when this first all started to come down a hundred years ago, I thought this was my Pulitzer. I still think there's something major there. But I've got to give it to these guys, they covered their tracks. So I don't know what I can give you in the line of evidence that you might be able to use—at least, that you haven't seen yet."

"I haven't seen anything yet. Mostly I'm going on the article you wrote a few months ago about the major unsolved crimes in the city. The Dockside Massacre. So now I'm just starting out whacking the bushes, hoping there might be some low-hanging fruit."

Disappointment painted her face. "If there is any," she said, "I'm afraid it's going to be high up and out of sight. Frankly, I thought you might be coming to me because you had come across something new on your own."

"No such luck, sad to say. I think my boss, Mr. Jameson, basically sent me out to go fishing. I think he's worried about Wes Farrell in the next election. And yes, he knows it's a little early."

"Never too early," she said.

"Yeah, well. Especially when the first time the DA puts his foot in a courtroom, one of Farrell's partners is talking having his office recused for misconduct and suing him personally for damages."

"Dismas Hardy," she said.

"You know him?"

"I know everybody," she said. "It's my job. Also"—she broke another smile—"don't forget that this is the smallest town on the face of the earth. But that said, if your boss is trying to open this can of worms again and bring these guys down, that very fact is column-worthy. The war between the DAs."

"There's no love lost, that's true." Greene crossed his legs the other way. He suddenly realized that if the task Jameson had given him was to fire a warning shot across the bow of Dismas Hardy's ship, he didn't really need any new evidence related to the Dockside Massacre. He mentioned that the very idea that Jameson might be reopening those investigations—given that there was no statute of limitations on murder . . .

But Marrenas derailed that train of thought. "Before I run with that idea," she said, "I mean Jameson really going after these guys, which—believe me—is appealing on every level, it would be helpful if you had something new to bring to the party. Because I must tell you, I've looked and looked to try to find something to crack the thing. And then I looked some more. You'd think with that much firepower going on, something's going to have to pop up. There were, like, nearly two hundred shell casings out on that pier. Do you believe that? And five—five!—bodies. Beyond that, David Freeman died of internal trauma that same day after somebody beat him up, and Hardy's client, a guy named John Holiday, was one of the victims out at the pier. I mean, where was the evidence—*any* evidence—tying all this together? But Hardy was at his office all day: lots of witnesses, no doubt about it."

"Let me guess," Greene said. "One of those witnesses was Phyllis McGowan."

Marrenas raised both hands. "Holy shit. I bet she was. It never ends."

They shared a pregnant look and held it a moment.

"It's unbelievable," she said. "Isn't it?"

"All those alibis," he said. "And they all worked?"

Marrenas nodded. "Every last one. Every fucking one of them."

"And no squish in any of them?"

She shook her head. "I doubt it. McGuire—I know all these guys like the back of my hand—McGuire, now deceased, was Hardy's brother-in-law. He was with his wife on a friend's boat out on the bay. Hardy, as I said, was at his office. Glitsky was with . . ." Suddenly she went silent, her brow furrowing.

"What?" Greene asked. "Who was Glitsky with?"

She rubbed both hands over her forehead. "Holy shit," she said again. "Can it be I'm just seeing this now?" She met Greene's eyes. "He was with Roake, picking out clothes for David Freeman to wear for his funeral."

"But maybe he wasn't there. Maybe neither of them were there."

Killing time while she pondered, she scanned the upper corners of her office. Finally she came back to Greene. "Maybe this isn't anything relevant, but at least it's a fairly large coincidence. Can it only be hitting me now?"

"What, exactly?" Greene asked. "I'm listening."

"Okay. Did you follow it a couple of years ago when McGuire, Moses McGuire, Hardy's same old brother-in-law, had his own murder trial for killing the guy who raped his daughter?"

"This sounds like a laugh riot of a family to hang with."

"Doesn't it, though?"

"That trial does kind of ring a bell."

"It should. It was a huge deal while it ran. I covered it every day. It didn't look good for McGuire—they had a bunch of eyewitnesses—but the jury acquitted. You know why?"

"He was with Glitsky out on the bay on his friend's boat?"

Marrenas broke a wide grin. "I see you're paying attention. Even though that's the wrong answer. Actually, though, it's pretty darn close to the right one. McGuire was with Roake, the same Roake who was with Glitsky for the Dockside thing."

"What was he doing with her?"

"They were, apparently, ahem, intimate."

"All day?"

"Enough of it that the jury bought it." Her eyes squinted down as she went silent.

"What are you thinking?" Greene asked.

"Just remembering. During Roake's testimony, McGuire's wife rushed out of the courtroom in tears, her husband having just been described as having betrayed her and all. I was there, as I said, and it was an amazingly convincing display."

"Or a hell of an act?"

"Well, I never thought so until now. Until just this minute. But . . ."

"But Roake might be the chip in the façade of all of this?"

"Well, if she is, she's well defended. But we knew that. What's new here is her connection to both these scenarios—the Dockside thing and McGuire. Both of them with many of the same players . . ."

Greene finished her thought. "And both of them relying on her for their alibis. And only her, right?"

"Correct."

"I really like this," Greene said. "At least, if for nothing else, then as an excuse to look her up and say hi."

"At least that." Marrenas drummed her fingers on the table, then raised her gaze to look straight at Greene. "I'm wondering if those connections alone could be a column. Prime the pump for you to talk to her."

"That would work. But it might also put her on her guard. Could you give me a day or two, see what I could stir up by talking to her? What do you think?"

"I think it's been several years already, between both the alibis. What's a couple more days going to hurt?"

GEOFF COOKE HAD been dead now for three years, seven months, and twenty-one days.

Ron was right, Kate thought. After this much time, nobody—not even her once best friend Beth Tully—was ever going to arrest her or anyone else for his murder. This in spite of Kate's certainty that Beth had intuited the truth but could never find a shred of evidence to prove it. Because there had been none.

This was because Kate had always been a world-class organizer, and she had never spent as much time and energy making sure about every detail of a plan as before the one she'd hatched the night that she'd sat with Geoff Cooke in his car in one of the Presidio's isolated parking lots and—with no hesitation when the time finally arrived—shot him behind his right ear with one of the guns Ron had brought home with him from Iraq.

She had always gotten along well with Geoff, and had actually been great friends with his wife, Bina, but Beth Tully had been closing in on Ron as the killer of Peter Ash—which of course he was. And if Kate hadn't been able to somehow shift the blame to Geoff, Beth would have arrested her husband for murder.

Kate couldn't let that happen.

She did not kid herself: the blame for much if not all of it, Kate realized, was hers. She had been the prime mover, giving in to a moment of fantasy and lust and seducing Peter Ash, which six months later had led to Ron's jealous rage and the actual murder.

So she carried the weight of Peter's death with her at all times, as well as Geoff's. But she had saved herself and her family and, if that were the choice, she'd do it again. In fact, if she only could, she would never have given in to the temptation to sleep with Peter, but again, that was in the past and forever out of her control.

She and Ron both knew what they'd both done, and there was no way to undo any of it. Now the shared secret bound them in a way that she never would have imagined. They had the never-ending literal power of life and death over each other, and this was a two-edged sword, enflaming the physical passion between them on one day, seeding resentment in their every interaction on another. But whether on any given day they hated or loved one another more, the intensity of the relationship never wavered.

Sometimes, to Kate, it seemed too much to bear.

Except she knew that through it all she loved him unconditionally:

he was the father of her two children, and they were in it all so deeply together that there could never be an escape.

Not that she wanted to escape.

She had killed for him and now he was her life.

She knew that it was somewhat to assuage her guilt, but also—since she had lost the friendship of Beth Tully—to connect with other human beings, she had taken to volunteering more or less anonymously three days most weeks at the Missionaries of Charity soup kitchen in Noe Valley.

Now, going on five o'clock and with her shift finished, she was sitting at a tiny table, drinking a latte at the Peet's coffee shop a few blocks from the kitchen, where she'd spent the day. Much to her surprise and delight, in the past couple of months since Ron had been elected, she had made a new friend—a woman of about her age and background named Patty Simmons. Another mother of two, the wife of a clinical psychologist, and an attorney who had given up her mergers-and-acquisitions practice to be a stay-at-home mom, Patty liked to describe herself as "fun and fancy," and in fact that was a pretty good description. Happily, Kate found that the two of them could, and wanted to, talk about anything.

And yet, up until now Kate had avoided dropping the "DA bomb" on her. But today they had started talking about husbands and the stresses of their work in a generic sense, and Kate had reached a level of comfort where she felt it was a good time to bring it up.

Plus she was still badly rattled by the talk she and Ron had had over their morning coffee the other day, where he'd not only accused her of trying to shut him down just in terms of how he ran his life and his business, but also stuck in the knife further, saying that she was some kind of nag who would never let him forget how much he owed her.

Since that talk, she'd been living in a state of constant cold fury. She'd gone so far as to fantasize about putting an end to all of this madness, to the way they lived. How? She wasn't sure. More murders? Another suicide?

Well, no. Of course not. It hadn't gotten to that, and if they were lucky, it never would. But still . . .

She was just wound up. The pressure cooker of how they were living, the reality of their daily life, and on top of that Ron having the gall to imply that she was somehow to blame—that her vigilance for them both was somehow cramping his style . . .

To hell with that.

But here, now, with Patty Simmons, maybe she could just talk things out a little—subtly, to be sure—with somebody who would understand.

And so she told her.

Patty was raising her café au lait to her mouth and stopped halfway. "Are you kidding me?" she asked, incredulous. "The actual district attorney? Ron Jameson? How can I not have put that together? I must have heard your last name at least once, right? I just never thought you could be *that* Jameson. I mean, working at the soup kitchen . . ."

"Well, it's not something I make a big deal about. DA is just a job, after all."

"Is that what *he* thinks? Your husband? That being DA is just a job?"

"No. Not at all, really. He views it more as a calling—the whole political thing."

"I hate it, no offense," Patty said. "I could never do anything like that."

"Me neither. But Ron thinks he's on a mission. Put bad guys in jail. Be fair to everybody in the criminal system."

"That all sounds pretty good. But you're going to be disappointed in me," Patty said.

"Why?"

"Because I didn't even vote. Do you hate me?"

"Not even a little. It's refreshing, actually. Especially when I compare it to Ron, where sometimes I'm afraid it's becoming his whole life. Like the only thing he really cares about."

"Well, I'm sure he cares about you and your children."

"I know he does, but . . ."

"What? You can say." She lowered her voice. "Your secrets are safe with me."

Kate broke a small smile, then sighed. "It's just that since the election—oh, what am I saying?—since far longer than that, it's just been all work all the time. We've been on a whopping three dates—play dates, if you know what I'm saying—in the last two months. He never gets home before eight, and more often than not a lot later." She put her cup down, made an apologetic face. "And listen to poor, poor pitiful me. I'm sorry. I just never get to talk about this stuff."

"You can talk about anything with me."

"I know. I'm so grateful for that." She paused. "But it's just . . . well, things are so different now."

"In what way?"

Kate sighed. "Before, when the kids were younger, both of them still at home, and Ron was working building up his business, I felt so much that we were doing everything as partners. He'd come to me with problems or strategies at his work, and I'd come to him when issues with the kids came up, and he was always there, part of our gang, going to their games, and concerts and debates. We were always in all of it, together. I mean, the priority was always the family, all of us. Which it just isn't anymore."

"Isn't he still pretty new at the job? Maybe he's just getting used to it."

"I know. I tell myself that was it. He's just learning the ropes, getting the ship righted, and after that he'll come back to the way we were. But I'm really not so sure, to tell you the truth. It worries me."

"Do you think it might help if the two of you went and talked to somebody?"

"You mean a counselor? For Ron, who is never wrong? Never. Plus, it would be a negative to the electorate."

"Well, maybe, but sometimes it can help." Patty broke a smile. "Says the wife of the clinical psychologist. That's my answer for everything. Go somewhere where you can talk things out with a referee."

Kate smiled back in return. "I'm not saying it's a bad idea. I'm saying I don't really see Ron laying himself out there for somebody he doesn't know to criticize him."

"It's not always like that. Or even mostly, for that matter. It's just talking, connecting, trying to define the stuff you both want to work on. Keeping these things rational and even logical." She shrugged. "I know it's something people have to get used to the idea of. Seeing a counselor. And really, I'm not trying to drum up business for my husband's colleagues."

"I don't think that." Kate shook her head. "It's just that in that scenario I'm afraid I'd wind up sounding like the complaining bitch, resenting her husband's success, jealous of the time he spends with everybody else, when really all I want is some of it. His time, I mean."

"That's not so unreasonable."

"*I* don't think it is, anyway."

"Well, you know, you don't have to see somebody else. You might just tell him, counselor or not. He's probably not even aware of how much he might have changed. Carl and I had a similar thing when he left his first clinic and went out on his own. After maybe half a year of me feeling exactly how you're describing your situation, I said, 'Hey! Remember me?' And it turned out, he did. Although, to be fair, it took him a couple of months."

"I'd take a couple of months."

"Well, as I say, he might not even know he's changed his behavior."

"Do you think that could really be it?"

"I think it's certainly worth finding out."

20

As WAS HIS wont, Hardy wanted to keep pushing and move things along. He'd always been a big believer in the line from Shakespeare's *Julius Caesar*: "There is a tide in the affairs of men, / Which, taken at the flood, leads on to fortune; / Omitted, all the voyage of their life / Is bound in shallows and in miseries." He thought that if ever there had been a tide at its flood, it was at this moment, with Phyllis poised to work with the two homicide inspectors and a crystal-clear theory—what Hardy believed to be the true theory—of the case, there for the proving.

But then that pesky human element reared its ugly head.

For all of her disapproval and dismay over her brother's purported actions, there still remained the question in the mind of Phyllis as to whether Adam had actually killed Hector Valdez in cold blood. Perhaps unwittingly she had come to accept at least a part of Adam's bedrock belief that ex-convicts as a general rule didn't get a fair shake at the hands of police.

Of course, Adam had told her. Naturally, Tully and McCaffrey thought he'd pulled the trigger. They were programmed to look at him as the most natural suspect, even if there was little or no physical evidence, and even if Celia Montoya had every reason in the world to have killed Valdez and afterward to run.

The bottom line was that Phyllis needed more time to think about whether she was going to help the police put her brother back into custody, and this time for murder.

It turned out to be a good time to entertain these doubts. The two cops were not working tonight. Both of them were busy with their own family stuff, to which Hardy grudgingly acknowledged they were entitled. Meanwhile, they might not even get to Phyllis the next day. Tully told Hardy that they had plans to take another crack at Rita, all alone, tomorrow, and might not even need whatever else Phyllis could supply.

Beyond that, Tully was not enthusiastic about the strategy of putting a wire on Hardy's secretary: not only was there great personal risk to Phyllis in pursuing that course of action, but Tully felt that Phyllis would not be able to pull off the deception with her brother. He would read something in her attitude and/or body language and would either close up or go on the attack, neither of which would move the investigation forward. And might, in fact, shut it down altogether.

No, Tully thought, their best shot was to use Phyllis's information all right, but use it as leverage against not Adam but Rita, who might very well freak out when she heard about another version of events that afternoon at El Sol, a version that named somebody else, or maybe even her, as the shooter, which meant that Rita was at least an accomplice. Under those circumstances, did Rita want to stick with what she'd originally said, or tell the truth and trade her new testimony for a deal with police?

Tully could get Rita to crack. *Now.*

So, like it or not, flood tide or not, Hardy was on hold.

Now he was sitting at a barstool in his kitchen, drinking away his frustration with a double Maker's Mark manhattan, regaling his wife and daughter with all of these details that were keeping things from moving forward. With a hard police press, he really felt that Adam McGowan could be in jail and his sister's case dropped by tomorrow or next Monday at the latest. It was all doable and so *right there*. What was everybody thinking?

When he stopped to tip up his glass, Rebecca walked the few steps over to where he sat and gave him a quick kiss on the cheek. "If I'm ever in trouble," she said, "I'd want you to be my lawyer. Just because nobody cares as much as you do."

Frannie piped in. "Except, Beck, you're never going to be in trouble."

"No, of course not. But if I were . . ."

"I don't care what your mother says. I'd fight to the death defending you," Hardy said.

Rebecca leaned over and planted another quick kiss on his cheek. "See?" she said. "To the death yet."

"How gratifying to know," Frannie said. "Although that would leave me in a bit of a lurch, would it not? With my beloved husband dead and all."

"It probably wouldn't come to it," Hardy said, "in the real world. Since the Beck isn't ever going to do anything wrong in the first place, either."

"Still," Frannie said. "What if she's unjustly accused? Then she'd have to go to trial and you'd have to defend her to the death."

"I think," Hardy replied, "we'll just have to hope that that won't happen."

"I'll add it to the list of things I pray for every night."

Hardy asked his wife, "You pray every night? I didn't know that."

"Most nights, anyway."

"What are you praying for?" Rebecca asked.

"The usual stuff: world peace, end of hunger, cure for cancer, no more racism. And now I've got to add the part about you not getting falsely accused of some capital crime so that your father has to defend you to the death."

"And how are those working out? The prayers."

"Actually, when you put it like that—focusing on the results—not so good."

"You know, given the track record," Rebecca said, "maybe I don't want to be on that list after all. Of what you're praying for, I mean. Maybe you could kind of just generally hope I don't get arrested."

"You're right," her mother said, "that might be marginally better."

"Whew," Hardy said in mock relief, "I'm glad we got that settled."

Once in a while, Ron Jameson felt that he caught a sense of what it would be like to actually be God. He'd gotten it today during his talk to the K of C, what with the steady rain of applause and the all but unbridled approval of the large crowd of successful men who had hung on his every word.

They loved him, loved his message—ambiguous though it might have been—loved the power he unapologetically exuded. He, in turn, was nothing short of magnanimous, sharing his thoughts, vision, and persona with them.

It hardly mattered what he was actually saying. What mattered was the connection between him and his audience. In that environment he could, in many senses, do no wrong.

And it followed then that whatever he had done to get him to this place, it would not have been wrong, either. Without pondering it too critically, he felt that at these times the rules of normal men simply didn't apply to him. Ron was part of them, the regular folks, but also above them in some fundamental way. He had the answers that they wanted; he had the solutions that could only be delivered by a strong and unwavering hand.

Up in his office after his driver-investigator Chet Greene had dropped him off, he loosened his shirt and untied his tie, told Andrea that he was not to be disturbed for any reason, and dropped off to sleep on the leather couch.

At 5:30 he woke up refreshed, then used the restroom and splashed his face with cold water. Returning to his desk, he reached for a couple of folders in his in-box, but after he opened the first one, his attention wavered in the wash of glory that overcame him.

He was sure of it: this was how God felt.

People waited on his every move. They parsed his words for their true meaning. They wanted nothing more than to gain his approval, in minor to major ways. The world—his world—in truth revolved around him.

Closing the folder, he put it back in his in-box, then got up and went around his desk. Walking across to the door, he stood still a few seconds, considering. What the hell, he thought. He could do whatever he wanted; that was all there was to it. He reached out and opened the door.

Andrea was sitting at her own desk, glued to her computer monitor, her fingers moving over the keys. He moved forward a couple of steps and knocked gently on her desk. "Got a minute?"

Half turning, she nodded. "Certainly."

"In my office?"

"Yes, sir." With no hesitation—his wish truly was her command—she pushed her chair back, stood up, and crossed in front of him and back into his office. Falling in behind her, he followed her in and closed the door. Stopping, she turned with a smile. "What's up?"

"Well"—he lifted, then rolled his shoulders, showing her a bit of a grimace—"I'm afraid it might not fall within your formal job description, but suddenly I've developed this crick in my shoulders going up to my neck and I can't seem to get it worked out. It's killing me, if you want to know the truth. I'm tight as a drum. I was wondering if you would mind trying to work out the knots a little bit. I could just get into my chair and . . ."

"Go," she said, stepping aside, guiding him around her. "I don't make a big deal out of it here at the office, but back rubs are one of my specialties. So you've asked the right person."

"I don't want to make you uncomfortable."

"Not going to happen," she said.

He went to his chair and, with a slight exaggeration of pain, lowered himself into it.

She came around behind him. "Cross your arms on the desk and put your head down."

He did as directed and felt her thumbs jab expertly into the muscles of his upper back. "There you go," she said soothingly. "I see what you mean. Tight as a drum is right. That's it. Just let it go. Tell me if I'm pushing too hard. There you go. Easy now. Just breathe and try to relax. There."

BETH TULLY HAD a dinner date planned with her daughter, Ginny, but Ginny was late getting home from her classes. This afforded Beth a window of opportunity to reflect on all that was going on, and as she sat in her living room with a glass of white wine, she came under the grip of a realization so strong that at first it made her dizzy.

The Valdez murder case, from which she and Ike had been so unceremoniously removed, was turning out in all probability to be not so cut-and-dried as it had originally seemed. In fact, Beth and Ike both now believed in an entirely different theory than the one they had begun with.

Whether they could prove it was another question.

But the point that had struck her so forcefully was that they had come to their new version of the truth by the simple expedient of continuing to pepper with questions those most closely involved.

They had discovered no new evidence. They had simply kept prodding the principals—in this case Adam McGowan, Mel Bernardo, and Rita Allegro—and a new truth had begun to emerge from the disparate stories that had come from the mouths of these witnesses. Only by playing those stories back one against the other were they able to better understand where they failed to jibe. And, in fact, what truth they might be hiding.

Of course, in her many years as a detective, and particularly since becoming a homicide inspector, she had broken the stories of many suspects, usually by presenting them with evidence that contradicted their testimony. Only rarely—if ever—could she remember a time when she and/or Ike had drawn a confession from someone or discovered some new theory because someone else told a different story.

And there was also the simple reality that murder cases were a commercial product. The Homicide Department was to a large extent judged and budgeted by its success with handling that product. Investigations had their own shelf life; they were not supposed to last forever. This was why, when Beth and Ike had been removed from the Valdez case, neither of them really lost any sleep over it. The issue had been decided; they had an indicted suspect. They would move on to another murder—and God knew they were never in short supply—keep busy, identify suspects, make their numbers. The past cases were closed and that was the end of it.

Except now, with a successful conclusion expected in the informally reopened Valdez case, she found herself unable to stop her brain's restless contemplation of the murders of Peter Ash and Geoff Cooke. She reasoned that if her professional time could be spared to revisit the supposedly closed murder case of Hector Valdez, it might be even more profitably used going back and getting some statements from the principals in Ash/Cooke, starting with Kate Jameson.

Beth knew that after all this time, if she showed up on Kate's doorstep with some questions, it would be a shock, to say the very least. Asking new or even old questions about Peter Ash and Geoff Cooke would seriously impact Kate's worldview and by extension her husband's. Kate might find herself compelled to tell Ron that those murder cases were apparently no longer closed: everyone knew that there was no statute of limitations on murder. And then Ron's reaction, whatever it might be, could prove instructive.

Where Beth had let herself become intimidated by Ron's position and power—essentially believing that, with the slightest of provocations or even none at all, the DA could threaten her job—she suddenly realized that she could wield some significant power of her own by going on the offensive. How, she wondered, could she not have seen this earlier? Ron Jameson would never dare interfere with her job if there was even a rumor that she was investigating him and/or his wife. In fact, the investigation might even serve as a kind of life and/or job insurance.

She didn't have to live in fear of him or be anxious about what he might do to her. Rather, she could bring her game to his court and see how he liked that.

Was she worried, she asked herself, that she would be getting in the face of someone she knew was a murderer? Hardly. She confronted killers every day in her job.

She heard a key turn in her front door and her wonderful daughter came around the corner into the living room.

"Hey, Mom."

"Hey, sweetie."

"What are you looking so happy about?"

"Am I?"

"Like you just swallowed the canary. Did something happen?"

"Not yet," Beth said, her smile now all but beaming, "but maybe soon."

21

HARDY FINALLY DECIDED to go ahead and file the motion for recusal against Ron Jameson that he'd written over the past week. All along, he had thought that there was little chance that the motion would prevail, but that wasn't the point: the filing alone, he thought, might put the district attorney off his feed for a while, and that at the very least might give the man pause before he tried to pull his bullying bullshit on other defendants.

It was a cold and clear Friday morning, and rather than mail the motion Hardy decided to walk the half mile or so from his office down to the Hall of Justice, where he would file the motion himself.

That process—essentially handing a few pages to a clerk behind a window—took him the better part of an hour, the wheels of justice at every level continuing to grind exceeding slow. He didn't know after all these years why this still had the ability to surprise him. Maybe because it had been so long since he'd done any kind of grunt work himself; he also wanted to believe that bureaucratically things must have improved. But this seemed to be a vain hope, at least this morning.

Out on the front steps, his breath forming vapor clouds in front of him, he hesitated for a few seconds before shrugging, making up his mind, and crossing Bryant. He didn't have any plan or expectation about what if anything he'd run into down the stairs to Lou the Greek's, but he could use a cup of hot coffee in any event, and you just never knew.

He stopped inside the doors and for a few seconds let his eyes adjust to the dimness. The place had its usual half dozen morning drinkers at the bar to his right, but all of the floor tables were empty. At the farthest-back corner booth, though, he recognized a familiar face and made his way through the empty room.

"Any room in there where an old guy can sit and rest his weary bones?"

Devin Juhle looked up at him in mild surprise, then slid over. "Hey, Diz. What brings you down here?"

"I had a recusal motion on our esteemed DA that was burning a hole in my pocket. It suddenly felt like a good day to go file it."

"You're going ahead on that?" Beth asked.

Hardy nodded. "I just did."

"That ought to liven things up over at the Hall," Juhle said.

Hardy wore a tight little smile. "It might at that. Stir the pot a little." He nodded across the table at the two inspectors. "Meanwhile," he said, "I'm not interfering with official police business, I trust."

"Not egregiously," Beth replied. "We're just about to head out to talk to Rita from El Sol again in the Valdez case. If that doesn't work out too well with her, we were talking again about the odds of getting Phyllis to wear a wire."

"Probably not much better than they were yesterday," Hardy said, "but still worth trying. I can talk to her if you want, but last time she seemed to think you guys were after Adam because he was an ex-con."

Ike grunted. "We're after her brother," he said, "because he killed Valdez."

Beth put a hand over her partner's. "I think we're all pretty much on the same team here. It's just a matter of breaking the stories, which ought to happen soon."

"Let's hope," Juhle said. "Although that's going to open its own can of worms with the DA."

"Probably," Beth said.

Hardy put in his two cents. "Not necessarily a bad thing."

Juhle grunted. "Easy for you to say."

EVEN DURING THE five years or so when she'd been defining herself as a full-time novelist, Gina Roake never stopped coming into her office for at least a few hours. Her goal was to put down a page of fiction every day, which, she knew, would result in a finished book every year. She hadn't exactly broken through commercially on any of her books to date, and the last offer from her publishers had been, she felt, just short of insulting, so she'd turned it down. Since that refusal, her agent hadn't landed another deal, so she was in limbo.

Which didn't mean that she had stopped writing. She still loved the process, coming in to work, making stuff up. Maybe she'd self-publish the next one.

This Friday morning she was in early, working on a new character based on her former law partner, lover, and (for about a day) fiancé, David Freeman. Although part of her felt that borrowing traits from a real person she'd actually known was somehow cheating, it also gave her the opportunity to reimagine her time with him and to tap into the emotions of the times they'd spent together.

She had long ago learned, when she was writing, to lock the door to her office against the intrusion of secretaries, paralegals, or associates who might wander in and catch her with tears running down her cheeks.

As they were this morning.

Her intercom buzzed and her secretary, Ally, told her that an Inspector Chet Greene from the DA's Bureau of Investigations was there and wanted to see her. He did not have an appointment.

"Did he say what this is about?"

"No."

The name was vaguely familiar to her, and in any event her personal policy was to cooperate with law enforcement whenever possible—always remembering that sometimes it wasn't—so she said, "I need a couple of minutes. Please ask him to wait and I'll ring you right back when I'm ready."

After first logging off her computer, she hung up, then dug out a Kleenex. Standing, she crossed over to her wet bar and threw water in her face, dabbing at her eyes. Well, she thought, at least she hadn't been outright sobbing. She looked in the mirror and declared herself fit to receive guests. Returning to her desk, she picked up her phone and told Ally to send the inspector back.

She recognized him right away as the guy who'd put the handcuffs on Phyllis here at the office a few days ago. Still, she greeted him cordially enough, shook hands, and asked him to take one of the comfortable upholstered chairs that made up her seating area, and she sat down across from him. "So, Inspector, how can I help you? I'm afraid that if this is about Ms. McGowan, you're going to want to talk to Mr. Hardy, who is her attorney."

"Well, no. It's not about her." He cracked a thin perfunctory smile and pressed on. "Actually, Mr. Jameson has assigned me to revisit some of our cold cases and see if we could profitably open some of those investigations and get them resolved one way or the other."

Gina sat back in her chair, her tears forgotten, her face closing down. "And you're here to talk to me about one of those?"

"Two, actually."

"Two? These were cases I defended, I presume?"

"Not exactly, no."

"Well, then, exactly how was I involved?"

Greene blew out a quick pulse of air. "Frankly, in both cases, you provided alibis that impacted the prosecution."

"What does that mean exactly: 'impacted the prosecution'? What were these cases?"

"Well, one of them, the first one, never got to trial."

"Really? So you're saying there wasn't enough evidence to take it to trial?"

"No. There was a ton of evidence. Hundreds of rounds of casings and bullets and five bodies. As I'm sure you realize by now, I'm talking about the Dockside Massacre."

"You're implying that I had something to do with that?"

"I am. I'm talking about the fact that you and Lieutenant Glitsky each alibied one another for the time of those shootings."

Gina cocked her head. "Really? And when was this, again, exactly?"

"You don't remember that?"

"What?"

"What you told police about that at the time."

"I don't know anything about the Dockside Massacre other than what I've read about it over the years. At the time, though, if I remember correctly, I was mourning the death of Mr. Freeman and I can't say I was thinking about too much else. My understanding and my memory was that the shoot-out was some Russian mafia situation over blood diamonds or something of that nature. How in the world do you put me in the middle of that—or anywhere near it, for that matter? It's absurd. You're essentially calling me a murderer, do you realize that?" Gina stood up. "I think, Inspector, that it's time for this interview to be over. Unless you've got a warrant of some kind. Otherwise . . ."

"You don't want to hear about the other case you figured into?"

"Not really, unless—"

Greene interrupted her. "I'm talking about Moses McGuire—your partner's brother-in-law—and about your alibi for the afternoon of the murder he committed."

"That's because he didn't commit any murder. A jury found him not guilty, Inspector. That's how we do it here in this country. And that makes it not a cold case but a closed case. I can't believe I'm hearing this. Mr. Jameson's seriously got you out looking to tie me to these two cases? And yet you don't present me with even the smallest show of new evidence in either case. If this isn't pure harassment, I don't know what is."

"It's actually a courtesy where Mr. Jameson is prepared to make a deal for immunity in your case—"

"Immunity from what?"

"Getting charged with murder, along with Hardy and Glitsky and McGuire."

"McGuire's already dead, Inspector. You're a little bit behind the curve."

"If you'd just—"

"I don't want any part of it. And I need you to get up and get out of my office before I call the real police—and don't think I won't—to get you out of here."

Greene got to his feet. "You're making a huge mistake."

"Nothing like the one you've already made. Now get out! Now. Get out."

• • •

"NO, REALLY?" HARDY said.

"Yes, really." Gina sat with one hip on the corner of her office desk. "I am still in a state of shock, if you want to know. I mean, how far can they push this without any evidence?"

"I want to say 'Nowhere,' but when you throw the rules out the window . . ." Hardy shrugged his shoulders. "In the normal course of events, they couldn't do a goddamn thing. But we all saw the way they moved on Phyllis, which had nothing to do with what they really had on her. They just wanted to piss in our beer."

"And now they're doing it again."

"I see it," Hardy said. "Imagine if the guy had lost the election, if this is his magnanimous self as a winner. I think he wants to wipe this firm off the face of the earth. And I don't know what we can actually do."

"Do you want to add this to your recusal motion?"

"What? What do we want sanctions for? Interviewing a witness? Offering her immunity? Nothing wrong with any of that. Except for how it might play in terms of our business in real life. If he's going to put these innuendos out there . . ."

"A lot more than innuendos."

"Okay. I won't fight you there. A lot more."

Gina's intercom rang and she picked it up. "Send him on down," she said.

Half a minute later, Wes Farrell was with them, and two minutes after that he had hoisted himself onto the other corner of Gina's desk and was shaking his head in anger and disbelief. "Not to sound like an egomaniac," he said, "but this is all my fault. It's all because of me. I've got to bail on you guys and get you out of the line of fire."

"That's no solution," Hardy snapped back. "Then he just wins. And it wouldn't work anyway. That would just embolden him."

"Maybe," Wes said, "or maybe we just live to fight another day."

"That whole 'fight another day' argument doesn't exactly sing for me, Wes."

Gina nodded. "Me neither."

"Well, I appreciate the loyalty and show of support," Wes said, "but I thought that me joining up with the firm would be lucrative and fun, and now it's looking like a whole lot of neither." He looked over at Gina. "He actually accused you of murder?"

"Yeah, or close enough to it. Evidently I was part of the Dockside Massacre, blasting away at a bunch of Russian mafia guys. Or something."

"Don't forget me," Hardy said. "I was there, too. Either shooting my client or helping him get shot by somebody else. Maybe Abe."

"He's saying Abe was in it, too?"

"Yep." Gina nodded.

"How was he allegedly involved?"

"Because he wanted to get his job back in Homicide, so he had to kill Barry Gerson."

"Seriously?"

"That's their story and they're stickin' to it. But fortunately nobody will ever really know about it, because I made up a story that alibis him for the time in question. We were together picking out David Freeman's funeral suit while all the shooting was going on."

"And you weren't in fact doing that?"

"Of course we were. David had just died that day, for Christ's sake. Abe and I spent the whole afternoon at his place. Mostly me crying and him picking out shirts."

Farrell boosted himself off the desk and paced over to the window, then turned. "Honestly, the first thing that comes to mind is that I should withdraw from the firm. That ought to take the pressure off of you both for your connection to me."

Hardy shook his head. "I think it's too late for that, Wes. Like it or not, we're all in this together. Jameson's got the big lie going and he's going to keep telling it until it starts sounding like the truth to a lot of people—even without any evidence. If you started your own firm, he'd just find another way to try to put you in the mix and bring you down. The only way out, if you want my opinion, is that you retire from the practice of law, and even that probably wouldn't work. And somehow I've got the feeling that's not what you had in mind anyway, is it?"

"Not really, no. I thought I'd go another lap or two."

Hardy nodded with approval. "There's my man."

"So what do you think the next move is?" Gina asked.

"That's a good question," Hardy replied. "Since we've seen him do it before, I don't think we can rule out the grand jury. He goes in there and spins his magic web of a fairy tale, and maybe we find ourselves indicted."

Gina whispered. "Jesus Christ, Diz. Are you talking for murder?"

Hardy bobbed his head. "Check it out. Barry Gerson was head of Homicide when all of that went down. So the massacre was, at the very least, a cop killing that has never been solved. He can ride that one a long way."

"I don't know," Farrell said. "I like to think that I'm a pretty cynical guy, but that's going pretty far. I mean, he can't really believe that you guys were part of a gang shoot-out that killed a cop, not to mention a few other people, and that you walked away from it scot-free."

"He can believe it," Hardy said, "but he doesn't really have to if he wants to move ahead. Remember, most recently, they had approximately zero in terms of evidence on Phyllis, and they indicted her. Why? Jameson decided it would be politically expedient, that's why. So imagine how much more he could get out of bringing us down for colluding to kill and actually killing another cop. If Jameson brings those people in—that would be us—and convicts us after all this time, he's a fucking hero. He doesn't even have to convict us. Just putting us on trial ought to do the job for a lot of people."

"Except," Wes countered, "that the whole thing is indefensible. The entire idea of it."

"He's not on the same moral grid as most people," Hardy said. "I think we'd be smart to keep that in front of us at all times. Beth Tully—you may both know Inspector Tully—believes that in actual fact he's got his own bona fide murder on his résumé. I'm talking in-your-face, one-on-one, first-degree murder."

"Who'd he allegedly kill?" Wes asked.

"Peter Ash. I'm sure you remember."

"Sure, but I thought that was . . . what was his name? Jameson's law partner, right?"

"Geoff Cooke."

"That's it."

"Well, evidently, according to Tully, it wasn't it. It was Jameson."

Gina finally spoke up again. "So wait. Tully says Jameson literally killed Peter Ash?"

"Yep. Although she can't prove it, and she doesn't have a grand jury to make her case to. But she's certain."

Gina looked from one partner to the other. "Holy shit."

Farrell let out a breath. "Maybe you ought to take a rain check on submitting your recusal motion, Diz. Give things a little time to cool down instead of forcing him to think about doing something stupid or reckless or both."

"Good idea," Hardy said, "but too late."

22

On what might have been another planet in a completely different universe, Beth Tully and Ike McCaffrey sat across a pockmarked wooden table from Rita in a laundromat around the corner from El Sol. The witness had just finished telling her story for the third time, and this time she had wavered anew on the whole question of where Adam McGowan had been when she'd heard the shot. She seemed to have forgotten whether she'd earlier said he was standing up or crouching down by the cash register. Neither did she remember if Adam had responded to Mel asking if everybody was all right or if she just imagined the whole thing.

Clearly it was nerve-racking. Rita was starting to realize that she should not have agreed to come back for another interview without Mel nearby. They'd already done this, hadn't they? They must be suspecting something, trying to break her testimony. Rita picked little splinters from the table in front of her and cast her eyes hopefully first to Beth, then to Ike, as though seeking approval for the job she had done.

From the expressions on the faces of the inspectors, that approval would not be forthcoming.

A study in disappointment, Beth raised her eyes and held Rita's gaze. Sadly. She shook her head ever so slightly, looked over at Ike, shook her head again, then finally came back to Rita. "Okay, on another topic, Rita, roughly how long after the shot was it before Celia came out of the office with the gun?" she asked.

"After the shot?"

"That's right."

"I don't know for sure. Pretty much right away, I think."

"A couple of seconds, maybe?"

"Something like that. Two seconds. Or three."

"So. Hardly time for Adam to get from behind the bar and back into the office."

"Right."

Ike was suddenly all impatience. "You're saying he didn't go into the office?"

"I never said he went in until after Celia left."

"That's what you said. He was either crouching behind the bar or standing there."

"One of them, yeah."

"Rita," Beth whispered gently, "what if I said that Adam told his sister that he went into the office before Celia left?"

This news clearly rocked her. She sat back in her chair, at a loss. "He said that? When did he do that?"

Beth kept up the soft press. "We talked to him the other day and the story he told us doesn't match what you told us. Or what Mel told us, either, for that matter."

"No," Rita said. "That was what happened."

Beth didn't try to hide her disappointment. "Rita," she said, "you're digging yourself a hole here that's going to be too deep to climb out of. And then we won't be able to help you."

"But I didn't do nothing wrong. Mel neither."

"Here's the thing," Beth said. "The way it looks now is that the three of you—Adam, you, and Mel—you're all in this together, trying to cover each other's stories. But they're not hanging together, Rita. So what somebody's been telling us isn't the truth. What that leaves is that all three of you were in it together, deciding to kill Hector and put the blame on Celia."

"No." Although it was decidedly cold in the laundromat, Rita ran a hand over the sheen developing on her forehead. "That's not how it was. We didn't plan it, me and Mel. That wasn't us."

"Well, you're going down for it just as much as if you planned it all out together," Ike said, "unless you want to tell us what really happened.

Then we tell the DA that you're a cooperating witness, not a suspect or a defendant."

Beth picked up that thread. "You understand what it looks like right now, don't you, Rita? With you and Mel each sticking to your two different stories. It looks like you're both, independently, covering for Adam and what he did. Which makes each of you just as guilty as he is in the eyes of the law. When we arrest him, we'll be bringing you and Mel in at the same time. Just as though you all planned it together."

"Unless," Ike added, "you tell us what really happened."

"And then what happens to Mel?"

"Well," Beth said, "if he comes clean and corroborates your story—and this time, telling the truth, he'll do a better job at it—then you'll both be witnesses for the prosecution, not co-defendants with Adam. That's a huge difference."

Rita hung her head as though it were hanging on by a thread. Closing her eyes, she sighed, then looked up at the inspectors again. "It was just . . ." she began. "I mean, after it was done, there wasn't any choice. We had no idea what Adam was going to do before he just did it, but afterward, when he came out with Celia and the gun, and Hector dead in the office . . . he told us how it would all be good if we just stuck together. And then, when Celia ran, it seemed to everyone—even you police—like she had killed Hector in a fight between them and it all would work out for us."

In spite of, or maybe even because of, Gina Roake's near-violent reaction to his accusations and offer of immunity, Chet Greene felt that he had hit a nerve: the woman might not have been actively involved in the Dockside Massacre—or even given a false alibi in the Moses McGuire case—but he felt that she was sure as hell guilty of something.

Back in his cubicle in the Hall of Justice, the inspector spent about an hour googling whatever he could find about either of the two cases, and found the pickings surprisingly slim. The *Chronicle*'s coverage of the Dockside Massacre pretty much hewed to the party line that it had been a turf battle between some private security guys and a bunch of Russian mafiosi who'd been particularly adept at covering their tracks. Even

Sheila Marrenas's original take in the *Courier* hadn't been able to find a connection that had any traction with anyone in the local legal community. In none of the articles in either newspaper he read did Greene so much as come across any accusations against Hardy, Glitsky, Roake, or Freeman, to say nothing of McGuire.

At least the McGuire trial coverage, most recently, acknowledged Roake's connection to the suspect, his shocking and unexpected alibi, and his eventual acquittal. And of course his representation by Dismas Hardy. However, since McGuire was Hardy's brother-in-law and Roake was Hardy's sometime law partner, those connections were hardly earth-shattering or even provocative.

Still, Greene had convinced himself that there must be something here. And he thought he knew where he could go next to find out what it might be.

So, for the second time in two days, he found himself at the *Courier*'s building, walking down the long and empty hallway to the office of Sheila Marrenas, whose door was open. Chet stood outside for a few seconds watching her in profile as she worked on her computer. She struck him as even more attractive than he remembered. Stepping forward, he tapped on the door and she jumped slightly—fetchingly—at the interruption before breaking into a welcoming smile.

"Inspector Greene," she said. "Tell me you found something."

He smiled back at her. "Chet," he said. "And not much. But I thought I'd take the chance and see if you were free for lunch, where you can tell me where I could've looked but didn't."

She stole a glance at her monitor, paused a second or two, then hit a few keys on her keyboard. "I'll have to be back in an hour to get this done by my deadline," she said.

"An hour's doable," he said. "If you'd prefer, we could stay here, but I thought lunch might be nice."

"No question. Lunch is nice. And the best Thai place in the world is just down the block, if you like Thai."

Chet raised his hand as though taking an oath. "Thai is my absolute favorite."

• • •

"Okay," Chet said, "let's count it off. The Thai iced tea is the best ever, the shrimp curry is the best ever, the satay is the best ever, and the pad thai is tied for the best ever."

Marrenas popped a shrimp into her mouth. "Told you. What a nice idea to have lunch. I don't do much lunch lately. I should make it a point."

"Well, with this place this close, I know I would."

"But maybe you wouldn't if you were going out of business."

Chet swallowed. "That sounds depressing enough."

Marrenas shrugged. "You live with it day-to-day. But that possibility is pretty much a constant for the past few years. If I've still got the same job a year from now—and that's with twenty-five years of columns behind me—I'll be shocked. Or, frankly, even if there's still a physical newspaper every day. Our readership is already sixty percent online, so the end is definitely in sight. Sorry, I don't mean to be a downer, but it's why I don't do a lot of lunches anymore."

"Well, then I'm doubly glad we did this one."

"And we haven't even gotten to what you really wanted to talk about, have we?"

Chet looked at his watch. "I guess we had a lot of that other real-life stuff to cover. I've really enjoyed it."

"Me too."

"And you still don't have to be back for fifteen minutes."

Truly surprised, Marrenas looked at her watch. "Well, damn. So what can I tell you?"

"How about some of the background on these cases involving Gina Roake?" He went on to tell her about his interview with Roake that morning, then his follow-up checking on the two cases on his computer. "But there was next to nothing on the people we talked about yesterday—Hardy, Glitsky, Roake," he concluded. "Except you seemed to have a lot, though little of it made the papers."

"That's because back in the day—even as recently as McGuire's trial—we weren't supposed to run a story unless we had a credible source for it. So a lot of this stuff, in my opinion, was real as a heart attack, but we couldn't run it because it was hearsay or rumor or somebody else's opinion, but it wasn't viewed as hard news."

"Actually," Chet said, "that's exactly what I was hoping. When we talked yesterday, it seemed like you knew a lot more than whatever made it into the paper, and, that being the case, you might still have a record of it."

"No might about it." She reached across the table and touched the back of his hand. "I probably should have given you a little more guidance about where to look, but I figured Gina Roake was as good a place as any. At least, to get a feel for what you might be up against."

"And she was good for that. But she wasn't into giving me any more context. Period. She knew nothing about nothing."

"That's Gina all right. Tough as fucking nails."

"So who else should I talk to?"

"Let's get back to my office," she said, "and I'll give you whatever I've got. On one condition, though."

"What's that?"

"If you get your hands on something real, I'm going to want the scoop."

Chet broke a big smile. "Do you guys still really use that word, 'scoop'?"

She grinned back at him. "Absolutely."

"Well, then, you'll absolutely get the scoop as soon as I get one."

"Deal."

DEVIN JUHLE SAT behind the desk in his office with the door closed. Across the room, he had a large whiteboard mounted on the wall. Nine of the sixteen lines were filled in with active homicide cases, with the names of the victims and the inspectors who reported to him and had been assigned to those cases. This was about the average number that he lived with, although he'd had it go as low as three and as high as all sixteen.

Now he was trying to figure out what he was going to do with the new information he'd gotten from Beth Tully and Ike McCaffrey. It was one thing, he knew, to talk to his troops out of the office and wax philosophical about some of the moral, ethical, and logistical issues that made up the lives of homicide cops. It was another thing altogether to assign inspectors to work a case that technically was already closed. Because that meant that somebody had screwed up and had arrested the wrong person, or at least hadn't arrested the right one.

And when the person who had screwed up happened to be the short-tempered, autocratic, egomaniacal district attorney—the highest-ranking and most powerful lawyer in the city—the pressure was even greater this time to get it right. Because to get it wrong again would be perceived as a definite slight against a man who did not brook much in the way of criticism.

In fact, almost undoubtedly, if his inspectors weren't right this time, Juhle could see himself becoming embroiled in what would become a political battle, as though he were taking sides against the new DA when in fact all he was doing was trying to run his department efficiently, to identify and arrest the guilty, to avoid rushes to judgment, and to live by the rule of law.

As if Ron Jameson cared.

No: for the DA, all that would matter was that Juhle had supervised an investigation that should have already been closed because he'd declared it to be so, and that explicitly called into question the DA's decision that Celia Montoya had killed Hector Valdez.

Except that—uh-oh—it sure was beginning to look as though it hadn't been her at all.

It had been an ex-convict named Adam McGowan.

Just today, his two inspectors had gotten statements from two eyewitnesses that all but eliminated doubt about whether McGowan was the killer of Mr. Valdez. The inspectors were pushing to make an immediate arrest of McGowan based on the new developments. They were motivated to move quickly, because they realized—probably rightly—that their two witnesses were themselves in imminent danger from McGowan. If he even got a whiff that they had changed their stories to implicate him in the murder, he might very well kill them, too.

They had to get this man off the streets as soon as possible.

But as soon as they did that, it would get ugly very fast. And the basic situation with Jameson wouldn't be helped by the other indignity he'd suffered today, which was Dismas Hardy's filing of his recusal motion, news of which had swept through the Hall like a hurricane. Yes, it was going to get very ugly.

Juhle looked out his high windows, heard the howling of the wind outside. Taking a deep breath, he finally stood up, picked up a black Sharpie, and went around his desk. He took another few seconds, then sighed and wrote on Line Ten: *Hector Valdez/Tully & McCaffrey*.

Right there for the whole world to see.

God help him.

Picking up his phone, he punched in some numbers and waited for a ring, then a second one.

"Tully," she said. "What's up, Dev?"

"I'm on board with you on Valdez," he said. "Go pick him up."

23

"CityTalk"

by Jeffrey Elliott

As District Attorney Ron Jameson gets to the end of his second month in office this week, the question of his basic competence to handle the rigors of his position, especially after the events over the past few days, has never been more in doubt.

Regular readers of this column will remember Mr. Jameson's decision to fast track the investigation into the gunshot murder of a Mission District bar manager, Hector Valdez, pinning the crime, without much show of evidence or credible witness testimony, on a 19-year-old undocumented woman named Cella Montoya. Only now are the tragic consequences of his actions in this matter beginning to become clear.

To recap: Rather than let the homicide investigation into Mr. Valdez's death proceed at its natural pace, with extensive witness interviews and the analysis of crime scene evidence, Mr. Jameson went around the regular SFPD inspectors assigned to the case and then sought and obtained a grand jury indictment against Ms. Montoya, who—fearing arrest because of her undocumented status—had fled the city in the immediate aftermath of the shooting.

Subsequently, Ms. Montoya was arrested in Ukiah and taken into custody on the murder charge. She was scheduled to be returned for trial to San Francisco the following afternoon, but instead she hung herself that evening in her cell.

This would be tragic enough if the story ended here. It was entirely possible, after all, that Ms. Montoya had committed suicide rather than face a trial and a lengthy imprisonment; or perhaps she felt guilty about the murder of Mr. Valdez, and took her own life out of remorse.

But what if she hadn't killed Mr. Valdez? What if this whole chain of events was a direct result of Mr. Jameson's rush to judgment based on faulty witness testimony? What if Mr. Jameson's actions and decisions, and those decisions alone—first targeting and then arresting an innocent young woman—had driven Ms. Montoya to a state of despair from which the only escape was taking her own life?

When I first became aware of this possible interpretation of events and the alternative reason for Ms. Montoya's suicide—that is, as a direct consequence of Mr. Jameson's intrusion into the case—I found them compelling as a theory. But I told my source that unless Mr. Jameson was flat-out wrong in focusing on Ms. Montoya as a suspect, which forced her to run and led to her arrest and, arguably, her suicide, then he could not be held to blame for the way the tragedy played out for her.

Then, last Friday night, the original homicide inspectors whom Mr. Jameson had effectively removed from the Valdez case arrested a new suspect on this same case (incidentally, without a warrant, thereby circumventing our esteemed DA). Adam McGowan, who had recently been released after serving seventeen years in Avenal State

Prison, was positively identified in statements by two of his associates at El Sol as the actual killer of Mr. Valdez.

If only Mr. Jameson had waited until the SFPD inspectors had done their jobs and finished their interviews with witnesses before he'd named his own suspect. Would Celia Montoya's story have turned out differently? Would she still be alive today?

No one can say for sure, of course.

But the district attorney, who is already facing a recusal motion and a civil suit for other misconduct since he has taken office, might do well to consider the rule of law before he bends it again to suit his own purposes.

24

At 10:00 on Sunday morning, Dismas Hardy went outside to pick up his newspaper. The cold spell continued and—strangely for San Francisco in the middle of winter—had even gotten more severe. The sky was a cloudless deep blue. The shadow of his house behind him blocked any warmth from sunlight, and the outer pages of the paper crinkled slightly with a rime of frost.

He hustled back inside to the warmth of his house and sat down at his dining room table, where Frannie had poured him a cup of coffee. They'd had a bit of a physically satisfying morning that had kept them upstairs until this relatively late hour, and now Frannie, who almost never cooked, was frying eggs and bacon and toasting English muffins.

Hardy sipped at his coffee and opened up the paper. "Are you okay in there?" he asked. "Anything I can do?"

"I'm good. You read your paper and enjoy your coffee. I'm content to be pleasing my man."

"And that you are."

"I know," she said. She turned at the kitchen counter, met his eyes, and placed her palm over her heart. "And for the record, just between the two of us, I'm pretty pleased myself."

He nodded. "Good to know," he said. "So good to know."

"CityTalk" ran two columns wide on page three and Hardy read it once as fast as he could, said "Listen to this," and then read it again, aloud.

When he finished, Frannie said, "Well, that ought to get the bastard's attention. I'm assuming you might be somehow related to this mysterious source."

"I'll never reveal it, and Jeff won't, either. But I think he's got it about exactly right. It's true that we'll never know for sure, but I've got to believe that she would never have killed herself if Ronnie boy hadn't put the crosshairs on her back."

She came in with the plates and put them in their places. "Did you know that they've already arrested Phyllis's brother?"

"I did. Although who they got from the DA's office to charge it remains one of God's mysteries. But anyway, Beth Tully called me yesterday, which is when I called Jeff. She was a little nervous now that the word's out to God and all about it, to say nothing of going around Jameson, but she did the right thing. No way could they have let Adam run around free for another weekend. He would either have absconded or maybe even killed the witnesses who turned against him, or both. In any event he's in custody now, and that's where he belongs."

"Even if Phyllis asks you, you're not going to be defending him, are you?"

Hardy shook his head. "Never."

"Phyllis isn't pushing for that?"

"Not even close. First of all, there would be a huge conflict. Besides, this whole experience has kind of been a wake-up call for her. It turns out her brother is really not a very nice person. She kept wanting to believe that he was going to change his ways—I mean, right up until Tully and McCaffrey showed up to arrest him."

"And this time they're pretty sure they got the right guy?"

"As sure as they can get. Plus, that little bonus on the gun."

"Which gun was that?"

"The one that he shot Valdez with." He took a bite of bacon and chewed for a moment. "He'd wiped his fingerprints off of it before he gave it to Phyllis, but he either forgot or didn't know that when he'd loaded the thing he'd left a print on a casing. Jameson was in such a goddamn hurry that even when the lab told him they had a partial print on one of the casings that was too small for the fingerprint computer, he didn't give them the time to do a hand check against any possible suspects. His position was 'Her prints are on the gun. Screw it, that's enough.' Now Len Faro has gone back and checked that partial against Adam and got himself a match, big as life. So, as an ex-convict, Adam is screwed on the weapons charge alone. The bottom line is he's going to prison again, maybe for the rest of his life. And this is a good thing, believe me."

"I do. And what about Ron Jameson?"

"Well, at the very least, he's got some 'splainin' to do. Worst case for him, or best for me, is maybe the judge who's got my recusal motion will read Jeff's column this morning and get a little ex parte idea of what a crappy lawyer and even worse human being Jameson is."

"But never forget, he is still actually the sitting DA."

"Maybe not for too much longer."

"Okay, maybe not. But while he's got the position, he's got the power. It would not be smart to forget that."

"I never would."

"Don't be sarcastic with me." She gave him an exasperated look. "The point is, he's nobody to treat lightly, and yet you decided to pick on him as your personal project."

Hardy, mock offended, slid back in his chair. "Hey! He's the one who picked this fight. I was minding my own business . . ."

"Plus campaigning for Wes."

Hardy waved that off. "That, too. But really, that was just business as usual, trying to get my man elected. Nothing personal about Ron Jameson. But this thing with me and him started when he went after Phyllis, who is, after you, possibly the sweetest woman in the world."

"And what's happening with her now?"

"What do you mean?"

"I mean the charge against her. Accessory after the fact, isn't it?"

"Well, since the person she was allegedly an accessory after the fact to is now dead and presumably innocent of the murder, and since they've gone ahead and arrested a whole different person for that crime—I'm talking Adam now—Phyllis is clearly not guilty of being an accessory to a murder committed by Celia, and that's what she was indicted for. So, at the very least, that case has to be dismissed and they've got to start over. And I can't believe that with all that's happened, even Jameson would have the balls to do that."

"And after how his inspectors manhandled her, that's not exactly going to be another feather in Mr. Jameson's hat, is it?"

Hardy allowed himself a small grin. "Sadly, you may be right."

"And you're still not worried?"

"Not too much, no. By any rational standard, I've got to believe I've taken this round."

"Yes, but how about the next round? Taking one doesn't mean you've beaten him."

"Well, for the time being, what's he going to do? I've got all the cards here."

"But he's got all the power of his position. And apparently no scruples about how he wields it. That strikes me as a dangerous combination."

He put his hand over hers. "You're right. And I'm not taking him lightly. Really. He's got my full attention. I'm just glad we landed a punch or two. Maybe that will give him pause the next time he's tempted to screw around with how he's supposed to do things. That's all I'm hoping for."

If Ron Jameson thought he'd been nearly apoplectic with anger and frustration when he'd first read Jeff Elliott's column after the wake-up call he'd gotten from Chet Greene this Sunday morning telling him about it—and he had been—those reactions and emotions were mild as a spring shower compared to the rage he battled now as he faced his two children.

Aidan was now a sophomore at Stanford via St. Ignatius, randomly home for the weekend, and Janey, still living with her parents, went to Mercy High School. Although neither of their parents were even remotely religious, both kids had finely honed moral sensibilities from their years in Catholic schools. When Aidan first saw the "CityTalk" column, it seemed to hit him right between the eyes. No doubt, it hadn't helped that Ron had folded up the paper when he was done with it and put it in the recycling bin so that his son, when he finally got up, had to go looking for it.

Ron was in the den watching football when he heard his son's first exclamation from the kitchen: "Holy shit." Then, a minute later, from the doorway, the front section of the paper gripped tightly in his fist: "Holy shit, Dad. Are you kidding me? Did you hide this thing outside so I'd never see it?"

Ron muted the television and turned in his chair. "Watch your mouth, Aidan. Your mother and sister are still asleep."

"And what? I'm not supposed to say 'Holy shit'? Whoa! My mouth is a way bigger problem for the family compared to my dad making the dead-wrong call on a murder case and driving this poor undocumented girl to commit suicide?"

"That isn't what it was. It was nothing like that."

"What else could it be? Look at it. Were you ever going to tell us about this? Or were we just going to pretend it never happened?"

"No, it happened all right. And it's a tragedy. But also it's just politics, Aidan. I didn't do anything other DAs haven't done a million times. This is the way you have to play the game—"

"The game? This isn't a game, Dad, this is some girl's life. And you just decided she was the one you—"

In her pajamas, Janey appeared behind her brother. "What did he do now?" she asked.

"Now?" Ron turned all the way around. "What do you mean, 'now'?"

But Aidan ignored that question, whirled around and slapped the paper, folded to the "CityTalk" column, at his sister. "Did you see this? Did you know about this?"

Now Ron was all the way out of his chair. "Give me that." His tone was low and ominous. "Goddamn it, Janey, let me have that right now."

"Who's got to watch his mouth now?" Aidan said.

"It's going to be more than your mouth in a minute," Ron said.

Aidan brought his palms up as though ready to spar. "Oh yeah? Bring it, Dad. Come on."

Janey had stepped back and, speed-reading, had already picked up the gist of the story. She came around her brother's side again, holding up the paper. "This is not how you do things, Dad," she said. "Did this girl really kill herself?"

"Celia," Aidan said. "Her name was Celia."

Janey snapped at her brother. "I know her name, Aidan." Then, to her father: "Why didn't you just wait and let the police investigate a little more? I mean, Celia was just the wrong person, it sounds like."

"It looked one hundred percent like she had done it. Everyone agreed on that."

"Who's 'everybody'?" Janey asked.

"My inspectors, my advisors, everybody. And it still isn't so absolutely clear it wasn't her. It still might have been her, and this new arrest is just a smoke screen to embarrass me."

"Let me get this straight, Dad," Aidan said. "This girl Celia is dead but the big issue is you might be embarrassed? Is that really what you're saying?"

"Of course that's not what I'm saying. My heart goes out to that poor girl, but she shouldn't have run in the first place."

"God, Dad. Again?" Janey was completely revved up by now. "Again it's her fault and not yours? Don't you see any of this? What's this job done to you?"

Ron pointed a finger at both of his children. "Are you listening to me? It's not this job, except to the degree that it gives my enemies ammunition. And obviously they've got friends in the press ready to jump on any accusation against me, no matter how far-fetched. This is not about me and my job. This is about my enemies trying to take me down, and that's all it is."

"What it sounds like to me," Aidan said, "is you becoming super-paranoid."

"You have no idea, either of you, the pressure that I'm dealing with every day. If you look at what this Jeff Elliott says in the column, there's still no proof of anything. Some cops have gone behind my back and dug up an alternative suspect to make me look bad. And what I'd like to see from my two children is just a little show of loyalty and gratitude. I'm not the bad guy here. And I don't have to listen to this crap from my own kids. You don't like living under this roof, even if it's only for a day, and you don't want to follow my rules here, you're both welcome to find someplace else to hang out, find another—"

Kate suddenly appeared in the doorway behind the kids. "What is all this shouting?"

25

First thing on Monday morning, Lieutenant Devin Juhle once again found himself sitting in the back booth at Lou the Greek's with Beth Tully and Ike McCaffrey. Everyone was drinking coffee. Adam McGowan was being arraigned for the murder of Hector Valdez this morning, and the two inspectors were planning to be in the courtroom for the formality.

Juhle didn't blame them for their apparent euphoria. They had, after all, reclaimed a high-profile case as their own and were both feeling their oats. But there were other issues they would be wise to consider.

"Well, of course I'm glad for you both," Juhle said. "I really do think you got the right guy this time. I can't help but ask, though, how in the name of God did you find an assistant DA who would actually file this case? I mean, it's one thing to put handcuffs on the guy, but he doesn't go to court without a complaint, and you don't get a complaint without the signature of an ADA, and—given the political ramifications—I can't imagine an ADA crazy or suicidal enough to sign off on this without clearing it with the boss. And Jameson would never cut his own throat this way."

Ike and Beth shared a look. "Well, Dev," Beth said. "I have two words for you: Mike Wendler."

Juhle gave her a baleful eye. "You're talking Marine Corps Reserve colonel Mike Wendler? The single most tenacious, irreverent, and politically incorrect homicide prosecutor on the planet?"

"The same," Ike said. "Twenty years on the job, unbeaten in court, and never made head of the unit because they can't let him out in public without fear of massive embarrassment."

Beth added, "We started to explain how the case was all screwed up by the previous arrest and he said 'To hell with it, this guy's guilty of murder and I'm going to charge him.'"

Juhle nodded. "I hope you explained the kind of trouble he was walking into."

"We did," Ike said. "You know what he said? And this is a quote, Dev: 'Will there be gunfire? Because it's only trouble if somebody's shooting at you.'"

"Okay," Juhle said. "But he could be fired for this."

"As if he cares," Beth said. "Word is he's going to retire in a few months anyway, and if they fire him first, the severance package with his seniority would be more than a year's pay. So, bottom line, I've got to believe that, since it's now in the system in front of God and everybody, Jameson's stuck with it."

"Well, one way or the other," Juhle said, "all I'm saying is you might want to skip the courtroom this morning and lie low for a while, let the political side of this blow over and revert to business as usual. Give Mr. Jameson time to formulate some kind of response to cover himself. Maybe he'll even apologize or—"

Beth snorted with derision. "As if."

"It's not impossible. Maybe he'll learn something from all this."

"Maybe," Ike shot back, "he'll flap his arms and fly to the moon."

Juhle gave them a reluctant but acknowledging nod. "Well, either way, you don't want to rock his boat too much. If I were either of you, I'd make it a point to stay out of his sight."

"Dev, come on," Beth said, "what's he going to do to us in the real world?"

"I don't think you want to find out."

Beth and Ike exchanged a look.

"What?" Juhle asked.

Beth shook her head. "Nothing."

"You want my opinion," Juhle said, "that's a pretty loud nothing." He sipped some coffee. "How about if I say 'Pretty please'?"

The answer seemed to fall to Ike and he spoke up. "We had so much fun with this one, and it turned out so well, we've been talking about taking a look at another cold case."

"How cold?"

"Couple of years."

"Actually, it's not really, technically, a cold case. It's more like this one, where they closed it but we think they got the wrong guy."

"We *know* that they got the wrong guy," Beth put in. "*We*—not me personally, but the department—*we* got the wrong guy."

"That would be me you'd be talking about, then." Juhle's tone had picked up some asperity.

"No, it's all of us who went along," Beth said.

"And who's your new bad guy?" Juhle asked. "And while we're at it, meanwhile, where is this wrong guy now, in prison? In which case you could just turn it over to the Innocence Project and get him out in a few years."

"That would be a good idea," Beth said, "except in this other case the alleged perp isn't in prison, because before we could get him he killed himself."

"Those pesky damn suicides." The light finally coming on for Juhle, he squirmed a bit in his chair and lowered his voice. "You're talking Peter Ash."

Beth nodded. "Yes, sir. I am indeed. And Geoff Cooke, since they're related, if you're keeping score."

"I am, and let me just say for the record that that's a really awful idea."

"We just want to talk again to a few people," Ike said.

"Same kind of thing we did in this case," Beth added. "See where it leads us."

"If memory serves, and I believe that it does," Juhle said, his voice now barely above a whisper even in the nearly empty room, "at one point you were talking about Mr. Jameson himself as a viable suspect in that investigation."

"That's correct." Beth was leaning in across the table to hear him. "But then Mr. Cooke's suicide knocked that off the rails. Except that I think there's still a hell of a lot of doubt about whether it was, in fact, a suicide."

"Didn't Patel"—this was Dr. Amit Patel, the medical examiner—"call it a suicide?"

"Not exactly," she said. "Suicide/homicide equivocal." She pressed on. "So to say that there was no doubt is actually not too accurate."

"So essentially you're saying that you want to pursue your investigation into Mr. Jameson regarding Mr. Cooke's death?"

"Not exactly." Beth looked over at her partner, got a nod, and went ahead. "My gut feeling, Devin—and it's gut but not uninformed—is that Jameson's wife, Kate, realized that I was on the verge of arresting her husband for Ash's murder . . ."

"Really? On the verge?"

Beth nodded. "This close. I think I can build a convictable case on Kate, who had no alibi for the time Cooke was killed. And once we get her for Cooke, we go after Jameson himself for Ash."

"I've looked over her file," Ike said, "and it's complicated, but the evidence is all there. We think if we get some of Kate's story on record, she's going to trip herself up."

"Like our witnesses here on Valdez," Beth added.

Juhle finally straightened up on his bench, picked up his coffee, then put it back down. "And what, may I ask, is going to induce this woman Kate to talk to you about this again when it's already closed and ancient history and her husband is the goddamn DA?"

"She used to be a friend of mine, Devin. We were college roommates. I can get her to talk to me, and I'll have a wire."

"And she'll just give it up?"

"Not so much that as she'll make a mistake, yes. She's arrogant and competent, but naïve. She'd never believe I'd do something so underhanded as to trick her by wearing a wire. She might even be tempted to actually admit what she did."

Juhle nodded. "So let me get this straight: you want to go interview the wife of the city's district attorney and get her to confess on tape."

Beth nodded back at him. "And even if that doesn't happen, Devin, she'll contradict something she said earlier and we'll get to chip away at that until we break her story."

"And what about when her husband comes home that night and she says, 'Hi, honey, guess who came by today for a little chat about the death of Peter Ash?' Then what do you think happens to you two, aside from probably losing your jobs?"

"He wouldn't dare," Beth said.

"You're saying Ron Jameson—our own Ron Jameson—wouldn't care if you interrogated his wife? I would beg to differ."

But Ike was shaking his head. "He can't fire us without looking like he's guilty, Dev. So right now, on the heels of Valdez, we've got a window where we can go at him."

Juhle sulked for a few seconds. "You really think he's a killer, Beth? Our elected DA is a stone-cold killer?"

"Absolutely. And so's his wife."

Juhle rubbed his forehead. "Jesus." Letting out a heavy breath, he held up a hand for a moment, as though trying to stop the onslaught. "If you've got a file with righteous evidence," he said, "the way to proceed is we need to get in touch with the attorney general's office or the FBI, or both. I contact them, not either of you, and we give them what we've got so they can start their own investigation. Good?"

"No," Beth said. "I really want this one, Dev. I've been dealing with this stuff for the past couple of years and I need some closure on it."

"Well, I'm sorry, but that's simply not happening. What's going to happen is we've got to stay completely out of any investigation like this one. That's the only way it will work: objective and thorough. And no nonsense at all about you deciding to talk to your old roommate, wire or no wire. That's just not in the cards. But meanwhile I've got to think about the timing on this."

Beth nodded but clearly didn't like it. "Whatever you do, Dev, quicker would be better."

"Jesus." Juhle hung his head and sighed again. Glancing at his watch seemed to galvanize him. "Well," he said, "time flies and all when you're having fun. And I still think it's a lousy idea, but if you're still going to court, you've only got about five minutes. You'd better be jammin'."

• • •

Not that the coffee was particularly good, but Juhle lingered to finish his tepid cup and pay the check. He wanted to give his inspectors a head start so he wouldn't have to continue arguing with them about what had already given him a headache.

He wasn't any kind of a fan of Ron Jameson, but the idea that the man might in actual fact be a killer had never really crossed his mind. It was true that the "CityTalk" column hadn't painted him in a very sympathetic light, but on the scale of acceptable behavior among elected officialdom there was a vast difference between bureaucratic incompetence, arrogance—even corruption—and murder.

To say nothing of what could happen to him personally: not just his job, but—if he was going to go paranoid—his physical safety if he pursued this investigation into the city and county's chief law enforcement officer.

Lost in these thoughts and walking outside into the bright and cold morning, he had stepped off the curb and started to jaywalk across Bryant without so much as a glance toward the oncoming traffic on his left, when an earsplitting honking of a horn threw him backward and almost knocked him over a quarter of a second before a black Ford F-250 pickup went whizzing by where he'd just been standing as somebody yelled out the passenger window: "Watch where you're going, asshole!"

When he caught his breath, he walked down to the crosswalk and waited for the light to change. He was still shaken when he got to the metal detector station just inside the entrance of the Hall of Justice and the cop there looked him up and down and asked him, "Was that you and that truck?"

"Yeah."

"Close one."

"Tell me about it."

"You all right?"

"Yeah. Maybe a lot older than I was a minute ago."

"Jaywalking's not a good idea."

"Never again." Juhle picked up his gun and his keys from the box where he'd put them.

By the time he got off the elevator on the interminable rise to the fourth floor, his breath had more or less returned to normal. He said hello to Marta, the receptionist parked out in front of the hallway back to his office, and she gave him an ambiguous look that he took as a warning and prompted him to lean over and ask quietly, "Everything all right?"

She swallowed. "The chief's gone on back."

"The chief?"

"Of police," Marta clarified.

"Chief Lapeer?" he asked unnecessarily, since there weren't two chiefs of police.

"Yes, sir."

Walking around the corner to his short hallway, he saw that the door was open even though he—as always—had left it closed when he'd gone out.

So she'd let herself in.

A visit from the chief was unusual, to say the least. Vi Lapeer had been to his office no more than four times in his years as lieutenant of Homicide, and every other time she had come, it was not to party.

He steeled himself and walked through the door.

Chief Lapeer was an African American woman now in her mid-fifties. She had been an assistant chief in Philadelphia before landing in San Francisco and did not suffer gracefully the passage of the years. She wore a short graying Afro, her dress uniform at all times, and—except for a light touch of lipstick—no makeup to hide her face's spatter of freckles.

She had been sitting on the corner of Juhle's desk and stood as soon as she saw him.

Stopping his forward motion, he snapped to attention and gave her a quick salute. "Chief," he said.

She nodded. "Lieutenant." Ostentatiously consulting her wristwatch, she added, "Banker's hours today?"

At the inauspicious opening, Juhle cleared his throat. "I was with a couple of inspectors over at Lou the Greek's, ma'am. If I'd have known you were coming by, I would have cut that meeting short. What can I do for you?"

"Well, I'm afraid it's not good news. Would you like to come in and sit down?"

Since his legs had gone a little weak under him with the "not good news" disclaimer, he decided to take her up on her offer. Coming abreast of her and then past, he took one of the small fold-up chairs that sat between the whiteboard wall and his desk. Looking up at her where she stood, he adopted a neutral expression. "So what's up?" he asked.

"What's up is the question of how you've been running this detail lately, which I'm afraid has been unacceptable. No doubt you've read or at least heard about the 'CityTalk' column in yesterday's *Chronicle*?"

"Sure."

"Perhaps you'll remember that the column described how inspectors under your supervision decided on their own initiative to continue with an investigation that had already been closed because a suspect had already been indicted by the grand jury and apprehended."

"Except that that suspect turned out to be not guilty, ma'am."

"I don't think that's been established by any means, Lieutenant."

"With all respect, ma'am, we have a far more legitimate suspect in custody for the same crime who's probably being arraigned as we speak."

"Who is still presumed innocent, although that's not the point, either."

"My inspectors . . . Excuse me, but if that's not the point, what is? They have identified and arrested a homicide suspect who very likely killed Mr. Valdez. That's their job."

Lapeer drew a breath and let it out. "Their job, though, is not to undermine the authority of the district attorney and to pursue cases that have taken another tack through the system."

"The system, in this case, ma'am, got it wrong."

"Possibly, although again not certainly. But in any case, rather than you or your inspectors going to Mr. Jameson and sharing with him your doubts about the indictment, you went ahead and unilaterally gave your inspectors permission to act at cross purposes to the grand jury, the result of which was to embarrass the district attorney and, in fact, to undercut the reputation and credibility of law enforcement as we do it in this city and county. This lack of coordination and cooperation between the departments in this building, Lieutenant, just cannot be tolerated. It's bad for morale, it's bad for the public, and it's bad for the whole system."

"But mostly," Juhle, unable to stop himself, said, "it's bad for Ron Jameson."

"Well, it certainly isn't good for him. I see you understand that very clearly. Which unfortunately speaks to the political overtones that are part and parcel of this thing."

"You're accusing me of approving my inspectors' investigation on this case for political reasons?"

"To discredit Mr. Jameson. I'd have to say that is the general conclusion."

"By whom?"

"Mr. Jameson and Mr. Crawford." Leland Crawford was the mayor of San Francisco. "And as you know, I serve at the pleasure of the mayor."

"So did he send you here for this scolding? I'm duly chagrined."

"I'd advise you not to get smart with me. This is not just a scolding, Lieutenant. I'm here to put you on administrative leave effective immediately and pending a disciplinary hearing at a later time to be determined. You absolutely should not have let these inspectors run amok with an ongoing investigation. It's poor leadership, it's poor judgment, and it's something that I cannot condone within my police department."

26

Phyllis held her landline phone tightly in her grip until she heard the busy signal and realized that she'd been standing in her kitchen and had left the message at work that she—again—would not be in.

She didn't know why. A day off wasn't anything she'd particularly been thinking about, even as she'd gone to bed last night. And then this morning she'd had her coffee and a croissant as usual and then suddenly just felt she couldn't come in and face Dismas and the rest of them.

They'd arrested Adam over the weekend. It now seemed likely—even to her—that he'd both shot Mr. Valdez and laid the blame on Celia.

And why now did she feel so guilty?

Surely it wasn't her fault, any of it, except for being perhaps nearly terminally naïve. She had thought she was doing some good by being a way station in their so-called underground railroad. And, true, she had helped dozens if not hundreds of desperate people, many of whom now undoubtedly had created new lives for themselves and their families.

And yet, if she hadn't stepped in to help Celia . . .

Would she still be alive?

She found herself sitting at the kitchen table, her hands clasped in front of her. Her shoulder still throbbed dully where they'd dislocated it. More gratuitous violence that she hadn't seen coming.

At least they'd spared her the horror and indignity of having to be an active participant in Adam's arrest. Of the absurdity of having her wear a wire. Of betraying her only living relative. Although they would now want her to testify against him, recount the story he'd told her about the shooting. Be part of the prosecution team that would send her brother to prison for the rest of his life.

Is that what he deserved?

For killing someone in cold blood, of course, she thought. You couldn't let someone who did that stay on the streets where he could do it again. Even if the victim was a dealer of drugs making more of his living off human trafficking. An evil man keeping Celia in sexual slavery. Should Adam stay in prison forever for taking Valdez out of the gene pool?

She knew that Adam had never really had a chance. Abandoned by their father, raised by a mother who barely had enough wits and discipline to keep herself alive, much less a rowdy young man without a role model.

Was that an excuse?

Apparently without a thought, though, he'd allowed the police to arrest Phyllis, to put her own life and freedom in jeopardy.

Her own brother, willing to sacrifice her and anyone else who stood in the way of what he wanted or thought he needed.

But he seemed so sincere, so honest, so good, even. Trying to help Celia escape. Convincing Phyllis that this is what they had to do. It was the right thing.

She was such a fool to have believed him. To have played into his hands.

What was the matter with her?

She didn't know. All of this was so far outside of her experience. Was that another flaw in who she was? In her long life, could she have done more to understand how people really were? Capable of evil as well, sometimes, as good?

What was the matter with her?

She just didn't know.

AT THE FREEMAN Building, one flight up from Hardy's office, a bit of a festive atmosphere prevailed about the "CityTalk" column. Wes Farrell had ordered in Chinese and Glitsky was also around to help Treya get her workstation set up, although he did not file things in the same way that she did and was really much more hindrance than help.

When the food arrived, it was far too much, and they invited Hardy and Gina both to come up and join them for lunch.

Wes had for the longest time been well known for his position against the standard office desk. He thought a desk caused a needless separation between people that, besides, fairly screamed inequality of station. So he used an old library table that doubled nicely as a dining surface.

They were all sitting around it, separating the chopsticks, when Hardy's phone rang at his belt. Because it was his private investigator, Wyatt Hunt, he picked up with his usual jaunty "Yo." But as he started to listen, his expression grew more serious right away. "You're shitting me," he said. And then he listened some more.

GINA WAS INCREDULOUS. "She fired Devin Juhle?"

"Administrative leave," Farrell said.

Glitsky looked up from where he was working on a sudoku game on the couch. "Same thing," he said. "Whatever you call it, he's not coming back to Homicide, I'll tell you that."

"But he was great," Treya said. "Some say almost as good as the legendary Abe Glitsky."

Abe shot her a look. "Let's not get carried away."

"But seriously, why Devin?" Treya asked.

"That's what makes the guy so dangerous," Hardy said. "He's not dumb."

"What guy are you talking about? I thought you said Lapeer did it."

"Well," Wes said to his secretary, "that's true enough, as far as it goes. She actually pulled the trigger. But it wasn't her idea, I promise you. This is Jameson going to the mayor and the esteemed Mr. Crawford moving it on down the line. That's the only thing it could be. Crawford's not exactly pro-cop in any case, so this also played directly into his hands, where he gets to take a stand against our rampant police state."

"But the main thing, Treya," Hardy added, "is who he's really sending a message to, which would be Inspectors Tully and McCaffrey, but maybe, most of all, us."

"Us?"

Glitsky put his newspaper down and shook his head in disagreement. "Maybe not us most," he said. "I think most is Beth Tully. But no doubt we're in the mix."

"I need a scorecard here," Farrell said. "What's this about Tully?" he asked.

"Well," Hardy said, "she definitely went off the reservation by building the case on Adam McGowan, as we all saw from 'CityTalk.' So she brings in the real goods and rubs Jameson's face in the shit he's created. And let's face it, she got the right suspect and he didn't, so he can't really come down too hard on her—directly, anyway—although he certainly can send her a message, which would be not to interfere with the way he runs his department. Don't second-guess him on his decisions and, above all, don't even for a second forget that he's got the power to lay her and her partner off anytime he wants. So taking out Devin was a warning. She wants to cross him again, she does so at peril to her own job, and McCaffrey's while she's at it."

"What a bastard," Gina said. "How could people have voted for him? That's what *I* want to know. And now how can they want to keep him in after the 'CityTalk' thing when they see what a clown he is?"

"That's one of the enduring mysteries," Glitsky said, "but I'm afraid—and Diz will back me up on this—this thing actually hits a little closer to home than Beth Tully." Since everybody was hanging on his every word, he continued. "Never mind the details how, but Diz and I both got connected to her through this McGowan case, first Phyllis and then Adam. So there's little to no doubt in Jameson's mind that we are probably Jeff Elliott's source for the column, and in fact he's right."

"All true," Hardy put in, "but the real issue is way more serious. All of us here should know this, since I predict it's going to be part of our lives for a while, maybe a long while."

"That sounds ominous enough," Farrell said.

"Not to get everybody freaked out," Hardy replied, "but the real issue is that Tully has another cold case she's interested in." He hesitated for a long few seconds, then let out a heavy breath. "She believes more than that Mr. Jameson is corrupt. She's pretty convinced—no, she's absolutely sure—that he killed a lawyer named Peter Ash a couple of years ago."

"I've heard that before," Farrell said, "but that rumor got pretty well squashed during the campaign, didn't it?"

"Well, maybe. But not for Beth."

"Did she find some new evidence?" Gina asked.

"More like a new approach," Hardy said.

"And she somehow thinks she's going to be able to do this, re-kick-start this investigation . . . how?" Farrell asked.

"Maybe not at all now." Hardy shook his head either in admiration or frustration, or both. "That's why laying off Devin was such a good strategic move. Tully and McCaffrey were going to try to work the Peter Ash case under the radar, the way they had handled McGowan. And they had at least Devin's tacit approval if not complete support. Then they spring it on Jameson when it was a done deal, maybe through the state attorney or the FBI or other jurisdiction." He shrugged. "But now . . ."

Glitsky picked up the narrative. "But now with a new lieutenant handpicked by Lapeer and under the mayor's thumb, good luck with that. Now both of these inspectors might find themselves on administrative leave as well. Or worse: just let go. At anytime and for any one of a number of fabricated excuses, none of them having anything to do with Ron Jameson."

"You got to admire him," Farrell said. "He is one slick son of a bitch."

"That he is." Gina nodded in agreement. "And I'm starting to think I should be taking him a lot more seriously."

"That's not totally inappropriate, Gina," Hardy said. "And, at the risk of sounding paranoid, I don't think this thing today with Devin is the end of anything. I don't think Jameson's done being proactive."

"Which means what?" Gina asked.

"I hope I'm wrong and I don't exactly see how," Hardy said, "but I wouldn't be surprised if somehow we're up next."

27

Ron Jameson cleared his schedule on this Monday for a couple of reasons, not the least of which was that he didn't want to spend time out in public where he would have to listen to all the questions about the Celia Montoya–Adam McGowan situation. Andrea was not forwarding calls on the subject, either. That situation had resolved itself, Adam McGowan was being arraigned, so the thing was over, a done deal now, and he had nothing more to say about it. If he had to let a couple of days go by while he hung out in his office, then that's what he'd do. It would all blow over when it did, and he was simply going to let that happen. If he fell out of the news cycle for a while, so what?

After the abuse he'd taken from his own children, and even from Kate, at home yesterday, he had come down to the office in the afternoon and called the mayor and put into motion what he thought was an excellent solution—having Lapeer fire Juhle—to address the underlying issue, which was Beth Tully, who didn't know it yet but who was facing the end of her police career before too long. Jameson would just have to give that a little more time so it didn't seem so intimately connected to the Valdez murder, but before she could make any progress at all if she had any thoughts about revisiting the Peter Ash matter.

Basically, he thought, fuck her and the horse she rode in on.

Meanwhile he'd passed a very pleasant morning dictating seven different letters to victims of violent crimes in the city. Of course, he could have pulled up similar letters from the past on his computer and updated them, or he could simply have spoken into any one of his recording devices, but instead, he thought, why not take the opportunity to spend quality time with the lovely Andrea, who had been outraged at the unfairness of the "CityTalk" column, instead of with the harping and unwashed public?

Andrea understood that Ron had only been trying to act decisively and satisfy his constituency that he took his job seriously—that it wasn't really an anti-immigrant issue but rather that the scourge of the illegals was the crimes they committed, and that he, Ron, was right to have gone so quickly after Celia, who so clearly was guilty of something, even if it wasn't killing Mr. Valdez. Just look at the people she hung out with. And, by the way, she was pretty obviously working as a prostitute, wasn't she? Which in itself was a crime. And then killing herself, the coward's way out. Andrea had no understanding at all of all the sympathy this girl seemed to have generated in the city at large. If she'd have just stayed home in Mexico or wherever it was she came from, none of this would have happened. And to say it was Ron's fault was simply absurd.

The shoulder massage finally got his tight muscles to relax. He took her advice that he should lie down on the couch and take a nap. She'd continue to hold his calls. Oh, and he should remember to turn off his own cell phone, too. After all he'd been through in the last twenty-four hours, he deserved a little downtime.

Chet Greene had come into the office ramrod straight like a soldier reporting for duty, salute and all, but Ron told him to make himself comfortable, and now the DA investigator sat all but slumped on one of the leather chairs across from the couch on which his boss was sitting back, one leg crossed over the other.

"So no real luck?" Ron asked.

"That's kind of what I wanted to talk to you about, sir. I feel like there's got to be something there. I talked a bit to Sheila Marrenas, who writes a column called 'Our Town' for the *Courier* . . ."

"Sure, I know it."

"Well, she knows everything."

"More than Jeff Elliott?"

"At least as much. I get the feeling that they're kind of at war with each other on a permanent basis."

"So what about her?"

"She's who popped up when I googled the Dockside Massacre, so I went out to where she worked and asked her what she knew about it. Back in the day, this was going to be the big story of her career."

"But that didn't happen."

"No. The story as she had it just never came together."

"Dang," Ron said.

"Well, not entirely." Greene straightened up a bit and put an ankle on the opposite knee. "When I actually sat down with Marrenas, she got out her old files. It turns out that one of the Dockside Massacre victims, a guy named John Holiday, was a client of Dismas Hardy's."

"And that didn't make the papers? How could that be?"

"It didn't seem to have to do with anything. Hardy wasn't connected to Pier 70, the shooting site. He'd been at his office all day, with about a dozen witnesses. One of whom—you'll love this—was Phyllis McGowan."

"So if he wasn't a suspect, why did they even interview him?"

"Because of this Holiday guy. But that's the way this whole story seemed to go. Somebody would show up connected to somebody else, but nothing tied them to the shooting."

"What about Glitsky?"

"Same thing."

"In what way, exactly?"

"Well, because he wound up taking over as the lieutenant of the Homicide Detail when Gerson got himself killed, he's the one who most clearly benefited from the shoot-out. So naturally some cops—me, for example—had our suspicions. But he was alibied up the ying-yang. With Roake, by the way, in case you're keeping score."

"Roake and Glitsky?" Jameson came forward on the couch. "And this never made the papers, either?"

"Nope. Neither of them were at the pier."

"So where were they?"

"At her boyfriend's apartment. David Freeman. He got himself beaten and died the day before the shoot-out. So Roake's story is that she was with Glitsky at Freeman's apartment all afternoon, picking out his clothes for the funeral."

"Except if they weren't," Jameson said. "They ever find who killed Freeman?"

Greene shook his head. "Nope. Random mugging while he walked home from work."

"Shit."

"Yes, sir."

"Lots of stuff happening all at once."

"Seems so."

"Hard to believe it isn't all somehow related."

"That's what Sheila thinks, too. But she's just never been able to get any traction on proving it."

Jameson broke a small, tight smile. "Sheila now, is she?"

Greene smiled back. "What are you gonna do? Anyway"—the smile disappeared—"I went and paid a visit to Roake and she basically threw me out of her office. Oh, I forgot to say, there's one other player in all of this madness: Dismas Hardy's brother-in-law, Moses McGuire, now deceased. But he stood trial a couple of years ago for killing the guy who'd raped his daughter."

"And how's he part of this?"

"Well, it's not apparent he was any part of the Dockside thing, but he got acquitted at his trial because—you'll never guess—he was alibied by Gina Roake, who'd spent the day of the murder in bed with him."

Jameson sat all the way back on the couch. "Wow."

"Yeah. It's a lot of coincidence."

"But no real evidence."

"A couple of hundred rounds of casings from various ammunition, but other than that, nothing."

"I think it's interesting that all these people—with the possible exception of McGuire, who we don't know—make a living around the criminal justice system, so they're all experts at evidence and how to make it disappear."

"That *is* interesting. But we can't do much with that, can we?"

"I don't see how. But I'll tell you something: I'd give my left nut to get these people in front of a grand jury and watch them try to wriggle their way out. I mean, even forgetting all those other victims, this shoot-out killed a cop. Somebody should have given it an event number at the very least and beat the bushes until they had some real answers. Instead, we get the Russian mafia? Are you kidding me? Who believed that nonsense?"

"Pretty much everybody, it seems, sir."

"I want you to keep looking."

"Yes, sir."

"Go to your other skeptical cop friends. Find out who interrogated Glitsky and Hardy and especially Roake. I'm giving you my own special, personal event number. Take your Sheila friend out and let's see if there's something she forgot to tell you. These people think they can sue me, even maybe get me recused? Let's give them something a little more personal to think about. You know what happens if you're indicted for a felony, Chet? You lose your civil rights. You can't vote. Forget being a lawyer. I mean it, screw these people. I'm going to take them down. All of them."

"Yes, sir," Chet said. "Sounds like a good plan."

28

Tully and McCaffrey were sitting in the courtroom, waiting for the arraignment of Adam McGowan, whose line number had yet to be called even though it had turned into early afternoon, when Tully felt the vibration on her belt. God help her if her cell phone made a noise in the gallery; she'd turned it to silent mode before they even entered the courtroom. She knew that she couldn't be too careful on that score. Superior court judges had been known to have bailiffs impound a miscreant ringing cell phone and then to leave the bench, take the phone, and go out the courtroom doors, where they would send it skittering down a tenth of a mile of echoing hallway.

The text from Devin Juhle read: *Call me. Urgent.*

She poked her partner gently in the thigh and showed him the message, and the two of them got up and went out into the hallway.

Ten minutes later Tully knocked on a heavy steel door painted bright maroon a few blocks from the Hall on Brannan Street. Juhle opened it right away and let them in. It was a large open space with high windows for light and an assortment of sports, music, and computer equipment scattered around haphazardly, although by far its most distinguishing characteristic was a full-sized half basketball court that took up most of the room.

McCaffrey whistled with appreciation. "Where are we? What is this place?"

"My buddy Wyatt Hunt lives here, through that wall there. I've got a key."

"Lucky you," Ike said.

"Well, as it turns out, maybe not so much." Although Juhle clearly was striving for a light tone, the events of his day so far had just as clearly beaten him up.

The three of them were still standing by the back entrance through which they'd come.

"Anyway," Juhle said. "Thanks for coming down. I hope nobody followed you."

"Unlikely," Beth said. Then: "So what the hell, Dev?"

He nodded. "I know. I never saw this coming, I swear to God. Though maybe I should have. But, Jesus Christ, the guy wasted no time, did he?"

"Not a minute."

"And Lapeer just asked him 'How high?' when he told her to jump?" Ike asked.

"Not exactly," Juhle said. "He made his pitch to the mayor. She answers to him and takes it to me."

"You'd think she might stand up for her team," Beth said. "And by 'team,' I mean us troops slogging it out in the trenches, including you. I mean, what is wrong with this picture? We did the job they pay us for and got the bad guy here, didn't we?"

"That's how I read it." Juhle dredged up a small smile. "Obviously, she and you and I don't share the same idea of who her team is. Or what the job is, exactly."

"But taking you out," Beth said, "that's just wrong. If anyone should be taking the fall here, it ought to be us."

"Well, I appreciate the sentiment but, hey, the burden of command, right? I should have reined you in, apparently."

"This just completely sucks," Ike said.

"I couldn't agree with you more," Juhle replied, "but the reason I asked you to meet me down here is to let you know how the wind is really blowing. You'll probably be hearing some idiocy about why they're putting me on leave, how I've lost control of the detail, yada yada. But I wanted you to know so you'd get it straight from the horse's mouth—so you'd know that these guys, particularly Jameson, are dead serious. You piss him off even a little and it's at your own peril. And you two guys are way in his sights. That's why they're getting rid of me: because I couldn't control you the way I should have."

"But we . . ." Beth began.

He stopped her, raising his hand palm up. "No, listen up. The reason you need to know all this, like yesterday, is that obviously they're watching whatever it is you guys are doing. I wasn't completely kidding when I asked if anybody'd followed you down here. All the stuff we talked about this morning—going to the state AG or the FBI—I'm not sure that's the wisest course of action you could take. And, Beth, your original idea to go out and talk to people again who you'd already interrogated—needless to say, that's a complete nonstarter. If Jameson catches even a whiff of you sniffing around the Peter Ash case . . ." He ran out of steam.

"So you're saying we just drop it?"

Juhle nodded. "That's what I'm saying, yeah. The case has already been gathering dust for the better part of three years anyway. Give it a rest and leave it alone. And even then I can't say that you guys aren't in a whole heap of trouble already."

"So what do you want us to do, Dev?" Ike asked.

"If I were you, I'd lie low and let things simmer down a little for a while. It's not like there aren't other homicides on the whiteboard. Work those cases. Don't give them any excuse to come after you."

Beth harrumphed. "Or even notice us."

"Or even that, Beth. Right."

"So he wins. Jameson."

"This round. Maybe he does."

"And while we're on it," Beth continued, "let's not forget he won the last round, too."

Juhle shrugged. "He's got the hammer," he said. "What are you gonna do?"

Beth met Juhle's eyes.

"I know," he said. "It galls the shit out of me, too. And a hell of a lot of good that does me, doesn't it? I'm just trying to contain the damage to both of you. Although, frankly, it might be too late for that. But at least you might have a chance."

"I don't know if I want one under these conditions," Beth said.

"Well, that's your decision. But at least it would be you making it and not them forcing you out. At least promise me you'll think about it."

"You mean the lying-low part? Sure," Beth said, "I'll think about it. So will Ike, I'm sure. Won't you, Ike?"

"Absolutely. As long as it takes."

Beth took a beat, met Juhle's eyes again. "There you go," she said.

"Meanwhile," Ike asked, "any idea who's taking your place in the detail?"

"Not a clue. But whoever it is, he or she will have been prepped about you two."

"What a swell work environment," Beth said.

Juhle made a face. "Sorry about that, but that's what it is."

"I think we got the picture," Ike said. "So what are you going to do next?"

"I don't know. Take a month or two off. Wyatt Hunt—the guy who owns this place—he's got a PI outfit in town and he's been pushing me to come and work for him. So I might take him up on that."

"We are really sorry, Dev," Beth said. "This is just so not right."

Juhle shrugged. "I couldn't agree with you more."

29

Marcel Lanier was the homicide inspector—actually the acting lieutenant of Homicide at the time—who had investigated and written up the interview he had with Abe Glitsky in the immediate aftermath of the Dockside Massacre. After a lengthy career with the SFPD, he finally retired with the rank of deputy chief. Now seventy-eight years old, much of his working life had been spent in and around the Homicide Detail, and there probably wasn't a better-qualified or more credible witness to be found in the city. Chet Greene remembered him vaguely as a straight-shooting, humorless, and intimidating senior officer, but that had been a long time ago, and now, at first glance, he struck Chet, surprisingly, as much more sprightly and even charming, with bright blue eyes and a ready smile, clean-shaven, the hair on his head full and white. Bouquets of capillaries bloomed across his cheeks and over his nose.

He lived four floors up with his wife, Diane, in an apartment on Gough at California. There was a nice view to the west from the corner living room. They kept the temperature in the mid-70s and Chet had his jacket folded over the arm of his chair. The three of them chatted in the kitchen while the older man poured some Diet Cokes into glasses with ice, and when they finally sat down with the view, Diane disappeared.

Chet sipped at his drink. "So, Chief," he began, "thanks for agreeing to talk to me on such short notice."

The old man chuckled. "It's not like the dance card was exactly overbooked for the afternoon, son. I'm delighted to talk to another cop almost any time, even a DA investigator. I figure that's close enough. Anyway, if you don't stop me, I'll go on and on. And you said it was an old case, and it probably wasn't a too-successful one if we're here talking about it after all these years."

"Well, neither successful nor unsuccessful, really. Nobody went to jail over it. I'm just trying to understand a few details about why that was, since it was evidently a real mess."

"As you know, we've had our share of real messes without arresting anybody. I used to hate those damn things. Probably still would. You know somebody's out there and you just can't make the case. Used to drive me crazy. I'll bet, by the way, I'll remember the one you want to talk about."

"How about the Dockside Massacre?"

"Yes." Lanier's face broke into a smile. "One of my favorites," he said. "Although you're right: no arrests. But it was a monster of a case. We worked it for a month or two. But I think we came away pretty convinced that we got it all right."

"How was that? The Russian angle?"

"Russia, dope, cash, diamonds, you name it. Do you remember when they had their own helicopter to bring the gems up from the airport to their showroom? Pretty amazing time." His eyes actually seemed to twinkle. "That's how they all got away, the shooters. On the chopper. Then a charter plane to Moscow. At least, that's what we finally got to. And all of them presumably with diplomatic immunity, too, even if we could have identified them and put them on the spot. Which we never could do. So what happened? Did you get a new lead?"

"Not really. More like a couple of questions which may or may not be related."

"Okay. Shoot."

"Abe Glitsky."

Chet thought it was as if someone had turned down the light shining behind his eyes. "What about him?"

"Well, I've been going over the file, and you interrogated him in connection with the death of Lieutenant Gerson. It's not exactly clear to me why that was. Was he somehow involved with these Russians who were out on the pier? Or anybody else around the shooting?"

"The short answer is no. There was never any proof of that. And you're right, I went and talked to him myself."

"Were you guys friends?"

Lanier cocked his head to one side, the light from his eyes now completely gone. He put his drink down on a coaster on the coffee table between them. The intimidating man he'd once been suddenly had reappeared. "Are you accusing me of some kind of cover-up here?"

"No, sir. I'm sorry if I gave you that impression. I just haven't been able to understand why Glitsky was in the file at all if he wasn't some kind of suspect or person of interest."

"It's a little convoluted, but the bottom line was that he was investigating the Panos brothers in connection with this Russian diamond situation, and one of the brothers turned out to be a victim in the shoot-out. Evidently these guys resented Glitsky's closing in on them and threatened him. He never denied that.

"There was also speculation that some of their henchmen had mugged a lawyer and a friend of Abe's named David Freeman. So there was certainly some bad blood, but I never for a second thought Glitsky played any role in the shoot-out itself. He was a cop, for Christ's sake, like you and me, son. He didn't go outside the box to kill anybody, I promise you. But since he'd come up as a possible participant in the shoot-out, being thorough and following the book, I had to verify his alibi, which is what I did. And it checked out. When the shoot-out was happening, he was with Freeman's girlfriend picking out his funeral clothes."

"Gina Roake."

"That's right. Roake and he had the same story. And there was really no great suspicion of either of them. I just checked them off my list."

"Even though Gerson's death opened the door for Glitsky to get back to head of Homicide?"

A visible wave of fatigue passed over Lanier's features. "Actually, the person who took over as immediate head of Homicide after Barry died . . . that was me. And I didn't kill him to get his job. Abe came up to Homicide after I got promoted to deputy chief. And if you don't mind my saying so,

Inspector, if you think you'll find Abe Glitsky involved in that shoot-out, you are seriously barking up the wrong tree.

"And now, if you'll excuse me, I have another appointment coming up soon, and I'm afraid I'm going to have to ask you to let yourself out."

THOROUGHLY DEMORALIZED BY the turn in the meeting with Lanier, Chet almost called it an early day. This was hardly the way to impress his boss, and even less so the way to uncover new and critical evidence in an old murder case. One thing he could say for sure was that so far the two people he'd called on, Gina Roake and Marcel Lanier, were more than a little sensitive about what may or may not have happened and who had been at the shoot-out. If the two of them had been just a bit more relaxed and answered his questions equably, he would probably now be closer to thinking that there was, in fact, nothing there.

But neither of them had been even remotely sanguine, relaxed, or ultimately cooperative. Instead, both had basically overreacted.

Why?

The easy answer was that his questions made them nervous and remained, after all this time, a source of acute discomfort. With no physical evidence of any kind, Chet simply couldn't shake the conviction that this was because there was no statute of limitations for murder. Both of these people either knew or suspected something, but they didn't want to tell him what it was. Still, it was out there. He knew it was.

He was just going to have to keep looking.

BAYSHORE AUTOTOW IN Hunters Point owned the towing concession in San Francisco, a hugely lucrative venture for the company itself and the city that hired it. Situated on a large corner section of godforsaken land jutting out into the bay, just across from the parking lot at Candlestick Point, the actual headquarters building was low-slung, dingy white, prefabricated, and surrounded by its own enormous parking lot that was currently, this late in the afternoon, nearly filled with cars that had been towed, augmented with a healthy representation of the trucks that had towed them.

Chet Greene had dredged the name Dan Cuneo up from his memory bank because he distinctly remembered the animosity between Cuneo and Glitsky as a simmering issue from his own time in Homicide. As the details came back to him, he also had a vague recollection of a trial where Cuneo got slandered for making sexual advances toward the woman who was eventually charged with homicide. Try as he might, he could not specifically remember who the woman's defense attorney had been in that case, but he wouldn't be surprised if . . .

"Dismas fucking Hardy is who it was, the son of a bitch."

Cuneo hadn't mellowed much with age, although he had put on twenty pounds or so, all on his stomach. He wore a plain blue tie, a white short-sleeved dress shirt, and brown slacks. His sports coat was draped over his chair.

Now he was head of security for Bayshore Autotow, ensconced in a huge corner office with a nice view of the water, the Bay Bridge, and Treasure Island. The gig was possibly not as strenuous as it could have been, judging from the full drum kit that took up the back quarter of his office.

Cuneo had greeted Chet enthusiastically as a former brother-in-arms and they reminisced about the old days for fully fifteen minutes before Chet had felt comfortable enough to broach the name Glitsky and the question of who the defense counsel had been in his last case, eliciting Cuneo's explosive response.

"Those two guys, I tell you . . ." Leaving his exact meaning ambiguous.

"What about them?"

"What about them was that they were in cahoots setting me up. Which all turned out for the best, since I wound up here; but if this job hadn't come up right when it did, who knows where I'd be today? Doing home security most likely; maybe if I was lucky, Patrol Special."

Cuneo's random mention of the Patrol Specials sent a small electric jolt up Chet's backbone, since three of the victims at the Dockside Massacre had been employed as this special brand of rent-a-cop.

Chet knew that, anachronistic as it was, the Patrol Special program was still alive and well in San Francisco. Back in its vigilante heyday in the late 1800s, the city's fathers had realized that the regular police department could not adequately handle the law enforcement needs of the community, and so it had created a hundred privately owned jurisdictions—Patrol Special districts, limit three per owner—where businesses and neighborhoods could buy their own protection and security. Perhaps, even more unbelievably, Patrol Special officers wore uniforms that, except for a small arm patch, were exactly the same as the regular SFPD uniforms. They could carry guns and make arrests, too.

Chet had always thought that, even though officially sanctioned by the city, the Patrol Special program was essentially an opportunity for shakedowns and corruption.

And now Dan Cuneo had casually brought it up in the general context of Abe Glitsky and Dismas Hardy. "So if you don't mind my asking," Chet said, "did you know why these two guys were down on you?"

Cuneo sat back in his chair, his mouth set, a faraway look in his eyes. Under the desk, his foot started to tap as though he were playing a kick drum. Bringing his focus back to Chet, he took a breath, stopped the foot tapping, and came forward, putting his hands together and locking them on the surface of his desk. "How much do you remember about the Dockside Massacre?"

It was Chet's turn to be blown back in his chair. "You're not going to believe this, but that's what I'm here about today. I remember you had some issues with Glitsky."

Cuneo nodded. "Well, the short answer is that's why they had to get me out of the detail. Lanier and those other clowns, in my opinion, they'd covered up the murder of Barry Gerson and wanted to get Glitsky back up to Homicide . . ."

"I just talked to Lanier before I came here."

Cuneo let out a bitter little laugh. "Ha. And how was he?"

"Pretty unresponsive. He didn't want to talk about it."

"No shit. I bet not. He drank every drop of the Kool-Aid and never believed Glitsky was any part of it. Or Dismas Hardy, for that matter."

"But you did?"

Cuneo let out a long breath. "You want to know the truth? I don't really like talking about this anymore, either. It gives me a headache. Do you mind telling me why you're investigating this again right now?"

"My boss—the DA?—is interested. Dismas Hardy and Wes Farrell are both stirring up some shit, maybe even trying to get him impeached or otherwise removed from office. Jameson wants to take them out of the game before they get too far down that path, and I think he's smart to be thinking about it."

Cuneo let out another sigh. "I'm assuming you've heard about the Russian mafia version of what went down."

"Pretty much."

"All right, but maybe you want to put this in your pipe and smoke it. These are the plain, undisputed facts. Look who we know was at the pier that afternoon: Barry Gerson, three Patrol Specials named Nick Sephia, Julio Rez, and Roy Panos, and a murder suspect named John Holiday. And well, look at this, this guy's lawyer is Dismas Hardy. What the hell does John Holiday have to do with the Russian mafia? Zero, that's what. But what he *does* have to do with is the murder he's charged with, of an old pawnshop owner named Sam Silverman, who was a Patrol Special client. You following this?"

"So far, so good."

"Okay, so that's the real reason Holiday's at the pier. It's the only thing that makes any sense. Russian mafia, my ass. Holiday's being hounded by the Patrol Specials . . ."

"So he goes down to the pier, where he knows these guys want to bring him in or maybe kill him? Just being the devil's advocate here, but how does this make sense?"

"Obviously he doesn't think they're going to be there. He's there to take out Gerson." Cuneo pursed his lips. "The story's got a few holes, okay. But they're pluggable. You want to hear the theory?"

"Sorry. Sure."

"Okay, how about if Hardy ostensibly sets up Holiday's surrender to his pal Glitsky, who in theory is going to pass him off to Gerson to bring him back uptown to jail? These three Patrol Specials are there because Gerson has a whiff that he's getting set up and has asked them to come along as backup. He thinks Holiday's the bait, and he's not all wrong. Glitsky wants his job back in Homicide, and the plan is to hit Gerson to get it. But the ambush backfires when the Patrol Specials are there when Holiday and Glitsky arrive, and the shooting starts."

Chet sat back all the way in his chair. "But there's no evidence Glitsky was there. Or am I missing something?"

Cuneo somehow kept himself from sounding defensive. "I said there were some holes."

After a small pause, Chet asked, "Okay, how about Gina Roake?"

"How about her?"

"Well," Chet pressed on, "I understand that she alibied Glitsky for the time in question. Which means he alibied her as well. Do you think she was there, too? At the pier?"

Cuneo shook his head. "I don't know. Again, no evidence. But there was bad blood between her and the Patrol Specials."

"Why was that?"

"Because she thinks these Patrol Specials killed her boyfriend the day before."

"David Freeman."

"Right. Freeman. So Roake decides to join up with Glitsky and settle the score with them, and alibiing Glitsky to boot. Anyway, the point is, suddenly you got a critical mass of armed people and things go to hell in a hurry."

Chet considered the whole scenario for the better part of a minute. "And what about Wes Farrell?"

Cuneo shrugged. "Nothing. Not connected so far as I know."

"Moses McGuire?"

"Nope. Not familiar. What about him?"

"He's Hardy's brother-in-law and a loose cannon. Got himself arrested for murder a couple of years ago. Guess who was his lawyer: Hardy. And his alibi: Roake. Small world, wouldn't you say?"

Cuneo lifted his shoulders, let them drop. "If only we had some evidence putting these clowns on the pier. And, goddamn, I *know* they were there. Unless you want to believe that Holiday took out four armed and experienced cops by himself and got killed in the process. But I don't think that. And it wasn't any Russian mafia when we have so many locals who had a much better chance of being there, and plenty more good reasons."

"But there's still no proof that either Hardy or Glitsky or Roake or McGuire were even there?"

"Not that I've ever seen or heard of. It's a bitch."

"Well, let me ask you this, Dan. Supposing we keep working on this and Mr. Jameson decides to call a grand jury. Would you be interested in coming down and giving your two cents?"

Cuneo considered for a moment, his foot tapping again. "If you think I could help, although I'd like to have something besides all this conjecture to offer you. Those two guys—Hardy and Glitsky—pretty much ruined my career as a cop. And I loved that gig. But they got me accused of sexual harassment, and once somebody accuses you of that, you're toast, as you may know."

"I've heard about it."

"So?" He stood up behind his desk, and Chet followed his lead. "I hope I've been some kind of help."

"Quite a bit," Chet lied. "And at the least it was good to talk to somebody who didn't cut me off as soon as I mentioned what I was here about. You might be hearing from me again if we get a little closer."

"Sounds good," Cuneo said. "I'll wait for the call."

Abe Glitsky got off the telephone and fell into a kind of trance sitting in the reading chair in his living room. Outside his picture window, the dusk thickened and the streetlights came on.

He heard the garage door open and then close below him and heard the welcome sounds of familiar voices as his wife and kids ascended the outdoor steps that led up to his front door. On her way home from her work downtown, Treya had picked them up from the study club they both attended after school.

Glitsky admitted to one and all that it was a little weird that in his mid-sixties he still had two children living with him. Youngish children: Rachel was thirteen and Zachary eleven. He told himself that they kept him young, and it wasn't all delusion.

Without any conscious thought, he was up and opening the door as they arrived at the landing. For some reason—whatever it was, he'd take it—they both favored him with quick hugs as they went sailing past and turned back into their respective bedrooms.

"Hey, Dad."

"Hey, Dad."

"Hey, rats!"

Then they were gone and Treya was standing in front of him, smiling. "Hey, Dad," she said, "and if you say 'Hey, rat' back at me, I'll smack you."

"It would never occur to me," Abe said, straight-faced.

She stepped across the threshold and kissed him.

• • •

Back in his chair ten minutes later, Glitsky looked up as Treya appeared in the kitchen doorway with two steaming mugs. "I took the liberty," she said, coming forward and handing him one of them. "Plain old Earl Grey."

"My favorite, as I believe you know."

Lowering herself onto the couch across from him, she sipped her own tea and said, "You seem a little pensive."

"I'm a thoughtful guy."

"I know that. But you've been sitting there without moving a muscle for five minutes. Is everything all right?"

"Peachy."

"That good, huh?"

Glitsky raised his eyes, cast her a glance. After a small hesitation, he started in. "I got a call from Marcel Lanier. It seems he got a visit today from Chet Greene, who wanted to know what Marcel knew about the Dockside Massacre, especially as it related to me and Diz."

"Chet Greene's the guy who threatened Gina, too, isn't he?"

A nod. "Not exactly, and I don't think he got as far as threatening Marcel with anything. Apparently he just wanted to see if Marcel had been convinced that Gina and I had really been picking out funeral clothes for David Freeman. Marcel told him he was completely convinced, so there wasn't anything more to talk about after that, and Marcel said he kicked him out a little unceremoniously. But he—Marcel, that is—didn't feel real comfortable with Greene's tone. It was really like a bona fide interrogation, trying to dig up some dirt on me."

Treya took another sip of her tea, gave Abe a sympathetic look. "This thing is kind of heating up, hon, isn't it? First Gina, then poor Devin getting fired—and what's he going to do now?—then Marcel. Is this all because of those sanctions Diz filed?"

Glitsky considered a moment. "That's probably part of it, but more I think is the 'CityTalk' column and everything around that."

"Are you really worried?"

"Maybe I shouldn't be. I mean, it's been ten years. If they had anything, somebody would have dug it out and done something with it long ago."

"But . . . ?"

"But Jameson doesn't care about the rules. He's entirely capable—at least from everything I've seen, I believe he is—entirely capable of planting evidence, or producing bogus witnesses, or any other kind of cheating he can think of."

Treya said, "Up to and including killing his enemies."

"Well"—Abe ate up a few seconds drinking his tea—"I think that might be a bit of an exaggeration."

"Do you really? Didn't you hear what Diz said today at the office? Two homicide inspectors evidently believe just that. That he's a literal killer."

"Okay, but that whole proof thing . . . If Tully and McCaffrey had proof, they would have charged him back when the case was hot. But they didn't, so there's no point in theorizing that maybe he killed somebody else once upon a time. We just don't know that."

"I know you, Abe, and I think you do know it."

"Well, okay, good point. I admit, I think I'm pretty sure I know it. But there's a difference between knowing it and being able to prove it. And if you get that mixed up, you're on a slippery slope. Maybe the same one Jameson's on. I mean, look, I'm sure he believed on some level that Celia Montoya killed this Valdez character, but he shouldn't have made any move at all until he could prove it, or let Tully build her case. That's the rule, plain and simple. You don't do that, you don't belong in this business."

"But Jameson's already in this business. And it sure looks like he's coming after you and Diz and Gina and whoever else, and he won't be playing by the rules as he goes along."

"Yeah," Glitsky said in a somber tone. "It does look like that."

"So? What do you think you ought to do?"

Glitsky shook his head and sighed. "I don't know, Trey. I really don't know."

"He actually went and visited Lanier in person?" Hardy asked.

"He did. But remember that he came and visited Gina, too," Glitsky said.

"I'd never forget, but with Gina he was just fishing and offering her immunity if she'd help bust us. With Lanier he was actually doing an interrogation, hoping to break your alibi, which sounds more to me like he's building a case. Different situation entirely. Definitely turning up the heat if he's driving around town talking to folks."

They were sitting in Hardy's living room. Oak burned and occasionally snapped in the fireplace. Hardy had a large Riedel glass half filled with Handwritten Cabernet Sauvignon on the coffee table in front of him. Glitsky sipped at yet another cup of tea.

"So what do you suppose we ought to do?" he asked. "Treya asked me and I had nothing to tell her. Are we just supposed to wait around until he does something drastic?"

"I'm not really inclined to think that way, although I do see a little silver lining around the cloud here."

"What's that?"

"Well"—Hardy drank some wine—"so long as he's spending his time putting together some kind of legal case against us, I think we can rule out that he's also planning to shoot us down in the street. Isn't that heartening?"

"You think this is funny?"

"Actually, no. I'm just trying to lighten things up a little, since I'll think a little more clearly when with every breath I'm not afraid I'm going to get shot. But I must have forgotten for a minute that I'm talking to the ever-jovial People Not Laughing."

"You've been known to beat a dead horse, you know that?" Abe asked. "But all kidding aside, Diz, what do you think is going on here?"

"Well, he can't get us even if he goes to the grand jury, even if he gives us the greatest motive in the world to have been there, and even if that's the whole truth and nothing but the truth. He can't get us unless he's got physical evidence. You know this as well as I do, maybe better."

"So say he doesn't get his physical evidence and he can't get us going by the rules. Then he breaks them, wouldn't you say?"

Hardy shook his head. "We're not there yet. *He's* not there yet. We've got to let it play out."

"I hate that part," Abe said.

Hardy nodded. "I'm not too crazy about it myself."

GASPARE'S AGAIN.

Beth Tully was thinking she ought to buy shares in the place. At the same time she was thinking it would be bad luck if it turned out that the ten-table pizza joint on Geary was bugged for sound and Ron Jameson was listening in on everything that she said. Or if somebody—maybe Chet Greene—had a tail on her and knew where she was at every moment.

She was truly getting paranoid.

But not, she told herself, without some reason.

After all, when she'd gotten into work just that very morning—could that have been today?—the arraignment of Adam McGowan had been the only pressing item on her agenda. Devin Juhle had still been in charge of the Homicide Detail. She and Ike had a plan for investigating the murders of Peter Ash and Geoff Cooke that she felt had some reasonable chance of success.

Now, in the past twelve hours, all of that had changed. Even her partner, Ike, wasn't inclined to push the envelope on what they could possibly get away with. He still had a hard time believing that they'd been able to remove Devin from his post without any due process or even much discussion—without so much as a by-your-leave.

Chief Lapeer had just come waltzing in and swept him out as if he were a dust bunny cluttering up his office.

It had gotten Ike's attention. Even without one false step, he could be gone in a hot second. If the powers that be could dismiss their lieutenant out of hand, they could certainly find some excuse to dismiss him and Beth.

Sorry, he'd told Beth, but he had three children and a stay-at-home wife. He couldn't risk it anymore. While they'd had Juhle's support, he'd felt it was just on the closer edge of worthwhile to try to bring down big prey like Ron Jameson. Now, without that support, he and Beth could too easily become the prey themselves.

He couldn't live with that, so she was back on her own.

Ike hoped that she'd get the message loud and clear and just lie low, as she'd promised Devin she would.

She had promised, true, but had thought that Ike understood that she was being sarcastic. She had no intention of lying low. Ike had understood that, hadn't he? He must have.

But apparently not.

Beth didn't want to think about who Devin's replacement might turn out to be. Or about his earlier comment: "Whoever it is, he or she will have been prepped about you two."

This was a far from heartening thought.

She was sitting in a back corner by the pickup station facing out, so that she could have the entire place within her vision at all times. Navy SEALs and Army Rangers and other people who knew combat, she knew, tended to pick that seat as well, almost as a default. It felt like right where she belonged.

People had been coming in and picking up to-go orders at a rate of about one every five minutes for the entire half hour she'd been here. The four booths were full and parties of two to four sat at six of the floor tables. The Eagles were singing about living it up at the Hotel California.

Checking her watch, she wondered what was taking so long.

If she didn't come, then what?

What the hell was she doing here? she wondered. She should just get up and, taking a page from Ike's handbook, head home to be with her daughter and boyfriend.

And then the door opened and she forgot all that as Bina Cooke came in out of the biting cold, blinked a couple of times, saw her, and raised a tentative hand in a low-key greeting.

Crossing over, Bina pulled out the chair opposite Beth's and sat down. "Sorry I'm late."

"That's fine. You didn't have to come at all."

"Yes I did." Bina threw back the hood of her very stylish jacket and shrugged out of the rest of it, letting it hang where it fell over the back of her chair. She seemed to be ten years younger and much prettier—

exponentially prettier—than Beth remembered, though of course the last time she'd seen her, three years earlier, she'd just lost her husband and could barely contain her grief. Beth's image of Bina that day was of burning red eyes, sallow skin, and lank, lusterless hair.

Now, seeing Bina's well and no doubt expensively coiffed silver-gray hair, light makeup, high cheekbones, and flawless complexion, Beth thought that she could easily work as a model.

It threw her slightly, altering her perception—this woman was not some beaten-down victim.

Due to the circumstances and her physical appearance last time, she'd seen Bina as a destroyed shell of a human being who'd been buffeted by horrific events. Literally pitiable and, seen from any angle, Bina Cooke had exuded pain and disorientation. And because of this, Beth had considered any information from this woman to be suspect at best, hysterical and all but worthless. Bina was someone to feel sorry for, not a reliable witness. Certainly she was not a woman dealing from a base of power, either personally or professionally.

Sitting across from her today, this Bina Cooke was a different person.

"I told them I was waiting for a friend before ordering," Beth began, "so they let me save the table. Would you like anything? The pizza is great here."

"Anything you'd like."

Beth felt a sudden nervous fluttering in her stomach. This was a Rubicon moment, to be sure, and she shouldn't miss the significance of it. Excusing herself, she got to her feet and walked over to the counter, where she placed her order.

Back at the table, Beth slid into her chair. She stopped herself from thanking Bina again for coming down and instead decided to come right out with it. Leaning in a little closer, she lowered her voice and said, "As I told you when we talked, I'm considering reopening the case into your husband's death."

Bina knew this from their earlier discussion, of course, but at the actual verification that this was really going forward with a legitimate homicide inspector, she threw a glance at the ceiling, then closed her eyes and released what Beth took to be a grateful sigh. "Do you know how long I've been waiting to hear those words?"

"I think I do, yes."

"Tell me how I can help you. Whatever you want to know."

"Well, I thought we might start with the gun."

"The gun would be good."

There were actually three areas of possible discrepancy that Beth wanted to revisit concerning the death of Geoff Cooke: the suicide note, the fact that Geoff had been left-handed and shot himself on the right side of his head, and the gun he'd used. Her plan was to address all these issues afresh and prepare a file that she would somehow, surreptitiously, deliver to the attorney general's office. Of the three, the most provocative—and quite possibly the most provable—had to do to with the gun.

Beth again pulled herself in closer to the table, her voice barely above a whisper. "You told me during the last investigation that it wasn't your husband's gun that had killed him."

"Right."

"But he had the exact same kind of weapon that we found with him in the car."

"Yes."

"Do you want to refresh me on all of that?"

"It's not too complicated," Bina said. "Geoff was in Desert Storm at the same time as Ron Jameson—and, by the way, what is that guy going to have to do before people understand what an evil monster he is? Did you read about this poor girl he chased out of town so that she could get arrested and kill herself in jail? Sorry," she cracked a small, apologetic smile. "Off point."

"No worries," Beth said. "We're pretty much in accord about him. So . . . Geoff and Ron, they were both in Desert Storm."

Bina nodded. "And they both picked up a couple of these guns. Who knows exactly how these things happen or how they got them home. Anyway, they did. They brought back two each. Souvenirs. Just a minute, I've got my notes here." She dug into her purse and pulled out a few sheets of yellow legal pad paper on which she'd written her comments and ideas.

"Here it is. The guns were all . . . this is the thing. They were all exactly the same type of gun, called a Tariq nine-millimeter. It was made over there in Iraq. Evidently, according to my brilliant analysis here, they're basically the brother to an American-made gun, a Beretta M9."

"And both Geoff and Jameson brought two of them home each?"

"Right."

"And how do you know that?"

"What do you mean?"

"I mean, might one of them have brought only one home? Or kept three?"

"No," Bina said. "No chance. Right when they first got back here, after the deployment was over, sometimes they'd get together—actually, it was often the four of us—"

"I'm sorry. The four of you?"

"Me, Geoff, Ron, and Kate."

"Of course. Yes. The four of you." The reminder of her friend Kate Jameson's familiarity and comfort with guns sent a small shock wave running down her back. "Go on."

"Well, we'd all go shooting at the range some afternoons. You know, just for fun. And the guys would bring their Iraqi stuff along with their regular service weapons."

"And they had two of these Tariq guns each? And no more?"

"No. It wasn't like there was anything secret going on. We all shot all of them. Geoff had his two and Ron had his two. It wasn't like anybody was hiding one or more of them. Plus, they talked about them. There was really never any question about who had what. Why is that such an issue?"

"Because we've got a finite number of guns, four, that we're dealing with. You had two of these last time we were at your house, in your safe. Are they still there?"

"Yes."

"Okay, two to go. Ron's guns. One of them, he shoots Peter Ash on your boat that he'd borrowed, then throws the gun overboard into the bay, lost forever."

Bina whispered almost inaudibly. "Do you know that?"

"I do. But I can't prove it. Just bear with me, okay? All right. So we're down to one Tariq left. This is of course the gun we found in your husband's car. It has to have been Ron's, because there's no other option, but it has no fingerprints or anything else to put him together with it."

"But wasn't Ron—I so remember this—wasn't he at some deposition with, like, six other lawyers the whole night that Geoff . . . ?" She stopped and sighed again.

"Yes, he was. No question. He has a foolproof alibi."

"I remember," she repeated.

"But Kate doesn't," she said.

"Kate? No, Kate was my . . ." She stopped, her mouth all but hanging open in shock.

"She was my friend, too," Beth said. "One of my best friends. Have you seen her since?"

"A few times, right after. Condolences—you know. Never since. How about you?"

"Once. I told her I would come and arrest her someday. That kind of cooled off the friendship."

"So you're saying she killed Peter, too?"

"No. Ron killed Peter because he found out Kate had slept with him."

"Was that it?"

"That was it."

"Fuck," Bina said. "Unbelievable."

"I know. Isn't it?"

The pizza arrived and put the conversation on hold.

Bina started in after she'd swallowed. "Ron told me that he'd turned both of his guns in to the city."

"He told me that, too," Beth said. "But the city keeps close track of those things, and they had no record of anything like his guns in the log. I checked. And besides, it would have been only one, since he threw the other one in the bay. But there wasn't just one gun, either. There were none. He never handed in any guns at all."

"So what are you going to do with all this?" Bina asked. "What's different that you hadn't known before I came here?"

"The main thing is I think I see where I can cross Ron up, with him lying about getting rid of all of his guns. That could be huge. Beyond that, I wanted to make sure I had my facts straight on these guns. Next up, I'm going to get this file in front of the attorney general or the FBI or anybody else I can get to listen and make the case that Ron lied to a police officer when he told me he'd gotten rid of the guns and how he'd done it. We law enforcement types get a little snarky when we get lied to. Especially by the corrupt bastard DA. This is a couple of murders we're talking about. I've got to believe somebody's going to show an interest."

"If you need me again," Bina said, "I want you to know that I'm willing to testify about any of this."

"That's good to know, but be warned that it might be a while. The wheels of justice sometimes grind exceedingly slow."

"That's all right," she said. "I've already waited this long. I can go a little longer."

"That is so good to hear. And, Bina?"

"Yes?"

"I can't thank you enough for agreeing to come down here and meet with me like this. I realize how brutal this is, and I'm just so sorry it took me this long to figure out how to stay under the radar and get these cases back on track. Just keep your fingers crossed that I can move it on down the line."

"I will."

"Don't lose faith," Beth said. "I'm going to make something happen."

"I know you will," Bina said. "If only any of it could bring Geoff back."

31

Finally, on Tuesday morning, the fog rolled in and the cold snap broke. By 7:30, when Chet Greene left his house out in the lower Sunset District, the temperature had climbed to a near balmy 54 degrees, shooting for a high of 62 after the marine layer burned off.

The DA had reserved him for a morning pickup, because he was speaking at a Bar Association breakfast at the Olympic Club. But when Chet got to the Jamesons' gorgeous home on Washington Street at 8:00 sharp, his boss didn't come out the front door just as he drove up, as he usually did, so Chet pulled to the curb and waited.

After ten minutes, he called Jameson's cell phone, which rang twice before he heard the DA say hello.

"This is Chet, sir, and I just wanted you to know I'm out front of your house whenever you're ready."

"Sure. Thanks. But what's up?"

"I'm not sure what you mean, sir. You had an appointment, I believe with the Bar Association?"

"No. I canceled that. I didn't tell you?"

"No, sir."

"Yeah. Well, if I went and talked to all these lawyers, all I'd hear about down there is this Valdez case and how I shouldn't have second-guessed my cops about who killed him, so I decided I'd just blow them off. I'm tired of all that shit. I should have told you. Sorry. But since you're here, how about if I hitch a ride downtown with you?"

"Fine. I'll just wait out here until you're ready."

"Two minutes."

• • •

THE DA HAD barely settled into the backseat when he asked, "So are you having any luck with the Dockside stuff? I know what you told me about your meeting with Gina Roake, but weren't you going to talk to some other folks about that, too?"

Chet pulled away from the curb. "I was and I did—two of them, anyway—but I can't say it was the most productive day of my life. One of them, Marcel Lanier, thinks Glitsky and Hardy walk on water, which is a little strange to me, hearing it from a lifetime cop, since Hardy's a defense guy all the way. I mean, do you have any criminal defense attorney pals?"

"I can't say I do. But that's really neither here nor there."

"No. I know."

"What about the other guy?"

"Dan Cuneo, now running security at Bayshore Autotow. Completely different story. Couldn't wait to testify for us as soon as we found something for him to talk about. Or maybe even commit some friendly little perjury if we asked him to. Hardy and Glitsky evidently got him blackballed for sexual harassment of a witness that went public in the middle of one of his trials. Ruined his career here in the PD. He's still pretty bitter."

"I don't blame him, especially if he didn't do it. You get any feeling for that?"

"Not really, no. These days, you know, you don't have to do much to get slammed on that front. He might have said he liked her sweater or something, which she took to be a come-on of some kind."

"But he had nothing to give us?"

"No. He wasn't anywhere near the shoot-out. He just felt like somehow Glitsky was in it. And then Hardy's client was down there, too—John Holiday, one of the victims—so Cuneo figured Hardy must have been involved in it, too. He had this whole scenario worked out about what he thought had probably gone down."

"Which was what?"

"The short version is that Hardy negotiated a surrender of Holiday to Gerson but wanted Glitsky there to make sure it all played as it should."

"As opposed to . . . ?"

"As opposed to Holiday getting himself shot trying to escape."

Jameson chortled. "That didn't work out so well, did it?"

"No, sir. But the bad news is Cuneo didn't have any theory that fit with the other three dead guys, who all worked as Patrol Specials."

"Rent-a-cops. The diamond people."

"Essentially, yeah. But Cuneo didn't think they were there about diamonds. His opinion was that somehow they got wind of Holiday's surrender, when and where it was going down."

"How'd they learn that?"

"Unclear. Some leak out of Homicide. Not me, I swear."

"Never thought it was, Chet. Go on."

"So theory one is that Holiday had evidence that these guys had mugged and killed David Freeman, and he was going to rat them out, so they decided they had to kill him first."

"And they just happened to show up at the same time as Glitsky and Hardy and Holiday and Gerson? This is getting a little thick."

"I know. Theory two about how these guys are involved is a little better, but not much."

"Let's hear it."

"Gerson himself actually invited these Patrol Special guys along to back him up because he was afraid that Hardy and Holiday and Glitsky planned to ambush him, although Cuneo didn't know why Gerson might have thought that."

"Hardy wanted to keep his client out of jail, that's why. At the same time, Glitsky moves up to running Homicide and drops the case."

"Okay, maybe, except Lanier reminded me that Glitsky didn't take over Homicide until way later. But, in any event, theory two doesn't make sense, either, unless Gerson was dirty and tied up with these Patrol Specials, maybe even on a payroll someplace, which was unlikely, to say the least."

They stopped at a red light on Van Ness and both men went silent with their thoughts.

When they started rolling again, Jameson said, "But even for this guy Cuneo, it's all just theory anyway. He doesn't have anything we can actually use. Any physical evidence at all."

"I'm afraid that's true. But I've got a few more folks I thought I'd talk to as long as I've got your permission."

"Take as much time as you need. But while I've still got you here, is there anything at all you can think of that explains this John Holiday's presence on the pier? I mean, we don't have evidence that Glitsky or Hardy were there, because if we did, I'd be getting them indicted for murder right now.

"But Holiday, no question, he was there. He died there. So did Gerson and these Patrol Specials. What was Holiday doing there? Did he have something to do with these Russian diamonds?"

"I haven't run across even a rumor of that. No, sir."

"Well, then, if not that, why was he there?"

"All by himself, he was turning himself in to Gerson."

"Without his lawyer or anybody else to protect him? And out in the boondocks, where he is completely exposed? He had to have been smarter than that." Jameson blew out in frustration. "At least Hardy must have been there, Chet. It's the only thing that makes sense, given this Holiday character actually and in fact being there as part of the mix. And Glitsky tagged along because these guys run in a pack. Does that sing for you?"

"Except we can't put either Hardy or Glitsky there."

"Yeah," Jameson said, his brow furrowed in frustration. "There's that."

THE HEAD OF the Crime Scene Investigation unit, Len Faro, had been living for a couple of months with the rumor that he was going to move up a rank to lieutenant. This would be a significant pay raise that would make his life better and his pension larger.

When he got the call from one of the DA investigators, Chet Greene, wanting to talk about an old case, he said he'd be happy to, but in reality he greeted the news with mixed emotions. Greene's boss had already interfered enough with Len's department in the Valdez case, where he'd essentially shut down the investigation into the murder before Len had

had a chance to analyze the real evidence that would or would not implicate or exclude the woman Mr. Jameson had summarily indicted while he played politics.

Next thing Len knew, there was the "CityTalk" column, which was followed all too closely by the dismissal of Devin Juhle. That action had shocked Len to his core. He'd worked with Juhle since he'd come on in Homicide, and the man was competent, smart, honest, a straight shooter, and an all-around good guy.

None of which had helped him keep his job when push came to shove.

Although decisions within the police department were supposedly not subject to the whims of the district attorney, Len and many other of his fellow officers could not help but see Jameson's fingerprints on the travesty that had gone down with Juhle. Len didn't know all the details, but the timing was such that it all but inescapably had to do with Devin supervising the bringing in of a second suspect in the Valdez murder case. And, knowing Juhle, this was because they had something compelling on Adam McGowan.

But because this was embarrassing to the DA, the clear message was that Juhle should have somehow kept that arrest from happening. He wasn't being a team player. He'd let his inspectors run amok and hadn't protected the DA's reputation.

Somehow.

Never mind that Beth Tully and Ike McCaffrey—two stone-pro homicide inspectors—identified who was most probably the real killer of Hector Valdez.

And now, just when Len Faro was getting used to the idea that this lieutenant gig might be in his future, Chet Greene was coming around to talk about some old stuff. Which meant DA stuff. Which meant politics and very probably an end run around due process.

Shit.

Len knew Greene slightly from his days in Homicide and didn't have much of a feeling about him either way, which in itself was instructive. The terrifying thought briefly crossed his mind that Greene might in reality be coming by as an emissary to feel him out and maybe offer him Juhle's former position, which would get him his raise to lieutenant's pay, but under conditions that would range all the way from bad to awful.

And then suddenly here was a knock on his open door and Greene, to his credit, stood waiting with an expectant expression until Faro waved him on in. "Have a seat," he said. "I'm about to have my sixth cup of coffee and I hate to drink alone."

Greene broke a grin. "Isn't six kind of a big number?"

"It's all relative. I was doing fifteen a day and my doctor thought it might be a good idea to cut down, so now I try to keep it under a dozen. Besides, this Keurig thing"—he pointed to a small machine set up on a file cabinet under one of the bookshelves—"it's a miracle. Load up the cartridge, push the button, wait a half a minute, bang, you might as well be at Starbucks at a tenth the price. Did you say yes?"

"Sure," Chet said. "Living large."

"You won't regret it." He pushed the button. "So what can I do for you?"

"Jameson's got me looking at one of our old unsolved cases that's come to his attention recently. The Dockside Massacre."

"Hmm." Faro, killing a few seconds, scratched at his soul patch. "Good luck with that. I'd be glad to help you if I can, of course, but you've got to know that that one's been beaten to death over the years. You might as well be trying to hook up with the Zodiac."

"I've been talking to some people already and that's a little bit the feeling I'm getting."

"Why's your boss interested now, after all this time?"

Chet hesitated for a second before saying, "I don't really know."

Len raised an eyebrow as his internal bullshit meter flew off the chart.

"But some of it," Chet went on, "just between you and me, he could use some good PR after the flak he's been taking lately. He closes an old big cop-killer case and he's a hero, at least for a while."

Faro pulled one cup out from under the machine's spigot. "I guess it could happen. Black?"

"Black's good."

"You got any ideas?" Len asked.

"Not really. As I said, I've talked to some people, but the basic problem is that there's no evidence that proves anything."

Pushing the button on a second cup, Len nodded. "I remember. I worked that scene right afterwards and, believe me, it was a madhouse. Half the force was down there. Nobody could figure out what it was all about. We worked it for three days, the scene."

"And got nothing?"

"Mostly. Whoever the other guys were—the Russians, maybe—they knew how to clean up a crime scene. They must have been professionals with body armor, since apparently none of them even drew blood. Strout"—the medical examiner at the time—"had us sample every damn smear of blood on the pier, and all of it except for two small unidentifieds belonged to the bodies at the scene."

"And what about them? The unidentifieds."

Faro clucked. "Somebody got nicked or fell and scraped himself and bled a little, nothing like the gunshot wounds. And of course, even if there was a little blood and DNA, you could never prove how long it had been there. But in any event, no match with DNA on them, which makes sense if they'd just flown in from Russia and didn't stick around so we could swab them for a comparison sample anyway."

"So how many of these pros were there, do you think?"

"Nobody knows for sure. Four or five, and they must have come out shooting. We finally came to the conclusion that there must have been a delivery of diamonds involved, which the Patrol Specials were guarding."

"And what was Gerson doing there?"

"A mystery. Although arresting Holiday seems to be the consensus. But again, why then and why there? Nobody knows."

"Any sign about how they got away, these Russian pros?"

Len pulled his own coffee over in front of him. "You'll laugh, but the rumor at the time was the helicopter, except nobody in the neighborhood remembers hearing or seeing it."

"So what's that leave?"

"What do you mean? What does that leave what?"

"In terms of evidence."

"Well, not to get technical, but it leaves basically squat." Len blew on his coffee and sipped. Suddenly he put his cup down and threw a glance up toward the ceiling. "Except the largest collection of shell casings we've ever recovered from one scene. Which means we've got a pretty good idea of the ordnance that the guests brought along to the party."

Chet put his own cup down. "How many different guns? Any of them Russian?"

"Seven or eight guns, around there. I don't remember exactly. As to Russians . . ." The idea seemed to bring Faro up short. "It's funny, but I don't remember hearing anybody ask that question before."

"So what's the answer?"

"I don't know if anybody's ever looked for that specifically. Not that it would necessarily lead to anything. These were casings we're talking about, not the guns themselves."

"So best case," Chet said, "it might narrow down whether it was in fact probably Russians or probably not Russians. If they come in with diplomatic immunity, these Russian killers, that undoubtedly means they brought along their guns from the mother country, right? But casings, they could have got them anywhere."

"Right," Faro said. "Really no point in looking."

"You could eliminate about them being Russian."

"Not really. Not with certainty. Best I could get to is maybe. And even then, so what?"

"So what is you got a Russian casing or a hundred of them, it tells us something," Chet said. "But if they're not there . . . you see what I'm saying?"

Len nodded warily, noncommittal. "Who, for example, would the non-Russians have been?"

"Well, John Holiday for one."

"Okay. I can buy him."

Like a tell in poker, Chet brought one hand down over his mouth. "Other people," he said. "Locals."

"Or how about Russians who used American weapons?"

"Or that, sure." Clearly on a scent, Chet Greene went back to his coffee, took a sip, put the cup back down. "Let me ask you this, Len. Roughly how many of these casings are we talking about?"

Len couldn't suppress a chuckle. "I don't know if anybody's ever counted all of them, but I'd take a stab at around two hundred, four or five different calibers, and twenty or thirty shotgun pellets we dug out of the pier."

"Did you check them for fingerprints, or partials?"

"As a matter of fact, I think we did. I'm sure we had Gerson and Holiday because Gerson was a cop and Holiday had a sheet, so they were both in the database. One of the rent-a-cops, too, although I don't remember his name: Nick, or Rick. Doesn't matter."

With a growing intensity, Chet came forward in his chair, pushing his coffee cup aside. "How about casings with no prints? Any of those?"

"I would assume so. Though I wouldn't have cared much about them, would I? I don't really remember."

"No. Right. Of course. They don't tell you anything, except some pros would have known to wipe them before they loaded up."

"Yep."

"Okay, but here's the big one, Len: Do you remember if you got any prints or partials that you couldn't identify?"

"I'd assume so, on a sample that big. There had to have been some, I'd assume."

"And why wouldn't somebody's prints show up?"

"Because they weren't in the old database."

Chet brought the flat of his hand theatrically to his forehead. "Of course. The old database."

Before the lab went over to the federal database, about ten years before, the fingerprints of anybody who'd been booked in California—plus cops, other first responders, government employees, some medical people—could be found in the old database. Which left a large sampling unrepresented. When they'd gone over to the federal database, that problem disappeared.

"So," Chet said. "You're saying that basically no one's gone back since then and run the unknowns through the new database?"

"I would be very surprised if they had." Len tipped up his cup and finished his coffee. This was, unexpectedly, a rather fascinating turn. Chet was correct. This would be virgin, unmined territory.

God, Len thought, *I love this job*.

Chet Greene hadn't come down for any nefarious or political reason. He'd come down trying to lay his hands on evidence, and the unearthing of evidence was what Len Faro lived for—not his promotion or his pay grade but evidence. And why? Because bullshit walks, he thought, and guess what?

Evidence talks.

"I KNOW." BETH wore a mischievous grin. "I'm a bad girl."

"So bad," Hardy agreed. "I'm slightly afraid to be sitting with you, to tell you the truth."

"Same back atcha." Beth took in her surroundings—the low-slung sagging upholstered couches in the very back by some ancient Tiffany lamps, hard by the entrance to the bathrooms; about ten customers in the whole place, nearly empty here at nine o'clock on a Tuesday. "What is this place?" she asked.

"This, believe it or not, is the oldest bar in San Francisco, the Little Shamrock."

"I know that. I just got it on Google Maps and drove here. But what's your connection?"

"I'm the majority owner."

"You're kidding me?"

"I'm not. I try to keep a low profile around it, but I've found it's a good spot to pretend I'm not a working lawyer. Or where a cop like yourself can show up without anybody thinking it's a meet with an agenda. You want something to drink?"

"What are you having?"

"Macallan 12. If you like Scotch, it's hard to beat."

"Sure," she said. "Hit me."

Hardy got up, went around behind the bar, and poured out a couple of generous shots. In under a minute he was back, setting her glass on the low coffee table in front of her. She picked it up and knocked it against Hardy's own. "*Sláinte,*" she said, and lifted it to her lips.

When they'd both put their drinks down, Hardy met her eyes. "So your supervisor gets himself fired for making things uncomfortable for Mr. Jameson, then makes it a point to warn you and your partner off any of your own investigations, especially those that bring you into contact with the DA, and so the first thing you do is go talk to a witness on just such a case."

"I know," Beth said. "I told you I was a bad girl. I'm also starting to think I might have a small problem with authority."

Hardy broke an appreciative grin. "I'm getting that impression." He paused for a beat. Then: "So was it worth it, going back to your witness?"

"Mostly. I think so. Geoff Cooke's wife, Bina. She helped get my ducks lined up, at least. The main thing is that, first, she's motivated to testify again if it comes to it. Jameson definitely lied to her about what he did with his souvenir guns from Iraq. He didn't turn them in to the city, and they keep records of that. It flat out didn't happen. In fact, one of his guns is probably still in the evidence locker, since it's the gun that killed Cooke."

"Still," Hardy said, "that's not much. Maybe he lied. That's it?"

"He did lie to Bina. He also lied to me. If somehow he gets himself into a situation where he lies under oath to a federal officer—say, an FBI agent—that's a felony and he could go to jail."

"True, except that you can't really prove it—either that he lied or that it wasn't his gun—and even if you could make that case, so what? Who—I mean who in law enforcement—is this Bina going to give her testimony to? Who are you going to give yours to, for that matter? If Jameson gets any wind of what you've been up to . . ."

"Everybody's so afraid of that dick."

"With good reason, Beth. Especially if he's . . . if he's what you think he is."

"He's a literal cold-blooded murderer, that's what he is, Dismas. Same as his wife, Kate, although actually she may be worse. No doubt in my mind."

"Okay. If all that's true, then people are afraid of him for good reason, wouldn't you say? Hell, *I'm* afraid of him, if you want to know the truth."

"Yeah, but at least you've taken him on with the recusal and the lawsuit and being Jeff Elliott's source, to say nothing about talking to me."

"The wisdom of which is not yet apparent. But as for you, what are you planning to do with what you've got?"

"Just before he got canned, Devin suggested that me and Ike should get in touch with the AG or the FBI. Have them start their own investigation. I mean, this is a double murder we're talking about, which is some serious shit. Glitsky told me that he's got a reliable connection in the FBI who—"

"Wait, you've also talked to Glitsky on this?"

"I did. He's how I got to you in the first place, you remember. In fact, I'm expecting him down here with his connection any minute."

"Here? Now?"

She flashed him a not-quite-sincere "Gotcha!" smile. "No time like the present. The clock is ticking here." She glanced at her watch. "Pretty soon."

"And how did I get involved in this, again?"

"You're already involved, sir. It was Glitsky's idea. He thought that, no matter what, you'd want to be part of whatever is going down."

"Really?" Hardy seemed for a moment to be almost in a state of shock. "They're coming down here?" He looked down the length of the room to the front door, which opened as if on cue as Glitsky pushed his way in, another guy—in from central casting as an FBI agent—trailing in his wake.

FBI SPECIAL AGENT Bill Schuyler said: "I'll tell you what: he lies to me and he's got himself in a whole heap of trouble right there. It's a felony to lie to a federal officer, as all of you may know. If it gets to it, that ought to tie him up in a couple of knots. We could take him into custody on that alone. But I must say," he added to Beth, "you've built a pretty compelling narrative around him and his wife. I don't think I would have come aboard normally, even with Abe's gentle prodding, but this all sings to me. We've been aware of this guy for a while. Plus, now he's a sitting DA with an arrogance issue. It's a great opportunity. But I do see one potential problem and maybe it's a big one."

"What is it?" Beth asked.

"Well, we start sniffing around your old investigation, and even if he can't connect you to us, he's likely to put two and two together and realize that you, Inspector, have been the driving force here. You might want to be a little careful about your own safety until this shakes out."

"That's why I came to you," Beth said. "So it wouldn't look like it was me."

"But it *is* you," Schuyler said. "Sorry, but that's the simple fact of it."

"*You're* sorry?" Beth asked. "Is there any other way to take him into custody first?"

Schuyler almost smiled. "You mean just go pick him up because we don't like him?"

"Or," Beth said, "because he's committed murder."

"Yeah, well, as your lawyer friend here can tell you"—he nodded toward Hardy—"I'm not always wild about it, but arresting somebody just 'cause we don't like him, we frown upon that here in this country."

Hardy asked Beth: "What kind of file did you have on the Peter Ash case? You've said all along that you were close to pulling Ron in. You must have had something at least modestly compelling. I mean, some real evidence."

"I thought of that before we got here," Beth said, "but there wasn't anything until you put it together with the Geoff Cooke thing. And his lying about the guns. That's verifiable. That's on the record. He never turned any of those guns in, and they're distinctive." She turned to Schuyler and Glitsky. "If you can get him to tell you what he did with them . . ."

Glitsky said, "He'll just say that the evidence clerk didn't enter the serial numbers right or stole them himself. So there's no record? No clerical error. So what?"

"Do you think," Schuyler asked, "that you have something a little . . . firmer . . . on the wife?"

"Kate?" Beth blew out a breath in frustration. "She made two mistakes, maybe even three, but tying them to her specifically could be a little tough."

"Let me be the judge of that," Schuyler said. "What were they? The mistakes."

"First, Geoff Cooke was left-handed and behind the wheel in the driver's seat. Kate was sitting in the passenger seat, so she had to shoot him from there. He didn't hold the gun and shoot himself with his right hand."

"Okay," Schuyler said, dismissing that explanation out of hand. "But in fact it could have happened. Not likely, I'll grant you, but not impossible. What else?"

"Kate wrote a suicide note, as though it were from Geoff, and sent it to his wife on his computer. Her name is Bina, but he never, not once, wrote her and called her anything but 'Bean.' He didn't write that note."

"Correct me if I'm wrong," Schuyler said, "but that doesn't mean your friend Kate did, does it? Were her fingerprints on his computer?"

"No. There were no prints on his computer, not even his. It had been wiped."

"So somebody killed him. So he didn't kill himself. What about Ron?"

Beth shook her head disconsolately. "Ron's got a solid alibi for that night. Depositions with clients and associates. No chance it was him, though I'd love it if there was."

Glitsky finally spoke up. "You said she made three mistakes. What's the third one?"

Beth sighed in frustration. "The magazine in the murder weapon had two bullets missing. Which even now, as I say it out loud, I realize it's lame."

"What's the significance of that?" Glitsky asked.

"If you can follow me here," Beth said, "she needed the casing from that gun to match the casing found in the car so that she could then plant it on Cooke's boat, where Peter Ash was killed. That made it look like the same gun that Cooke had killed himself with was the one he used to kill Ash."

"Now you've totally lost me," Schuyler said.

Beth shook her head. "I thought I might."

"How about witnesses?" Schuyler asked.

"What do you mean?"

"Other people you were talking to. People who knew Ash or Ron or heard something."

"Sure. It was a big case. I've got a reasonable file."

"Well, with that," Schuyler said, "I'm willing to go out and do a little canvassing. I have to tell you guys that even if everything you're telling me is true, I'm hard-pressed to see a federal crime here. Jameson wasn't in office at the time, so I'm not even sure we can call this an investigation into political corruption. But for the moment let's let that slide and we'll call it interagency cooperation.

"You've made a decent case that Cooke didn't kill himself," Schuyler went on. "Okay, that doesn't mean that Jameson or his wife killed him, but somebody other than himself certainly might have, and at least that's a reason why the FBI ought to look into it. If anybody asks, it's plausible to say that the wife—Bina?—came to us and asked if we could take another look. And that keeps you, Inspector, under Jameson's radar, or we can hope it does."

"Great," she said. "No, seriously. Great."

32

The next day, for lunch, Ron Jameson decided to take a little risk.

Sick and tired of hanging out in his office, and without even a small inclination to go to any of his previously scheduled meetings, he felt he needed to get outside before he went completely batshit.

The risk lay in his decision to go to Sam's, a longtime favorite of his and Kate's.

He thought that she was working at her soup kitchen as usual on Wednesdays, but he was not entirely certain. It mattered because this was going to be his first real date with Andrea. He had requested a two-person booth that closed for privacy. When they got seated, he'd order a cocktail for both of them and then they could share a bottle of fine wine. And see where the afternoon led them.

With all the stress he was under, nobody could blame him.

He just didn't want the hassle of explaining to Kate if she did decide to go there for lunch that day, but the odds of that, he knew, were slim. If it came to having to explain, he could always just tell his wife that he needed to get out of the claustrophobic office and he'd invited Andrea along to coordinate his schedule and organize their respective workloads. It would all be vague enough to be true and she might not completely believe it, but it would play.

He had always, after all, been faithful to her up until now. She was the one who'd had the dalliance with fucking Peter Ash that had changed everything. He felt that if he went ahead and allowed himself to have a little extracurricular fun, she should shower him with the same understanding and forgiveness that he'd given her when he'd realized what she'd done back then.

In fact, if anything, truth be told, she owed him. Even if he got physically involved with Andrea . . .

But they weren't quite at that point. Not yet, anyway. There was ultimately deniability there because nothing overt had happened. They were just two working colleagues having a platonic date for lunch.

But the possibilities and the risk added a certain piquancy to the whole feel of the day. And what the hell, he told himself. Kate ought to cut him some slack. He'd earned a little quality time.

ANDREA WAS VALUABLE as a secretary because she had a keen eye for detail. In his office, after they'd finished going over his calendar for the next week or so, he proffered the invitation and she told him that she would love to go out and have a nice restaurant lunch with him. It would be a nice way to break up the day, and she was at his service, but . . .

"I think we'd be wise if we didn't drive down there together, Ron." This was the first time she'd called him by his first name. "People see us both get out of the same car and you never know where that's going to lead. You are a pretty recognizable face, you know. As you should be. But we need to be hyperaware of appearances, don't you think? You don't want to get tongues wagging."

"But why should they? We work together. If anybody asks, we just say we're talking about our work over a nice meal. People have business lunches all the time. There's nothing remotely salacious about it."

The smile she gave him carried a multitude of messages, all of which he found exciting. This discussion really was a private game they were playing. She knew exactly what he was talking about and was telling him that they should not kid themselves: this was a date. The cover story was a working lunch. But she knew that they were not in fact taking any work with them. This was an escalation in their relationship, and she gave him every indication that she was in on the game and on board with it.

"I just think it would be smart to be careful," she said.

Speaking of details, when he got to Sam's, he should remember to mention that he'd like a different booth from his usual, which had a small brass plaque inscribed *Ron & Kate, First Fridays*. That would certainly dampen the mood with Andrea.

And so he found himself alone in the alternative booth he'd reserved, waiting for his secretary. He was drinking an experimental martini with Hendrick's gin and a few drops of St-Germain, an elderflower liqueur in place of vermouth, which he found surprisingly delicious.

He'd told Stefano to be on the lookout for Andrea and to deliver her right back to the booth when she arrived. He couldn't miss her: she'd be the prettiest woman who came in the door, period.

Meanwhile, would Stefano please pull the curtain closed and let him enjoy his drink in peace?

CHET GREENE KNEW that he was being a pest, but couldn't help himself.

He didn't have any driving duties with the DA today, so first thing in the morning he'd showed up at the main evidence locker down by the police lab at Hunters Point. The workers there didn't seem to have the same sense of urgency that he felt, and it had taken him the better part of an hour to get his hands on the physical files relating to the Dockside Massacre, then another hour or so to personally connect with the DNA expert, Philip Nguyen, who explained to him that, unlike the fingerprint situation, in those days they didn't have a computerized DNA database, so they couldn't match DNA unless they had a comparison sample from somebody they wanted to check. Which Chet didn't have.

And even if he had a sample of, for example, Dismas Hardy's or Abe Glitsky's DNA to check against the blood sample, Nguyen could not possibly get around to his requested analysis for at least a couple of days.

And never if he didn't get some of Hardy's or Glitsky's DNA for comparison.

This was, after all, a pretty darned old case for there to be any real hurry. If Chet could bring him some samples, he'd get to it when he got a little time.

The fingerprint expert, whose name tag read *Pat Daly*, was marginally more cooperative, although she, too, was less than wholeheartedly enthusiastic.

It didn't really help matters that, after the initial round of fingerprint analysis back when the case was new, the casings—all 137 of them!—with either no traces at all or unidentified fingerprints, had been unceremoniously dumped back into a gallon-sized Ziploc bag. (The fingerprints that had originally yielded identifiable prints had their own bag.) The cards with the actual lifts from the various casings were all in file folders.

Pat Daly explained that this meant she would have to go through these one by one. Chet shouldn't feel like he had to wait around for the results. She could call him when she (eventually) got through them, if she had any results to share with him.

But this didn't fit in with how Chet was feeling. He was down here now, they had the casings, he'd wait here for something to shake out. After two more visits back to the front window to check on how things were coming along, Pat Daly finally let him come back to her workstation, with its computer with its database and her microscope.

She wasn't doing it in the most efficient way. First, she was separating the cards into two piles: the lifts that she thought could be entered into the computer, and the partials that she decided would have to be checked by hand, assuming there was someone to check them against. But she was including the previously identified latents. Chet gently pointed out that this was an extra and unnecessary step, since he was only interested in the others, the unknown prints or partials.

With a sigh of almost biblical proportions, Daly acknowledged that he was right.

It was slow going. Sometimes five to seven minutes per lift card.

Chet was pretty sure that if he tried to rush her it would only succeed in slowing things down.

ALTHOUGH HE HAD a full load of legal work on his desk, Hardy decided on more or less the spur of the moment that he was going to take the afternoon off. He was, after all, the managing partner of a successful law firm, and if he couldn't take a couple of hours to play hooky, what was the point?

Glitsky, being retired, had every afternoon off if he wanted to take it, and Hardy's suggestion that they take the thirty-minute ferry ride over to Sausalito struck a chord.

Now the two of them stood on the stern deck looking back over the wake as it churned up the bay behind them. They were just passing Alcatraz, basking in its own tiny ray of sunshine.

"This was a good idea," Glitsky said. "I ought to get out here on the water more often."

"Everybody ought to do that. In fact, they should make it a law. Mellow everybody out."

"A law that forces everybody to mellow out?"

"No. They'd mellow out by themselves once they started cruising around on the bay. You'd only need the law if people didn't want to do it on their own."

"Then you make it against the law not to cruise around on the bay?"

"That's the idea, but it wouldn't have to be every day. A few days a week ought to do it."

"To cruise or not to cruise?"

"Cruise."

"To keep everybody mellow?"

"Exactly."

"What if everybody didn't want to be mellow? What if people wanted to be intense and uptight and cut you off in traffic and work hard on stuff?"

"I'd feel sorry for them, but maybe they could get a special exemption. Except the people who cut you off. They should be locked up and possibly executed."

"That's a little harsh, wouldn't you say?"

"People would get used to it."

"Getting executed?"

"No, having to ride on the ferry. It'd be good for almost everybody."

"It's the 'almost' I'm worried about. What about if you get legitimately seasick?"

"On a little ferry ride like this?"

"Could happen."

"Rarely if ever, and if it did, we could write up an exception for those poor souls."

"Another law."

Hardy shrugged. "Looks like. But without them, you must admit, it's chaos."

"How about this?" Glitsky cast him a sidelong look. "Everything doesn't have to be a law. Did you ever think about that as a possibility?"

"Not too often. I can't imagine why I would. I'm a lawyer, in case you haven't been paying attention. The law is my life. Laws are good."

"Well, good laws are good, I'll give you that. Bad laws, not so much. Why are we talking about the law again, by the way? Remind me."

"It's such a good time?"

"Nope," Glitsky said. "I'm pretty sure that's not it."

THEY HAD MOST of an hour to kill before the return trip on the ferry, and now they walked along the Sausalito waterfront. Although the fog still lay like a thick blanket out on the bay where it was blowing in under the Golden Gate, the sun had followed them directly over from Alcatraz and now within this minuscule microclimate it was downright balmy.

"I don't know if asking Schuyler down was a mistake," Glitsky was saying. "He's a good guy and I thought it might be worth a try. I just knew that Tully going out and shaking the bushes on her own would be a problem."

"Not to sound negative, since that's mostly your job, but she's going to have a problem anyway, Abe. She wants to take Jameson down, and I don't blame her. Hell, I want to help her, which is why I agreed to meet with her last night. And you two as well, I might add, though I did feel a bit ambushed."

"Well, sorry about that, but if there's something to find on these murders—evidence-wise—I've got to believe the FBI has a better shot of coming up with it than one semi-compromised homicide inspector, and by that I mean Tully. But a better shot doesn't necessarily mean a good shot. Especially after three years."

"That's a lot longer than four days," Hardy said. He was referring to the truism among law enforcement that after four days, if a homicide wasn't solved, it probably never would be.

Glitsky stopped and looked over the water. "I wonder if we could be more proactive."

"I think we're already in that category. Wouldn't you?"

"Well, you've got your legal stuff, which is a step or two in the right direction, especially if you get a good ruling. But I'm thinking more if I got involved."

"How would you do that?"

"Well, I'm nothing, right? I have no official standing to interview anybody. And nobody can fire me. So what's to stop me from going out and talking, for example, to Kate Jameson . . ."

"Under what pretext?"

"No pretext. Straightforward. 'Here are some discrepancies in your story—oh, and by the way, your husband's story—that I'd like to ask you about.'"

"And why would you do that? She'd slam the door in your face."

"Well, it would take the heat off Beth, for one thing. Maybe let Kate think I'm working for you and somehow my interest is related to how her husband treated Phyllis or how he's going to handle her trial, if it comes to that. If he could back off on those charges, we could stop asking these pesky little questions about the murders they've committed. However she reacts to those kinds of threats—or how *he* reacts, for that matter—could be pretty instructive. Even if she refuses to talk, that could be instructive."

"If he backs off on Phyllis, then he's guilty?"

"Something like that." Glitsky raised and lowered his shoulders. "Just thinking out loud, but this guy needs to be in prison, not the DA's office.

And while we're at it, don't think for a minute that he's not keeping a keen eye out for rumors about you and me, too."

"I don't know about—"

Glitsky held up a hand. "I'm just saying it might be time to get on the offensive around this guy and keep him scrambling if we can."

33

Bina Cooke woke up from her afternoon nap with a migraine. She'd been suffering from them with some regularity ever since she got the word that her husband had killed himself. That was a little over three years ago and nothing she did seemed to make any difference.

This situation, she had come to believe, had come from an inability to obtain what they called closure. Even after all this time, it was inconceivable to her that her beloved Geoff had taken his own life, and no amount of grief counseling—and she'd had plenty—or therapeutic hikes with girlfriends or hysterical breakdowns had in any way made the stark truth of his death any more manageable.

He was gone forever.

Closure remained elusive because no matter what anybody said, Bina believed with all of her heart that Geoff had not committed suicide. Someone had killed him. In the immediate aftermath of the shooting, the San Francisco police, and particularly Inspector Beth Tully, had first bought into the idea that Geoff had killed himself, which Bina had rejected out of hand for several reasons, not the least of which were the purported suicide note—an email, for God's sake, in which he called her Bina instead of his usual Bean—and the question of whether he would have held the gun in his right hand. Impossible, she thought.

But perhaps most conclusively, he could not have shot himself with either of the Tariq semiautomatic pistols he'd brought home from Desert Storm. Those guns—both of them—remained in their safe here in the house.

They were there, locked up, even now. Therefore, he had not used one of them to kill himself.

Bina knew as an absolute certainty that Geoff had brought home two and only two of these souvenirs. They'd had at least a dozen discussions about them, about whether he should keep them, whether he should surrender them to the city's gun abatement program, whether they were anything he wanted to be reminded of.

But the main point was that he'd only brought home two of them.

The other person who'd done the same thing—brought home two of these esoteric foreign-made handguns—was their ex-friend and Geoff's former law partner Ron Jameson, now the district attorney of San Francisco.

Two guns.

Now one of Ron's guns was presumably where he'd tossed it after killing Peter Ash, at the bottom of the bay, and the other—the one found in Geoff's car after it had killed him—was in the evidence lockup as the suicide weapon.

So, Bina had reasoned at the time, Ron had to have been Geoff's killer. He'd killed both Peter Ash and her husband using one of these Tariq weapons for each. It was the only scenario that made any sense. The only one that took any account of the guns.

But then Beth Tully had discovered that Ron had a perfect alibi for the time of the murder. No fewer than six of his colleagues had testified that he had been continuously in their presence in the conference room of his law firm.

Ron could not have done it. But could he have had it done? And if so, by whom? Who could he trust enough?

That reality—so unbelievable and yet apparently true—had so taken the wind out of Bina's sails that she had essentially shut down her critical faculties about who had been the murderer. She didn't really care anymore who had done it.

What mattered was that Geoff was dead. If Ron hadn't killed him, then it must have been one of any number of his colleagues for a million possible reasons, and then the search for Geoff's murderer—Tully's job—would be exhausting and possibly futile police business. The search might, in fact, never end. For anyone involved, closure might never come.

And that is what seemed to have played out.

Until yesterday.

Until last night, when she'd met up with a clearly fearful Beth Tully at Gaspare's. And Beth had calmly laid out her solution, the only possible solution, to the mystery.

Kate.

In some ways, she was always the most obvious choice, except that from Bina's perspective, and probably Tully's as well, that had been flatly impossible. Neither of them had to even think about it to conclude that they had to eliminate Kate as a possible suspect. Kate, after all, was their friend. She was a good person, a doting mother, a gentle soul, absolutely incapable of violence, especially the murder of someone she'd cared about.

And yet Tully now had no doubt. She had had no doubt for a long time.

Kate.

Bina opened her eyes in the dark room.

The migraine had suddenly passed.

Gingerly, she swung her legs out of the bed and turned to sit up. Standing, she crossed over to the drapes and pulled them open and found herself looking down over the cottony top of the bank of fog that was still pushing its way inland. Above it, her house still basked in the late-afternoon sunshine.

Fingers at her temples, she blinked at the brightness, but she experienced no aura at the periphery of her vision, no strobe-like beams delivering bursts of pain. Suddenly, she realized, all was clarity.

Kate, she thought. Of course. Kate.

Still a bit nervous that the headache would return, she waited another minute or two to make sure she had regained her equilibrium, then left her bedroom and went downstairs and into the library, where she turned on the lights. Her safe was hidden behind a wall of books that slid out and turned when she pressed the secret button under the large mahogany desk.

She didn't remember the last time she'd opened the safe, but she'd memorized the combination and in under thirty seconds she was reaching in to pull out the first of the two Tariqs. Both were wrapped in blue velvet Crown Royal bags. Placing each one of them on the blotter that covered most of the desktop, she removed them from their bags and picked them up, checking them out one by one. Neither held a clip. The clips turned out to be stored in the back of the safe. Bina reached in and took them out, one for each gun, no extras, checking to make sure that they were fully loaded.

Wondering which weapon, if either, was in better shape than the other, she hefted them one by one, pulled the triggers, checked the actions. She wasn't particularly sure what she was looking for; her goal was to make sure that, when needed, the weapon would fire. They certainly had not been fired in several years.

She should probably take them to a shooting range, get them cleaned and test-fired.

Sitting down at the rolling leather-upholstered chair behind the desk, she held one gun in each hand, trying to decide which one she should use to avenge her husband's death by killing Kate Jameson.

CHET GREENE THOUGHT it might have been the longest day of his life.

It turned out that fingerprint specialist Pat Daly had all the personality of a hermit crab: she would only come out of her shell for the split second when they'd pull up a match on her computer, which happened 39 times out of the 137 lifted prints they were checking. The rest of the time she methodically sorted the other lift cards according to some arcane system of loops and swirls and bifurcations that he didn't understand.

Infuriatingly, Chet also came to realize that this was the second pass for the kind of identification they were trying to make. Last time, ten or so years ago, someone had gone through much the same process with all of the lifts and saved the matches, which included recognizable fingerprints for Homicide lieutenant Barry Gerson, Hardy's client John Holiday, and the rent-a-cops.

And then, all of a sudden . . .

Daly and Chet suddenly realized at the same moment that a bunch of the lift cards were different from the others. Same case number but no description of where the lift was supposed to have come from, and no technician's signature.

Chet sat back in his chair. "What the hell?"

"Probably just a technical error," Daly said. "The technician was in a hurry and didn't fill out the card completely. But they've all got the right case number and they're all in the same file. They have to be from this case."

"Pull these out," Greene said. "Forget about the others. Concentrate on these."

So by a little before 5:00 they were getting to the very last one of the thirty-nine lifts. This one, like all the others, turned out to be a match for a name—Jon Nathanson—that rang no bells with Chet at all. Who the hell was Jon Nathanson (four lifts)? Who, for that matter, was Debi Sullivan (three lifts)? Or Jorge Orosco, Stevie Sheppard, Tong Li (five, six, and one, respectively)? Could they have been involved in the Dockside Massacre? It seemed unlikely if not impossible. But if not, what were their fingerprints doing on these casings found at the scene? Or were these lifts from those casings at all?

He couldn't help but notice there were no Russian names, either.

Chet had a list of a dozen names now that were matched in the new database, and none of them were Hardy or Glitsky or anybody else they were with.

Beyond that, they had nine more unmatched lifts, regardless of the new and supposedly universal database.

"So I'm back at the front window at the lab, signing this huge bank box full of evidence back into the lockers. Have I mentioned that we got not even one familiar name with all the new hits?"

Sheila Marrenas nodded. "Once or twice."

"Unreal. But true. Anyway, of course there's a log-in/log-out page for all the files down there, but when I came in this morning I just scribbled my name, signing it out like everybody else because I was in a hurry, which is an unknown concept down at the lab."

"Okay."

"Okay, so on the way out, the day was shot anyway, and I'm just shooting the shit with the clerk there, wondering what could have gone on with these fingerprint lifts, so I ask the guy if he's got a record of other times people have checked out this pile of evidence. For any reason. Turns out there is, and it's on the computer by case number. So I ask if he'd mind taking a look, which of course he does, otherwise they wouldn't have hired him. Anyway, at last he comes around and punches up the number. And guess what?"

"I'm guessing a familiar name at last."

"Abe Glitsky. Seven years ago, when he was head of Homicide."

Marrenas squinted across her desk at him. "He signed out the massacre file?"

"Yep."

"What for?"

"It doesn't say. Just that he took it out."

"Out of the building?"

"No way to tell. He signed and took it out at the front desk one day, and two days later he brought it back and signed it in."

"Was there some kind of new and ongoing investigation at that time? Did they reopen the case for some reason?"

"Not that I know of. There was nothing I saw in the file. And this time I really looked."

"I believe you. What'd you find?"

"You want my opinion, Glitsky reopened the case himself; after all, he's head of Homicide, he can make that call. He's waited three years since the massacre went down. Nobody's even sniffing around it anymore.

"And remember, this is about when they were changing over to the new, bigger database, so Glitsky got wind of that and decided he needed to get rid of the casings without a database match. And then he substituted the same number of random casings from his local shooting gallery—a hundred and thirty-seven if you're counting. But even so, it wouldn't have been that hard to do. Oh, and he also threw away the hard-copy prints that they'd lifted but couldn't match. His, I'm thinking. And Hardy's. And maybe some others of their friends."

"Jesus."

"That's what I say."

"So what are you going to do?"

"I don't know what I *can* do. He's played this pretty smart. Even if I can get the DA to make a stink about it, Glitsky had every right to take files out of the evidence lockers, especially on dead cold cases like the massacre. Nobody was looking and he picked his time just right."

Marrenas leaned back in her chair and put her feet up on her desk. "That's what's been so damn frustrating about this whole case, Chet, right from the beginning. You think you're on the verge of finding some real evidence about who was down at that pier and what they all did, and then it all somehow goes away."

DUSK WAS STARTING to settle. Kate sat at Peet's, nursing her latte.

Things had gotten far worse on the home front since the last time Kate had talked to Patty Simmons after their soup kitchen volunteering last week. Of course, who could have seen or predicted all of the fallout from that awful "CityTalk" column, which seemed to have changed not only the public's perception of Ron overnight but also his own state of mind? It wasn't like him to be defensive, but he was snapping at everything and everybody. People didn't understand him. People should support him. People should understand the stress he was under.

The fight he'd had with Aidan was a good example. True, the boy hadn't given his father much of the benefit of the doubt about his motivations and decisions, but Ron's reaction, or overreaction, had simply been over-the-top. He didn't really want to make their children feel afraid of him and unwelcome in their own home. He didn't want to urge them to leave and stay away if they didn't agree with him. That was just ridiculous.

And when she'd more or less sided with the kids on that one, he'd exploded at her! Whose side was she on, anyway?

How dare he ask her that? She, who was his protector in all things. How could he even think it, what with everything she did for him every day? To say nothing of literally saving him from prison by her own bold move, just when it had to be done.

But this was the other thing that she didn't like to acknowledge: every time she thought about him getting angry at her, or taking her for granted, or yelling at her in front of the kids, her own reaction seemed to be getting worse and worse. Less and less tolerant and patient. That was not who she wanted to be, either.

But it seemed that now they were in some kind of downward spiral together. They were mostly polite to one another, yes, but she could feel the distance growing between them.

She couldn't let that happen. Not after everything they'd been through together, the secrets they held. They needed each other. Nothing would convince her she was mistaken on that score. They had to be a team.

But Ron had to do his part, to be integral to it. After all she'd sacrificed for him, she wouldn't tolerate him cutting her out of his life, and any hint of that brought her closer to a rage that she didn't feel she could control. She had, in fact, killed to save him. He had to know that she would kill again to protect him if the need arose, but he had to acknowledge her. He had to love her.

"Someone's deep in thought," Patty said.

Startled out of her reverie, Kate flashed a quick smile. "Not really. Just . . ." Her smile spread across her face. "Just deep in thought, actually."

"Would you mind if I join you?"

"Not at all. I was half hoping you'd stop by."

"Does that leave the other half hoping I wouldn't?"

"You're such a goof. Of course not. Sit down."

Patty pulled out her chair, put her coffee on the table, and sat with her own bright smile. "So, as the bartender said to the horse, 'Why the long face?' "

Kate shook her head. "Just a little worried about Ron, I'm afraid."

"Well, I noticed that they've been treating him a little rough in the news these past few days. But it'll probably pass. These things usually do."

"I know." She sipped at her coffee. "It's not the public stuff so much. He'll probably ride it out, as you say. But do you remember last week when I was talking about all the time he's not spending with his wife? That would be me, the wife, by the way. With all these problems he's got to deal with . . . I'm sorry. I know I'm whining."

"But you're saying he's spending too much time at work?"

A short, brittle laugh. "All the time is more like it."

"That's hard."

"I guess I just don't understand why he doesn't want to come home and be with me at a reasonable hour. I'm a great cook. I'm always ready to make dinner, or we could go out anywhere. All of those meetings can't be that important. The two of us are the solid, good part of our lives, and I'm afraid he might be losing track of that. Plus, of course, the new job and all that stress. But still . . . as you say, it's a little hard."

Patty drank from her own cup. "Do you have a night out together planned in the near future?"

Kate grimaced. "Maybe Easter, if he can make it."

"Really. That bad?"

"Probably not. I'm exaggerating. But not by much."

"Well, if he can't plan in advance, maybe you should just go by and surprise him."

"What? Do you mean at work?"

"If that's where he is."

"Well," she said with a chuckle, "that's a good bet."

"So?"

She shook her head. "I don't know. I don't want him to feel like I'm checking up on him or anything like that."

"You wouldn't be doing that. What's to check up on? He's in his office working, right?"

"Or out giving a talk someplace."

"From which he returns to his office?"

"Probably. Usually."

"You could call his secretary and find out."

Kate looked at her watch. "She's probably gone home by now. I gather that the staff at the Hall of Justice is pretty much nine-to-five."

Patty said, "It's your call. That was just a suggestion to shake things up a little, if you think it might help, as a kind of wake-up call. Let him know that you're serious about needing more of his time."

"It's really not a bad idea. I just don't know. I don't want to be the pushy wife, either."

"Well, nobody's going to think you're that. And there's no hurry. It certainly doesn't have to be today. It was just a thought."

"And worth considering," Kate said, then let out a heavy sigh. "I don't know why he has to make us go through this."

"Hey, he's a guy," Patty said with sympathy. "Odds are he doesn't even know he's doing anything. He might just need a good kick in the pants."

34

Beth and Ike spent the better part of Thursday morning and now the early afternoon at the Holly Park projects, one of the most godforsaken areas in the city. Everything about the place screamed poverty and neglect: the walls were riots of graffiti; the original grassy lawns had long since given way to plain packed dirt which served as the resting place of hundreds if not thousands of syringes; garbage of all kinds dotted the entire landscape and blew around in the gusting wind.

They were there because they'd been next up in the rotating game that all the homicide inspectors had instituted in the wake of Devin Juhle's dismissal. Chief Lapeer had not yet appointed anyone to take his place, and so assignments on new homicides fell to whoever was next up.

The latest victim was a twenty-one-year-old mother of two named Aretha Hood, who had been shot, presumably by her boyfriend, JaMason Lewis, in a dispute that Aretha's sister, Rayanne, characterized as over a candy bar—an Almond Joy, to be exact. Rayanne was the only witness in the case, as she'd been at her sister and JaMason's place getting ready to babysit while the young couple went out somewhere, when the argument had begun. JaMason had now fled.

Beth and Ike stood outside waiting for the arrival of the Crime Scene team and the coroner's van. As usual when responding to calls in neighborhoods like this, response time didn't seem to be much of an issue. It seemed there had been another homicide in a part of town with a better tax base that had assumed priority. It had already been four hours since they'd called in the request for the van. They knew that it could arrive any hour now.

And then, suddenly, *mirabile dictu*, an unmarked car with its bubble lit up came into view at a far-off corner, and two minutes later they were saying hello to Leonard Faro, head of Crime Scene Investigations. Faro was dressed as usual to the nines, in a dark olive Italian suit, thousand-dollar shoes, and a cashmere overcoat, soon to be covered for entry into the crime scene by a jumpsuit and booties. His soul patch hung like a well-trained bug of some kind under his lower lip, and he exuded enthusiasm and competence.

But as soon as he'd gotten the lay of the land from Beth and Ike, a wave of frustration seemed to flow over him. "So where are my peeps?" he asked them. "I headed out here a half hour ago and I thought they were way ahead of me."

"Not yet, Len," Ike said. "Nobody here yet but the station guys holding the fort, and us."

"Darn. And I even gave them extra time, I thought."

"This place is a tough draw."

"Tell me about it." He started to walk back toward the flat with the police tape over the door but suddenly stopped, stood still a second, then turned back to them. "Might as well wait for the team," he said. "Who's the stiff again?"

"Young woman, African American mother of two, kids with the sister next door."

"Almond Joy addict, apparently," Beth said, straight-faced.

Faro nodded soberly. "Stuff's worse than Oxy. This is my tenth case this year."

"Really?" Ike asked.

"No, not really, dipshit." Faro shook his head in disbelief. "You ought to get out more, Ike. Really." Shifting gears, he looked around as if sweeping the place for witnesses. "But hey," he said. "I'm glad to see you two guys out here working in the field. I thought after the 'CityTalk' thing, you might have been going the way of Devin—which, your ears only, sucked."

"There's still plenty of time," Beth said.

"For the moment," Ike added, "we're flying low, hoping nobody sees us."

"Probably a good idea. Although I don't see how our esteemed DA can be down on you working a case that's supposedly closed when he's got his own inspector doing essentially the same thing, and on a much older case."

"Who's that?" Ike asked.

"Chet Greene."

Beth cast her partner a look, then asked Faro, "What's he looking at?"

"You remember the dockside case?"

"Sure," Beth said, "back in my childhood."

"Well, childhood or no, it's a murder case, so it's never going away."

"And what?" Ike asked. "Jameson thinks he's going to get it solved and resurrect his good name, such as it is?"

"Something like that. Although I think it's got a more personal edge."

Nerves kicking in, Beth shifted her weight from one foot to the other. "How's that?"

"Well," Faro said, "it's funny, because this comes back around, a little bit anyway, to you guys. The Valdez case and then the 'CityTalk' column?"

"Connected to the dockside thing?"

"Yeah."

Beth nearly jumped at him. "In what possible way could that be?"

Faro nodded, acknowledging her intensity. "I know. Cool, right? It turns out—according to Chet—that Jameson believes that the guy who leaked all the details of Valdez to Jeff Elliott for the 'CityTalk' column was a lawyer in town named Dismas Hardy."

"And he's somehow tied to the Dockside Massacre?"

"Yep. Tangentially. One of the victims, apparently, a guy named John Holiday, was one of his clients."

"And Hardy was there? At the pier for the shoot-out?"

"Nobody knows, but if Jameson could prove he was, Hardy's in big trouble."

"So that's what Greene is looking for, new evidence of some kind against this guy Hardy? After all this time?"

"Exactly. And just between you, me, and the lamppost, he might get it. At least, he's looking where no man has gone before." He looked from one inspector to the other, his eyes flashing with excitement. "But there's more, children, there's more!"

"Hit us," Ike said.

"All right. Hardy also filed a recusal motion and civil suit against Jameson for mistreating one of his clients, the sister of Adam McGowan."

"Phyllis," Beth said.

"You know her?"

"We arrested Adam," Ike said. "We ran across her."

"So that's another strike against Hardy. He's trying to get Jameson disbarred, maybe impeached. It's plenty ugly out there for both of them. And if he gets Hardy for the Dockside thing, the shit is really going to fly, because there is even more."

"Please don't make us beg," Beth said.

"All right. Because you've been paying such close attention, guess who Hardy is rumored to be hanging with in all of this?"

"Hunter Pence," Ike said.

"Good guess, but wrong," Faro said. "Anybody else? Anybody?" At their continued silence, he finally gave it up. "Abe Glitsky. Former deputy chief of detectives. Former head of Homicide."

Beth was the first to respond. "That's a hell of a rumor, Len."

"I agree. And let me hasten to add that it is still only a rumor. All parts of it. But if Chet finds evidence also putting Glitsky out on the pier, now we're talking all-out war. It's the kind of thing people could get themselves literally killed over."

Breathless, Beth could barely talk. "Lord."

"Lord." Faro nodded. "Yes, ma'am. Have mercy."

THE CRIME SCENE unit still hadn't arrived, so Ike went off to pick up some hamburgers for lunch. Faro invited Beth to wait in his car with him, out of the wind.

Beth wasted no time after she got in. "While I've got you here, Len, I wonder if I could bend your ear for a few minutes, where you can stop me anytime you want."

"Are you asking my permission?"

"Not really. I figure I've got you trapped. If you're not sick of the topic, I want to talk about the Peter Ash case. Which is also the Geoff Cooke case."

Faro shifted uncomfortably. "All I do—all the team does—is collect and analyze evidence, Beth. You know that."

"Fine. But I'm guessing you remember the main suspect in Ash before the Cooke suicide changed everything."

He blew out a short breath. "Jameson. Of course I remember."

"He did it. He killed Ash because Ash had slept with his wife, Kate."

"All right."

"You don't believe that?"

He shrugged. "It's, as they say, a colorable argument. Give me some evidence to prove it, though, and I'll be happier. Do you have any evidence at all to keep this thing alive in your head? Anything, I mean, that trumps the wealth of actual, physical evidence we got on Cooke? When you do, I'll be happy to listen anytime, anyplace. But forgetting Ron for a minute: we've got Ash's blood running in the gunwales of Cooke's boat; we've got casings from the same gun that killed Cooke on the boat as well; we've got a suicide note admitting that he killed Ash . . ."

"That was—"

Faro held up a hand. "Could have been better, yes. But a man who is about to put a bullet in his head may not act like he would otherwise. What else?"

"Two of those Tariq guns still in Cooke's safe, untouched."

Faro rolled his eyes. "So he had a third gun and didn't tell anybody."

She slammed her fist up against the dashboard. "No, he didn't! He didn't have a third gun. The third gun was Ron's. Goddamn it, Len. Can't you see this? This is wrong. The whole interpretation is wrong, and now this killer is the DA of San Francisco and we're all going to be riding on his back into hell."

"That might be, Beth. It might be. Find me anything and I promise you I'll jump on it with both feet, but in the meantime I'd stick with your partner's idea: Keep a low profile, don't make waves. Especially if what you believe turns out to be the truth. You think Jameson's just going to lie still and let you expose him?" He paused and nodded in understanding but clearly felt there was nothing he could do without his stock-in-trade, which was evidence. "I'd let it go, Beth," he said gently. "I really would let it go."

BINA FELT DOWNRIGHT silly with the red wig on. The other stuff wasn't so bad: the khaki hiking pants and matching shirt from REI, the hiking boots that were such a long way from her usually modest heels. No makeup at all. She had taken out her contacts and wore her glasses.

Invisible, she thought, and at the very least unrecognizable as who she was, in plain sight.

She carried the guns and the magazines in Geoff's old briefcase. When she got to the firing range just off Highway 101, she found parking there to be easy and took a spot just to the right of the entrance.

Inside, she filled out the form to get on the range and handed her driver's license to the clerk, who, as she had hoped, didn't check it against the information she had written on the form, but merely put it behind the counter to be returned when she paid her bill and left. She had a moment of panic when the clerk showed so much interest in the magazines because he seemed to be able to tell that the guns hadn't been fired in a long while. He should really check them out, maybe clean them a bit, before letting her go back into the shooting area.

But it was nothing: just a friendly guy.

She told him that her husband had recently died. He hadn't used the guns in several years, and now, with him gone, she thought it would be smart to be proficient with the weapons for her own protection. You couldn't really ever be too careful.

She never mentioned the guns' provenance in Desert Storm.

When she was ready, and because she'd told the clerk that she hadn't done any shooting at all for quite a while, he gave her a little list of things to remember: Wear the ear protection at all times; don't ever point the gun at anybody, even for an instant; don't forget to rack the first round into the chamber, because it wouldn't fire if you didn't;

watch out that you didn't get pinched by the recoil; use two hands when firing.

Cake. She'd done all that dozens of times.

This time, though, the whole experience had a surreal quality. Was she really here, doing this? Her migraine had not returned over the last two days.

Putting on her ear protection, she slammed the magazine into the butt of the gun and remembered to rack the first round.

Stepping up to her shooting lane, she held the gun with both hands extended at the target and pulled the trigger.

Bang!

Even with the headphones, the gunshot was louder than she remembered from when she used to go shooting with Geoff, and packed much more of a kick. She knew what they were talking about when they reminded her to watch out for getting pinched.

Bang! She breathed out in a rush, settling into the rhythm of the so-called double tap: two shots in quick succession, recommended in all the reference books as the preferred method of firing if you wanted to make sure that your target would be well and truly dead.

Bang! Bang!

Bang! Bang!

35

At 5:45, Hardy sat behind the desk in his office talking to Beth Tully on the firm's landline. "You've got to be kidding me," he said. "Chet Greene did what? And how did you find out about it?"

"Len Faro came by a crime scene we were working today down at Holly Park, and we just got to chatting because of the coincidence of this apparent connection between the Valdez case and the Dockside Massacre ten years ago."

"And what is that, exactly?"

"Well, apparently, at least what Greene wants to get at, is you."

"Me? What about me? How can there be any connection to me?"

"Evidently you had a client who was killed there?"

"Sure. John Holiday."

"So it's true?"

"Absolutely. This has never been a secret. John apparently went down there to turn himself in to Barry Gerson on a murder rap he was facing. He did that on his own and against my advice, which you won't be surprised to hear happens all the time."

Beth was silent.

After a long moment Hardy said, "Did he supposedly find any evidence that I had been there? And the answer to that has to be no, since I wasn't. And don't get me wrong, I've heard rumors about this over the years, of course. But I had half a dozen people at the office who testified at the time that I'd been here working all that day. David Freeman, my partner, had just been killed, for God's sake. We were all shell-shocked, sitting around with our hearts broken. Why did I want to be down at that pier with a recalcitrant client? I had other things on my mind that day. I don't know how those rumors even got started, much less how they still have enough legs to spark another investigation. What did Greene think he was hoping to find?"

"According to Faro, something to tell Ron Jameson about, evidence-wise, to threaten your credibility, probably because of those motions you're waiting on."

"He's grasping at straws, Beth. He's not going to find anything because there's nothing to find."

Beth sighed into the phone. "Well, good. But I thought you should know that this was going on. I also wanted to tell you that it's not just you, either. Evidently, Abe is somehow in the mix as well."

Alone in his darkened office, Hardy closed his eyes against a rush of adrenaline. "Wow," he whispered into the mouthpiece. "And how, again, are they justifying all this?"

"I'm thinking that they hope they'll get their justification later if they find something while they're fishing. Then, after the fact, everybody agrees it was good that they looked, right?"

"But only if they find something, which they won't." Planting the seed just in case, he added: "Unless they plant something incriminating. But they're still left with all the witnesses who swear we were with them. I'm talking Abe, too. We've been through this drill before, you know. He was with my other partner, Gina, at David Freeman's apartment, picking out a suit for his funeral. Nobody's ever had anything that puts him anywhere else. Like down at the pier. And you know why? Because he wasn't there, either."

"That's good to know. But I thought all this was something you ought to know about. Jameson and Greene are seriously looking to get you and Abe compromised at least, maybe even arrested."

Hardy forced a chuckle. "Well, I'd say there's little to no chance of that."

"That's good to hear. But still, be careful."

"Always," Hardy said. "And you too."

"I will."

• • •

THURSDAY NIGHT, AND Treya was working late, still getting settled at her new workstation outside Wes Farrell's office. Both of the Glitsky children were at different friends' homes for dinner, so Abe was alone at home, half dozing on the living room couch, when the deep gong of the doorbell slapped him all the way awake. Getting to the door, he checked the peephole, saw a familiar face, and opened up.

Hardy wasted no time with pleasantries. "In these troubled times," he said with some asperity, "you might consider leaving your phone turned on."

"I have considered it. I concluded that I didn't want to. And I'm retired, as in not working anymore, so who's going to stop me? In fact, isn't that the whole point of being retired? You don't have to do stuff." He stepped back to let Hardy in. "And what is so troubled about these times, other than the usual?"

"You want the short version?"

"Sure. Should we sit down?"

"Might as well."

They did, Glitsky in his reading chair in the front room, and Hardy across the way on the sofa.

"So," Glitsky said, relaxing back into the chair. "I'm listening."

When Hardy finished several minutes later, Glitsky was sitting forward, elbows on his knees, hands clasped in front of him. The scar through his lips shone on his dark face. His brow was furrowed, his blue eyes nearly hidden under the deep scowl. "Is it never going to end?" he asked.

"Apparently not."

"Did Beth say where the good Inspector Greene was looking to find this purportedly new evidence on the pier?"

"No. But there's only one place he could have."

"Where's that?"

"Has to be casings or DNA," Hardy said. "Those are really the only possibilities. Weren't there a few hundred casings left out there?"

"At least."

"And they never came back to us on any of them."

"Right."

"I'm thinking Greene must have gotten the idea from that 'CityTalk' column. They got McGowan's fingerprints off the casings on his murder weapon. Maybe he came up with the idea that there might be prints they'd missed the first time around because they weren't in the old known-criminal database, if you remember that."

Glitsky's lips went up a centimeter, almost all the way to a smile. "Of course I remember. Although I wiped my ammunition when I loaded, so it wasn't an issue for me."

"Yeah, but I don't think I did. Or Gina, for that matter."

"I wouldn't worry about it," Glitsky said.

"But I do. If they take another pass at all the lifts from those casings, who knows what they'll come up with? Fingerprints, as you know, being oil-based, they don't go away."

"I'm vaguely aware of that. But that issue has been taken care of."

"I don't see how—"

Glitsky held up a hand. "Diz! Trust me here. Fingerprints aren't a problem anymore. I have it on the highest authority."

Hardy looked at his friend for a long moment. "You sneaky bastard," he said at last, with real admiration in his voice.

Glitsky inclined his head an inch in acknowledgment.

"So what about DNA?"

"Unless they know who they're trying to get a match with—like, for example, you or me—realistically, that's probably not happening."

"I got cut on the hand, you know. It bled pretty good."

"Honestly, I wouldn't worry about it. It's possible, of course, but I'm predicting they're not getting a swab from me or you. Right?"

"Okay, so what else could it be? Greene must think he's on some kind of hot trail."

"I don't know. Better men than him have tried to tie us in on this and had no luck. But I admit, it's worrisome. I don't see Jameson backing away from any of this just because of lack of results on his first round of looking."

"I don't, either. So . . . you know what you said yesterday about going on the offensive a little more with this guy? I think it may be time."

"It might be at that. What are you thinking?"

"I'm thinking about your friend Bill Schuyler. I think it might be the time for Jameson to understand that he himself is the target of an active FBI investigation into the murder of Peter Ash who, P.S., he actually did kill. Schuyler gets him to lie under oath about what he did with his guns—whether or not he can prove it's a lie yet—suddenly the heat goes way up under him. There's a real danger of him getting arrested at any time. At the very least, he's going to be distracted from trying to put us out at Pier 70."

Glitsky chewed at the side of his cheek. "Yeah, okay, but what about Beth Tully?"

"What about her?"

"Well, in a perfect world, we didn't want to expose her as the source of Schuyler's case, remember? That's why we had him going around and talking to other witnesses first so Jameson would think that they've been building a case against him for a while with no reference to Tully."

"Yeah, I remember all that."

"And?"

"She's a big girl, Abe. And the prime mover on Jameson. I say we call her and let her make the decision. If she's on board, Schuyler moves in close for the hit."

"ARE YOU KIDDING me?" Beth asked them both. She was on the speaker on Hardy's cell. "I'm the one who's been pushing this thing forward all along. You want to go after the son of a bitch now, you are totally welcome and you have my complete blessing."

"Okay," Glitsky said. "But we don't want to downplay this. It could be dangerous. As in physically dangerous."

"Hey, guys," she said. "This just in: I'm a cop. I work homicide. Everything I do is physically dangerous. Thanks for calling with the update, but I say let's rock and roll. I'll take care of myself. Got it?"

"We got it," Hardy said. "Thank you."

"No worries," she said. "Keep me informed."

She hung up and Glitsky said, "I love that woman."

Ron Jameson's intercom squawked at 9:36 and Andrea, her voice somewhat shaky, said, "There's an FBI Special Agent Bill Schuyler here to see you, sir."

"Does he have an appointment?"

"No. He says it's official business."

"Well, I've got some official business, too. I'm supposed to be where at ten thirty?"

"The Mission Rotary, sir. Inspector Greene is picking you up in a half hour."

"Yes, well, please tell Mr. FBI that you'd be happy to make an appointment for him, say Monday or Tuesday next week, and I'll be happy to talk to him then."

"I will."

"Good. Thank you."

Hitting the switch to end the connection, he swore in frustration at the interruption and pushed himself back away from his desk. Getting to his feet, he crossed over to the window looking down on Bryant Street, then suddenly turned in irritation as his intercom chirped again. Crossing the room and picking up, he said, "Andrea, what the hell?"

"He says it is personal and urgent, sir."

A moment later the man stood in the doorway. He was wearing a charcoal business suit. The bulge of a gun was just visible under his left arm. In his right hand he held out a badge. His expression was at once weary and angry. Andrea, in a formfitting red dress, hovered in the background behind Schuyler, trying to look around the intruder so that she could somehow wordlessly convey her apologies to her boss.

"Thank you for seeing me, sir," Schuyler said. "I'm here to ask you a few questions on an investigation we're conducting."

"What investigation? Into what?"

"Into the death—the murder, actually—of one of your acquaintances from a few years ago. Peter Ash."

Ron settled a glance on Schuyler, then flashed a look around him to where his secretary was still waiting nervously, patiently wringing her hands. "It's all right, Andrea," he said. "You can get the door. Mr. Schiller—"

"Schuyler."

"Mr. Schuyler and I ought to be done with whatever he wants to discuss shortly. Would that be accurate?"

A non-smile. "However long it takes."

"All right. Still"—he looked behind Schuyler—"Andrea, the door." She reached in and pulled the door closed behind them.

"What do you want?" Ron asked. "I barely knew Peter Ash. I've got a speech to give in less than an hour. And what the hell is the FBI doing, investigating an ancient homicide here in San Francisco? That case is long closed."

"Yes, it is." Schuyler reached into his coat pocket and took out a cell phone. "Recording," he said into it, giving the place and date, Ron's name, and the subject of his investigation, Peter Ash. He put the cell phone in his shirt pocket, sat down on the side of a wing chair, and started back in. "So you closely followed the original investigation into the murder of Peter Ash?"

Ron picked another chair and sat. "Of course I followed it," he said. "I'd met the man socially a couple of times. He seemed like a good guy and he was a fellow lawyer here in the city as well. A colleague. And then it turned out that one of my law partners killed him. So, yes, I'd say I had a little bit of a passing acquaintance with Peter Ash. And I don't have any idea how I can help you with your investigation."

Schuyler ignored the comment. "Your partner, I take it, who allegedly killed Mr. Ash, was Geoff Cooke?"

"That's right. Partner and good friend, I might add. But I don't know about the 'allegedly' part. There didn't seem to be any doubt about that at the time."

"You mean Geoff Cooke killing Peter Ash?"

"Yes."

"And you and Geoff Cooke had been friends a long time, isn't that right? In fact, you were in Desert Storm together, were you not?"

"Yes. Although what does Desert Storm have to do with the price of beans?"

"Well, while you were over there, you both picked up a certain gun as a souvenir."

"All right. So what? Why are we talking about the guns we took home? There was nothing illegal in it. Are you saying Geoff and I did something illegal?"

"No, sir, I'm not. I'm asking you about firearms that you and Mr. Cooke brought back to the United States. First Mr. Cooke. It is true, is it not, that to your knowledge he brought back two handguns?"

"Well, yes, as far as I know, but—"

"And you, sir, you also brought back two of the same sort of handgun. Could I ask you where your handguns are now?"

"Look, I'll be happy to cooperate with you. I've just got a speech to give"—he checked his watch—"in about twenty minutes now, and they'll hate me if I don't show up. So let's cut to the chase: How can I help you?"

"Thank you. I believe we were on the guns you brought back from the Middle East. A Tariq, I believe it's called. Is that right?"

"Yes."

"And how many of these did you bring home?"

"Two."

"And do you still have these guns in your possession?"

"No. Neither of them."

"What happened to them?"

"A few years ago, after one of the school shootings, we just decided to get rid of them. We didn't want them around."

"Was this before or after Peter Ash was killed?"

"I don't remember. If I had to guess, I'd say before."

"And how did you get rid of them?"

Ron appeared to be trying to remember. "We turned them in to the city. We have a gun abatement program, and I took the guns down and dropped them off just downstairs. Actually, it's coming back to me now. I think this was the summer before Ash was killed."

Schuyler took a moment, then asked, "So you turned in both of them?"

"Yes."

"And did they give you a receipt for these guns?"

"They might have. I don't remember. Probably."

"So you don't remember if you kept it? A receipt."

"No, I don't remember. I don't know why I would. It would just have been more paper clogging up my life. I mean, who'd care? I probably just tossed it. But I really don't remember."

Schuyler nodded with satisfaction. He was sure he'd gotten the felony lie he wanted from Ron Jameson. Proving it might present some challenges, but this was, he thought, a good start, and in any event would certainly put Jameson on notice that he was a true and valid target of this federal investigation. There would be no record of his guns having been turned in. Jameson might argue that a clerk had never signed them in or had stolen them, but this was not as easily accomplished as one might think.

Beyond that, the simple fact that he had lied at all meant that he was hiding something. This vastly increased the likelihood, in Schuyler's mind, that he was guilty of something, all the way up to and including murder.

And if they didn't have him yet, he thought, at least they were on their way.

AT A LITTLE after 2:00, Chet Greene dropped his boss back at the Hall after his Rotary gig, then pulled into his reserved space behind the building and checked his text messages. The first message he'd received from his fellow investigator Don Hancock, at around noon, had simply said: *Acquired.*

Which meant that after a three-hour wait, he was now moving, on foot, following Dismas Hardy from the time he left his Sutter Street office to wherever he was going for lunch. Chet had done his homework and knew that Hardy went out to lunch in one of the city's downtown restaurants almost every day, walking to and from his office. And today, thankfully, seemed to be no exception.

Ten minutes later another text came in: *Sam's.*

Not really the biggest surprise in the world, Chet thought.

The plan that he'd devised was to get a sample of Hardy's DNA so that he could deliver it to Philip Nguyen at the police lab for comparison to the unidentifiable blood samples from Pier 70. Since Hardy would undoubtedly be aware of Chet if he showed up anywhere near him, he'd had to recruit his younger colleague Hancock, who was relatively new to the office and hence probably unknown to Hardy, but who was pretty sure that he knew Dismas Hardy on sight. Hancock was only too happy to get involved in something that smacked of real investigative work that did not include a desk.

The last message, ten minutes ago, read: *Occidental Cigar Bar & Grill. Home run. Pick me up.*

The home run in question turned out to be the cigar that Hardy had indulged in after his lunch. Don Hancock had followed him from Sam's—where on his way out, he'd surreptitiously also pocketed Hardy's wineglass as he passed the table he'd eaten at—down Belden Alley to the Cigar Bar, and ordered his own Cohiba while Hardy smoked and chatted with a couple of guys with whom he seemed to be right at home.

A half hour later, Hardy left his well-chewed and finished cigar in the ashtray on the bar, and Don had let him go outside with his pals before he put his own cigar out, then casually walked down to the back of the bar where Hardy had been sitting.

The DNA-laden spent cigar disappeared from the ashtray into the Ziploc bag in Inspector Hancock's jacket pocket.

JaMason Lewis came back home to his crib on Friday morning and by the early afternoon, his common law sister-in-law, Rayanne, had convinced him to turn himself in to the police, and then she had called Tully.

It turned out that JaMason was terribly sorry that he'd killed Aretha, the mother of his children. The whole thing had been a mistake. He hadn't meant to shoot anybody. He was just trying to make a point, get the woman's attention, and also—not incidentally—get his half of the Almond Joy. They'd bought the king size anyway, both bars plenty big for one serving, and Aretha had been trying to lose weight, so really JaMason had just been trying to help her in that endeavor. Aretha had told him more than once to make her stop if she seemed to be thinking about eating more than one at a time.

And then the gun went off.

Not his fault, really. A total mistake.

The two cops—he didn't know: maybe they could somehow give him a pass on this one, since he so obviously didn't mean to do it. Did they really have to take him downtown? Beth explained to him that, as it turned out, they did.

"I mean," he had argued politely, "I mean, unless something really weird be going down, this shit ain't likely happening again. I just can't see it."

"Yeah, well . . ." Ike said, and snicked on the handcuffs. "Next time, just a thought: Maybe don't pick up the gun."

So Beth and Ike, though not exactly in raucous high spirits due to the inherent tragedy of the situation, were reliving the humor of it all at their front-to-front desks in the Homicide Detail when Ike looked up and his expression went from smile to serious in a half second as he rose and brandished a salute. Beth, following his lead standing up anyway, turned and nodded as Chief Lapeer approached, followed closely by Grayson Brill, deputy chief of detectives, and Lauren Weeks, whom Beth knew to be the lieutenant of HR.

This, she knew, was an execution squad.

In spite of herself, she couldn't suppress a half-swallowed chortle.

At the sound, Lapeer turned and fixed her with a deadly look. "Is something funny, Sergeant?" she asked.

"Probably not."

"That's the right answer. There's nothing funny going on around here at all. I suppose that after what happened to Lieutenant Juhle you both might not be surprised to see me."

"No, ma'am," Ike said. He looked helplessly at his partner.

Lapeer went on. "I thought that putting Lieutenant Juhle on administrative leave might send a bit of a stronger message to the troops down here, mostly including yourselves. But I see that it hasn't had that effect."

"He let us do our job," Beth said. "And that's all we've been doing now."

"Well, unfortunately, that's patently untrue. You both seem to be fixated on working outside the chain of command."

"Without Devin," Beth said, "there is no chain of command in here, Chief. We've been dividing up the work as it comes in."

Lapeer's nostrils flared. "I know what you've been doing. And it's the same kind of politically motivated shenanigans that led me to relieve Lieutenant Juhle."

"With respect, ma'am," Ike said, "that was not political. We don't have a political agenda down here. In that case, we simply identified a more viable suspect than the one who'd been indicted. And we made a case, I might add, which was charged by Mike Wendler, an experienced member of the district attorney's Homicide unit."

"And what about the Peter Ash case? A case, I might add, that's been closed and considered solved for over three years now."

"What about it?" Ike asked. "We're not working on that case."

"No? That's funny. Because I have it on unimpeachable authority that there is an active investigation going on in that case—an investigation, I might add, that could only have originated in this office and whose aim is, once again, to embarrass or humiliate Mr. Jameson. And if that's not political, I don't know what is."

"All right," Ike said, "but the plain fact is that we're not investigating that case."

Beth cleared her throat. "I'm sorry, Ike, but that's not quite accurate." She flashed him a "Forgive me" look and went on. "Okay, the other day I went and interviewed Bina Cooke, the wife of the man accused of killing Peter Ash."

"And why would you do that?" Lapeer asked.

"Because that was my case when it went down and I'm still convinced that we settled on the wrong guy. And I thought Bina might supply me with a few answers."

Ike suddenly appeared shaken to his roots. "Beth?"

"I know. I'm sorry."

"I'm afraid that sorry does not cut it under these circumstances. The net effect of this investigation is once again to embarrass the DA—"

"Excuse me, ma'am, but I don't want to embarrass the DA. I want to arrest him."

Lapeer skewered her with a look, then turned to Ike and the rest of her audience behind her. "That's about as clear as I could hope it would be. I rest my case."

Coming back around to her two inspectors, she said, "I'm asking for your shields and your guns right now, pending the administrative hearing when we get it scheduled. You are hereby relieved of your duties. I've got a couple of officers waiting outside who will escort you out of the building. Your behavior—especially yours, Inspector Tully—is an embarrassment to the department. Inspector McCaffrey, I'm sorry you seem to have gotten caught up in the middle of this, but the fact that you did reflects poorly on your character and judgment as well."

37

Ron Jameson sat comfortably back in the chair behind his desk, thinking: Okay, they fired the bitch. That was good, but it isn't going to be enough.

It had been over three years and he should have taken care of her long ago, when he'd originally wanted to.

Except that Kate had convinced him it wasn't necessary. The case was closed and Geoff Cooke, not Ron Jameson, was the killer.

End of story.

Nobody in the real world, Kate had told him, even gave the matter a second thought anymore.

And Ron had proven Kate correct by not only running for DA but winning. He was now, effectively, the establishment. If anything, Beth Tully's continuing shrill belief in his guilt could be spun as almost a kind of mental illness on her part. She was not a danger to Ron or to anyone else, and he shouldn't waste any time worrying about her.

But today, with the visit of Special Agent Schuyler, he realized that she was still a very active player and a legitimate threat. In fact, if she'd gone out of the normal channels and straight to the FBI, which she evidently had, she clearly hadn't lost any of her passion for bringing him down as the killer of Peter Ash.

She was a driven woman and had to be stopped.

The Schuyler visit had bothered him as an inconvenience, sure, but not because he thought there was any real chance of a reopened case convicting or even charging him but because it meant that until Beth Tully was truly out of the picture, and forever, he would never have peace in his life. She would always be there, pecking at the edges of things.

She was never going away unless he made her go away.

He could do that. He'd done it before.

He'd figure out how. It would take him a couple of days, tops.

Then he'd act. Get the damn deed done.

OUTSIDE HAD SETTLED into full dark. Ron had been sitting, fantasizing and planning, at his desk for most of the past hour, and finally he'd pushed his chair back, stood up, and crossed over to the windows. Behind him as he stood looking down on Bryant Street, the green shade of the banker's lamp on his desk dimly illumined the office.

He barely heard the knock on the door and looked at his watch: 6:30.

"Yes. Come in."

Andrea stood backlit and silhouetted in the doorway.

They'd come a long way this past week, from the shoulder massages to the romantic lunch they'd had behind the curtain at Sam's. The first tender kiss as they'd gotten up together, nearly bumping their heads in the limited space, laughing and then not laughing and then their lips meeting. Barely. Quickly. Then over.

Phenomenal.

But no acknowledgment of any kind as they'd arrived, separately, back at the office that afternoon. Or since, even today.

"Are you all right?" she asked.

"I'm good," he said. "I thought you'd gone home."

"No." A pause. Then: "I'm still here."

"I see that."

He heard her sigh. "Long day," she said.

"Tell me about it."

She moved inside from the doorway, lifting her hand, holding something, although he couldn't see what it was. "End of the day. End of the week," she said. "I thought maybe you could use something special to drink."

"That's very sweet of you. I think I might. Please, come on in."

She stepped forward, then turned and closed the door behind her. He heard the soft click as she pushed in the lock.

Turning back, she held up something he couldn't identify in the low light.

"What is it that's so special?"

She moved a few steps closer and held up the bottle. He imagined he could see her smile. "Have you ever heard of Pappy Van Winkle's twenty-year-old Kentucky bourbon?"

"Only by rumor. Is that really it?"

"It is." She moved over to his counter, pulled out a glass, and poured.

"How much did you pay for that, Andrea?"

"It doesn't matter. It's for you. Whatever it is, it's worth it if you like it."

"I'm sure I will. But really, what does it cost?"

She sighed again, came up to him and handed him the glass. "About two thousand dollars."

"No!"

Delighted, she broke a small laugh. "Yes."

He took a sip. "Oh my God."

"You like it?"

"It's amazing." Taking another sip, he said, "You didn't have to go out and buy something like this, you know."

"Yes, I did. I wanted something special. I'm so glad you like it."

"You should pour yourself some."

"Maybe I will," she said. "After."

"After what?"

She reached up and put her hands behind her head, and in the next second her red dress fell off her shoulders and floated down to the floor.

"After."

38

Ron slept in until 9:30 on Saturday morning.

There was a covered breakfast tray—coffee, orange juice, lox, bagels—on his bedside table, with a rose and a note: *Enjoy your rest. Sleep in. You've earned it. I love you. Kate.*

Pouring himself a perfect cup of coffee from the thermos, he plumped up his pillow and leaned back against it. For a moment, unbidden, he flashed on the events of the night before.

First the incredible and unexpected time with Andrea.

Then somehow, as he'd promised Kate he would, he'd made it home in time for dinner, with a bourbon cocktail as soon as he came in the door to cover the Pappy Van Winkle's. Heading upstairs right away to shower and change. "I'm sorry, I'll be quick. But sometimes the people I've got to deal with in this job just make me feel dirty."

Kate understood. The duck breast dinner had been fantastic, the wine a delicious Oregon Pinot Noir from their cellar. No heavy conversation, thank God. A lot of Janey talking about her teenage life. Afterward, Janey had a date and he and Kate had snuggled together watching their old favorite, *Blue Bloods,* in the family room.

Both of them sleeping by 11:00.

He knew he'd been lucky. He also realized that he had better put some priority on giving Kate some real quality time soon or things with his domestic situation might fall apart. He was pushing things to the limit, he knew, and maybe already even beyond it, but the simple fact was that the time he spent at home with Kate and Janey couldn't hold a candle to the pure rush and excitement of his life at the office.

And it wasn't just Andrea, as satisfying as that was turning out to be.

He also had the tireless and loyal Chet Greene at his beck and call. And through Chet—because he was a former homicide inspector with great credibility—Ron felt that he had the confidence of the entire staff of the DA's Bureau of Investigations. The mayor and the chief of police were also turning out to be surprising allies as he worked to get his administration established. It turned out that his predecessor, Wes Farrell, hadn't been the most tough-on-crime district attorney in the city's history, and he hadn't endeared himself to the police department or the mayor's office. So Ron had a definite advantage there.

In short, he was finally living the self-actualized life that he'd always known that he deserved. He was important. He wielded real power. When he talked, people listened. And when he gave a speech, they cheered.

This was who he was always meant to be.

But he could not let himself forget about Kate. Really, no matter what else he thought about her, there was no escaping that she had to be part of whatever it was that he was becoming. She knew and kept his biggest secret, as he did hers, and that connection bound them as nothing else ever could.

He could not allow himself to think that he was getting bored with her, with their life together. That could become a self-fulfilling prophecy, and he could not let himself go there. Kate was, after all—as he was—capable of murder. They were equals. Best not to forget that, even for an instant. She was a force of nature in her own right, his partner and protector. She was a lioness, ever vigilant in guarding her pride, her nest, her mate.

It would not be prudent to neglect Kate.

He had to give her some attention. It was only smart.

"I CAN'T BELIEVE you managed not to mention this FBI issue last night," Kate said.

"It wasn't easy, actually. It took all my willpower not to bring it up, but after the week I've had, I didn't want to have another heavy conversation at home about the job, especially with Janey there. I figure she's heard enough about that to last her for a few months. I didn't want to put her—or you, for that matter—through the worry."

"I think that was a really nice decision."

"Thank you. That's because I'm really a nice guy, underneath it all."

"Not so underneath."

"Well, that's nice of you to say so."

He squeezed her hand. They were strolling toward the Golden Gate Bridge on the paved walking path that ran along the bay at Crissy Field. The sun had broken through a half hour before and now the temperature was flirting with the 70s.

"So," she came back to their topic. "Are you worried?"

"About the FBI? Not really. The bureau has no chance of putting the whole thing together. Thanks to the brilliance of someone I know," he said, "there are no new facts to hang any charge on."

"So why did this special agent come around to your office?"

"Half of it, hassle value. The other half or more, Beth Tully, may she rest in peace."

"May she rest in peace? You're not saying she's . . . ?"

"Dead? No. Sadly. I meant may she rest in peace in her new employment, whatever that may turn out to be."

"God," Kate said. "For a minute there, I thought something had happened to her."

"Well, she did get relieved from Homicide. Which may be the next best thing."

"And you think she's the one who got the FBI involved?"

"Absolutely. She's always glommed onto that gun question."

Kate's voice took on an edge. "Let's not forget to mention that she's right about that, Ron. It's the only flaw and she thinks if she picks at it enough, it's all going to come undone. In a way, I feel a little sorry for her."

"Well, I don't, I promise you. She could have just left all of this alone."

"No. Being her, she couldn't. And now look what's happened to her."

"Well, you'll pardon me if I'm a little more concerned with our lives than with Beth Tully's. All of this should be so over. It ought to be clear, even with the FBI looking at it, that nothing new is coming out. Why does she care so much?"

"Because she thinks I betrayed her. I mean personally. And we were friends. Now we're not and never will be again. I hurt her."

"Okay. That's one I understand. Losing your friendship. I don't know how anybody could live if they were your friend and then weren't anymore." He squeezed her hand again. "I'm including present company."

She looked up at him, her eyes pools of relief.

"Really," he said.

After a few more steps, she asked him, "Do you mean that?"

"Completely. Could you ever doubt it?"

"I don't know."

Ron stopped and turned to look into her eyes. "Kate. Really, truly, seriously. If you weren't in my life, if you weren't the most important thing in my life, I have no idea what I'd do. Maybe just shrivel up and die. I mean it. You are my whole world."

She moved into his embrace.

"Are you okay?" he whispered.

She nodded against him. "It's just that, especially since the election . . . I mean, we don't get anything like the time together that we used to. I thought that might be how it was always going to be from now on. That was the way you wanted it."

"No. I've just been swamped. I know things kind of got away from me, and I'm so sorry. I've got to dial it back. Figure out how to do it better. Better for us, I mean. The last thing I want is less time with you." He pulled away slightly, lifted her chin with his index finger, and kissed her. "I love you," he said. "That's the whole story."

KATE PULLED THE sheets up around her. "Don't be upset," she said.

"Easy for you to say." He sat on the side of the bed, his feet on the floor.

"No, it isn't, really. I think we're just out of practice."

"It's not like we used to have to practice to stay good at it."

"No, I know. That's not what I meant. Maybe it's that you've got so many other things on your mind, making love isn't the main one right now." She patted the bed. "Hey, come here, lie back down. At least we can hug."

"I'm just so afraid I'm letting you down."

"You never let me down. This stuff happens, that's all."

"Not to me."

"Well, then your memory isn't working so well, either." She patted the bed again. "That was kind of a joke. Come over here."

He sighed.

"Please," she said.

He turned to look at her. "It's not going to work, Kate."

"We're in bed together, Ron. That's working enough right there, don't you think? And we've had such a good day so far. Let's not let this ruin it."

"It's not ruined," he said. "It's just . . ."

"What?"

"Nothing," he said. "Nothing."

39

It was not Hardy's favorite thing that on the first warm and beautiful Saturday afternoon of the calendar year, he was indoors sitting at the big round table in the Solarium. It was also not a personal highlight moment to acknowledge that in his haste to sidetrack Ron Jameson and his meddling in the Dockside Massacre case, he had probably caused Beth Tully to lose her job.

When he'd heard from her, hungover, a few hours earlier, he decided to invite her down to neutral ground to find out exactly what had happened. He'd then called Abe to give him the news and invite him, and Abe had put in a call to Bill Schuyler.

And now, here they all were.

"The guy moves fast," Schuyler said. "I'll give him that."

Hardy nodded soberly. "I should have seen that coming, with how he pushed things along on Devin Juhle. I am so sorry, Beth. I feel like this is all my fault."

"How could it be?"

"Well, it was more or less my idea to move things into the fast lane. I don't know what I was thinking—maybe that Jameson would panic and do something stupid. That we'd have some leverage we've been missing to take him down. Like no record of him ever turning in his guns."

"That wasn't a bad idea," Schuyler said. "I already went down and checked out the log-in book for every gun turned in all around the relevant months—in fact, the whole year. It's true: nothing. Unfortunately, though I believe in my heart that he's lying, we need more if we want to get anywhere close to proving it. The good news, if you want to call it that, is that he's got me motivated, and I intend to keep looking."

"What are you going to do?" Abe asked.

"I like the idea of keeping him aware that there's an active FBI investigation going on and he's in the middle of it. That's got to get his full attention. He's already shown that he's the kind of guy who can't just sit back and let events unfold. He gets pressured, my guess he's going to do something."

"Ha." Beth laughed without humor. "Tell me about it. So meanwhile, while we're waiting, what are we supposed to do?"

"Who are 'we'?"

"Well, me, for one example. You're telling me I'm supposed to just sit around and wait until he does something else?"

Schuyler and Glitsky exchanged a glance.

"The short answer is: Absolutely," Schuyler said. "In fact, if anything, you just back off and lie low. He's already made his move against you."

"That's my point. He's going to think I'm sitting at home, licking my wounds. How about if I just keep the pressure on, as you say, Bill? Get up in his face somehow? Instead of just rolling over like the passive little woman he expects me to be?"

"I don't think that's exactly how he thinks of you," Hardy said.

Schuyler grimaced and said, "I appreciate the offer, and I know where you're coming from, but you can't do that. You start hassling him or his wife, he could lock you up. Meanwhile, I'm bringing in a couple of my colleagues to talk to some of the witnesses from back then, plus one of our tech guys for phone and computer stuff. When Jameson knows we're turning up the heat, my hope is that he's going to suddenly remember some tracks he forgot to cover, and then he's going to fix everything, because that's who he is."

Beth, sitting slumped in her chair, her hands folded in front of her mouth, didn't like this solution. "So I just hang?"

Glitsky said, "You don't have a badge, Beth. What do you think you could do?"

She took a moment to consider. "How about I go talk to Kate?"

"That's exactly what I'm saying you shouldn't do. You shouldn't even think about any of that. You're not a cop anymore—at least, not for the time being. You're a private citizen."

"That's my point. I wouldn't be impersonating an officer. I'd just be a—"

But Schuyler was shaking his head. "Abe's right. You get threatening around his family, he's not going to make that distinction. He'll get you pulled in on any number of charges."

"You don't want to be in custody under his watch," Hardy said. "Really. Bad things can happen. Ask my secretary about it."

Beth looked around the room. "You guys are a big help."

Schuyler said, "I know how you feel. I don't blame you. But I think we've got him moving now, maybe even running scared. We're going to tie up the knot. I can feel it."

"Somebody's got to talk to his wife," Beth said. "She's the one who killed Geoff Cooke."

Schuyler nodded. "That's our plan. Plus, we interrogate again anybody else you want to recommend. You wouldn't be completely out of the loop. We'd definitely want your input."

Beth gave the FBI agent a flat glare. "It's bad luck to bullshit a bull-shitter," she said.

40

Janey was going through a religious phase and so she, Ron, and Kate all went to Mass together at St. Dominic's on Sunday morning. The weather had become downright unseasonable, and when they came out of the church, it was still and warm.

After Mass, the three of them repaired to the Balboa Cafe, where they all had the justly famous burger on a baguette with fries. Ron and Kate had a couple of mimosas each, clinking glasses "to us" like newlyweds. Several of the other diners recognized Ron, but only two people came over to say hello and interrupt their lunch, and both of them had voted for him and let him know it. They also wanted him to know that they were still with him.

After lunch—by now it was early afternoon—Ron drove the family back to drop them off at their house, where Kate picked up the other car to drive herself and her daughter to Janey's cello recital at Mercy. Ron would have loved to attend with them—he'd only found out about the recital that morning—but unfortunately he'd already made plans and now needed to get a jump on his workload for the following week. Janey should give him more warning when this kind of stuff was coming up; he would have put it on his calendar if he had known about it. He hated to miss it.

Parked across the street and a couple of houses down from the Jameson home, Bina watched Ron's black Audi park in the open space at the curb in front of their house.

Damn it! she thought. All three of them are together.

Although it wasn't part of her original plan, she wouldn't mind so much if she had to include Ron in her business today, even if he really hadn't played a role in Geoff's death.

But whatever she had to do with Ron and Kate, she knew she could never shoot Janey.

Nevertheless, she had a good view as she watched them get out, laughing and joking with one another. They walked up the path to their front door and all of them went inside.

She had all the windows down against the heat.

And whether it was the heat or her nerves, or both, she was sweating like crazy under the wig. There wasn't anything she could do about it now.

In fact, she only now was starting to realize, the whole camouflage outfit she wore was wrong for such an unexpectedly balmy afternoon. Wrong for today.

And then the family all being together—she hadn't planned for that. She hadn't planned enough, she was starting to realize.

A Sunday was a bad idea, too, she now knew. Tomorrow, Kate would almost undoubtedly be home alone.

She had the loaded Tariq hidden between the folds of the *Chronicle* on the seat next to her. She quickly scanned the street in both directions, then flipped the newspaper open to check that the gun was still there.

Of course it was. Where could it have gone, after all?

Closing the paper over it once again, she looked across at the house. Sucking in a heavy breath, she blew it out and wiped the sweat along the edge of the wig.

A second black Audi was suddenly backing out down the driveway, getting to the street, turning in her direction. Kate was driving, with Janey in the passenger seat. Talking to one another, neither of them even glanced at Bina as she sat there in her nondescript silver Jetta.

The sight of Kate, happy and engaged, almost made her physically sick with a blast of rage.

Waiting until they got to the corner and made the turn, she sighed deeply once again, dug the keys out of her pocket, and turned on the ignition.

This was the wrong day, she realized. Everything about it was wrong—the weather, the timing, her clothing.

Everything.

And now she'd been sitting here, wearing a red wig, for the better part of an hour. Somebody might have noticed her already, she realized, lying in wait all this time on the street.

She had to get out of here and rethink what she was going to do.

She was still going to do it, of course. That was not going to change. Not ever.

But she wasn't going to do it today.

WHEN HIS WIFE and daughter pulled out of the driveway and turned the corner, Ron placed the call he'd been waiting to make all day long.

"Thank God," Andrea said. "I thought you were mad at me."

"How could I be mad at you? I just got hung up here at home."

"You're not still, are you?"

"No. I just got freed up. I need to see you."

"I know. Me too. I miss you so much. I haven't been able to think about anything else. When can you be here?" she asked.

"I'm leaving now. Fifteen minutes?"

"All right," she said. "But hurry. Please."

"I'm on my way."

YEAH, RON WAS thinking. So much for not getting it up. Today he'd pretty well made the point with Andrea that there was nothing wrong with him or his performance.

No problem with that today. No problem twice.

Lord, was she hot.

And while he was at it, driving home from out here in the Richmond District, he hadn't realized how close Andrea lived to Beth Tully.

He didn't know how he was going to do it exactly, but since he was already out here, he might profitably spend a few minutes getting the lay of the land.

His original thought was that he'd show up when it was dark, then just knock on her door and wait until she opened it. This would probably be a fine way to go as long as he could guarantee that she would actually be home and not, say, in the middle of a party. One roommate opening the door was something he was sure he could handle, just in terms of the deed itself, but a second victim would probably complicate things. Things being equal, he'd prefer to avoid it.

Another basic problem was that, since about ninety percent of the buildings out here in the Avenues were two flats, one on top of the other, she probably lived in that kind of place. And if that was the case, there would be some issues about getting away unseen. To say nothing of finding a parking space close enough to park and then drive away quickly.

He turned north off Geary onto Seventeenth Avenue and slowly cruised down the street. She lived on the west side, about halfway to Clement, exactly the jam-packed environment he'd thought it would be. He couldn't help but notice that there was no free curb space, no place to park on a random Sunday afternoon.

He slowed down when he got to her address, which, except for the color it had been painted, was exactly the same as all of her neighbors' buildings.

He could, of course, simply call her and under some pretext ask her to meet him to talk about all these issues that had driven a wedge between Beth, Kate, and himself. She was wrong to believe that he had killed Peter, wrong to believe that Kate had killed Geoff.

Couldn't they just get together and have a civilized discussion? He could explain away all of her doubts.

But calling anybody nowadays was always a problem. There would be a record of the call no matter what type of phone you used; it was unavoidable.

And, as an experienced, dogged, and cynical cop, Beth would be aware that he was capable of turning a clandestine, private meeting in a remote place into an ambush.

As the sun lowered, he tapped his hand with frustration on the steering wheel.

How to actually do the killing hadn't been so hard to figure out with

Peter Ash, he thought. Peter was a trusting soul and, stupidly, had had no suspicions when Ron, *whose wife he had slept with*, suggested they go out on the bay in Geoff's boat to smoke a cigar and drink some fine Scotch. To Peter, that had sounded like a good idea—a bonding moment, for Christ's sake.

The idiot.

But Beth?

Beth would not buy it or anything like it.

And whatever he did, it would have to be soon. By roping the FBI into this long-dead investigation, she'd already done enough damage, and to think that she would stop there was simply not credible.

She was in this for the long haul, and she had to be stopped.

41

FIRST THING MONDAY morning, just after he'd sat down with his coffee in his cubicle, Chet Greene looked up to see the eager young face of Don Hancock coming back through the office toward him.

"Hey," the young newcomer said cheerily.

"Hey yourself. What's going on?"

"That's what I came back to ask you. Any word on the DNA?"

"Not yet. The clerk told me it might be three or four days."

"Four days!" Hancock couldn't believe it. "They put the sample in the machine, if you got a match, it spits out an answer in about five minutes."

"I think that actually putting it into the machine is the bottleneck," Chet said. "I was there on a fingerprint question last week and every single step took ten minutes. It took ten minutes for her to stir her coffee. I thought I was going to wind up killing her. Drag it out for ten minutes. See how she liked it."

"Yeah, well . . ."

"I'll let you know if they get something."

"Thanks."

Hancock hesitated.

"Anything else?" Chet asked.

Nodding, he said, "Do you get that kind of work a lot?"

"What kind of work is that?"

"You know. Kind of a close tail. Go to Sam's. Eat a great lunch and then steal your target's wineglass before the waiters can clear it. Then hang out while he smokes a cigar afterwards and so you've got to have one yourself." He added with heavy irony, "Tough detail."

"Some people hate that kind of thing. Tedious and boring."

"Not for me. How does anybody hate that? It's like playing hide-and-seek and capture the flag at the same time. You get any other work like that, you can give me a call anytime."

"I'll keep that in mind. Though I've got to say, stuff like that doesn't come up all the time. That was actually my first time pulling a sample like that."

With a show of disappointment, Hancock went on: "Well, anyway, I thought it was way cool. Your guy Hardy never made me, never even noticed I was alive. I just sat there eating my sand dabs ten feet across the way from him. And, by the way, the sand dabs were worth the whole day all by themselves. No matter how the scan comes out."

"It would be better if it comes out with a match."

"Well, sure. I didn't mean—"

Greene held up a hand. "No worries, Don. Something like it comes up again, I'll give you a call."

"So if we do get a match, then what?"

"Then Mr. Hardy's going to find himself in a whole deep pile of shit. Like a murder rap."

Hancock's mouth hung open for a second or two before he closed it. "Wow."

"Tell me about it," Greene said.

THE THING WITH Andrea was out of control.

Not that Ron was complaining.

As soon as he'd gotten in, she came into the office and closed the door behind her, both of them knowing they couldn't let it go too far right there and then, but laying the groundwork for as soon as they could get away with it.

She'd gone back out and gotten behind her desk just in time. Two minutes later Chet Greene knocked at the hallway door and was standing in front of her with a satisfied look on his face.

"He's going to want to talk to me," he said. "We got him."

Ron Jameson appeared in his office doorway. "Hey, Chet. Who do we have?"

"Dismas Hardy."

"You're kidding me. Really? After all these years?"

Chet nodded. "I just got the call from the lab five minutes ago." All enthusiasm, he outlined the surveillance and collection of Hardy's DNA from the Sam's glass and, mostly, the butt of the cigar Hardy had smoked. "Bottom line," he concluded, "we never had a comparison sample on him, essentially since nobody even looked. Can you believe that?"

"I can, given all the guy's pals in law enforcement. Nobody was motivated to a take a swab and just run it against the samples. This is some great detective work, Chet."

"Thanks."

"And didn't you say there was more than one? Unidentified sample, I mean."

"Yeah, there was one other one that wasn't Hardy."

"Glitsky?" Ron asked. "Might as well run down all those rumors. If we had both of them together, it would be better. Not that it isn't plenty good now. We've got Hardy at the pier; that's huge. Although Glitsky would be a terrific bonus."

"We might try to run down a comparison sample on him the way we did with Hardy. Getting him to agree to a swab voluntarily is probably a long shot, to say the least."

"Well, if you ask him and he doesn't cooperate, that's something right there, isn't it? Why wouldn't he, if he's innocent?"

"Right."

"I'm saying that if we're going to take this new information to the grand jury, it would be better if we had these two guys together in a conspiracy. And even without Glitsky, you've got something you can now use to press the shit out of Hardy. He says he was never on the pier. The DNA says he was. Hmm. I think the grand jury goes for the evidence, not the denial."

On a roll, Ron went on. "Plus, his alibi witnesses, all of whom work for him," he said. "That's a coincidence, huh? So we throw a little perjury threat into the mix and see if anybody remembers things differently. This is good work, Chet. Awesome work!"

• • •

KATE LEFT HER house at around 9:30, walked the block up to Fillmore, and had to kill a half hour at the Starbucks because the flower shop didn't open until 10:00.

The delay didn't bother her in the least.

She felt better—more connected and valued—than she had at any time over the past several months.

Finally, she and Ron had had a good couple of days to clear the air about real stuff, the lack of communication that was driving them apart. They were back to being a team, having each other's back, and most importantly, even enjoying each other's company.

Never mind the lack of success in the bedroom.

He had so much on his mind, was living under so much pressure. And, truth be told, she had probably pushed him a little before he was truly relaxed and ready. They were out of practice, that was all. They'd weathered these storms before, several times. Next time she would just be more patient and maybe more creative, and their sexual life would go back to the way it had been.

The worst was over.

When the flower shop opened, she finally settled on an early spring bouquet of gorgeous Peruvian lilies in a clear vase. It was large enough that it was a bit awkward to carry, but again, that didn't bother her. Nothing was going to bother her today. She wanted the present to be big enough to make a statement.

When she got home, she went straight to the Audi in the garage and fastened the bouquet in place with the passenger seat belt. She checked her watch: 10:45.

Right on time.

When she'd asked him at breakfast about what his day today was looking like, Ron had told her he'd be stuck at the Hall doing all the paperwork that he hadn't finished when he'd come in the day before.

Which was perfect for her plans: surprise him with flowers to brighten up his office and his day. Then break him away for a nice lunch together. If he was too busy, she would understand, of course, but Patty Simmons was right: you needed to break up the routine if you wanted to keep things fresh in your marriage. In your lives together.

And Ron had given her every indication that he was open to her being a greater presence in his life. Early in their marriage, they'd gone to lunch together at least once a week. Maybe, she thought, it was time to establish a new custom along those lines.

The DA job didn't have to be all that consuming.

Between traffic and parking, it took her a half hour to get to the Hall and then another fifteen minutes to get through the metal detector line at the front door, up the world's slowest elevator, and down the long hallway to the DA's admissions window, where miraculously there was no line. She nodded in greeting to Linda Coelho, whom she'd met several times now.

"Lovely flowers," she said.

"Thank you."

"Do you want me to call your husband and tell him you're here?"

Though there was no one else around them, Kate leaned in and lowered her voice. "I was kind of hoping I could just walk in and surprise him. Would that be okay?"

Coelho looked at the flowers, decided they posed no threat to the health and safety of either the DA or the staff, and pushed the button to unlock the door.

The first door to Ron's office was down the hallway to the right, but it was closed.

Kate knocked quietly, received no reply, so she knocked again and finally turned the doorknob.

Somewhat to her surprise, the door opened right up.

Andrea was not at her station.

Kate took a couple of steps inside and put the bouquet on the corner of Andrea's desk.

"Hello," she whispered.

No answer.

The door to Ron's inner office was closed as well. Kate straightened up and heard what sounded like some kind of a thumping noise and then a groan.

Crossing over to the door, she put her ear up against it and heard similar noises.

They could only be one thing.

She tapped on the door. "Ron."

The noises stopped.

Then Ron's voice: "Just a minute. Be right with you. Who is it?"

"Ron. Ron? It's Kate."

"Kate?" As though he couldn't imagine how it was possible that she was there. "Just one second."

"A second's up." She banged on the door again. "Ron!"

The door clicked as it unlocked, and then it opened and Ron stood in front of her, his shirt still somewhat untucked, the very picture of conjugal guilt. Inside the room, over Ron's shoulder and behind his desk, similarly disheveled, Andrea stood looking downcast like a schoolgirl waiting to be scolded.

"This isn't what . . . I mean . . ." Ron began.

But Kate would have none of it. She whirled around, reaching for the first thing that came to hand: the bouquet she'd brought in with her. Picking it up off the desk, without any hesitation, she lifted it high above her head and threw it down to the floor at Ron's feet, where it exploded in the enclosed space with the sound of a small bomb.

Kate then screamed in anger and frustration, took one last look at the damning tableau, and ran out the door and down the hallway.

Between the cleaning crew and trying to calm Andrea down, it took Ron nearly an hour to get down to his car and another twenty minutes to make the drive home.

Kate's car was already parked in front of the garage along the side of the house. Pulling up behind where she'd parked, he sat for a moment trying to collect himself, to plan an approach that might possibly undo even a little of the damage. He could tell her that she had misunderstood. That Andrea was having problems at home and that he . . .

No.

The less mention of Andrea, the better.

Whatever card he played, the theme was apology. He was sorry. It would never happen again.

She had come on to him and he had at first tried to hold her off and . . .

Andrea again. Not a good idea.

The important thing, he would tell her, was that he loved her. That was the fundamental truth between them. They were each other's soul mate.

Okay, he had fallen. He should probably admit that.

He would make amends. Nothing like this would happen again.

He was sorry. Sorry, sorry, sorry.

That's how he had to play it.

He had to keep her from letting their secret out to punish him. Had to make her promise to keep it sacrosanct between them. He would keep secret the truth about her and Geoff, too. They were still and forever bound in that tradeoff. That was the important thing.

And other than that, he was sorry.

Sorry was the ticket.

Taking one last ragged breath, he opened his car door, got out, and somehow, shakily, made it to the side door that led into their kitchen.

AT HER DESK in their study, Kate turned to see Ron come to a stop in the doorway.

"I thought I should come home," he began. "I am so sorry."

She didn't answer.

"What are you doing there?" he asked.

She turned back to the legal pad she'd been using. "Writing a letter."

"Who to?"

"Beth."

"That's not a solution, Kate. We can talk this out. Beth isn't part of it. This is us."

No reply.

"Tell me what you want, Kate," he said, taking a step toward her. "Whatever it is, I know we can still make it work."

Another step.

"Please," she said. "Don't come any closer."

He stopped. "Whatever you want. I promise. From now on. I'll quit the job. Whatever. I am so sorry. So very sorry."

"It doesn't matter."

"Sure it does. We can make it work again. We just have to—"

"No," she said.

"Yes, we can." He took another small step.

"Stay back there!"

"I just—"

"You just nothing." She turned around to face him and lifted her hand from her lap. She held the gun she'd taken from their safe as soon as she'd come home. "How fucking dare you?" She pointed the gun at the center of his chest and pulled the trigger. Then pulled it again.

Ron went down on his back.

She waited to see that he was perfectly still, a little less than a minute. Then she put the barrel under her chin and pulled the trigger a third time.

42

To: Sergeant Beth Tully

Inspector, San Francisco Homicide Detail

Dear Beth:

Please tell my children that I love them.

I am writing this letter in longhand, in my own handwriting, so there won't be any question about its authenticity. Just so there's no ambiguity, this is a confession to murder and a suicide note.

I want you to know that you were right about everything. I'm sorry that we had to stop being friends. Maybe if you had not been a cop, I could have just told you, as I'm telling you now. But I felt like I had to protect Ron and that you wouldn't understand that.

Forgive me.

Forgive me for seducing Peter Ash and starting this whole horrible cycle. Ron is not stupid and he found out what I'd done. Because he is a complete narcissist, he couldn't stand the idea that I'd been unfaithful to him and he plotted to kill Peter because he was jealous.

He probably should have killed me instead. I started it.

But no matter what, I couldn't let Ron be charged with Peter's murder—it would ruin our family and the lives of the kids. And suddenly I saw another way out.

Forgive me for killing a really good man, Geoff Cooke. As you know, it was Ron's gun that killed him, although apparently no one else except you believed that.

Geoff did have only the two Tariq weapons from Desert Storm. They are probably both still in their safe at their house. Bina would know.

Of course, we never handed Ron's guns in to the abatement program. One of them he dropped into the bay after he shot Peter, and the other is in the police department's evidence locker on Geoff's death.

After all I had done to save ourselves, our lives, and our marriage, today I discovered that Ron was betraying me. With his secretary. Could it be more of a pathetic cliché? Can he think so little of me? Whatever it was that I thought we had together, whatever bond we had created, all of it was a lie. He deserves to die. And I can't bear to live. Not anymore.

Forgive me for causing you and the rest of the world so much trouble. It would probably have been better if I'd never been born.

Your once best friend,
Kate Jameson

BINA SAT ON one end of the large red-leather couch in her well-appointed living room. "What are you telling me?" she asked. "What do you mean, Kate killed herself?" But of course this was a rhetorical question. There could be no other meaning but the plain truth. "When?"

Beth, no longer working in Homicide but, because Kate's letter had been written to her, very much in the loop, sat on the other end of the couch. "Today," she said. "A few hours ago. She shot Ron before she turned the gun on herself."

"You're saying she killed him?"

"He's dead, yes."

Bina's hand covered her mouth. "Oh my God."

"She also confessed in writing that she shot Geoff and made it look like he killed himself." She leaned over toward Bina. "The main takeaway here is that your husband didn't kill himself. Definitely now, without any question."

Bina brought her hand up to her eyes, wiped at the tears that were forming. "I never thought he did, you know. Never. He would never have done that to me. To us." She stared across at Beth. "Why did she do it? I mean, why now?"

"Apparently, Ron was having an affair with his secretary and Kate found out about it. After all she'd done for him—putting her own life on the line to frame Geoff and get Ron off the hook for Peter Ash's murder—she just couldn't take it anymore. He was betraying her after all she had done for him? That, finally, was enough. She couldn't forgive it anymore. In any event, it's going to be all over the news tonight, and I thought I'd give you a heads-up. Are you going to be all right?"

"Yes." The simple reality was kicking in. When she spoke, it was in a half whisper, almost to herself. "In fact, I'm probably better than I've been over the past few years. Knowing for sure, that is. Not that it will bring Geoff back, but knowing he didn't leave me . . ."

"That would be good to know."

"It is. I can't tell you." She dabbed at her eyes again. "And Kate is dead, too?"

Beth nodded.

"I hope this doesn't sound terrible, but I'm glad."

"I think that's forgivable. She got herself all turned around."

"I thought about killing her myself, you know. I probably shouldn't tell you this, but I was going to go to her house and shoot her dead with one of Geoff's Tariqs."

"When were you going to do this?"

"Maybe as early as tomorrow."

Beth sat stock-still.

"You don't believe me?"

"No, I do believe you."

"I even had a disguise. I didn't necessarily want to get caught, but really I didn't care what happened to me. As long as I could punish her, since it didn't seem like anybody else was going to, even though after our talk at the pizza place, there wasn't any doubt that she'd killed

Geoff. So I figured that punishing her would fall to me. You can't just let a person shoot somebody you love and then walk away. I really would have done it."

"I believe you. And that makes me doubly glad you're not going to get that chance."

"Me too, thank God. Me too."

PHYLLIS SAT RAMROD straight on the first few inches of the chair in front of Hardy's desk. "So what are you telling me?" she asked. "Are they dropping my case?"

"Not immediately, but I'm filing a motion to dismiss as soon as I can get it written and I'm guessing that the new administration, the new DA—whoever that turns out to be—is going to want to distance the office from the chaos of the past couple of weeks, which would include your case. There's really no point, to say nothing of any political advantage, in pursuing it."

Phyllis sat quietly for a few seconds. "You know," she said, "I never thought poor Celia actually killed Mr. Valdez. She just needed help getting out of town, like so many of the other people I'd been working with. That was the point to me. I probably would do the same thing again under the same circumstances."

"That's because you're a saint, Phyllis."

She barked out a one-note laugh. "Hardly that. Or a hero of any kind, either. I'm not trying to help criminals escape. But so many truly innocent people are being treated so unfairly. I had a young woman last week, for example . . ."

Hardy held up a hand. "Wait a minute. You're still actively doing this?"

She nodded, as though surprised by the question. "Of course. The problem isn't going away. If anything, it's getting worse."

"Okay, but—"

This time she raised her hand to stop him. "No. Listen. This woman—Rosa, twenty-three years old—came here to the US with her mother from El Salvador when she was three. She's perfectly fluent in English and has a nursing degree from UOP. She works at Kaiser here in town. Did you know they had an ICE raid there last week? At Kaiser! And picked up eight undocumented DACA kids. Fortunately, she was on a different shift and they missed her in the sweep.

"And I really shouldn't call them kids," she went on. "These were all working young adults. Skilled, English-speaking, taxpaying, sometimes home-owning young adults. I mean, really? Working at Kaiser? And these people pose a risk to our society and ought to be deported?

"But in any event, Rosa had to get out of here or get picked up and sent back to El Salvador, where she knows exactly nobody. Now she's trying to get to Montréal or maybe somewhere farther west in Canada, but first she had to get out of the city immediately, so I drove her up after work to a supposedly safe house in Vallejo. Fingers crossed. But I'm going to keep doing this as long as they need me to. Just so you know. I mean, if it's going to affect the charges against me. I don't want to get you or the firm in trouble."

"I'm not worried about me and the firm. Or you, for that matter. Especially if we get some stability in the DA's office."

"Do you think that will happen?"

"Well, more than we've had lately, anyway. As you say, fingers crossed."

Phyllis sat back in her chair and cocked her head, birdlike, as though she was about to say something.

"What?" Hardy prompted her.

"Just that it's all so fragile, isn't it?"

"What's that?"

"Life. The way things work. A few little changes and suddenly things start to fall apart. It doesn't feel like the same rules we all grew up with, does it?"

"Still close, one hopes," Hardy said. "But you're right. It's damn fragile."

BY ITSELF, A sitting DA's violent death would have caused its share of political turmoil and fallout in San Francisco, but the fact that Ron Jameson was also revealed to be a murderer who had killed his colleague Peter

Ash set off alarms all over the place, most notably in the office of Mayor Leland Crawford.

In that environment, it suddenly became bad form to be perceived as Jameson's close ally, and clearly the best strategy to limit the damage would be to find a scapegoat who could shoulder the lion's share of the blame.

In his press conference the day after the murder-suicide, Mayor Crawford could not give high enough praise to the efforts of homicide inspector Beth Tully, who had never wavered in her search to identify suspects in two murders, one of whom was the DA himself, and the other an ex-convict, Adam McGowan. Inspector Tully's tireless and gutsy approach had earned her the enmity of Jameson and also of the chief of police Vi Lapeer, and had resulted in her being removed from the Homicide Detail—along with her lieutenant, Devin Juhle, and her partner, Ike McCaffrey.

As soon as the mayor had learned the true facts, he took immediate steps to reinstate those three stellar members of the police department, and to dismiss the administrative hearings that they were all facing, clearly because of the personal vendetta waged by Jameson and Lapeer.

The mayor would also be looking into Chief Lapeer's connection with Ron Jameson's campaign and with his administration since his election. Without calling for Lapeer's outright dismissal at that point in time, he opined that it might not be too early to begin talking about instigating a search for a new police chief, one without the stain of complicity with a corrupt DA sullying that person's record.

It was ten days after the murder-suicide, and the former chief assistant district attorney, a career prosecuting attorney named Amanda Jenkins, now sat behind the enormous tabletop desk in what had been the office of Ron Jameson. When the mayor had approved her assignment as district attorney, he had told her that, barring any truly egregious shenanigans, she was going to keep her hands on that job until the next election. What the city needed was a calm, firm, professional hand running the office without hysteria or a political agenda.

Now, Jenkins looked with a practiced prosecutorial eye at the lanky frame of one of her inspectors, Chet Greene, sitting across from her. Chet all but exuded political agenda, having explained already to her in this interview that not everything Ron Jameson did had been wrong.

In fact, in his opinion, damn little if anything had been wrong.

Chet wasn't even remotely convinced that Mr. Jameson had in fact killed Peter Ash. Who was to say, he argued, that Ron's wife, Kate—an experienced murderer who had clearly admitted to killing Geoff Cooke—hadn't also killed Peter Ash? After all, she had successfully framed Cooke for the same thing. What was to stop her from casting the blame on her husband in her suicide note and then killing him so that he would never even have a chance to offer his own defense?

Ron Jameson was a good man, even a hero. He would never have killed anybody.

But in the meantime—the real reason for this meeting—Jenkins was about to give Inspector Greene more bad news.

She shook her head in what she hoped was a sincere show of disappointment. "I know it must seem compelling," she said, "but it—"

"It's totally compelling," Chet interrupted. "It absolutely proves that Hardy was at the pier. He needs to explain that if he can, at the very least."

"I don't know why he'd have to do that. Do we know *when* he was there, Chet? Do we know it was the day of the massacre?"

"He was there."

Amanda broke a thin smile. "I'm not saying he wasn't, Chet. It's entirely possible. What I'm saying is that your DNA match doesn't really prove it one way or another."

"Well, then, that's why we need to interrogate him. Hard."

"Except that you've already told me that the evidence file is hopelessly corrupted."

"That was because Glitsky took it out of the evidence lockup and I'm betting he tampered with the bullet casings."

"You're betting? I don't think betting cuts it here, Chet. And if he tampered with the bullet casings, who's to say some DNA—Hardy's or Glitsky's or somebody else's—didn't get tampered with by someone else, maybe even planted back in the file. And maybe whoever that was, that tamperer, forgot to sign it out." She moved some papers around on her desk, then met his eyes and spoke quietly. "You know, Chet, it seems like ever since I've been here in this office, there's been this recurring rumor that Hardy and Glitsky were part of the Dockside Massacre thing. If you want my opinion, it's because something in the cop mind-set—forgive me—recoils at the idea of a defense attorney being pals with a cop. If that's happening, the two of them must be up to something no good.

"I think it's time we put this thing permanently to rest. As a lifetime prosecutor, I can guarantee you there's not a judge on the planet who is going to admit evidence from that locker, especially once you explain your tampering allegation."

"But I—"

She cut him off. "You can't have it both ways, Chet. Either it's a pristine file or it's corrupted, and you've already made the argument to me that it's the latter. Which means the DNA, such as it is, doesn't matter. However it got there, planted or bleeding out on the pier, it doesn't matter. It has no bearing. Don't you see that? If I'm wrong, please fill me in on where, because it's clear as day to me."

"So we just drop it?"

She gave the thought a second or two. "Yes. We just drop it."

"It kills me," he said. "We are so close."

"Actually, Chet, we're no closer than we've ever been." Then: "We've got to let it go."

"Forever?"

"Yes, I think so," she said. "Forever."

EPILOGUE

WITH HIS LOVE of all things arcane and esoteric, Hardy was thrilled with Frannie's choice of locale to have the firm's retreat dinner, a terrific South of Market restaurant called Trou Normand, because it would give him the opportunity to wax eloquent about stuff nobody knew about, one of his favorite endeavors.

They had the whole place reserved for this Friday night in mid-April, and his partners, colleagues, and employees ought to start showing up any minute, but he was already engaged in a conversation with the first arrivals, Don Peek's secretary, Kathleen Mavone Wheeler, and her boyfriend, Eric, about the meaning of the name.

"I speak a little French," Kathleen said, "and doesn't *trou normand* just mean "Norman hole"? Which, if I may say, would not be among the top ten food-related names I would pick."

"Ah," Hardy said, "but that's the beauty of it. It means Norman hole all right, but what does that refer to?" His eyes sparkled. "What's the hidden meaning?"

Eric leaned in. "The Norman hole," he said. "Are you sure we want to know?"

Hardy gave him a quick stern look—how could someone not want to know a factoid?— then followed the scowl with a conciliatory smile. "I think you will. You may have heard that they typically eat a lot of food at their meals in Normandy, possibly even to excess. It's kind of the ritual there. You just keep eating until you can't do it anymore. Butter, meats in cream sauces, cheese for dessert. More and more and more."

Kathleen put her hand to her midriff. "This is starting to sound a little iffy."

Hardy held up a hand. "It gets better. Because finally you're done. You can't eat another bite. But of course there's still some more dessert items and maybe some other food on the table. So what do you do?"

"Stop eating," Kathleen said. "Just an idea."

Hardy gave her a deadpan look. "No, no, no. And here's where the genius of the French kicks in. Normandy happens to be the home of this terrific apple brandy called calvados."

"Something I know at last," Eric said with real enthusiasm. "I love calvados."

"Okay. You're going to love this next part, then. You can't eat anymore. You're completely stuffed. So what do you do?"

"Slip into the vomitorium for a couple of minutes?" Eric asked.

Hardy shook his head. "That was ancient Rome. This is modern France and a way better solution to the same problem. You get yourself a large shot of calvados and you drink it off all at once. This makes a fire in your throat as it burns its way down and finally the fireball creates a hole in your stomach that allows you to have another few bites of food. And that hole is, of course, called the *trou normand*."

"Wonderful," Kathleen said.

"I can't wait to try it," Eric added.

"I don't know if I'd recommend that," Hardy said. "But it is a hell of a good thing to know about just on general principle." He looked at Kathleen. "Just don't tell Wes Farrell when he gets here. He hates it when I hit him with obscure French stuff."

"You have my word," Kathleen said. "No French with Mr. Farrell unless you give us the all clear."

IN ALL, INCLUDING employees, boyfriends, girlfriends, and significant others, there were five full tables of ten.

Hardy sat with Frannie on one side of him and their daughter, Rebecca, on the other side next to their son, Vincent (not a member of the firm or even a lawyer), with Glitsky and Treya directly across from them. To his right, Wes and Sam presided over their table of young associates, while Gina did much the same on his left with some of the older ones: Graham Russo and his wife, Sarah; Amy Wu and her husband, Jason; Don Peek and his new bride, whose name Hardy couldn't remember. (It occurred to him that maybe for some reason Peek himself was the cause of Hardy's inability to remember the names of the women around him.)

Over in the corner, his investigator Wyatt Hunt sat with his wife, Tamara, and the rest of a group they called the "irregulars": steady contract workers, though not technically employees of the firm. Good people, hardworking, and well trusted.

And there was Phyllis, over at Norma's table with the other admin staff. Much to Hardy's surprise and delight, she had a male guest with her—whose name was another victim of Hardy's apparently failing memory—and almost every time he caught a glimpse of her, she was smiling.

A slight lull descended, and Frannie reached out and put a hand gently on his arm. "It's probably getting to be time that you said a little something," she said.

Hardy gave his wife's hand a reassuring pat and nodded. Picking up the snifter that was down to its last quarter inch of VSOP, he clinked his spoon against it, then clinked it again until the room had gone completely quiet.

He got to his feet. "I want to thank you all for coming here tonight to help us ring in the newly reconstituted edition of Freeman, Farrell, Hardy & Roake. As all of you know, it's been a challenging launch, to say the least. But I'm happy to say that we've weathered the opening storms and now are looking at smooth sailing well into the future."

He paused to cast a glance over his own table and then, after a bit of hesitancy, the other tables. The silence gathered in the crowded room.

"You know," he said, his voice sounding thicker.

He stopped.

After a small eternity of ten or twelve seconds, a woman's voice finally called out from the side of the room: Phyllis, suddenly on her feet, raising her own glass. "I'd like to propose a toast to Mr. Hardy," she said, "the sine qua non, which he'd like us all to know means 'without whom, not.'

Which is exactly what he is, the man without whom there is no firm, there are not so many friendships, there is not so strong a team. So let's raise a glass to Mr. Hardy."

The rest of the room came to its feet, applauding.

Hardy stood in a kind of shock, nodding at his place in mute acknowledgment.

Unbelievable, he thought, trying to take it all in, also trying not to let his emotions get the better of him.

After all he'd been through from his early cop days, patrolling with Abe; losing his first son, his first marriage ending in divorce; then his new life with Frannie and their children; connecting with David Freeman; becoming a full-time lawyer; surviving Pier 70; and finally all the cases . . .

All the clients and all the cases. Even up to the war he'd waged with Ron Jameson.

And now here he was, a success in every way that mattered, clearly revered if not loved by his applauding firm, by all of his people.

Unbelievable, he thought again.

Absolutely unbelievable.

ACKNOWLEDGMENTS

For various reasons, this book was a bit more of a solitary creative effort than many others. I knew that I wanted to tie up several hanging elements from disparate past Dismas Hardy books, and so I wasn't in as much need of background material and/or knowledge of the technicalities of the law as I usually find myself when the idea of the novel began to percolate.

That said, these things are never produced in a vacuum, and as always I turned at the outset to the triumvirate named in this book's dedication—my consigliere, legal consultant, and great pal Al Giannini; my fantastic agent, Barney Karpfinger; and my still-darling bride of thirty-five years, Lisa Sawyer.

I'd also like to acknowledge the team of folks who work with me on a regular basis and help these books make it to publication. Anita Boone, my assistant for over twenty years, is simply the best at what she does, which is keeping organized the sometimes bewildering and chaotic life of the working writer, making certain that deadlines are met, promotional material is up-to-date, emails and other correspondence get dealt with, and so much more. Handling all of my social media, a large part of today's publishing industry, is the talented and tireless Dr. Andy Jones. Also, on the hard-print side, my two personal editors, Peggy Nauts and Doug Kelly, have given the final polish to many of my books, including this one, and I'm very grateful to them for finding those last little glitches and dispatching them so completely.

The next generation—my daughter, Justine; her husband, Josh; and my son, Jack—continues to inform and hopefully enrich these novels, whose relevance would be suspect indeed without that input, sensibility, and insight.

I'd also like to give a nod to three of my writer colleagues—Max Byrd, Rob Leininger, and C. J. Box—who in different ways and all unwittingly have helped to keep the inspirational well for this book filled to the brim. Thanks, guys, just for being who you are.

Generous contributors to various organizations have purchased the right to name characters in this book. These people and their respective organizations are: Katy Peek, El Dorado Court Appointed Special Advocates (CASA); Andrea O'Riordan, Serra High School Fund A Dream; Kathleen Wheeler, the Sacramento Point West Rotary Club; and Paul Simmons, the Yolo Land Trust.

I'm very grateful for the enthusiasm and support of Simon & Schuster/Atria Books and particularly Peter Borland, Daniella Wexler, and publicist David Brown. Working behind the scenes for the success of these books is the top flight sales group of Janice Fryer, Wendy Sheanin, and Colin Shields. It is a pleasure and privilege to work with all of you. Thank you so much.

Finally, I love hearing from my readers. Please feel free to stop by my website and say hello—I really do answer my email.

Thanks for buying my books!